For President and Country

JAMES TINDALL

Look for the following novels from this author:

Jagged Grass (Book I, Seminole Trilogy)

The Transparency (Book II, Seminole Trilogy)

Indian Law (Book III, Seminole Trilogy)

Sun God's Treasure (Book I, Sun God series)

Alas Omega (Book II, Sun God series)

See these and other books by the author at www.drtindall.com

AUTHORS NOTE:

This is the first book of the Jackson Black Spy Thriller Series.

For President and Country

A Jackson Black Spy Thriller

Book 1

James Tindall

JAMES TINDALL

Library of Congress Cataloging-in-Publication Data

Tindall, James

For President and Country/James Tindall

p. 342

ISBN: 978-1-7372476-8-5

Published by DTP Publishing, Denver, Colorado

Printed in the United States of America

10 9 8 7 6 5 4 3 2 1

ISBN: 978-1-7372476-8-5

DEDICATION

To my siblings Bill, Deloris, and Lin,

And to Dessie and Ruth

and,

to my friends in the intelligence and spy communities.

Disclaimer:

Most of the locations mentioned herein are real. While the many other geographic settings mentioned are also real, any description or likeness of characters that resemble persons living or dead or media driven is entirely coincidental.

CHAPTER 1

THE plane touched down at Podgorica airport, five miles south of Podgorica, Montenegro. Total flight time from Washington DC, including almost a five-hour layover in Newark and similar one in Vienna had been twenty-one hours. Jakson was tired but shook it off while making his way through customs and then to a private sedan waiting for him at passenger pickup. He was relieved to see that it was Mitch, head of the Tactical Technology Office for DARPA (Defense Advanced Research Projects Agency). He and his covert colleagues simply called it T-Group. The TTO engages in high-risk, high-payoff advanced military research that emphasizes a systems approach to the development of air and land systems, as well as advanced processors and controls. Many countries who know about DARPA and other intelligence agencies around the world, including MI6 wish they had such an advanced technology operation to call upon. One of the top global financial magazines had called DARPA the agency that had shaped the modern world, especially regarding weather satellites, GPS, stealth technology, voice interfaces, drones, personal computers and the Internet. They have even gotten involved in pandemic vaccines. Their list of innovations follows a long track record of success and has inspired world governments to launch similar R&D enterprises. Being under military control, it stands alone and for special operators from all branches of service, especially Green Berets, Navy Seals, and Delta Forces, DARPA provides unparalleled technology and weapons for specialized clandestine missions. It stands independent of other military research groups and reports to the senior Department of Defense management with loose ties to the CIA. It is deliberately kept small and honed to a razors edge. Best of all Jackson thought, it was indispensable to CIA operatives on missions like his. Mitch had been with them for fifteen years and was the go-to guy for tactical innovations for field operatives. Secretly, he headed T-Group; the best of the best for high-tech gadgets used by operatives. His technology had saved Jackson's life multiple times in the field. Mitch had paid his dues with a PhD in Physics and Engineering at the top of his class out of Georgia Tech. He was fit as a man could be. It was required to adequately test the experimental equipment T-Group designed. There was no room for error in the field; it was always life or death. Having spent a few years behind enemy lines in the Middle East and with CIA teams and field operatives, he found out what worked and what didn't.

"Jackson Black, old friend," Mitch said. "Are you ready to save the world again?"

"For President and Country," Jackson replied. "You know how it goes. What do you have for me?"

"I was briefed by the director; we have come up with something new given the mission parameters, although you wouldn't know to look at it. Briefly, it's the baddest ass bike you've ever seen. Of course, we have added a few enhancements."

"Why did you choose a bike?" Jackson asked.

"I knew you used to race and are adept at handling them.

Given the weather, potentially tight turns, and mountainous terrain, the group thought it would work better for you than a rental car. By the way, that envelope contains the latest travel information on your target. The director said to pass it along."

"Hmmmm," Jackson mused, quickly perusing the contents. "How far is it to Budva?"

"About twenty-five miles once you're on the road," Mitch responded. "It will just be getting dark when you arrive. The target is staying at the Hotel Slovenska Plaža. He's being watched until you arrive. You know how it is."

"Yes, don't I though."

"What's this guy done to deserve you?" Mitch asked. "Or can you tell me?"

Jackson looked at Mitch as he drove. They had just pulled up to a small warehouse. Their eyes locked. Jackson was never supposed to tell anything about a mission, but in this case, he owed Mitch. It was time for some payback.

"I'll simply tell you that this target has already bought a dozen countermand devices that can decapacitate our nuclear power plants, but what is worse is he has somehow acquired both a nuclear missile and the codes for it."

"Russian?"

"We suspect so."

"Target?"

"DC."

"I know you're not supposed to tell, but thank you," Mitch said. "I'll tell Julie to get out of town."

"No one else," Jackson said.

"Understood," Mitch replied. "Any idea on timing?"

"We believe he may have or shortly will have the countermand devices," Jackson said. "We are hoping he doesn't get rid of them before I can follow him to the missile. We know that he needs to meet someone to obtain the codes."

"I know you've done your homework," Mitch said. "What do

you think it is?"

"My hunch is it is one of the older ones because they would be the easiest to get in a manner of speaking. The Sickle or Topol SS-25 was first put online in 1988. Russia has been phasing it out, which is why one could easily get lost in the shuffle."

"I hate to ask but what is the yield?"

"From 550 to 800 kilotons."

"My god," Mitch whispered. "That will take out all of DC and Baltimore as well."

"I agree," Jackson said. "Almost everyone within a three-mile radius will suffer instant death, out to eight miles if down wind. The radiation spread will be uncontainable. Buildings out to twenty-five-mile radius will suffer damage and people will suffer radiation poisoning. The food chain will be interrupted, and God knows what else."

The two men had exited the car; two agents lifted a roll-up door admitting them into the small warehouse.

"Whatever it takes," Mitch said. "Get him. This should help."

"That's one badass looking bike," Jackson gasped.

The front suspension fork and rear swingarm of the bike, along with the edge were a deep candy-apple red satin finish, the rest of the bike was a flat black with carbon fiber cowlings on each side that covered every part of the motorcycle, including the engine blending into the bottom of the curved tank. The front rims were a dual chrome and black color, the rear rim a satin black.

"Don't drool over it too much," Mitch said. "Take a seat on it and put on this helmet. Now pay attention. It is equipped with mini missiles controlled from the heads-up display. Look at that wall as if you're cruising. You'll notice the display in your helmet visor. This mini screen shows all the enhancements at once – heat seeking mini missiles, smoke, flamethrower, NOX system, night vision mode, and pistol storage set up for your favorite, the P228 and five magazines, all positioned to enable you to ride, extract and shoot at the same time."

"Like chewing bubblegum and walking," Jackson smiled.

"Precisely. Get off the bike and let's walk over here. You'll get to see my greatest brainchild."

"If something here is his greatest brainchild, it must be awesome because Mitch was nothing short of brilliant," Jackson thought.

"Drew, would you sit on the bike and turn on the SM?" Mitch said.

The two men had walked about thirty feet away, looking at the bike.

"Activate SM," Mitch called out.

All at once the bike disappeared. Straining, Jackson could only see about two inches of the top of the helmet and four inches below the bike frame and part of the bottom of the tires where they met the concrete.

"How did you do that?" Jackson asked incredulously.

"By now you have guess that SM is stealth mode," Mitch responded. "The bike was built for stealth from the ground up. It's simple really. I installed several dozen mini cameras along each side of the bike and on the leather jacket and helmet. Take a walk around it."

While he did his walk around, Jackson noted that the view he saw reflected what was on the opposite side of the bike, no matter where he positioned himself.

"Pure genius," Jackson muttered. "How does it work?"

"As I said before; quite simple," Mitch responded. "What you are seeing is a 3-D hologram projected from a high power, miniature transformer embedded under the cowling. I call it VRC or Visually Reflective Camouflage. It's ninety percent efficient during the day and almost 100 percent from dusk to dawn. Note that the taillight is inset forward from the rear curvature of the fender. Only someone directly behind you can see it. The turn signal lights are on the rear of each side of the cowling. They have laser rangefinders built into them with a mini-missile directly adjacent to each one. The cowling has the look of carbon fiber, but that's only the skin, below it is reinforced, layered Kevlar that will stop armor piercing rounds up to a .338 caliber.

"I'm speechless," Jackson managed to say. "Dare I ask the capabilities other than the weapons?"

"Get back on the bike," Mitch commanded. "Put on the helmet and look in the top right corner of the display for the two set of letters Pb and Pr. To request any command simply say PB or PR, mini missile, etc. Wait before you do."

Mitch stepped up beside the bike and turned a small lever from A to UA.

"Go ahead," Mitch said. "Practice the commands only your voice can activate them. Say the command in letters or words followed by on."

"PR on," Jackson said. "The PR is blinking green; PB on; it's blinking green too."

"That means it's active," Mitch said. "Do you know what they mean?"

"No."

"The PB is parachute for the bike and the PR is the parachute for the rider. The others are NV for night vision, etc. Here's a list. Familiarize yourself with all of them."

"Wait!" Jackson exclaimed. "You mean to tell me this bike has a parachute?"

"Yes," Mitch said. "It has four attachments when it's activated. They are at these points. The parachute for the jacket is built in. Not steerable but it will keep you alive. Pay particular attention to this switch. Think of your M4 when you take the safety off. Rotate it downward to 'A' to arm the bikes enhancements. The UA, rotating it back up, is unarmed. In the UA position, the bike is just like any other bike on the road. And, even if the switch is in the 'A' position, it remains unarmed unless your voice is heard by the built-in artificial intelligence."

"You've outdone yourself," Jackson said, grinning.

"I try," Mitch said. "The bike takes unleaded and as you have noticed, is belt driven. My friends at County Choppers helped develop the frame, which is a cross between a Harley Davidson Sportster and the Indian Scout with an elongated frame and as you can see, the handles and grips attached to the front suspension bars have a sleek, swept-back design that barely clears the Kevlar gas tank. We tweaked it after they delivered it to us. Top speed is 138 miles per hour unless you engage the NOX. That will take it up to about 185 miles per hour, but make sure that you are on a long straightaway before you do. Oh, the range is 200 miles, you can get another thirty miles by flipping this switch to the reserve."

"Does this thing have a toothbrush?"

"Not quite," Mitch grinned. "Just go over this manual and make sure you understand everything. Once you're done, we will go over it all again. This bike was built to help keep you alive."

For the next hour Jackson sat on the bike with his helmet on, reading through the operating manual. It was very short and complex but easy to understand given his previous experience.

"Julie," I need you to go to our mountain retreat for the next three days. Don't ask me why. It is imperative you get out of DC immediately. Tell no one else. Take the kids and go. Make up whatever excuse you need to work from home."

"I cannot just up and go on a whim," Julie replied.

"You must trust me love," Mitch whispered, looking over at Jackson, watching him go through the instructions. "Dark Babylon."

That was the family code for an imminent emergency. Julie knew instantly there was no time to argue.

"Kids, come here," she yelled. "I understand. Explain it all later."

"I will," Mitch whispered. "I love you, now go."

"Drew," Mitch yelled over. "Go dark."

Suddenly, the entire facility inside went dark. There was absolutely no light. Walking around the back, the taillight was clearly visible, but not overly bright. The headlights were triple LED, putting out an amazing 8,000 Lumens on high beam.

"Night vision on," Jackson spoke softly into his helmet. Instantly the lights went out, dousing the room in total blackness. He was able to see ahead without distraction and could easily make out the several people in the large space. He hadn't noticed before, but the helmet switched from typical night vision to thermal when he turned his head back and forth.

"Light's," Mitch commanded.

"What's up with the night vision?" Jackson asked.

"I should have mentioned that," Mitch replied. "The vision switches from normal to thermal depending on the surroundings. For example, if it is pouring rain, it will automatically switch from low-light imaging to thermal for better visibility, since thermal has better identification in poor visibility conditions. If you prefer thermal in certain situations just say thermal on."

"I cannot wait to get this thing on the road," Jackson said. "I have a few questions to clarify things. Would you clear them up for me?"

"Certainly," Mitch said.

During the next hour, Mitch clarified all the workings of the bike to Jackson's satisfaction while he practiced using all of the controls. Finally, both were assured of Jacksons skills to operate it.

"It will be dark soon," Mitch said. "Your contact in Budva has the target under surveillance. Leave now and you can get a feel for the capabilities in daylight and dark."

"Which way is best?"

"Tap Budva on your GPS screen," Mitch said. "There, the fastest route is M-2.4. It will take you near Sutomore on the coast. It's southwest of us then, follow it up through Stefan and keep going northwest to Budva. It's about thirty-five miles with a toll somewhere along the route. The road will go from sea level to about 2,500 feet in elevation and back down to sea level. There are only few straightaways but lots of tight turns and very mountainous terrain. Have fun and don't wreck my bike. I expect it will be returned in pristine condition."

"Yes sir," Jackson said as the men rolled up the door and he sped off into the setting sun.

He made it to Virpazar, southwest of Lake Scutari. Riding over the almost two-mile long bridge Jackson gunned the bike and it literally flew down the highway. At one point he thought it was going to launch itself airborne when he engaged the NOX. The belt drive propulsion was extremely quiet. It was almost like the exhaust pipes on the motorcycle had been built like a firearms suppressor. It was nice to feel the wind whipping around his body. There was nothing like the feeling of freedom on the seat of a motorcycle. It reminded him of the Loudon Challenge he had competed in multiple times, the longest running motorcycle race in the U.S. However, this terrain was reminiscent of the Pikes Peak International Hill Climb motorcycle competition, the race to the clouds as the competitors called it, although Montenegro was much tamer. He couldn't help wondering how this bike would perform in those races. Memories of joys long past clouded his mind of the comradery with other racers, adrenaline rush, and tight turns fraught with danger. It seemed like a lifetime ago.

Darkness had fallen and he decided to try out the night vision and engage the stealth mode. Going through Tunel Sozina, he passed several cars. Based on their reaction, he was certain they had not seen him. Suddenly in front of him was a two-car roadblock. Four men stood in front; automatic weapons at the ready.

"Mitch," he called on his comm. "Roadblock ahead. Who knows about this mission?"

"Only the director and me," Mitch replied. "Don't stop. We'll figure out who later."

Jackson spoke into his helmet, "Missiles fire."

The two cars parked in their inverted 'V' formation exploded into one large ball of fire; they were blown off the road. The men who had started firing their automatic weapons, died instantly.

"Wonder who the hell that was?" Jackson thought. "If I'm getting shot at before I begin the mission, I better stay on my toes."

Nearing the coast, he turned right as directed by the signs onto E851 and headed toward Stefan and through to Budva beyond. Traffic was light so he decided to switch from night vision to his headlights and try out the high beams. They were incredible. The highway was bright as day, the bike purring along a more tortuous path, which seemed easy to traverse with the brightness of the high beams. He passed through a few small towns and could see a large glow slightly off to his left, far ahead. Having passed through Petrovac and then Stefan, he was certain it was Budva. He was getting hungry and gunned the bike through twists and turns along the coast until he descended into the city. Slowing down, he made his way off Jadranski Put onto Slovenska Obala and another quick left into the parking lot at the west end of Hotel Park. The staff was very friendly. He quickly checked in and made his way back to the lobby. Near the end of the parking lot, he met his agency contact whom he had worked with before. Sharon watched him approach and climbed out of her compact hatchback.

"It's good to see you again Jackson," she said.

"And you," Jackson said, giving her a small hug. "What's our target been up to?"

"He arrived about noon," she said. "I've been tailing him around. So far, he simply took a walk along the walkway adjacent to the beach, had a late lunch, and retired to his room. I have another agent watching him. Looks like he's in for the night."

"Anything else?" Jackson asked.

"From the conversation we picked up he will be meeting the seller tomorrow."

"Any thoughts about him?"

"He appears very cunning and is super paranoid," Sharon replied. "I should also mention that the file on him notes he is very fit and somewhat of an expert with a handgun so, I wouldn't underestimate him."

"I couldn't imagine doing so," Jackson said, perusing the file. "This is the infamous Russian colonel who castigated the Russian president on television. Interesting."

"And if anyone could get their hands on a Russian missile and its launch codes, it would be him," Sharon said. "Colonel Grigori Ivanov, former head of the 31st Missile Army in the Strategic Rocket Forces. I'm sure he has low friends in high places."

"At least enough to get his hands on that hardware," Jackson said. "With those credentials he has more than enough contacts to procure and protect such a weapon. Didn't I read somewhere that he also was a former Spetsnaz commander?"

"Correct," Sharon replied. "To the best of our knowledge, he was with the SVR RF, their foreign intelligence service that was formerly the First Chief Directorate of the KGB. We have not substantiated it, but they are supposed to have their own top secret elite special force within their operations department or what is known as Directorate Z for Zaslon. I believe that means shield. Anyway, we know almost nothing about them. They are the best kept secret in the Russian army and intelligence."

"I have heard about them," Jackson said. "The mere existence of the group within SVR has been denied by Russian authorities but I would not discard the rumors of its existence. Lunadi spoke to me about them long ago. His information, which I do not know from where he obtained it, hinted that the group is assigned to execute very specific special operations overseas. So, it appears we have an ex-colonel that was involved in their special operations. Not only that, but special intelligence operations and who also served with units in charge of nuclear ICBM's. That's a potent mix."

"The director thinks so," Sharon said. "I would agree."

"Then, we must assume that with his former Spetsnaz connections, he has more than enough mercenaries to protect his assets."

"Bingo," Sharon said. "Like our own ex-special forces members who get hooked on adrenaline or can't keep a steady job and who have offers from around the globe for people with their kind of experience."

"Is there a place to eat nearby?" Jackson asked.

"This way."

The two walked up Slovenska Beach a short way and entered a traditional looking restaurant. Requesting seating outside, they walked through the main restaurant. Jackson admired the large wood beamed and tongue and groove ceilings, all-natural wood. Entering the garden area, it was about a third full of tourists and locals enjoying the Montenegrin and Balkan cuisine while they sat quietly in conversation overpowered by the natural beauty of the Adriatic Sea in front of them. The covered rectangular tables were adjoined with wooden benches akin to park benches. A soft breeze from the sea was warm and inviting. Jackson was happy to see meats of all kinds and barbeque on the menu, as well as sea food, stews, and the traditional Balkan cuisine he had experienced on earlier missions. He was starving. He ordered a Serbian salad, a steak and a cup of stew. The meal was delicious. Afterward he ordered fresh fruit with ice cream and a cup of coffee.

"Didn't you say this was a Chinese restaurant?" Jackson asked.

"No," Sharon said. "It gets its name from Chinese, a fine jade or gem, Lim."

"Interesting,"

Sharon raised her hand, motioning to a man who had entered the garden area; he strolled quickly over.

"Hi Sharon. You must be Jackson, extending his hand as they shook. I'm Art.

"I am Jackson Black, pleased to meet you."

Jackson suddenly felt old. Art was a young, mid-twenties man with a quick smile and exuberant energy. He was guessing it hadn't been that long ago that Art had finished his highly specialized training at the Camp Peary Naval Reservation (officially, the 9,000-acre Armed Forces Experimental Training Activity, or AFETA), near Williamsburg, Virginia, and nicknamed "The Farm," by those who attended. Originally it was a WWII naval construction training center for training Seabee's battalions, and later a POW camp for German prisoners, but run by the CIA since 1951. It was bordered on the east by the York River and not too far away to the west lay the James River. It was a perfect location to conduct land, sea, and air operations special training. He tried to recall his history. The CIA was founded in the fall of 1947 and carried on the wartime heritage of the controversial and mysterious Office of Strategic Services, the OSS. Training was mostly designed around special intelligence collection and covert action.

Most of the personnel in the newly formed CIA were comprised of OSS veterans. When Jackson had taken his training, it was called the Special Activities Division, SAD, and before 1962 the Special Operations Division, SOD. In

2016 the name had changed to the Special Activities Center, SAC. The names changed but the responsibility for covert operations and paramilitary operations remained the same. Although the missions had changed due to terrorism and global flattening arising from development of the Internet and other technologies, the SAC had been divided into two separate groups, the Special Operations Group (SOG) for tactical and paramilitary operations, and the Political Action Group (PAG) for covert, political actions. The SOG's that were assigned paramilitary tasks include covert operations, espionage, special operations, special reconnaissance, counterterrorism, direct actions, targeted killing, hostage rescue, black ops, and guerilla/unconventional warfare. Their members are known as Paramilitary Operations Officers (PMOOs) and Specialized-Skill Officers (SSOs) that are primarily comprised of former Special Forces officers, Green Berets, Army Rangers, Delta Force officers, Navy SEALs, and Marine and Air Force special operations personnel. Despite what the general public perceived about such personnel that was flamed by various news reports around the globe, all SAC and SOG operatives must hold at least a bachelor's degree, many having master's or even law degrees. The duties these personnel carry out are so demanding, hazardous, and specialized that there are generally fewer than one hundred members at any given time. Their missions are also very secretive. The excitement in Art's voice and demeanor was evident. Jackson wondered if this was his first assignment.

Sharon and Art were talking quietly between bites while Art hurriedly ate the food Sharon had ordered for him.

"How is our target?" Jackson asked discreetly so others would not overhear.

"He's turned out his lights," Art responded, leaning back on his bench. "He's in a second-floor room on the south side. I walked to the park and watched another hour. His room remained dark."

"Art says he had a phone call; the buy meeting will take place tomorrow about midday," Sharon said.

"Any idea where?" Jackson asked.

"He kept talking about a Trope or something like that," Art replied. "I apologize but my Russian isn't up to par."

"I think I know what that is," Sharon interrupted. "It's a small bar east of here right next to the beach."

"The one with all the shaded bamboo reed umbrellas?" Jackson asked.

"Yes, that one."

"I noticed when we passed by that it had two floors," Jackson said. "The upper floor has two-person tables covered by typical outdoor beach umbrellas. The bottom floor is the main bar area with four-person tables and directly around it for a couple of rows are permanent bamboo reed Tiki-type covers over tables that seat two. The stools beneath each have three legs of wrought iron curvature designs at the base."

"That's amazing that you remember such detail just from walking by," Art said. "Your reputation is much deserved. I hope that someday I will be able to be as good."

"It's simple situational awareness," Jackson replied, trying not to be embarrassed by the attention. "It just takes practice."

"Could you give me a hint?"

"Lunadi, my mentor told me to use at-a-glance for situational awareness. They teach it at the Farm but differently. Each time you look at a scene, try to remember more and more about it. The more you do it, the better you'll get."

"Thanks, I'll work on it."

"That brings us to tomorrow," Jackson said. "Because there are two floors, we will need to cover both. Any suggestions?"

"Two of us could be together on one level and the other on the next," Sharon suggested.

"Gregori is no novice," Art said. "We need to position

ourselves in such a way he doesn't suspect. Sharon and I could sit at the bottom level and you on top. If he sits there, you could come join us and vice versa."

"You're learning kid," Jackson said. "I like your thinking. If we play it wrong, he will be onto us. So, let's try this. Art, you keep your distance and follow behind. Sharon and I will be too far away from him for him to see us. Once he is seated, we get seated on the same level then, you come join us. It will prevent him from seeing us move if we're already seated, which would arouse his suspicions. You need to be certain that he does not see you tailing him so keep your distance."

"Good idea," Sharon responded. "This man is extremely paranoid. Especially with such a critical deal going down so stay on your toes."

Morning came earlier than anticipated. Jackson was up at 0500 and out the door. He met Sharon and Art briefly in the parking lot at their small, champagne colored surveillance van. After the rendezvous of the target with his seller, the goal was to follow the target to the missile. The three agents were concerned because they didn't expect the target to be close. There was no telling where the missile was, but they needed to clear the first hurdle — not being detected by buyer and seller at the meet.

"First thing first," Jackson said. "Let's sync our comms. Remember one specific protocol; never touch your ear or raise your hand toward your face when you talk. It's a bad habit. Besides, these comms cannot be seen. Insert it in your ear canal and forget about it."

"I find it difficult to do that, but I'll try to remember," Sharon said.

"Do," Jackson retorted. "On this mission particularly, your life will depend on it. Now, let's test the new toy Mitch gave me. Art, stay by the van and when I wave my hand, talk about something, anything. Sharon, you walk that way twenty-five paces. I'll do the same toward the beach."

The three took up position and Jackson waved his hand.

"When I was a kid, my dad used to beat the crap out of me. One day I disobeyed, and he hit me in the head with a ten-inch crescent wrench. It ...."

Jackson cut him off and they joined each other back at the van.

"How did you do that?" Sharon asked. "I heard him like I was standing next to him."

"See this little button on the lapel of my shirt?" Jackson asked. "It's a miniature laser mic good for about three hundred feet. It picked up the vibrations from Art's voice on the glass. Works damn good."

"Another question," Sharon asked. "Art, did your dad actually do that to you?"

"Yes, he did," Art smiled.

"Now I understand your dysfunctional personality," Sharon replied, giggling.

"Art," Jackson said. "Take up your position and get an eye on target. It could be a long day."

ALMOST thirteen hundred miles away in Moscow, sat the Senate Building, commonly called the 1st Building inside the Kremlin complex. The room was immaculate and ornate with a deep, rich walnut wood reaching from the floor to about seven feet above. Directly behind the ornate matching, polished wood desk trimmed in gold was the presidential standard, carved from ivory and trimmed in white and gold with a center dark red crest and inset within an oval framework of rich walnut. On the left side of the desk was the flag of Russia and on the right, the flag of the president. There was a bookcase on either side of the desk framed in walnut and glass and two windows on the right side, separated by another bookcase. The curtains were a deep rose gold, pleated, touching the floor, a deeply curved oval shawl running between them at the top. They were as ornate as the rest of the room, tassels hanging from the edges. Directly behind them was white shear coverings that let in light but not prying eyes. Two, gold trimmed, walnut chairs with an embroidered pattern and color matching the curtains sat directly in front of the desk, a richly columned table between them, also trimmed in gold. A large conference table trimmed in the same fashion and capable of seating eight sat in front of the desk at the opposite end of the room. Directly overhead was an inset vaulted ceiling featuring an inlaid lattice design, all white exposing an earth-toned, sand-colored paint in the opening hanging just in front of the desk and was equidistant from the opposite end of the room where two elaborate, crystal chandeliers hung. From the top of the molded ceiling, past the lattice work dropping down, the ceiling flattened to merge into end and side blocks painted white with gold trim. The office was the type most would drool over. Seated behind the desk was Russian President Nikolai Sokolav and head of the Foreign Intelligence Service (SVR) Andros Gusev, their faces taught, veins popping on their foreheads.

"You're telling me one of our ICBM's is missing," President Sokolav said. "This is disastrous."

"Yes," Andros replied. "It's one of those we were retiring. It has a 750-kiloton nuclear warhead."

"Any idea who took it?"

"It had to be one of our own. We are attempting to narrow it down, but so far nothing. Look Nikolai, maybe you should talk to the American President."

"We cannot risk that at this point," the President said. "It's not him I'm worried about, it's the leaks. They're already blaming us for the fiasco in the Ukraine. It was they who constructed more than thirty bio-weapons labs there. They know as well as you and me that we would not let that stand."

"Yes, I agree," Andros replied. "We need to do something."

"Do you think the Americans know what's happening?"

"Some of my agents have been tracking a small team in Budva," Andros said. "They are onto something; we don't know what. My intelligence says they were seeking for countermand devices that could interrupt their nuclear power plants. Word is they were made by the Chinese but got away from them."

"Can you identify any of their agents?" President Sokolav asked.

"Oh yes," Andros replied. "The leader is Jackson Black."

"He's their best from what I've heard."

"Indeed," Andros replied. "We have multiple scenario's modeled after his exploits in our training exercises. He's the best there has ever been."

"If he's there, they likely know something dire is going on," Sokolav said. "Aren't you acquainted with the CIA director?"

"Yes. We have developed some rapport during the last several years."

"Can we trust him?"

"Yes, I think so," Andros replied. "However, if we mention anything to him, he will most definitely tell President Armstrong."

"Well, at least it would be secret and not reach their congress who have been pushing for war during and after the last disastrous leader. Damn, what a joke he was. Any thoughts?"

"Finding the nuke is a win, win for both sides," Andros responded. "Their defense contractors and congress have been pushing for war. If this missile is launched and hits American soil, they'll get their wish. We must prevent that possibility at all costs. What would you like me to do Nikolai?"

"First, contact the CIA, face-to-face, no calls. Second, keep working on who may have taken the nuke. Put all the power of the SVR on it. Third, if you can help their agents in any way, do so, but discreetly. Divulge that to their director. Once you get things going with the director and President

Armstrong, schedule a face-to-face with all of us. War will not profit either of our countries, only the greed of the defense groups and the idiots in their congress. Anything else on the agenda?"

"Do you remember the criminal group the British were trying to put the lid on?"

"Yes. I thought they took care of them."

"Well, it wasn't them, it was another group that controlled them that is even more sinister."

"How can that be?"

"They control very advanced technology and are seeking what all of them do, world domination."

"How much truth is there to this Andros?"

"I'm afraid it is very real sir. My source, who died in one of my agent's arms, said they are trying to replace global leaders. I'm not sure how, but you may not be safe. I would double your security and use only those men you have known for years. If any of them seem suspicious, you must replace them until I can get a better handle on this."

"Very well Andros. You must do the same, but first, let's get this other business taken care of."

Andros sat for a moment, beginning to ponder the best way to go about his newly assigned task.

THE Director of the Central Intelligence Agency, Phillip Ross, was sitting on a park bench in the Ellipse south of the White House, a habit he had picked up from Dakotah. He wondered how he was doing. Having just come from a meeting with President Armstrong, he wanted to relax and clear his thoughts before heading back to Langley. His security had fanned out and ever alert, stopped a man that wanted to approach the director.

"I have a message for the Director," the man said with a slight Russian accent, holding out his cell phone.

The agent took the phone wanting to make sure it wasn't an

explosive device, "Hello. Who is on the line?"

"It is critical I speak with the director. My name is Andros."

"You stay here," the agent told the messenger, walking to the Director.

"Sir, there is an Andros on the line. He says it's urgent he speak with you."

Phil shot a surprised look at the agent; he reached out for the phone.

"Andros, how are you?"

"I am well. We have a problem and need to meet in person."

"Are you referring to the SS?"

Andros was surprised but didn't let it manifest itself in his voice.

"In part," Andros said. "There is also another matter, but we need to have a face-to-face. It's not something we should discuss over the open air."

"Agreed," Phil replied. "When would you like to meet?"

"I'm already in Washington. I'm sitting with two of my security agents on the steps of the Lincoln Memorial. Can we talk now?"

Phil looked toward the memorial. He could barely see the top of it from where he sat. Andros must have flown all night to meet him. It left little doubt about the meetings importance.

"I'll be there in about twenty minutes. Give this phone back to the courier and bring him along. Let's hustle."

The small group began a rapid walk out of the Ellipse and across Constitution Avenue. Approaching the Washington Monument, still early enough that it cast its shadow west toward the reflecting pool, they headed west and crossed 17th St. NW along the north side of the World War II Memorial. Once around the memorial, they walked quickly along the north side of the Reflecting Pool. It was 800 yards to the Lincoln Memorial steps. Nearing the memorial, Phil could see Andros with his two-person security detail on the steps to the right side. He picked up his pace and a few moments later, the security for both men had fanned out, the courier taking his place among Andros's men.

"It is nice to see you again Phil," Andros said, holding out his hand; the two shook.

"Great to see you as well. Let's have a seat."

The two sat down on the steps, looking furtively about which was their habit. Both had seen action in the field and were long-time masters in the spook game.

"What's the urgency?" Phil asked.

"I'll get directly to the point," Andros said. "I'm sure you already know about someone high jacking one of our nukes."

"Yes. We have our people on it now. Do you know who it was?"

"We are digging into it. It must be one of our commanders from a missile company. Who, we do not know."

"I'll save you a lot of time. It is Grigori Ivanov."

"I would have never thought. He seemed always one of our patriots, always the hardliner. So, it would appear he wants to launch the missile and start a war."

"It looks that way, at least that is what we surmised, the President and I."

"I come to you in peace," Andros said. "We do not want war and we will try to stop this maniac." Andros waved one of his men over and whispered in his ear. The agent walked away quickly, already on his phone.

"What did you tell him?"

"The name you just gave me and to find him. Also, to tell President Sokolav."

"He is currently in Budva, Montenegro. Apparently to meet with the seller of the codes to launch the missile. We have a team following him."

"Do you have enough assets in the area?" Andros asked.

"Only a surveillance team and our best man."

"Ah, you refer to Jackson Black. We have always been

intrigued by him. He is the best of the best is he not?"

"We think so, which is why he drew the assignment."

"I am prepared to offer you all the assets we have in the near area as an overture of good will. If things get nasty, you will need them."

"I am not sure where this will go," Phil said. "But I accept your offer. The one thing I need to know is if we cannot control the situation, we will have one of our submarines launch a cruise missile attack to stop the launch. Would you and President Sokolav back us up with that?"

"That is why I came to you," Andros said. "You are aware of the hostility between your congress and Russia. We both know there has been a lot of false narrative toward my country at their behest. They want war and neither you nor our president's do."

"Correct," Phil replied. "It is unfortunate that President Armstrong inherited such a bunch of wimps, whiners, and woosies to do the bidding of the U.S. government, but it is what it is. Like you, we do not want war. Only fools dare to tread there."

"That is why I came to you personally," Andros said. "We could ill afford this going through open channels. We prefer that you and I, along with Presidents Armstrong and Sokolav work together. We must stop this maniac."

"Then we are in agreement," Phil said. "And the missile strike if needed?"

"I will talk with President Sokolav. He will likely approve but may want a monitor aboard your submarine. I assume, based on our intelligence in the area that it is a Virginia Class?"

"Correct. I'm sure you already know it is the SSN Montana."

"Ah, the commander is a good man. That is a Block V with the Virginia Payload Module isn't it; up to forty Tomahawk cruise missiles. Do you think that is enough firepower?"

Both men grinned, relieving tension.

"If it isn't, we're in big trouble my friend. I will present your proposal to President Armstrong within the hour. I believe in the interests of both our countries that he will agree. Let's communicate directly. What is your codeword?"

"Let us call it Dark Horse," Andros replied.

"Now, what is the other issue?" Phil asked.

"I hesitate to bring it up," Andros said.

"Why?"

"Because I do not want you to think I'm crazy, but I will proceed. Our intelligence has collected data that points to a criminal enterprise on a global scale. If you recall the group that the British MI6 was working against and finally, at least on the surface, defeated — this group supposedly controlled them. The intelligence we received says the group MI6 took down was sacrificed once the command group was in place."

"They killed their own people to begin a new project? Phil asked.

"Our agent believes so. He was killed delivering the message. What we were able to vet was that the command group uses high technology incorporated with biohacking and cloning with the potential to replace key world leaders. This whole missile issue may be a moot point if these guys are operating already."

"Holy hell," Phil gasped. "They could replace any of us and control everything."

"Exactly," Andros said. "We have already taken precautions and suggest you do the same."

"Thank you, friend," Phil said. "I'll get on this right away. Meanwhile, communication will be strictly between us and then, relayed to our groups. Agreed?"

"Yes, agreed."

The two men shook hands, and the small groups went their separate way. Phil's mind was racing. He called for a vehicle to take him to the White House then, called the President's personal assistant.

"Martha, I need an immediate audience with the President.

It's of critical nature. I'll be there in twenty."

"Yes sir," Martha replied. "I'll inform him and will move back his next meeting."

"Thank you."

President Armstrong was sitting on one of the sofas in front of his desk in the Oval when Phil arrived. Martha closed the door behind him while Phil walked to the other sofa opposite the President and sat down.

"What's the emergency?" Bill asked.

"Sir, it is confirmed about the missile. The Russians have offered to provide additional assets if we need them to recover the missile and stop Ivanov."

"What do you think?"

"It's a good idea sir. If things go south, we do not have enough men on the ground to contain it. Also, if we need to perform a missile strike, they are on board, but may want an observer on board Montana."

"Hmmmm. We know they have the plan anyway so what's the harm. Keep the monitor constricted to specific areas. What else."

"This is going to seem farfetched, but they lost an agent who provided vetted intelligence about a global criminal enterprise who is using biohacking and cloning that could replace global and even corporate leaders. They apparently were the main umbrella group of the group that MI6 destroyed."

"What?" Bill exclaimed. "That's insane. Do you mean to tell me that someone could abduct an important official and replace him or her and no one would know?"

"It would seem so sir. President Sokolav and Andros have already taken precautions. I suggest we do the same. I'll put our intelligence groups on it discreetly, but it would be foolish not to react, at least until we can vet the information."

"Quite right," Bill said. "What is Sokolav doing to prevent this?"

"They are using only those agents they've known for over a decade. He believes that if one of them has been replaced there will be a tell in mannerisms so that they can stop any takeover or abduction. Additionally, they will stay out of locations frequented by too many people that they cannot control."

"Can we stop this group?"

"I'm not sure sir. For now, we need to take all the precautions we can until we learn more about them."

"Make it so," Bill said. "Watch your back."

"You do the same sir."

PRESIDENT Sokolav picked up his secure sat phone. Looking toward the door, he motioned his SBP officer to close it. Ivan had worked with him for over twenty years in different roles, but always as his personal security. Sokolav had gotten him appointed to the Presidential Security Service (SBP) upon taking office. Under the control of the Federal Protective Service or FSO, his longtime friend in charge of it had graciously allowed his request.

"What did he say," Nikolai spoke into the receiver.

"The director just phoned me. They have agreed to our help; I have a continent of SVR agents already deployed. They will be nearby in whatever capacity needed."

"And the monitor if a strike is needed."

"They also agreed but will restrict the monitor to certain areas of the vessel."

"If they do not succeed, I want this traitor eliminated."

"It will be as you order sir. The operation is Dark Horse. I will keep you posted. Take special precautions in public sir."

"I will. Thank you."

President Nikolai Sokolav called Ivan over.

"I want you to begin carefully checking out the men in the SBP who are around us. I'm unable to tell you why now but something strange may be going on. Any of them could be a potential threat no matter how much you trust them. Do you still carry a backup?"

"Certainly sir. Since you became president, I carry two, as well as multiple daggers."

"Good. Keep them close and loaded. I'll tell you more when I know more. Where I go, from now on you go."

"I understand Mr. President. Is there something you wish me to look for among the SBP agents?"

"That's just it. I do not know what to look for. Anything suspicious such as habits, memory recall, or a change in physical mannerisms or speech. Be watchful for anything you think may be out of place."

"I will do so discreetly sir. I'll begin right away."

"Good, open the door for my next visitor. Stand behind the secret mirror and watch us like a hawk. There are some very critical issues we are involved in right now. We cannot afford to fail. Sometimes I wish I had not run and won the presidency. This is one of those times."

"I will do so sir. And sir, strong men always have such feelings. Your choice was the correct one."

ART picked up Grigori as he crossed through the park behind the hotel. Jackson had made it clear the man was not a novice so he tailed at such a distance that he could barely keep his target in site. When Grigori reached the ocean walkway to head toward the previously confirmed meeting place, he turned right instead of left. Both Jackson and Sharon had taken seats on each of the levels of the beach bar.

"Something is up," Art spoke into his comm. "Grigori turned the opposite direction."

"That's not totally unexpected," Jackson replied. "Either he is trying to throw off a potential tail or he made arrangements for another meeting location."

"But I've monitored his phone every minute," Art said.

"You've got more to learn kid," Jackson responded. "Arranging a meeting at another location could have been done before he arrived or as simply as leaving a note at the hotel desk for someone to pick up."

"What do I do now?" Art asked.

"Stay on him but keep your distance. Pretend you're looking at something on your phone as you walk. We're on our way. I wanted to get in a morning run anyway. Sharon, coming down."

"Roger," Art said. "He is walking along the Slovian Coast Road. Wait, he's turning down a path to the beach."

Sharon and Jackson began a slow jog toward Art, headed along the ocean walkway. Jackson had not realized how beautiful the Budva Riviera was until now. It rivaled the French Riviera although on a smaller scale. It was bounded by mountain ridges running all the way to the sea on the east and west. The geography formed a horseshoe shape. The water just offshore was called Luka Budva. The meaning of Luka, 'bringer of light,' was particularly apt today. Cascading ripples filled the small bay. There were no waves; sunlight danced across the water with a display of greens, turquoise, and blues. Aloft was a clear blue sky, cumulous clouds floating like soft, white cotton, moving gently in the direction of the breeze blowing from the Adriatic. Along the beach were swimmers of all types, small boats getting ready for a day in the water, and photographers and tourists headed to Sveti Nikola Island a mile offshore to the south. Thousands, perhaps millions of years ago, the island had joined the mainland, but the sliver of land was now submerged, like a long underwater reef visible from the air and boats seeming so close to the surface but buried in the deep. Today was a beautiful day, one of those days the soul could easily get lost in. Sharon bumped his arm when they slowed to a walk.

"Look," she said. "There's Art."

"Where is the target?" Jackson asked.

"Sorry, I snagged my comm on a branch," Art replied. "He just sat down. He's looking around."

"Is that him in the brown wicker chairs with the yellow cushions?" Sharon asked.

"No, he's further out in the light gray wicker chairs," Art replied. "He's wearing a fedora and a dark maroon shirt."

"Got him," Jackson said. "We're going to the bar area and will get a seat outside. Join us after we sit down.

Sharon and Jackson walked toward the bar. The counter was typical of those along oceans, heavily lacquered wood to protect it from the salt air. Sharon spoke to the hostess asking if they could sit in the wicker chairs facing sea. She nodded saying she would be right out with their order. Jackson noticed that the area was paved in pebbled concrete slabs, a tan color, no doubt to match the outdoor furniture. Sitting down, he briefly glanced toward the target, noticing that the chairs, a light gray in color, again matched the concrete slab they sat on. It was almost as it the slab, circular in nature, where it joined the jetty to walk out further, was added as an afterthought. Art waited about six minutes and joined them, sitting across the table from the other two. It was a perfect surveillance arrangement, two chairs on one side and one on the other with a small wicker table between. It was easy for Jackson to look past Art without the target realizing he was being watched. Jackson turned on the small laser mic in his lapel and adjusted it toward the target just as waitress's brought drinks to each table. Oddly, everyone was having beer served in heavy glass mugs with handles. A man who had been sitting just south of them suddenly stood and joined the target.

GENERAL Misha Titov sat down opposite Grigori, carefully glancing around. He was head of Strategic Missile Forces in the Ministry of Defense for Russia.

"We are both taking a huge risk," Misha said.

"True," Grigori replied. "But think of the rewards. You will become the next iron man of Russia and I'll be your second in command."

"This attack will sever the head of the snake," Misha said. "I'll gain the presidency from the moderate Sokolav, and Washington will no longer be a thorn in our ass. It will be a decade before they recover."

Misha picked up his mug of beer. "Here's to success."

"Did you bring what I asked?"

"Yes."

Misha reached into his pocket and retrieved a USB flash drive, handing it to Grigori who pulled his phone from his pocket and attached a USB Type-C male to USB Type-A female adapter to it, plugging the flash drive into the female end. Almost instantly he had accessed the file and perused its contents.

"Excellent," Grigori said. "This will do nicely; I'll be able to quickly input it through the launch panel."

"Did you bring what I asked for?"

"They were too cumbersome to bring with me but here is one of them." He motioned to a man who had been standing near the bar area. It was one of his agents who walked over with a small duffle bag and sat it down beside the general. Misha sat the bag on his lap and slowly unzipped it, caressing the contents within. It was the countermand device. He zipped the bag closed and sat it beside him.

"Where are the rest?"

"They will be at this location," Grigori said, handing him a piece of paper. "I will meet you there. On the back side of the address is the account to transfer my half to. The buyer agreed to the $25 million, yes?"

"He did," Misha replied. "I told him we could sell him the missile and launch codes as well, but he had no interest."

"That's strange," Grigori said, going quiet while the waitress brought more beer. Watching her go, he glanced around and leaned closer. "Perhaps they could not afford the price."

"I don't think so," Misha said. "He was the head of some

criminal enterprise and said he had better ways of orchestrating the outcomes they desired. Anyway, I'll relay the meeting address and his men will be there to collect the other eleven devices and wire payment. Is the location secure?"

"Yes," Grigori said. "I'll have a dozen men inside, more outside."

"I'll send you a half dozen more just to be on the safe side," Misha replied. "This man gave me the creeps, although I don't think he'll be a problem."

"Not to worry friend," Grigori said. "Whether you become the next iron man of Russia or not, you'll be well compensated. I assume the $30 million for the missile payment was received on schedule."

"It was. Thank you. How were you able to pay so much?"

"It wasn't my money," Grigori replied slyly. "Let's just say we have friends who think similarly to us who are more than willing to do what should have been done years ago. Don't worry. You are safe. Your name was never mentioned."

"Keep it that way," Misha said, his eyes narrowing. "We have too many years and too much money in planning to fail now. At any rate, I'll fly to the meeting location. Are you still planning to drive?"

"Yes. I need to make it look like the vacation it's supposed to be. After all, we need distractions from our stressful jobs occasionally, neh?"

"We do and I must say you chose an excellent one and this beer is superb. I have never been here before. I must come for a vacation myself.

For the next hour the two men chatted about basic everyday life and how Russia had changed and how they hoped it would change once they were in power. General Titov arose and walked away. His security detail followed behind once he reached the walkway. They had stood waiting and watching, quietly out of the way near the bar area.

Jackson had seen them and immediately knew who they were. After a few minutes, Grigori left as well.

"We need to get this recording to the director right away," Jackson said. "Let's get on it."

They paid their bill and walked back to the surveillance van about five hundred yards to the east. Stepping into the back, Sharon made a satellite connection to the directors' office. Once secure, the audio file was sent via encrypted satellite phone. Due to its compatibility with GSM, commonly referred to as Global System for Mobile Audio File, the technology enabled the handset to be used much like a mobile phone. The audio format was initially designed for telephony use in Europe and was optimized for recording vocal audio, especially telephone conversations. It was no wonder it had made its way into spycraft.

MEETINGS with the president were becoming much more frequent for the director, but that happens when the world begins to fall apart.

"What's so important we need to meet at 0500?" President Armstrong asked, closing the door, and taking a seat on the sofa.

"You need to hear this Bill," Phil said, laying the digital recorder on the desk and pressing the play button.

"So, we have three issues," Bill replied. "The first is the missile crisis to take out our government. Second, an overthrow of the current Russian government is being planned; the missile strike will solidify that. Third, the countermand devices have reared their ugly head once more. This is becoming disastrous. Solutions?"

"I believe this is something we should discuss privately with my counterpart and President Sokolav. With your permission, I have a secure communication set up on this sat phone."

"Are they ready for a call?"

"They are waiting for your go ahead."

"Very well. Make the call."

Almost five thousand miles away, a secure phone began to ring in President Sokolav's office. Both he and Andros were looked at it while it rang.

"Dark Horse. President Armstrong, you are on speaker with me, Andros Gusev head of SVR, and President Sokolav."

"I am here along with Director Ross. Good day to both of you. I want to warn you that what we are about to say is looking like nothing short of disaster for both our governments."

"I understand," President Sokolav replied. "Andros has brought me up to speed on the initial issue. We will help in whatever way we can."

"Thank you," President Armstrong replied. "It is time to combine our forces to thwart this danger. I want to warn you that what you are about to hear may come as a shock."

"Very well," President Sokolav said. "What is it you wish to say?"

"It is not what I will say, but a recording we just received," President Armstrong replied.

"From your agent Jackson Black?" Andros queried.

The president looked at Phil.

"I'll fill you in shortly," Phil whispered.

"Correct," President Armstrong responded. "The recording is between Grigori Ivanov and another party. We are working on the identity. Here goes."

Phil pressed the play button on the digital recorder. While it played, President Sokolav and Andros looked at each other, surprise registering on their faces. They had not realized that a critical situation had arisen that could result in a coup against Sokolav. President Sokolav was gripping a pen with such force that his knuckles turned white; the pen snapped in half. His face was red with anger. He would have been embarrassed had this message come from someone else, but

33

he knew through back channels that President Armstrong had already weathered an attempted coup by the Speaker of the House. He looked quietly at Andros when the recording stopped. President Armstrong gave them a minute to gather their thoughts.

"Did you recognize the voice of the other man?" Phil asked.

"There is no need to work on identifying him," Andros replied. "With your permission President Sokolav, who nodded his head. The man is General Misha Titov, Head of our Strategic Missile Forces. I would have never suspected him of treason. What do you propose?"

"We need to work together," President Armstrong replied. "Our concern is that your government does not change. More importantly, we need to stop the missile launch and get those countermand devices back. They can be used against any nuclear plant, not just ours."

"What would be our first step in your opinion?" President Sokolav asked.

"We know what they are planning Mr. President," Phil interjected. "We do not yet know where the next meeting is. I suggest we combine our field agents. Our man will track them to the location. However, given the circumstances and to discover how widespread the general's network may be, we need to capture him alive. Of course, he would be transferred immediately to your control if our men caught him."

"I agree," President Sokolav said, nodding to Andros. "If our men are present, we should have him in our custody immediately. Whatever the situation, you may not keep him for interrogation. Agreed?"

"Agreed," President Armstrong said. "And what of Grigori Ivanov?"

"Put a bullet in his head once the missile is located," Andros said. "He is a traitor to us and a threat to you."

"But what about knowledge of the coup network?" President

Armstrong asked.

"The knowledge we extract from General Titov will be sufficient," President Sokolav responded. "Damn, what a mess."

"You got that right Mr. President," President Armstrong replied.

"Does the general have a plane you can track?" Phil asked.

"He does, but I have already checked," Andros replied. "It is at the airport of station and has not moved. Wherever he is, a private plane is in use. Perhaps your field agents can obtain that information."

"I'll put them on it right away," Phil said. "Once we find out, I'll contact you and you'll be able to disperse your men."

"My hunch is either Budapest or Bucharest," Andros said. "I'll have my men fly in discreetly to the Arad airport. That will put them about halfway between. If the location is other than what we suspect, we will modify our strategy."

"Understood," Phil replied. "I'll get my men on it right away."

"President Sokolav," President Armstrong said. "I suggest we let our two directors do their jobs and you and I can remain on standby as needed."

"I agree," President Sokolav said. "It is a pleasure working with you. We need to end this treason quickly."

"I couldn't agree more President Sokolav," President Armstrong replied. "Both our countries futures are at stake. There are far too many madmen in the upper echelons of both."

"Then we shall need to physically excise a few."

CHAPTER 2

JACKSON'S stealth bike was screaming down the road. They had discovered from the flight plan that General Titov was headed to Bucharest. Grigori had a two-hour head start by car. The surveillance van would not be able to keep pace with him, which meant he would need to refuel a couple of times at local petrol stations. Unless Grigori and his men stopped for a meal, he would not catch up until they were near Bucharest. He opened the throttle, hitting 95 mph on straightaways, which there were few. The bike was in stealth mode; he passed vehicles one after the other. They were oblivious to his presence until he passed. His exhaust at this speed was no longer quiet. He noticed passengers in his rear view looking around for the sound. Almost all of them looked skyward thinking it was the sounds from a jet. When negotiated sharp turns, his knees were almost hugging the asphalt. He began to remember the thrill during his days in the races and kept pushing the bike harder and harder.

"Do we have a satellite fix on them yet?" he asked.

"They are approximately one hundred miles ahead of you," Art replied. "We will send you updates as we get them. Wait, they're stopping at a petrol station and what appears to be a small restaurant. They're going in."

Jackson knew they would get a bite to eat and stretch some. He should be able to close the distance by about thirty miles. The belt drive was so smooth that there was no vibration, even at 100 miles per hour, which he hit in several places along the way. At this rate of speed, he would also need to stop for fuel. About two hours later a light on his gas gauge indicated the fuel had switched to the reserve.

"Art, are there any petrol stations nearby?"

"About ten miles up on the right according to our feeds."

"Roger that."

About seven minutes later, Jackson pulled into a small station, which only had two pumps. He had taken the bike out of stealth mode about a mile before. Quickly opening the fuel cover, he filled the bike and went inside to pay. Grabbing a soda, he quickly swigged it down. He noticed a young girl admiring the bike and then walk away. Suddenly, the hair on the back of his neck began to tingle. Something was wrong. Getting back on his bike, he slowly looked around as if he hadn't a care in the world. About fifty yards away, pulled beneath the thick canopy of a large tree were three racing bikes. The riders were staring through the low hanging branches directly at him, not realizing he had spotted them. Jackson put on his helmet like nothing was the matter and squatted down behind his bike pretending he was checking the engine, although it was hidden by the cowlings.

He could clearly see the bikes and riders. Everything was black, the bikes, leather clothes, and helmets; the weapons strapped to their sides stood out clearly. Semiauto machine pistols, the Russian PP-2000 in 9mm with a folding stock and lanyard to hold it in place.

"This had to be part of a rear guard in case someone came along. They would be too good not to know he was on the hunt. After all, American's stood out like a sore thumb when their helmets were off. Straddling his bike, he cranked it with the electric start; it was so quiet they wouldn't be able to hear it. Suddenly, he gunned the bike and was almost a quarter mile down the road before the pack pulled out behind him. He had immediately engaged the stealth mode and seemingly disappeared before their eyes, too stunned to react as quickly as they normally would.

"Jackson, we detect three bikes behind you," Sharon said.

"I picked them up at the station. They are a rear guard, either Russian soldiers or mercs. Either way, Grigori will now know he is being followed. Keep an eye on him."

Jackson knew he could just park and let them pass without seeing him, but that would put them and perhaps other contingents between him and his target. No, better to deal with them now rather than later. Just before rounding a curve to the left, bullets began ricocheting off the pavement. They had to be guessing where he was; he knew they couldn't see him. Looking at his console he had four mini rockets loaded, front and rear. Rounding the curve, the road was straight for almost a mile ahead of him. He leaned forward to reduce the wind resistance and activated the mini rockets, their heat seeking infrared homed in on the three bikes behind. He decided to use only two rockets. The round dots with the cross hairs locked onto two of them and he said, "Launch missiles." The flame from the rockets pinpointed his location and the riders fired, bullets impacting all around him. But it was too late, in seconds, two of the bikes disappeared into flames, shrapnel propelled in all directions; they disintegrated. The third rider didn't hesitate. It was just another mission. He sped forward. Jackson instinctively knew the man would not give up. Bullets were once again striking everything around him, but he was too far ahead of the other bike for them to do much damage.

"I need to take him out," Jackson thought.

He downshifted several gears without touching the brakes to slow the bike. The Russian agent had closed the distance quickly and was reloading. Jackson had removed his P-228 from the hidden compartment and stuck it through the stealth barrier. The agent was stunned. All he could see was the shrubs and trees to his right and the gun that seemed to be riding along with them. His eyes widened in fear; Jackson gave him a triple tap. The man was dead before he hit the asphalt, his bike skidding off the road and striking the railing of a small bridge, catapulting end over end several times before it came to rest on the highway, bursting into a fiery inferno.

Placing his P-228 back into the hidden console, Jackson sped forward, going as fast as his years of racing would allow.

"Be aware there are two police cars in pursuit. They passed the first two bikes. That means they are after you."

"Roger," Jackson said.

He knew that Russians like Grigori had law enforcement in key places under their influence throughout Eurasia. No matter what predicament such a man found himself in, he could always count on such to perform needed services, either in return for a favor, for money, or promise of death. It was only a few minutes before the police were visible behind him. His best option was to let them pass so he decided to pull over. The cars, lights flashing, went roaring by, two BMW M3's. They were fast. He watched until they disappeared around the next bend and began his journey.

"Jackson, they set up a roadblock around the bend in the road," Art shouted in excitement.

"That means they have infrared," Jackson said. "They saw me and now lay in wait."

Reaching the bend that turned sharply left, Jackson pulled off the road and walked along the edge. Staying low, he pulled out his small monocular and surveyed the roadblock.

The two cars had parked in a shallow 'V,' front to front. One of the officers was sitting in his car looking at a screen, obviously for the heat signature of the bike. Jackson knew the longer it took him to decide, the longer it would take to catch up with his target who by now was hell bent for leather to Bucharest. There was only one thing to do. Jackson walked back to his bike and turned on the ignition but did not start it. He pushed it along the left side of the road until he was sure the rockets would clear the underside of the low hanging branches. Next, he locked the mini rockets onto both vehicles and launched them. The force of the explosion blew the police cars off the road turning them into fiery coffins. He cranked the bike and sped past the cars, mangled from the force of the explosion. He hit 110 miles per hour and began taking sharp bends like his life depended on it, but it wasn't his life it was the lives of over six million people in the National Capitol Region of the United States.

"Too bad the missile couldn't just strike the congress when they were in session," he thought, grinning at the idea. "They were as useless as they come anyway."

He knew he could not let his feelings for the traitors in the halls of congress affect his judgement. The determined look on his face seemed to be set in concrete; he pushed the bike to its limits."

Back in the crises room at the White House, President Armstrong, Vice President Vince Reisner, and CIA Director Phillip Ross were watching the satellite feeds.

"Damn that man can drive," Vince muttered.

"He can at that," Phil whispered back.

The satellite feed was also being piped to Moscow where President Sokolav and Andros Gusev were admiring the skills.

"How fast did he take that curve?" President Sokolav asked.

"About 80 miles per hour," Andros remarked. "The limit is fifty."

"I can see why he is their best," Sokolav said.

"Yes, he is," Andros said. "We can trust him. His care is for the people, he defies their government."

"Then why does he work for them?" Sokolav asked.

"Because the President, Vice President, and the Director are his friends, and they are honest. If they remain in power, he will continue to do so. And they will be reasonable for us to deal with."

"Are our people in place to help them?" Sokolav asked.

"Yes," Andros replied. "They left Arad an hour ago. We don't know where the meeting is, so we wait on standby."

"They will tell us, yes."

"Yes, Nikolai. They need our help as much as we need theirs."

THE motorcycle was almost on its side, Jackson's left knee pad rubbing the pavement when he went around the sharp turn.

"You're gaining on them," Art spoke into his comm. "Think you can slow down a little. The general's plane just landed in Bucharest. We have a man on the ground there. He'll try to tail him to the meeting location. You have heavily armored vehicles coming your way. There is a cut off road about a quarter mile ahead. Take that to the right, a mile down, go left and in another mile, left again. It will lead you back to the main road."

"Roger," Jackson replied, muttering to himself. "This is beginning to be a royal pain in the ass."

"What was that?" Sharon asked.

"Nothing, just talking to myself."

The cut off roads were straight as arrows. Jackson put the bike on the red line. About three minutes later, he had pulled beneath the overhanging branches of some large trees waiting for the armored vehicles to pass.

"You are clear," Art said. "They just cleared the curve heading away from you."

Jackson gunned the bike, riding like the devil himself. Both he and his bike were beginning to get covered with road grime. Heading into a heavy rainstorm, he was clean once again. Cold and wet, just the way he liked to travel. He had already passed the border of Montenegro, through Paricin, Serbia; Vidin, Bulgaria; and into Romania. Passing east of Craiova, Romania, he remained heading east on E70 until he got stalled in a construction zone. It was then that he noticed them, about eight cars back. Two blacked out, metallic gray BMW M8's, the new luxury competition coupe model with a whopping 617 horsepower. With phenomenal handling and a blistering 0-60 time; they were going to be tough to deal with. There was just enough light from the darkness of the clouds to see the two men in the front of each vehicle. The passenger would be the shooter; the driver would keep the pedal to the metal as the old saying went. He was not currently in stealth mode, so they could see him as clearly as he saw them. They sat and waited patiently; the wait time interminable while the work crew let only one vehicle through at a time.

Rain began to fall again, the clouds growing darker. It would not let up anytime soon. The wait while each car was let through lengthened. Jackson began to feel the adrenaline rush because he was next in line. He gunned the bike forward at a reasonable speed. He did not want to telegraph that he had noticed the hitmen. There was a small curve in the road a few hundred yards ahead. Once he got to the other side, he turned stealth mode back on and pushed the bike to full throttle, redlining it. He began to wonder how they had found him and if they worked for Grigori or someone else. They had to be working for the Grigori or perhaps the general. It didn't matter, both were on the same team. His speed kept his face shield clear of rain, the bike throwing up a rooster tail of water behind it as he sped along. He passed cars like they were sitting still. Although he was invisible to them, the trail of water was not.

"There are two bogeys' back at the construction site," Jackson spoke into his comm. "Have they cleared it yet?"

"Roger," Art responded. "There are two fast moving vehicles approaching you from behind. It looks like they are slowly closing. They will reach visible range in thirty."

Jackson didn't like the sound of that. He was far enough ahead that the hitmen would have a difficult time following him, even with a tweaked out M8. He either needed to take a different route or keep the bike near the redline.

"Jackson," Art spoke into his earpiece. "There is another construction site ten miles out of Alexandria on DN6 or E70, not sure what the road signs say. You either let the bogey's pass or take an alternate route. There is only one. Take Highway 51 out of Alexandria and merge onto Highway 26 just south of Smârdioasa then, go northeast on a small jog to Bragadiru, pick up 506 heading southeast and merge onto Highway 5C at Bujoru. You'll head northeast again through Giurgiu onto their Interstate 5, which will take you right into Bucharest."

"What's the downside?"

"You'll lose about forty-five miles. But, because of the construction zone, you wouldn't catch Grigori anyway."

"Download the route to my GPS."

"Will do," Art replied.

The small display on the bike's console blinked and instantly displayed the new route.

The rain had stopped by the time Jackson reached Smârdioasa and turned onto the next highway.

"Jackson," Art spoke into his comm. "We have an issue. The two bogeys are following you."

"How the hell do they know where I am?"

"Unsure," Art replied. "Is it possible they put a tracking device on your bike?"

"I haven't left it long enough for anyone to do that."

Jackson began to think if there had been a place where a tracking device could have been put on. It would certainly explain the quick response and finding his location by the people who had been chasing him. Suddenly, it dawned on him, there had been a sexy young teenager admiring the motorcycle at the petrol station just before his encounter with the other bikes. Traffic was light, almost non-existent. He pulled over to the side of the road by a group of shrubs that partially hid him from traffic. He took a couple of steps back, picturing in his mind where the girl had stood near the pumps. She would have approached from the pump side so they would partially hide her from my view while paying for gas. Looking carefully at the bike, there were only two or three places a tracker could be attached quickly. Because of the cowling, it would need to be attached to the metal. He got down on his hands and knees and checked the rear frame around the back tire and belt drive. Nothing was there. Then, he checked the bottom of the bike around the main frame. Next, he looked near the top of the front suspension forks where they disappeared behind the headlights and under the fuel tank. He was baffled and stepped back. It had to be here, there was no way they could have found him so quickly.

Jackson slowly walked around the other side of the bike, comparing it to the previous side. It looked identical. "Wait," he thought. "The other side has an air intake."

He walked back around the bike and examined the air intake, which had four red, metal ribs sweeping back toward the rear of the bike at a forty-five-degree angle and beneath them, a mesh stainless steel screen that disappeared under a circular cover blending with the rest of the bikes cowling. Getting down on his hands and knees, he looked as far as he could along each rib, downward under the cover. There it was, on top of the second rib, a blinking green light. He shoved his hand between the two ribs and, barely able to reach the device, pulled it free. It was the half the size of a deck of playing cards with a magnetic back that held it tightly.

"Why did you stop?" Art asked. "They are about twenty miles behind you and closing fast."

"I found the tracker," Jackson replied. "I'll be on my way in a minute."

He looked in the small spare compartment on the left side of the cowling and retrieved four mini missiles, loading them into their small launch tubes. He was off like a shot, screaming down the highway. Passing through Bujoru, he reached the other side of Balariile ten miles later and found a petrol station with two cars at the pump. They were tourists heading toward Bucharest. Discreetly, he placed the tracker beneath the rear bumper of one of the sedans. When they pulled away, he filled his tank and headed out after the sedan, looking for a location where he could lay in wait. About four miles ahead, when entering Vedea, Highway 5C changed to Arsache Street. It turned quickly right and then sharply left. The shooters would need to turn in their seats and look far enough to their right to see him. He gambled they would be looking toward the direction of the tracker. There was a small market not more than two-hundred feet from the turn. He gunned his bike hard, parking behind a box truck with a clear view of the corner. About fifteen minutes later, the two M8's sped by. Putting the bike in stealth mode, he pulled out not far behind them.

"Art," Jackson said. "I'm behind them. I need to take them out. What is your satellite showing?"

"There's a five mile stretch between Malu and Slobozia with a couple of shallow turns. It's all farm fields. That's your best shot."

"Roger," Jackson replied.

He kept his distance a quarter mile back from the two cars who were closing on the sedan. Passing through Malu, there was almost no one on the road.

"I need to take them both out at the same time," Jackson thought. "He slowly increased speed until he was about five hundred feet from the tail car, pulling into the oncoming lane. Two miles out of Slobozia, he came to a screeching halt watching his targeting monitor when the M8's turned right around a shallow curve. He launched two missiles and watched their tail fire and smoke streak toward the targets. Three seconds later, both cars exploded. He slowed when he passed each, making sure the occupants were dead. Satisfied, he gunned the bike toward Bucharest.

ANDROS was sitting beside President Sokolav when the phone rang.

"Yes, director," Andros said.

"We have them," Phil said. "The general's plane arrived at Coanda in Bucharest. We've been tailing him. From the airport he traveled to a restaurant on Spătarului."

"What is he doing?"

"He is just sitting there."

"How long will it take for your men to reach it?"

"They'll be there in thirty minutes," Andros replied. "Is there a bar nearby?"

"Yes," Phil responded. "It's halfway down the block on the east side near the intersection of Strada Spătarului and Bulevardul Carol I. Why do you ask?"

"They will want to seal their treason with a drink," Andros replied. "I suggest you slowly filter your men into the bar. I will do the same."

Andros hung up the phone. "We have the traitor located Nikolai."

He quickly made another call, giving his men orders and directions.

A team of eight SVR agents were at once on their way in the back of a small box truck followed by another team of four in two sedans. All in civilian clothes, there was an air of confidence in how they handled themselves. They double checked their weapons, attaching suppressors. This was to be a quick in and out.

"Men, we will be working with the Americans to capture a traitor to our country. Look at his photo carefully, passing it around. This man is the CIA operative we will work with. Take care not to shoot him or his men. He is after Grigori Ivanov, this man, another traitor, but we are not to shoot him. We need General Titov alive. If they get him before we do, they will turn him over immediately. Do you understand?" The men nodded agreement.

Jackson had been directed by Art to the location. The general remained where he was, quietly sitting in his car. It suddenly became clear that this would be a night meeting.

"Jackson," Art spoke into his comm. "I'm going to patch you through to the SVR team. Standby."

The comm crackled softly; a man spoke English with a heavy Russian accent.

"Jackson. You may call me Anatoli; we friends in Dark Horse, neh?"

"Yes,' Jackson confirmed. "I am in the bar now. It looks like your man will wait until dark to meet. It is important not to kill Grigori or General Titov."

"Yes, confirmed," Anatoli replied. "I have same orders. I have twelve men with me and how many you have?"

"I and three others," Jackson replied. "We are all wearing darker colored baseball caps with Romanian flags or crests on them. Most of us have black or chocolate brown leather jackets."

"Thank you for the information," Anatoli said. "My men are wearing darker colored sweaters and beanies with an American sports team on them."

"Good to know," Jackson replied. "I'm in the bar now. It's low light, wood herringbone patterned floor, dual toned green wall and white ceiling. There are several rooms. A game room with small round tables and chairs, a side room with picnic style tables, and the main area. It has small round tables with an open door beyond to the bar. Entering the bar and liquor serving area the restrooms are to the left. I'm sitting in the corner of the main room, chocolate brown jacket."

"Very well," Anatoli said. "I will filter my men in. Where is Grigori?"

"Our team has him spotted a block away. I figure he will make his move in less than an hour."

During their conversation, Jackson had noticed a man casually looking at him from a table closer to the bar. He was wearing simple sports coat and slacks. The only thing that stood out was a gold ring on his finger with the initials CD. "Must be the initials of his name," Jackson thought.

After a couple of minutes, the man stood to leave when a couple waved at him from the door. They somehow seemed out of place to Jackson who doubled his observation efforts.

A few minutes later, a man in a dark gray sweater took a seat by Jackson.

"I am Anatoli."

"I am Jackson Black."

"So, I meet the famous spy at last."

"Not sure about the famous part, but glad to meet you."

The two men nodded imperceptibly at each other, glad to be identified so that when bullets began flying, they wouldn't shoot each other. During the next ten minutes, Anatoli's men slowly filtered in and ordered drinks. Two took up positions in each room. Both teams having identified each other, they sat quietly feigning tiredness from a long workday. Their comms were on the same frequency. When the targets walked in, the operatives appeared oblivious to them. Such training was a primary part of spycraft if one desired to stay alive.

Grigori walked in with seven men. He grabbed a table beneath an array of posters of famous bands, Kiss, Metallica, Motorhead, and others attached to a dark wood backing. Two of his men sat at tables on either side. and Anatoli's men outside reported another four. Suddenly, word of General Titov's car pulling up out front shifted their focus. The deal was about to go down. General Titov walked into the room and glanced about, not an ounce of fear. He was well over six feet tall and muscular. Two security agents stood next to him, another four spread out around the bar.

"This is not going to be easy," Jackson muttered under his breath.

"It never is," Anatoli replied. "When do you want to move?"

"Let's listen to their conversation. That will help us decide."

Jackson trained his small laser mic onto the wall directly behind the targets table. Within a few seconds, every agent could hear what they were saying.

"Are you sure this is a safe place?"

"Relax Misha," Grigori replied. "I have used it before. The crowd here is low key and won't notice us."

"Do you have the devices?" Misha asked.

Grigori nodded to one of his men.

"Send one of your men with him. They will transfer them to your car."

Misha signaled to one of his men who walked over; Misha whispering something in his ear. The two men walked out followed by another from each group.

"I sent Mikail because he is familiar with the devices. The funds have been wired to your account."

"Yes, I saw that. Thank you. Our plan is moving forward, gaining momentum. We will begin a war with the west and unseat President Sokolav. Let us toast."

The two raised their vodka shots, bumping the glasses, immediately gulping the entire shot. The strength brought tears to their eyes while they slightly coughed.

"Damn!" Misha exclaimed. "That is strong."

"But we are men, right? We can handle it."

Grigori waved over a waitress to order another round. It was then when he noticed something out of place. He caught the eyes of two men at the bar who immediately looked away. A trap.

"Give me your pen and I'll write down the address I spoke of," Grigori said, raising his eyebrows to give Misha a heads up while beginning to write the note.

"We are being watched, be cautious."

Misha read it without any indication something was wrong.

"By the way," Grigori said. "I have that brandy you wanted. I picked it up in Paris. I'll have my man get it for you."

Grigori motioned for his lead agent to come over and whispered in his ear. The agent stood and walked around the table as if exiting, speaking orders into his comm. Their men inside and out moved about as normal. The agent suddenly thrust the table on its side while Misha and Grigori rushed for the door, his 9mm pistol hurtling slugs at the Russian and American agents near the bar and at Jackson and Anatoli. Every agent was firing his gun at another. Anatoli and Jackson dove behind their table, turning it on its side, using it for cover while they returned fire. Half a dozen agents from each side lay dead or wounded writhing on the floor while remaining agents began making their way through the bar to the main door. Grigori's agents had taken a position across the street and rained a hail of bullets at the entrance. They were being shot at from all sides and slowly began to retreat from one car to another. Jackson had lost sight of Misha and Grigori when he heard shots around the side of the bar.

"Cover me," he said.

"I will comrade," Anatoli replied while shoving another magazine into his pistol, without losing motion, and firing three quick shots pinning Grigori's men down.

Jackson ran around the side of the bar, jumping over two wounded agents, not taking time to see who they were. All he focused on was the large sedan with the door closing. It began moving toward him. He raised his P-228 and put two quick shots into the windshield above the steering wheel and the repeated the pattern on the passenger side. The agent who had opened the door hadn't made it to the other side of the car and began returning fire. Jackson responded with one shot to the head; the man fell dead in his tracks. The sedan, almost hitting Jackson who dove out of its path, crashed into a parked car; Jackson scurried to quickly open the back door, dragging the occupant from the seat, throwing him face down on the pavement. He quickly pulled the man's hands behind his back and put on zip ties. It was only when he sat the man against the back wheel of the car that he realized it was Misha.

"Damn," he muttered under his breath. "I've got to find Grigori."

The gun fire subsided quickly while Grigori's men made it to their get-away vehicle. Jackson searched the car and then the trunk. The countermand devices were all there; he let out a sigh of relief.

"At least something had gone his way," he thought.

Seeing one of his men, he motioned him over.

"Watch this man and get some others over here to carry the devices."

Jackson slowly made his way back toward the street checking on the men who had fallen. They were Anatoli's agents, wounded but alive. On the street and in the bar were four dead agents of Grigori's. Both Anatoli and Jackson had each lost a man.

"Ah," Anatoli said, as he rounded the corner. "You're alive. It looks like the two big fish got away. Do you have satellite tracking them?"

"Come, follow me," Jackson said.

The two men walked back to the sedan. The agent had placed Misha in the back seat.

"I have a gift for you my friend," Jackson said.

Anatoli leaned down, looking into the car.

"Very good my friend. We have what we came for, but your fish got away."

"For now," Jackson replied. "Art, do you have them?"

"Yes, they are heading for the Băneasa regional airport to your north. The satellite is only picking up helicopters on the field. One has a heat signature and getting hotter. My guess is that is your target."

"Do you have a helicopter at your disposal?" Jackson asked.

"Yes," Anatoli replied. "I will have it pick you up here."

He walked away shouting orders and making a call.

"Hal," Jackson said. "Take care of the bike. Round up all the men and get out of here. It won't take the Sector 12 police long to arrive. Load up the wounded and get the hell out."

"The helicopter is going to touch down in the parking lot of the Grand Hotel Bucharest. It's six hundred yards west."

"Hal," Jackson yelled. "Come with me then you can have the bike."

Jackson strapped his helmet on, jumped on the bike; and Hal held on precariously when Jackson gunned the bike, burning rubber and screeching onto Carol Boulevard. He was pushing the needle into the red while downshifting gears making it to the parking lot of the hotel in less than three minutes. Jackson climbed off the back, Hal's eyes staring wide, filled with fear.

"Okay, take it back," Jackson said handing Hal his helmet. The sounds of the helicopter could be heard approaching while Hal sped away, panting into his comm.

"Are you okay?" Art asked, hearing the heavy breathing.

"That man's a lunatic," Hal spoke. "I thought he was going to kill us both."

"You're safe with him," Art replied, laughing. "You should see him drive alone. He rides the razor as they say."

Jackson stood at the edge of a small field in front of the hotel, the wash from the rotors pushing on him. The helicopter came to a hover three feet above the grass. The door opened and a helping hand grabbed Jackson's forearm and pulled him quickly inside.

"Art," Jackson screamed above the noise. "Patch into the pilot's headset and guide him to target."

"Roger"

Grigori had gotten into his helicopter and headed northeast. They had a half hour lead. Art was directing the pilot on the path they were taking.

"Where are they headed Art?" Jackson asked.

"They have a straight line of flight at 67-degrees east northeast."

"If I recall there is nothing but marshland along the coast," Jackson said. "Is the path deviating?"

"No, straight flight. Satellite shows a small island along the path. It's Bile."

"Isn't that Snake Island, where the Russians took some Ukrainians prisoner during the war."

"Yes," Art replied. "It had a small settlement of about fifty or so people, but our last intelligence said that it was deserted. Not a surprise since they need to bring in food and water from the outside."

"Is the satellite picking up anything?"

"There is a heat signature in a small group of buildings near the center of the island. We're also picking up probably twenty men."

"Find out if Anatoli has any men in the area?"

The man with the CD ring pulled his cell phone out.

"I'm afraid we lost our opportunity sir," the man said. "There were too many American and Russian agents."

"Damn!"

"What should we do now?"

"We know where they are going, get your other men ready. This will by your last opportunity. Do not fail. We need him dead or alive."

THE Oval Office was gloomier to Phil while he trudged along the hall, not wanting to inform the president about what was happening. It would be another meeting with the Russian President. It always amazed him how a crisis brought together strange bedfellows who had been long-time enemies. He was quickly admitted to meet the president who was already seated with the Vice President and Jonas Rothman, Secretary of Energy.

"Good morning, sirs," Phil said. "I have news. They caught General Titov, but lost Ivanov. They are tracking him as we speak. I've asked them to pipe it in here when they have more information."

"What about the countermand devices? Jonas asked.

"We took those into custody and handed the general over to the Russians."

"And Jackson?" Bill asked.

"He's hot on Grigori's tail, but I need not explain the risks to you."

"Art told us it looks like Grigori is headed to Snake Island and that it's heavily guarded," Vince interrupted. "How long will it take once he reaches there to arm and launch the weapon?"

"I talked to the Russians, and they said perhaps thirty minutes."

"How far away are they?" Jonas asked.

"About thirty minutes out," Phil replied.

"That give us one hour," Bill murmured.

The men leaders looked at each other. All had been friends with Jackson. He had saved each of their lives numerous times. They were now confronted with weighing his death. Jonas broke the silence.

"We have known Jackson for a long time. He is our friend. I have known him longer than all of you. If he were here, he would tell you without hesitation that the lives of the people are more important than any one man."

"I do not know him as well as you do, but when the President and I met him at the airfield I asked him why he still did this work," Vince said. "He told me for the people."

"Vince, get me Admiral West and the Chief of Naval Operations on the horn."

"Gentleman, it is crunch time. We need to be on top of this."

"Agreed Mr. President. Andros Gusev, head of SVR and President Sokolav are waiting sir."

"Let's get to it then," Bill said. "Mr. President and Andros. Good day to you sirs. On with us are Admiral West, Chief of Naval Operations Tom Riley, VP Reisner, Director CIA and Secretary of Energy. As you are aware, we have a critical situation for all of us."

"What do you need from us Mr. President?" Sokolav asked. "And thank you for capturing our traitorous general."

"More than happy to oblige," President Armstrong replied. "You are by now aware that Ivanov is headed toward Snake Island. Do you have any special operators that can team up with Jackson Black to try to stop this maniac?"

"I have a dozen men on the way," Andros interrupted. "They are developing a strategy as they go, but I do not need to tell you that time is short."

"Understood," President Armstrong said. "I understand your man is on board the Montana."

"Yes, Mr. President," Sokolav replied. "He was put aboard yesterday. Thank you for your hospitality. I have instructed our navy to clear the area. Only the Montana remains. It is my hope we do not need to use her."

"We hope the same thing Mr. President," Armstrong said. "The goal is to retrieve your missile if possible. At the same time, we cannot allow such an incident to occur. Admiral West, are you hearing all of this?"

"Yes, Mr. President. Chief of Naval Operations Samson has already relayed the coordinates of the target and they are locked on pending your orders sir."

"President Sokolav and Andros, please help us all you can. We are linking you to our men on the ground. If you have a link, let's all watch that too. President Sokolav, estimate the arming time as closely as you can and relay it to your man on the Montana."

"I understand Mr. President. We will wait until seven minutes before estimated launch time. Your commander in Montana needs to use that time as impact."

"Did you get that Admiral West?" President Armstrong asked.

"Yes. I heard President Sokolav. Information is already being relayed to the SSN Montana. God help us all."

"Alright gentlemen, we have live feed from both satellite and the Russian helicopter."

"We are linking you to our Spetsnaz," Andros said. "They are approaching the island from the west."

"Alright, showtime," Phil said.

Video feeds to presidents of both countries had come to life on large monitors to watch progress of the operation.

THE SSN Montana, a Virginia Class sub, commanded by Captain Jesse Reed had spent too much time for his taste reaching the Black Sea. Both Russians and Americans had planned together. Using Article 12 of the Montreux Convention that governs passage of naval warships through the Bosporus and Dardenelles Straits between the Aegean Sea and the Black Sea, they had posed as a Kilo Class Russian sub rejoining their base. The requirement to pass through the straits during daylight and on the surface did not sit well with Captain Reed, but orders were orders. They had picked up the Russian observer from a small boat at the beginning of the Dardenelles Strait, Captain Ludis Belsky from the Russian Black Fleet. The Turkish government had been notified and everything went according to plan. Of course, the SSN Montana was required to paint Russia's emblem on its mast. It now lay quietly, three hundred feet below the surface, seven miles from Snake Island, Bile as it was currently called.

They had entered the mouth of the Dardenelles Strait near Seddülbahir. It was forty-five miles through the strait before the sub could submerge again. Captain reed hated the exposure. Just over 125 miles later they entered the Bosporus Strait, the city of Istanbul standing like a sentinel at its mouth. The captain knew that unseen spies along their route would report the subs movements to their handlers and the information would trickle upstream until it reached the desk of the intelligence agency the asset worked for. Not wanting to risk further exposure, the Montana submerged again twenty-two miles later, heading to its destination about two-hundred seventy-five miles away. The Russian monitor, Captain Ludis Belsky was an affable man; one you could easily make friends with. He had a keen eye and was very humorous and outspoken, much different than most of those in the submarine service who took their jobs very seriously.

"So, Captain Reed," Ludis said. "Now we wait."

"Yes Captain, now we wait. Perhaps we should look at the satellite images and make sure we have our bases covered."

"That would be wise captain," Ludis replied with a grin. "After all, we both want to keep our rank."

The images of the island were laying on the chart table. They studied them for several minutes.

"The heat signatures are here, in this main complex in the middle of the island," Captain Reed said. "But there is also this small group of buildings on the east end near the docks. How well acquainted are you with this missile?"

"I know it well," Ludis replied. "I used to work on their warheads. Like you, I think that this should be the primary target. But . . . he paused.

"But what?" Reed asked.

"I know this Grigori Ivanov and have read his file," Ludis said. "He is shrewd and cunning, as well as ruthless. He may have set up this heat source on purpose."

"You think he is decoying us from the real target?"

"Perhaps," Ludis mused. "What if the missile is here, in this longest building by the dock? Just west of the four buildings with the green roofs. And here, to the north, the other building with the light-colored roof. I think it would fit in either."

"You are saying we need to take out everything, every building."

"Is your capitol not worth it?"

"Yes," Reed replied. "CSO, here please."

"Ah yes, your combat systems officer," Ludis smiled.

"Yes captain,"

"Look at these satellite photos," Reed said. "Do you already have the Tomahawks set for strike?"

"Yes sir, per the Admirals orders you passed along."

"Captain Belsky says this Grigori fellow is sneaky. So, we cannot afford to fail. The fate of DC and its people are on the line. I want you to specifically coordinate an attack on each building."

"That's a lot of Tomahawks sir and money," the CSO said.

"Yes," Captain Reed replied. "But like our friend Captain Belsky observed, Washington DC and the surrounding area and its people are worth it."

"Let me do some quick calculations sir."

The two captains stood looking over the CSO's shoulder while he began marking target coordinates and made the necessary calculations.

"Okay sir. With your permission we need to launch a total of eighteen sir. That will make certain there is complete destruction."

"See to it. Lock in the coordinates and be ready to fire at a moment's notice."

"Yes sir."

"Do you have that many Tomahawks on board?" Captain Belsky asked surprised.

"I'm sure you know my friend the answer to that," Captain Reed replied. "We have forty of them."

"Ah," Ludis mused. "The payload module with four more tubes each with seven Tomahawks. I was not aware this boat was one of those."

"It is," Reed replied. "Thus, we have sufficient for this mission. I'm hoping our people and yours get to him so that we do not need to launch."

"We will know within the hour, neh?"

The presidents of the U.S. and Russia were watching the operation while it unfolded, like slow motion feedback during a sports game. Satellite feeds showed Jackson already on the island. He had managed to quickly scale the seventy-five feet from the water to the top. Waves and sea spray bounced over the bow of a Russian Project 02510 BK-16 approaching Jackson's position at 75 miles per hour. A team of eight SVR Spetsnaz ready to disembark. The feed was also being piped to the SSN Montana that had rose to its launch depth. Ideally, a night operation would have been best, but the safety of night could no longer be afforded with mad man Grigori intent on launching the nuclear missile at Washington DC.

Jackson had been dropped off on the west side of Snake

Island and managed to lower a rope for the Spetsnaz team. They used a grapple gun to throw up several more ropes for a quicker ascent. They met Jackson two minutes later at the top.

"I am Sergeant Melor Dominik, Spetsnaz commander, call me Melor. You are Jackson Black, yes?

"Yes, good to meet you Melor. We are rather exposed here, so this is going to be quite dangerous."

"It is what we train for," Melor responded. "Am I correct that you believe the missile is in those buildings?"

"Satellite feed shows a heat signature in them," Jackson said. But I have been told to expect a potential decoy."

"I understand," Melor replied. "We have been told same. Let us first clear those buildings and then, move to these by the dock area." He was pointing to his small computer screen.

Presidents Sokolav and Armstrong, with their respective staffs watched intently. They could hear everything being said.

"You and I will take the southwest corner here. Two of my men will move to the northwest corner and the other five will approach along the west side of these two buildings."

"That is a sound plan," Jackson said. "We don't have much cover."

"We will slip along the edge of the cliff until we are in position," Melor said. "Then, we will need to sniper crawl as close as we can. Do you know where their men are?"

"We are picking up heat signatures from about a dozen men inside this longest building. There are another fifteen men between there and the boat docks near the green-roofed buildings."

"Hmmmm," Melor mused. "I think you are correct. This first building may be a decoy, but we cannot risk bypassing it."

Melor and Jackson began their approach once the remaining members of the Spetsnaz team had moved into position. The uneven ground worked to their advantage while they sniper-crawled about 150 yards to their assigned station.

"Whenever you're ready," Jackson said.

"Move in," Melor spoke into the comm.

The team of nine men ran quickly the last few yards and began working their way around each building to the entrances. Entering various doors at the same time they encountered a dozen armed men. The gunfight was fast and furious. Bullets thudded all around the inside of the buildings while the Spetsnaz and Jackson returned fire.

A gunman came around the corner, his gun leveling at Melor's head. Jackson took him out with one bullet in the forehead with his pistol.

"Thank you, my friend," Melor grimaced, a bullet hitting the wood next to his head and splintering into the side of his cheek.

The two moved steadily toward the northwest end of the building while the rest of the team made a pincer move toward the center. Above in the metal rafters, a sniper began firing. One of the Spetsnaz took him out quickly with automatic fire. The sounds from their suppressed weapons were in stark contrast to the staccato firing from the AK-47's the enemy was using.

"Jackson," Art spoke into his earpiece. "There are six men coming in from the east. They are almost to the building."

"Roger. Melor, we have six uninvited guests coming from that side."

The team members had made their way to the center of the long buildings, having cleared the smaller ones. There was no missile and no evidence of one. Jackson and Melor realized too late it was a decoy. Valuable time had been lost. The entire team moved to the east side of the building and out into the sunlight. Immediately a hail of gunfire erupted.

"Jackson, a hangar door is opening on building four near the docks, we see a missile emerging on tracks."

"Roger," Jackson replied, looking across at Melor. "Get your men out, we will not be able to make it to the missile before launch."

"Отступить," Melor shouted to his men. The 'fall back' order was clearly understood.

The SVR team moved quickly, laying down a hail of gunfire that killed or wounded the remaining assailants in sight. Jackson had been pinned down and circled around behind the entrance; one of the men had managed throw a grenade that exploded nearby severely wounding his left leg. A sinking feeling came over him while he put a tourniquet above the wound to stop the bleeding.

"Admiral," President Armstrong said. "You have authorization to fire."

"Captain Reed. This just came in sir."

"Did you verify it?"

"Yes sir. It is authentic."

"Very well. CSO!"

"Yes sir."

"Did you make those firing coordinate adjustments?"

"Yes Captain. I can fire at once on your command."

"Fire!"

The CSO went through the firing sequence and within seconds, 18 Tomahawks were on their way to target.

Grigori had input the codes and his launch engineer had prepped the missile. The entire end of the building was a giant door. It opened at the push of a button and his men began pushing the missile and its carrier down the short section of track to the outside so that the launch would be unimpeded. He had a smile on his lips for a brief instant while his men pushed the missile out. It was raising to launch position when the smile disappeared from his face.

Both presidents watched the approaching missiles and the satellite feeds. The men with President Armstrong glanced at each other knowingly.

Jackson had made it to the corner of the long building and saw Melor about to descend the rope to the fast boat at the bottom of the cliff. Their eyes locked. Melor felt a great sadness; he saluted the man who he had quickly come to admire. Jackson looked to his left and could see the missile slowly raising to launch position, almost a quarter mile away. There was no way they could have closed the distance fast enough. The breeze on his face felt refreshing; he looked skyward.

He could see the missiles streaking toward the island clearly now and would have expected no less. The wound to his leg made it impossible to be where he needed to be on time.

No one noticed the three helicopters approaching the north side of Snake Island from Zatoka, out of Ukrainian airspace. Reaching the island, they hovered just above water level at the bottom of the cliffs.

Watching the missiles approach, Jackson knew there was nowhere to run. He took a last, deep breath, inhaling the scent of the ocean breeze, his eyes on the sky, a smile creasing his lips. His thoughts were of Li Na. It was a perfect day to die.

The Tomahawk missiles struck just as flames began to exit the tail of the nuclear missile. The missile and men around it were instantly obliterated. Every building on the island was leveled; Jackson's limp body hurled through the air from the force of the first missile impact over a hundred yards away. He landed in a heap while the remaining missiles struck, one where he had stood. The entire complex of buildings was destroyed.

The smoke from the explosions had scarcely settled when

the three helicopters rose from the bottom of the cliffs and landed atop the island in the northwest corner. Four-man teams in white biohazard suits stepped from each helicopter and quickly assumed a grid search pattern, walking swiftly over the uneven terrain. Two hundred yards later they found what they were looking for.

"We found him. Mostly intact."

"Two men ran at a dead run from the nearest helicopter, stretcher in hand. They quickly put the limp body onto the stretcher and ran as fast as they could back to the helicopter. Within fifteen minutes, the operation was ended; the helicopters rose and descended to twenty feet above the Black Sea, heading back to Zatoka.

"Mission accomplished sir," the man wearing the CD ring said. "We have the package."

"How bad is it?"

"Better than expected sir. You will be pleased."

"Make all haste to the hospice. I do not need to tell you that we need him ready as quickly as possible."

"Understood sir. I will take care of it."

"I am sorry for the loss of your agent," President Sokolav said. "I know that he was a great asset and will be difficult to replace."

"Thank you, Mr. President," Armstrong said. "At least we stopped the crises. Thank you and your men for your cooperation and let us stay in touch. Perhaps we could visit each other."

"That would be a good step," President Sokolav responded. "I will have my people contact yours. Again, my condolences. Good day sir."

The men in the Oval stood looking at each other, both relief and sadness overcoming them.

"I don't know about you, but I could use a stiff drink," Phil said.

"Agreed," Vice President Reisner replied.

A double shot of bourbon was poured in each of their glasses.
"To Jackson," President Armstrong said. "He was my friend, and I will miss him and his unwavering loyalty."
"He sacrificed all to save us," Jonas responded.
"To a valiant patriot who never failed the cause," Phil replied.
"Here, here," Reisner said.
The glasses tingled when they touched each other, the men gulping down whiskey while contemplating the sacrifice of one good man so that thousands could live.

CHAPTER 3

THE body was placed in a tub of ice while the helicopter flew to the hospice. The core temperature was adjusted to just above 50 degrees. Also wrapped, the head was kept at precisely 51-degrees Fahrenheit. Any potential injury that continued would be greatly slowed. The tourniquet was removed, and the wound immediately stitched. There were no less than twenty metal fragments from the grenade embedded in the leg that were deftly removed and sutured.

"Make sure you stay within temperature norms," Dr. Bramahh said. We need the body as intact as possible, and damage minimized."

"Yes sir. All critical temperatures are being maintained."

"What about brain functioning?"

"It is there, but at a low state. He likely has some trauma."

"Is he alive?" Bramahh asked.

"I believe so sir. At least the brain functioning indicates it."

"Luckily, he was thrown from the blast area. Call and have the surgeons ready. We will be there in ten minutes."

"Yes sir."

Doctor Bramahh was double checking the body and making sure every wound and location was marked for the surgeons.

He was unable to see the back side of the body, but the surgeons would take care of that.

The surgical team was standing by when the body was brought in and placed on the operating table. The doctors immediately stabilized the patient and made certain oxygen and blood were flowing to the brain and that blood pressure was controlled. Having been removed from the ice and the head piece removed as well, the body temperature was slowly increased to normal. A portable X-ray had been wheeled in and the body was checked for broken bones. The left leg was broken. The wound was left open for access while the doctors reset the leg, antiseptically cleaned and dressed any small wounds or abrasions and then, put a cast on it with an access port to monitor potential infection. The open wound area where the tourniquet had been removed, had been sterilized and sutured.

The team of surgeons next turned the patient over, using a molded table that cradled the patient on the top when it turned. They found three wounds on the back and quickly cleaned and sutured them. One was a metal fragment from the grenade that had lodged near the L4 vertebrae. The wound was carefully inspected; it was determined the fragment was clear of the nerve; it was removed, and the wound sutured like the others. It was then that the chief neurosurgeon walked in.

"Is he ready?" Dr. Karpathian asked.

"Yes doctor," Dr. Bramahh replied. "All wounds have been sutured and cleaned. He is ready for implant."

"Let's finish then," Dr. Karpathian said.

Scalpel in hand, Doctor Karpathian deftly made a two-inch long horizonal incision just above the C1 vertebrae at the top of the spine. On either end of that incision, he made a matching vertical cut. Another surgeon folded back the skin with a clamp, so the neurosurgeon had access to the nerve center of the body. Great care was taken while the surgeon made the necessary cuts and from the tray next to him, picked up a small half-inch square biochip. It looked much like a credit card chip with two very tiny wires protruding from the back side. Using his deftly practiced technique, he delicately embedded and hooked the wires into the spinal cord. The chip was powered by the iron molecules of the blood. It would never run out of energy as long as the patient was alive.

"Doctor Bramahh," Doctor Karpathian said. "It is time for you to test the device."

Doctor Bramahh used a voltmeter with very small leads to test the circuitry of the chip and ensure it was implanted and functioning correctly. He next picked up a twenty-cc syringe from the tray and injected its contents one inch from the chip, just around the edge of the spinal cord.

"What is that?" Doctor Karpathian asked.

"It is nanobots of metallic carbon. The chip will be able to manipulate them at our will. "

"Is that enough of them?"

"He will be given several more injections in different parts of the body. They will complete the amount necessary for programming."

"Excellent," Doctor Karpathian said. "The boss will be very pleased."

"Doctors," a fellow surgeon said. "He appears to be functioning normally. It is time to test his functions."

"Very well," Dr. Bramahh said. "Inject him with one cc only and watch his vitals."

The surgeon injected one cc of 0.1% adrenaline so there would be no side effects. It began to work almost immediately.

"His brain functioning is increasing slightly," the surgeon said. Heart rate is slow due to the ice bath. Blood pressure is normal. Heart rate is 48 bpm."

"Good," Doctor Bramahh. Let his core temperature return to

normal then, induce the coma.

The temperature of the body slowly rose to normal. An anesthesiologist next administered Lorazepam that would ensure sedation for more than a few days. The drug was longer acting than Versed with no active metabolites. Medically induced, the body would remain in deep sedation of the brain so that it would reach a level called 'burst suppression.' The brain would be completely quiet for several seconds and alternate with very, very short bursts of activity. It would all be recorded by an EEG. This would give the brain vital time to rest and heal and allow administering of the remaining nanobot injections. The final injections would make the body a slave to the chip and easily controlled by Doctor Bramahh.

Day by day, the doctor and his staff worked on fine tuning the chip to Jackson's body. They increased the number of nanobots in his blood and kept his life functions in normal range while he lay in a coma. They slowly masked his memory with inputs of their own.

"How is progress on your patient?" Antonio asked.

"It is going well," Bramahh replied. "I am seeing some interesting responses to our treatment."

"In what way?"

"I'll put this in lay terms as much as I can. Do you remember the battle for men's minds introduced by the Russians in the early 1950's?"

"Of course," Antonio replied. "We have been seeking such results for decades."

"They and the Americans never perceived the magnitude of the problem. I mean we can model mass human behavior but the battle for the mind has eluded us unless the asset is so drugged, they perform for more drugs. I have overcome the barrier. I'm certain of it. Brain warfare is now ours, along with cloning and control of leaders of governments and nations."

"You mean you can make an individual do what you want them too under any circumstances."

"Exactly," Bramahh replied. "It all has to do with keeping them in a controlled state. Not through brain perversion techniques that the Russians first began with. The Americans were not far behind and watched the Russians for decades, as well as trying their own experiments with hypnosis and drugs such as Demerol. All of them had their place. In fact, everything their intelligence agencies tried was immoral and illegal, not that we care. I went back to the original Russian research and some classified documents we were able to obtain from early CIA research as well. They pointed to some groundbreaking accounts of mind-control techniques that, although crude, didn't pan out, but that no man could resist. One CIA report even discussed an unhinged scientist that had made several major breakthroughs. Hell, the American freedom of the mind versus Russian mind control became more of a dividing line than the old Iron Curtain, although the general populace was never aware of it. Then, in the 1960s the use of psychedelic drugs became prevalent. It was then that controlling the mind began in earnest."

"So, what are you telling me?" Antonio asked. "Are you telling me that you did what others could not achieve?"

"Better," Bramahh replied. "I have achieved for you complete mind control of any subject, although it takes extensive work to achieve on a subject-by-subject basis. I have eliminated the need for threat. Let me delve further into history and you will see the great benefit we now have. Let us go back to 1953 when the CIA director approved MK-Ultra, a top-secret CIA program for covert use of both biological and chemical materials for the specific goal of mind control. The intelligence we obtained demonstrates that their experiments centered around behavior modification through electro-shock therapy, hypnosis, polygraphs, and radiation, as well as the use of a wide variety of drugs, toxins, and chemicals. Their

71

experiments relied on volunteered subjects and those forced to volunteer through coercion. Some were even unaware they were participants. They gathered mentally impaired subjects, soldiers, criminal psychopaths, and dregs of society to conduct their research on. In short, they preyed on the most vulnerable members of American society. Prisoners were at the top of the list because they were willing to give consent in exchange for commuted sentences or extra yard time. A former crime boss wrote of his experience in the program stating loss of appetite, hallucinations, shape changes, paranoia, and sweeping violent feelings. He talked of nightmares, blood coming out of walls, other prisoners turning into skeletons, and inanimate objects taking the shape of an animal like the head of a dog. The point is, such reactions do us no good. If we are going to control someone, they must remain lucid and able to make cogent decisions."

"I agree," Antonio responded. "Without that ability, they are not any more valuable to us than a drug addict."

"It's laughable that it didn't work, and any doctor should have noticed it," Bramahh said. "But they didn't. The Americans were so terrified of the Russian LSD program because of their lack of knowledge of it that they became desperate. When the CIA began experimenting with LSD, they noted it could be potentially useful in gaining control over a person's body. So, in late 1953 a group of ten CIA scientists met at a cabin in the forests of Maryland. I think it may have been at Camp David, but I have no way to prove it."

"Yes, I remember," Antonio said. "It was first known as Hi-Catoctin and built as a camp for federal government agents and their families by the Works Progress Administration. They could have gathered there without undue notice."

"Precisely," Bramahh replied. "Anyway, after much discussion, the group knew the only way to understand the value of the drug was to experiment. That led to widespread use of the drugs by the agency dumping it into the inner cities and making careful notes of what happened. What they noticed was that it inhibited that part of the brain that controls pain and gives the user a euphoric feeling. Once they understood that, it was a matter of time before they graduated to prescription drugs such as Demerol and others so that they could control the user better, hopefully without the addiction side effects."

"But Demerol is an opioid," Antonio said. "Wouldn't it also become addictive."

"Yes. And that is what they had to work around. It's quite simple really, which is why we and others initially missed it. You see, euphoria is a state of pleasure that lets one experience the feelings of well-being and happiness, as well as excitement. The CIA hit on this very quickly with the new drug. We know that certain drugs can cause this feeling and that certain natural activities can also cause the same feeling. These of course being exercise, socializing with friends, laughter, music, dancing, and other activities. But the best part is that euphoria is caused by chemical reactions in the brain through the involvement of many receptors and neurotransmitters that are responsible for the feeling. Scientists and doctors are quite familiar that the interaction of dopamine with other neurochemicals in the brain is the surest cause of euphoria. Let me give you an example; continuous aerobic exercise such as running, releases dopamine within the nucleus accumbens. The result is a state of euphoria by increased biosynthesis with three other neurochemicals: anandamide, beta-endorphins, and phenethylamine."

"You're getting over my head doc," Antonio said.

"Bear with me and you will see where I'm going. Let me explain each of them. The accumbens is simply a hook-shaped expansion of the anteroventral region of the striatum that curves under the lateral ventricle and into the ventral half of the septal region. It is important because it is the medial olfactory area; the layer of gray matter in the brain connecting the optic chiasma and the anterior commissure where the latter becomes continuous with the rostral lamina. In other words, we can feed the system through this path."

"You mean with your control drug?" Antonion asked.

"Drugs," Bramahh replied. "Now for the other parts of the concoction to mix in. Anandamide is a neurotransmitter. It is part of the body's endocannabinoid system and can be provided by hemp plants. It binds a drug to the cannabinoid receptors, the very same receptors that the psychoactive compound THC in cannabis acts on and for that matter, any other psychoactive compound. This is important because it creates joy, delight, and euphoria."

"So, if you inject someone with your mix of drugs, they will be happy?" Antonio asked.

"Yes, happy to obey. Let's move on to the beta-endorphins, which are an endogenous opioid neuropeptide and peptide hormone that is produced in certain neurons within the central nervous system, as well as the peripheral nervous system. The body produces two other endorphins: α-endorphin and γ-endorphin. My theory, as well as that of others is that they work symbiotically in the body. Finally, we come to phenethylamine, a trace amine that acts as a central nervous system stimulant. In the brain, it regulates monoamine neurotransmission by binding to the trace amine-associated receptor 1, what doctors refer to as TAAR1, while inhibiting vesicular monoamine transporter 2 in monoamine neurons. It's important because it is an integral membrane protein that transports monoamines, particularly neurotransmitters such as dopamine, serotonin, and other compounds. You see, they all link together."

Doctor Bramahh was beaming, exultant in his accomplishment. But he could see that Antonio was perplexed.

"What I am telling you is that I can embed a very small

stainless tube into anyone and manipulate injections from it through the chip so that he or she will do whatever we want without question for several months at a time. Before he or she runs out of the drug concoction, we bring them in, sedate them and refill the tube. The person in question will never know it is there. We could perform the same operation on the cloned leaders or even kidnap the real leaders and perform it on them. Either way, we have total control.

"You make it sound easy," Antonio said. "How can we test it?"

"That is the easy part," Bramahh replied. "Jackson will be coming out of his induced coma in a week. We will bring in a prisoner and tell him to perform whatever task you wish on the convict."

"Very well," Antonio said, with an evil grin. "I will test your theory. It had better work."

Doctor Bramahh gulped.

SEVERAL weeks later, Jackson awoke in a rehab center, wondering how he was alive?

He had been awake for several hours and had eaten and drank several glasses of orange juice. The room was simple. It had the bed he was laying in, a small chair in the corner kitty-corner to his right and another chair against the wall to his left. Sunlight was streaming through a window as he watched floating particles of dust that never seemed to settle while they floated about. He could see outside; his attention focused on a pair of pigeons, the sun reflecting off their neck plumage that shown a brilliant green and purple above the gray of the rest of their wings and the pinkish white of their feet. Feeling relaxed, he slowly lifted the sheet covering his legs. There was a cast on his left leg. His other leg had bruises and there was evidence of stitches that had been removed from various lacerations that appeared to be almost fully healed.

The door opened and a medium built man walked in. He had jet black hair and matching mustache. The sport coat and matching ensemble he wore was immaculate, a dark blue with brass buttons, maroon leather elbow pads and khaki-colored pants with casual shoes. Without a word, he pulled the chair up next to the bed and sat down, his brilliant blue eyes staring at Jackson.

"It is so good to finally meet you Mr. Jackson Black. Permit me to introduce myself. I am Antonio Raven of CLUB DREAD. It took me years for this precise opportunity to develop, to help the CIA's foremost spy. We re-created you to work for us. Well, fortunately we did not need to recreate you. We simply brought you back to life. Do you remember the missiles?"

"Vaguely."

"A rogue general was going to launch a nuclear missile and kill thousands in your country," Antonio said. "We knew you would be there to stop it and used our influence in various ways to help. So, you see, we helped you save those thousands of lives."

"And what do I owe you for that?" Jackson asked.

"Unlike governments, we don't just help people and turn them over to someone else. We are a private enterprise. Tell me, what is your life worth?"

"A lot, just like it would be to anyone else I suppose," Jackson replied, his eyes scrutinizing the man. "Why do you ask?"

"You have two options, Mr. Black," Antonio said coldly. "We can put you back where we found you and in the same condition or, you can work for us. I need not remind you that had it not been for us you would now be dead. You have lacerations all over your body, shrapnel wounds from a grenade, a couple of bullet holes, a broken leg from your encounter, and severe head trauma with bleeding on the brain. Yes, were it not for us, you would be quite dead."

Jackson sat staring at Antonio. Through the doorway, he

could see at least six armed guards, all staring directly at him. He began to feel uncomfortable. Antonio's was also staring at him, unblinking. For now, he knew he had little choice.

"But aren't you my friend?" Jackson asked, the chip doing its work. That is how I remember you. How long will you need my services?"

"I think about six months," Antonio replied, thinking why did he ask me that? "Unless you think that is too much time to repay us for your life. Excuse me."

Antonio went out the door and spoke to Doctor Bramahh. "Why did he say that about me being his friend?"

"The chip is working. We gave him memories that the two of you were friends for a long time."

"Damn good work Doc."

He walked back into the room.

"What do you want me to do?" Jackson asked.

"You will comply with any command we give you," Antonio replied. "Feel the back of your head, near the base of your skull. Beneath the stitches is an embedded chip. With my phone I can induce severe pain or kill you as I deem necessary. If you work for us voluntarily, there is no reason to have me exercise such control. Besides, it is not my wish. I hope that we can remain friends, at least colleagues."

So, it was no accident he was here! He watched closely while Doctor Bramahh entered and bent over, whispering into Antonio's ear. He could not hear what was being said but saw Antonio playing with his smart phone, moving his finger on the screen, obscured from his view. Jackson felt kind of happy, despite the circumstances. He smiled for no reason, catching the doctor looking at him who whispered again to Antonio. He had an overpowering feeling these men were his friends.

"Bring him in," the Doctor said.

A man with a hood on was led into the room, his hands cuffed behind him. The guards seated him in the other chair in the corner.

"Permit me to introduce myself Mr. Black. I am Doctor Bramahh. My team and I saved your life. How do you feel?"

"I feel fine, happy. Although I do not know why?"

The doctor shot Antonio a knowing look.

"What do you think of traitors?" Antonio asked.

"They should be shot," Jackson said. "Anyone who would betray his country will betray anyone they meet."

"That man, nodding to the hooded figure, shot one of your agents and is planning to kill your CIA director, among others. The director is your friend, neh?"

"Yes, he is," Jackson replied looking at the man with the hood, a tint of anger in his voice.

The doctor laid Jackson's P-228 next to his right hand. He picked it up, hand quivering and pointed it at Antonio.

"Maybe I will not work for you," Jackson said, the guards training their weapons on him through the doorway. "Maybe I'll go back to work for ...." His voice trailed off. "My boss."

"I have been your boss for a long time," Antonio said. "Do you not remember? Right now, you need to decide. Either shoot the good doctor who saved your life and me or, shoot the traitor."

Jackson thought at the speed of light. Without hesitation he shot the man through the head once, blood and brains spattering against the wall and then, in the chest twice. In less than two seconds the man was dead, blood dripping onto the floor. Jackson tossed the pistol to the end of the bed out of his reach. It was the death all traitors should get. Yet, he was confused; things in his head seemed unclear.

"See, already you have done the world a great service," Antonio remarked. "The beginning of a long trail of traitors that will die at your hands. You will do many countries a great service. They are misguided, but it is necessary."

"What is CLUB DREAD?" Jackson asked. "I do not recall it in my work for you."

"That is because it has been a secret, divulged to only those with a need to know. It refers to Criminal Leaders Using Biohacking for Destruction, Ransom, Extortion and Domination. You will recall that one of your friends from British Intelligence ran into a group that was eventually destroyed. They were merely messengers. They served their purpose admirably and would still be alive but became too greedy. Like the stock market, they were driven by fear and greed. In the end it was their undoing, and it became necessary that we eliminate them. They were an obligatory sacrifice for a means to an end. You see, out of chaos we create order. That is what you will help us do. You can see the havoc being created by the new world order nonsense. We are the cure to make sure those goals are never achieved."

"But are we any better than they?" Jackson asked.

"We are superior in every way," Antonio said. "We must be to survive. We will put countries back on track managing themselves and behind the scenes we will wield control. It will not be for world domination, but control of resources and debt."

"So, it's all about money," Jackson said.

"Exactly," Antonio replied. "We will control the central banks globally, and governments through their leaders. What if I told you that China would turn into a democracy?"

"I'll believe that when I see it," Jackson muttered.

"It will happen, and you will help us," Antonio said. "You are going to put in place the leader that we will control that country and within eight months, China will turn, despite what you may believe now."

"How much do you think you are capable of controlling?" Jackson asked. "Do you really think the governments of all the countries will let you get away with it?"

"Have you ever heard of CLUB DREAD before today?" Antonio asked.

"No, I have not!" Jackson exclaimed.

"Neither have they," Antonio said, smiling softly. "It is difficult to dismember an organization no one knows anything about don't you think? We control the largest global banks, almost every major drug cartel, and every large criminal organization in the world. When we tell them to do something, it is done. Governments fail because they want control. Hell, the first thing any leader does is go after more control the instant they become a leader. Free or dictator it matters not. When they do so they diverge from rational thought to a lust for more power, more control, and more money. It is this character trait that has let us prosper. There was a man sitting on a park bench in DC. Do you really think he shot himself twice in the back of the head, that it was suicide? We did it because he got too greedy and failed to follow orders. CLUB DREAD has infiltrated every government and every corporation that can influence large numbers of people. More importantly, you will help us with the last and most critical ones. You are the most skilled in your profession and we will utilize those skills."

"What for? To dominate the global economy and steal people's money, to starve them into submission?"

"No, we seek to save lives," Antonio said. "Quite simply, dead people don't pay taxes and we need those. For hundreds of years politicians and bureaucrats have stolen taxpayer dollars for their own agendas. They will no longer do that. We will, but that money will be put to good use."

"You're telling me you're going to be philanthropists?" Jackson laughed.

"Don't laugh my friend," Antonio said. "What would you say if we cleaned up Chicago and other large cities. Instead of sending billions of dollars overseas, the money will be spent within the country of origin for better housing, healthcare, and jobs. The cities will become more prosperous and create untold billions in wealth."

"That you will manage and control?" Jackon said.

"Precisely!" Antonio exclaimed. "Poor people don't pay taxes or contribute significantly to society. We will change that, and we will reap the rewards."

"But it is still about control," Jackson said.

"Better that we do as planned, than let politicians' rule for decades longer where the only wealth goes with them while the poor remain poor. And cities slowly sink into a derelict condition. Slowly, we will get rid of drugs too."

Despite what Antonio represented, it sounded too good to be true. He couldn't help thinking that it made sense and was logical until greed reared its ugly head. Raven explained in concise detail how CD had influence everywhere. They were biohackers who had succeeded in storing consciousness in digital form, perfecting manipulation of brain and body through radical experimentation. Their agenda — to replace world and corporate leaders with bio-hacked clones that they alone controlled. The microchip installed in Jackson, although vastly improving his performance, also allowed CLUB DREAD control. The man sitting next to his bed made it quite clear what Jackson would do for them. His tone was level, almost friendly, sinister; he was a villain, nothing less. "I need to escape. I must get this chip out," Jackson thought. "For President and Country; for the fate of humanity!

The guards supervised the removal of the body while they were talking. A couple of people came in and cleaned the blood from the wall and the floor, leaving it spotless. The pungent stench of blood that had filled the air was gone. A nurse entered, along with another doctor whom Jackson had not seen before.

"I will leave you now," Antonio said. "We will continue our discussion later, perhaps over dinner. It is important for your health that you let the nurse and doctor monitor your body functions. You are far too valuable to us to let your health slide any at all. I will send for you later."

Jackson watched him pick up the pistol from the end of the

bed and walk out the door, handing it to one of the guards, two of whom remained behind to watch over him. It was not going to be easy to get out of this predicament. He was trying to think back to what happened. All he remembered was the missiles in the air. Suddenly, he felt a sharp stab to his arm. The nurse had sedated him.

HONG Kong was bustling. The sidewalks were crowded with people plodding to work. Li Na and Jackson had a very secluded place on the fringes of town near the waterfront. Her old boss, who she occasionally did work for had given it to them. Not even the intelligence agencies knew its whereabouts. The upper level was comprised of a large bedroom, kitchen, bath and huge living room area where the two hung out and practiced martial arts and swordsmanship. Li Na was sitting on the sofa next to the wall, staring out the small windows into the harbor. Her hand began trembling.

"Did you hear what I said?" Phil asked.

"Yes, I heard you," Li Na replied, a single tear flowing down her cheek. "Do you have a copy of the video I could watch?"

"I cannot let you have it," Phil said. "Sorry, but it is very classified."

"I understand," Li Na said. "Will you keep me updated if you learn anything else?"

"I will. And once again, I'm so sorry to bring you such tragic news. We know how close you both were."

She sat for several hours letting her emotions get the best of her. Her athletic frame quivered from the loneliness and sadness that set in. They had been like peas in a pod, and she knew if she lived ten lifetimes, she would never find another man that would suit her the way Jackson did. The deepness of their love was unmeasurable. Three hours later, she bolted out of her sadness and took a seated position in the middle of the room where she meditated for the next two hours, letting the wholeness of the universe enter her body. Her eyes suddenly opened wide; the feeling was not there. She knew that Jackson was somehow alive. But she needed proof to calm her soul and quiet the trembling's and fear that came with it. Her satellite phone had a scrambler so no one, not even the CIA could pinpoint her location. She began calling her network of intelligence agencies beginning with the Hong Kong Police, Chinese Military and others. Li Na knew that finding any video footage of what had happened was a shot in the dark, but she had to try. The CIA was always very careful to disguise their operations and make sure other satellites were not in view. She suddenly remembered another source. Jackson had saved his life multiple times so a favor was due.

COLIN Archer was sitting in his flat contemplating his latest assignment that had ended with the enemy dead and critical British secrets recovered. His fierce gray eyes stared out the window, watching the falling rain. It would be another dreary London day. At six feet with an athletic build, he was a handsome, rugged looking man. He could handle himself well in a fight and was an expert pistol marksman. His parents had died when he was three and he had ended up in an orphanage. At the age of four, a couple adopted him and had trained him in intelligence, fighting, shooting, and tech skills all his life. When he was twenty-one, he had been introduced to leaders in MI6, the agency who had placed him in the hands of his foster parents and who were their agents. It was all so organized. He had been trained throughout his life to work for the agency and when the opportunity came, it was a natural fit. He had few friends because in the spy business friends didn't live long. He was a loner and a womanizer and like many in his trade, had little empathy, but for the few friends he did have, he would move heaven and earth to come to their aid whenever needed, and they his. It was like an unwritten code. He was pulling his umbrella from its stand when his phone rang. Looking at the number, he didn't recognize it. But because of his work, he knew it was not a spam call. Cautiously, he answered.

"Archer," he said, hearing faint breathing on the other end. It was like there was a hesitancy during which the voice fought for a reason to talk to him.

"I do not know if you remember me. This is Li Na."

"Of course, I do," Colin responded. "How are you and Jackson?"

"That is what I want to talk to you about."

Colin suddenly got a sinking feeling in his stomach. Something had been bothering him all morning, now he sensed it.

"What's wrong Li Na?"

She told him about the phone call with the director and the missile strike that had taken Jackson out.

"My meditation and senses tell me he is alive," Li Na said. "But the video that the CIA has cannot be sent to me so, I am unable to vet what they have told me."

"I don't think they would lie to you given Jackson's status with them," Colin said. "But ..."

"But what?"

"Sometimes video feeds from satellites do not show all the details. There have been times when we thought a mission had failed or an agent was killed, and it turned out not to be the case."

"Would you have access to satellite views of that area. It was Snake Island."

"That is the one that was in controversy with the Ukraine and Russia. You may just be in luck. We launched a new intelligence satellite a few days ago. It would have been in that precise area on the day you speak of. The Americans do not know of its existence yet and may not find out. I will not promise you anything, but I will dig into it. Let's assume that I have the feed, can you come to London? We will sit and view it together."

"Yes, I will leave immediately. I have flown the route many times."

"I will be there in twenty-four hours after a three-hour layover in Paris."

"Very well," Colin said. "I will attempt to get access to the feed."

Rain was falling in torrents when Colin made his way to MI6. The streets were jammed with the workday rush, made even slower by the downpour. Walking past security with his normal morning pleasantries, he bypassed his office and made straight for the computer intelligence group. Henry, the groups top expert was sitting at his desk drinking early morning tea.

"I'm glad you're here," Colin said.

"Not you again," Henry said. "You're bound and determined to make my intelligence career a short one."

"This is of critical importance," Colin said. "I need a favor. I need you to pull a feed for a man that has saved my life and yours more than once."

"Ah, Jackson," Henry said. "What did he do this time?"

"The CIA said he was blown to hell," Colin replied, whispering. "I'm not convinced, and neither is Li Na."

"The legendary assassin?" Henry asked quizzically, his eyes darting to the ceiling.

"Yes her," Colin said. "She will be here tomorrow. Can you pipe the feed to your flat so we can watch it there?"

"I can pull it down to analyze it," Henry said. "You're playing with fire here."

"I know," Colin whispered back. "But if I'm right, we will need to be on top of this. It's something that has been nagging at me since we took down that nefarious criminal group months ago."

"You think this is related?" Henry asked.

"Not sure," Colin said. "But it has all the ear markings, and we need to be sure, one way or another."

"Alright," Henry said. "Let's pull it up and see what our new satellite saw. What are the coordinates?"

"Snake Island or Bile as they call it," Colin whispered in his ear, looking furtively about.

"You're kidding right?"

"No."

"Damn, my career will be shorter lived than I thought and yours too if they find us digging around there."

The feed was pulled up and was crystal clear. The missiles were detected from launch to detonation.

"Well look there," Henry gasped. "What do we have here?"

"What?" Colin asked.

"Look! A body was thrown through the air. And there, see those helicopters? Those cannot be the Americans or Russians. Theirs are bugging out from the west side of the island just after the missiles hit. These came before the missiles struck, hovering near water level in the lee of the island. Look, they're landing now. Look at those white suits, they're looking for something. They're picking up a man on a stretcher. Leaving now. This is sinister indeed."

"Can you get a copy so we can analyze it in your flat tomorrow morning?"

"Yes, I can make an algorithm that will copy it and then, we can reconstruct it on my end. I dare not tell you this must be our secret."

"For now," Colin said. "If it is what I suspect, I will need to take it up the channels to the foreign secretary and he will take it to the Prime Minister. I pray I'm wrong."

"What do you mean?" Henry asked.

"I think the group we took down was a subservient group to a larger, more capable group."

"If that is true, God help us," Henry said. "They were the most nefarious group I've ever dealt with."

"You should prepare some new tricks just in case."

"Hmmmm," Henry mused. "First things first. Let's get this done and then see where it takes us in the rabbit hole. Besides, I must admit that I'm eager to meet this renowned assassin,"

"Careful what you wish for," Colin grinned. "I hear she leaves no witnesses, ever."

"Then we must take care not to offend her," Henry smiled back. "Seriously, we need to keep this very quiet."

"Quiet is my middle name," Colin said. "Let me know when it's safe.

Li Na arrived at Heathrow Airport, having only a small carry-on bag; she grabbed it and rushed through the terminals to the taxi departure area. As soon as she was in the cab, she called Colin.

"I just arrived," she said. "Tell me where to go."

"The address has just been texted to you," Colin replied. "Keep an eye out for tails. You should be okay, but you know the drill."

Giving basic directions to the driver, about forty-five minutes later she was dropped on the corner of two adjoining streets. Making sure the cab was out of sight and no one was following, she walked two blocks over and one up until she found the address. She rang the doorbell; Henry had watched her walk to the door via his outside cameras. He had been told she was a beautiful woman but seeing her in person took his breath away. With a hand shaking with both nervousness and excitement, he opened the door.

"Welcome Li Na," he said, his voice quivering. When his eyes met hers, it was like she looked through his soul. Be very careful with this one he thought to himself. "Come in please."

"Thank you," she said, looking up and down the street before entering.

"Ah, there you are," Colin called out. "We have everything

set up. Your intuition was correct."

"Sit here please," Henry said, pulling out a chair.

"So, you found the video?" Li Na queried.

"Not only that," Colin said. "It is much more than we expected. Henry, let the show begin."

Li Na watched the video carefully when it began to play. Henry had slowed the speed so that every detail could be clearly seen while they searched meticulously through the footage for every minor detail.

"There, you see that?" Colin asked. "That is the missiles being launched. Freeze it, Henry. My intelligence sources say it was from the SSN Montana. It looks like 18 Tomahawk missiles. And there, see this, it is an ICBM getting ready to launch. We believe that was their target."

"They wanted it destroyed pretty badly," Henry said. "That's almost $15 million in hardware they put up."

"But how could a U.S. submarine get into the Black Sea?" Li Na asked.

"The only way is if they are cooperating with the Russians," Colin replied. "They would also need to disguise the sub as being Russian."

"We believe the missile was a nuke," Henry said. "Some leaked intelligence says it was aimed at DC. That could easily explain the cooperation. So, that's the launch itself. Let's back up the feed and you can see the beginning."

"Look, there please," Henry said.

"It looks like a helicopter at sea level approaching the island," Li Na said. "Yes, it is dropping off one man. Is that a boat approaching?"

"Yes," Colin said. "Henry was able to enhance the feed enough to identify it as a Russian Special Operations Unit fast boat. Now look closely. The man who got dropped off lowers a rope to the team below. There, they have climbed to the top and are having a discussion. Now fast forward to see them fan out and enter this group of buildings. Be mindful this is before the missiles launch."

"Can you recognize the man who met them?" Henry asked.

"Not yet," Li Na replied. "Move the feed forward please."

"Alright," Henry said. "Here they exit the building, and you can see an extensive firefight. It appears those occupying the island have the upper hand in numbers. There, an explosion by the door. And now, the entire team is looking toward the south end of the island then, they rush back to the cliff and descend the ropes to the fast boat again. It appears their leader is saluting the man near where the explosion occurred. He is frozen in the doorway and the enemy is retreating toward the ICBM on the south end near the docks."

"It is Jackson," Li Na gasped. "He is just standing there watching the missiles. Why?"

"We believe the grenade wounded him and he could not flee," Colin said. "But watch the footage when we move it forward. There, the first missile strikes between Jackson and the ICBM. Watch him carefully."

Li Na could see Jackson's body fly through the air, over what appeared to be a distance of about two-hundred feet. Then, the other missiles struck in rapid succession. When the smoke cleared, she could see Jackson's limp body laying where it had landed, clear of other missile strikes. Her eyes moistened while her heart leapt in her throat.

Colin and Henry could see that she was visibly moved and wanted to keep her spirits up.

"Look here now," Colin said. "You see these helicopters approach the lee side of the island. They hover until the missiles have exploded and then, look! They land and let off their men, all in white hazard suits. They form a grid search pattern and stop only at Jackson. They rush a stretcher and load him on it; they are off the island within a few minutes."

"What does that mean?" Li Na asked.

"I believe it is what your intuition told you," Colin said. "Jackson is alive, but those are not Russians or Americans that took him."

"What are you saying?" Li Na asked, leaning forward intently.

"I did not want to believe it," Henry said. "But Colin told me the wild story he had. A year ago, we busted this huge criminal organization. We presumed they were killed by our agents. They had infiltrated every intelligence group around the planet. We thought we had gotten all of them. Tell her Colin."

"I had a sinking feeling in my stomach the day this happened to Jackson," Colin said. "That feeling, after you called me, got me to thinking about all of this. Why would the Russians cooperate with the Americans? I believe because that was a nuclear missile they took out and that so many in America want a war with Russia that the person firing it was a rogue general but also that he was set up by an organization wielding considerable power. This is farfetched, but what if I told you that there is a criminal organization that controlled the one we took out?"

"That's difficult to believe," Henry butted in. "I mean it could happen, but like you say, it is farfetched."

"No, it isn't," Li Na said. "At least I don't think so. I was approached by a man about two months ago that told me his superiors would like to consider using my services. I told him to let me think about it but have not heard from him since. I don't know how he found me, but it made me suspicious. Continue."

"I think this group was in control of the one we took down," Colin said. "I began to wonder how we had succeeded since they seemed to be everywhere and then, suddenly, we knew all about them. I think the information was leaked so that we could bust them. After all, we knew very little about them. It was like the information we needed suddenly fell into our laps with little effort to obtain it. That would be impossible unless someone was aware of all the group's operations."

"So, you think there is a larger group that controlled the others?" Li Na asked.

"There has to be," Colin replied. "We couldn't have taken down the other group without someone knowing everything they were up to."

"Statistically," Henry said. "Colin is correct. It also means that this group, whoever they are, has a much larger network and much more capacity and capabilities. That's the scary part."

"But why would they want Jackson?" Li Na asked. "You saw the video feed. They went right to him and no one else then, took off."

"You know as well as we do that he is the best there is," Colin said. "I think they want to use his skill sets."

"Why?" Li Na asked, staring at the two of them.

Henry suddenly felt vulnerable, like she was going to kill him without mercy. Beautiful but deadly she was.

"I think they want to use him to get to large corporate or even government leaders," Colin replied. "I don't think it would be to kill them, but it's all guess work now."

"I can keep digging," Henry said. "I don't know what I will find, but we need to be sure. If it is as Colin suspects, higher authorities will need to be brought in. I have a suspicion this is a global problem, not a local one."

"Then I will do what I must," Li Na said. "I will track down the man who approached me and see where it leads. This couldn't be coincidence."

"What will you do?" Colin asked.

"I will find Jackson," Li Na said flatly. "I will kill anyone who gets in my way."

Henry swallowed; a dry swallow.

"We can help you," Henry said. "We tracked him to this location."

"What do you think they are doing to him?" Li Na asked.

"I know he will not cooperate with them without being

coerced to do so," Colin said.

"That would likely be impossible," Li Na replied.

"Perhaps less so than you think," Henry said. "With the use of chips and drugs governments do it all the time. They'll most certainly embed something otherwise they would not have chosen him. And anyone would be smart enough to know he would not willingly cooperate."

"I will take leave and help you," Colin said. "But we need another tech guy on Jackson's side."

"I know Mitch Daniels at DARPA," Li Na said. "He and Jackson are good friends. He will help us."

"I have heard of Mitch," Henry said. "It would be a pleasure to work with him."

I won't kid you," Colin said. "This will not be easy."

"Such matters never are," Li Na replied with a sly, evil grin. "We will do all that is necessary to find him. And if what you suspect is true, we will dismantle this new organization in the process."

DOCTOR Bramahh had once again sedated Jackson who was never aware of it. The chip had been programmed to block his short-term memory so that the medical staff could do anything they wanted. Each time he was sedated, he was hooked to EKG leads so that the organization implanted into his mind memories they wanted him to have. Memories that would override his past, replacing past friends and events with new ones. It was like he was a new person with only memories from his captors. The treatment had been ongoing since Jackson had been brought back from the dead. At last, it was complete.

"What are we looking at?" Antonio asked. "Will he work with us."

"As far as he is concerned, his past exists only as memories we implanted," Dr. Bramahh replied. "He will only remember that you have been his employer and friend for a long time."

"Is there anything that may override our control?" Antonio asked.

"If he were to suffer a severe impact of the chip or it were to be totally immersed in a liquid. Those are our biggest risks.

"He does perform rather hazardous assignments," Antonio said. "The ones coming up can become very dangerous."

"You worry too much. Injuries from such assignments are generally to the front of the body and lower back. He is tough and can handle himself."

"How can we test his obedience?" Antonio asked.

"I would say shooting that fellow in the recovery room was test enough. I couldn't believe how cold he was. You told him the man was a traitor and he snuffed him like one would a mosquito. Unbelievable."

"It was due to your chip and mind control techniques," Antonio said. "Still, I'd like to perform one more test. We need to be certain. We can afford no mistakes."

"Very well," Dr. Bramahh replied. "I will set up a scenario of a kidnapping. You will not only get to see him in action, but you will be able to determine how well we have programmed him."

The medical team and doctors had given Jackson a thorough check up. Each time they sent a command through the chip, it was obeyed like it was second nature. Then, for the next week, they made sure that he was in top physical form from his injuries. He excelled better than expected.

"He is completely ready Antonio," Doctor Bramahh said. "It is time for the test."

"Very well. Initiate it at once."

"Jackson, we have a problem," Illiac said. "Our boss has been kidnapped, held for ransom. The organization has refused to pay. The kidnappers stated they will kill him at noon today if the ransom is not paid. You are the only agent available for a rescue attempt. We know where he is; there are ten men guarding the compound and him. We need to execute an extraction immediately. The location is half an hour away."

"I'll need my pistol and a knife," Jackson said.

"They are on the helicopter," Illiac replied. "Let's move, hurry."

The two ran for the helicopter and boarded. Excepting the pilot, no one else was aboard."

The doctors and Antonio were already at the compound listening to the conversation.

"He took orders from Illiac like he's known him for years," Antonio said. "How?"

"The memory of Illiac was implanted through the chip," Doctor Bramahh said. "Now, time to execute the plan."

During the flight, Jackson had gone over the plans for the building and where the hostage was being held. The chopper landed about three hundred yards away in heavy winds blowing from the compound toward them. The clearing in the forest was surrounded by dense trees and undergrowth. Jackson and Illiac jumped from the chopper and began running toward the compound.

"I will catch up," Illiac shouted. "My ankle twisted when I landed."

"Let me help," Jackson said.

"No," Illiac yelled over the wind. "We have little time, you must go."

Jackson nodded and headed off through the trees.

"Antonio," Illiac said through his walkie talkie. "He is on the way. I hope you're sure about this. We don't want him killed."

"We need find out if he is as good as they say and if he will obey orders," Antonio responded. "Otherwise, he is of little value."

A few minutes later Jackson sat obscured in the tree line overlooking the compound. It was exactly like Illiac had shown him, along with the building schematics. It was fenced, with a guard shack at the main gate, several smaller outbuildings, and a long narrow building that had been used for shipping and manufacturing of computer chassis in years past. The windows were busted out, the walls sagging and the roof near collapse. There was a large room at one end and then, rows of smaller rooms where quality control and other operations had taken place. On the far end was what had been the main office on the only upstairs floor. It was there that Illiac's intelligence said they were holding the hostage.

He studied the layout for about twenty minutes to ascertain the whereabouts of the guards. He identified four outside and the one in the guard shack whom he would bypass. That meant there were at least another five guards inside the building. They looked like mercenaries and the way they carried themselves denoted they had experience. He slowly screwed his suppressor onto the end of his P-228. Cold and objective, he moved toward the first guard. The entire area around the buildings was covered with stacks of wooden shipping pallets, discarded equipment, and an occasional forklift, left to rot over time. Jackson worked his way to within about forty feet of the corner of the main building, slipping behind a stack of pallets. The wind and blowing rain kept his movements silent. When the guard passed, he quickly crept behind him, cupped his hand over his mouth pulling the man backward while he slid the tip of the dagger behind the man's earlobe and upward into the brain, twisting it as he thrust. Without a sound, he lowered the man to the dirt and drug him behind the pallets.

Having reached the end of the building, Jackson was moving toward the other side when two guards appeared directly in front of him, shocked looks on their faces. While they were grabbing their AK-47s, Jackson dropped both with one well-placed shot to each of their foreheads. Re-holstering his weapon, he dragged both behind a large piece of rusted equipment.

"Three down and one to go," he thought.

Looking back at the shack by the gate, the guard was still inside, looking away from the compound. The wind had picked up, but the rain was holding off. Jackson knew the other guard needed to be dispatched quickly. Once he saw the dead guards were nowhere around, he would sound the alarm. Jackson reached the far end of the building away from the office. The blowing rain turned into a downpour. Just when he rounded the corner, he almost bumped into the last outside guard. Without hesitation, he plunged his knife into the guard's throat. Both the guard's hands instinctively grabbed the gash, blood spurting between his fingers as he fell to his knees and then onto his side, a small gurling sound coming from his wound. Jackson dragged the body behind some pallets stacked close to the outer wall and placed one over the guard's feet.

"He makes it look so effortless," Antonio said. "You have to admire the man."

"He is moving into the toughest part of the test," Illiac said. "Rapid target identification and reflexes will be required."

"Hmmmm," Antonio mused.

Jackson circled back to the far end of the building where the large room was. He thought about where he would place guards if he were running the operation. They wouldn't all be together. Likely two would be roving and two in the room with the hostage.

"It was now or never," he thought, double checking his pistol and suppressor.

He crept around the edge of the room. The falling rain was coming down in torrents, obscuring the sound his feet made while he stepped over and around building insulation, broken glass and other clutter on the floor. The clouds and rain dimmed the natural light resulting in low lit surroundings much like a dive bar. Suddenly, he saw the glow of a cigarette. The guard wasn't more than twenty feet from him. A splintering piece of glass gave Jackson away; the guard turned, cigarette in his mouth, catching two bullets in the throat and chest, falling backward into the doorway of the room where he stood.

The rain began to fall even harder, the sound deafening when it hit the metal roof. Jackson made his way down the hallway. Obscured in the shadows, he was able to see two men at the end in a large space below the office. They were sitting, talking casually while playing cards. Jackson slipped into the last doorway before the room opened widely before him. Light was beaming from the windows in the upstairs office. There was also a light just beyond the two guards. With no other guards in sight, Jackson rushed the two playing cards, shooting each twice then, performed a combat reload as he bounded quickly and quietly up the stairs.

He kicked the door open and shot the guards in the head ending up standing next to the hooded hostage. Too late, he caught movement to his right out of his peripheral vision. It was a hidden guard who knocked his gun out of his hand. Without loss of motion, Jackson had drawn his knife and sidestepped to his left when the guard lunged with his own knife. Jackson sliced him across the throat and kicked him away with a right, side kick. The guard landed in a heap against the wall bleeding out. Quickly turning, he rolled and regained control of his pistol just as two more guards rushed through the door. Jackson dropped each with a double tap. Staying away from the hostage to ensure safety, he glanced around the room and through the windows to the floor below. Satisfied, he approached the hostage and removed the hood.

"About time," Antonio said. "These bastards kept threatening to kill me any second because no one was going to pay the ransom."

"How the hell did you end up here?" Jackson asked,

surprised.

"Lax security," Antonio replied while Jackson untied him. "Can't trust anyone these days. You saved my hide. I won't forget it."

"It's my job, right?" Jackson asked.

"Well, we won't make it a habit because I have more important jobs for you."

There was shouting coming from the end of the building.

"Up here," Antonio yelled.

His men came running up the stairs.

"Are you okay?" one asked.

"Fine thanks to Jackson."

Illiac, pretending to have a more severe strain was waiting below.

"I apologize I could not help you," Illiac told Jackson, looking around. "But looks like you did fine without me."

Antonio grinned. "Yes, he did quite well. Jackson, go back with these two and I'll see you in a while. I'll be okay; I have my guards now."

"Roger that."

When Jackson exited the building the two men stopped. Illiac had a small screen he turned on. Antonio watched the entire video from when Jackson entered the compound to the end.

"Damn, he is good," Antonio said.

"Now you know why he is called the best," Illiac said. "He didn't even flinch; the guards were as good as dead the moment he saw them."

"It is like he has a sixth sense for killing," Antonio replied. "What about our next target?"

"We are keeping tabs on him," Illiac said. "Our surveillance is almost complete."

"We will turn Jackson loose," Antonio said. "But make sure he understands not to kill the target, only those protecting him if necessary. Have your men remove the dead."

HONG Kong streets had a knack for casting shadows where none should be. Li Na had found the man who had approached her. Keeping her distance, she watched his every move. For some reason, he seemed oddly out of place. She was wary because her intuition told her the man had seen her. Caution was more than required whilst she furtively slipped between and around other pedestrians on the dark street. Her heart began to beat faster when her quarry slipped down a side alley. She had been there before. It was narrow and dark, serving as a delivery route for several stores. She let the handle of the Wakizashi under the left sleeve slip into her hand, catching the scabbard between her fingers. Glancing quickly about, she entered the alley, the hairs on her neck rose immediately. Her quarry was directly ahead; a man with a pistol had crept up behind her. Hearing the cocking of the double action pistol, Li Na whirled in an instant, the Wakizashi out of its scabbard, moving in an outward slice, tip down, severing the man's right wrist. Both his hands and the pistol dropped to the concrete. The blade continued outward and then flipping the tip upward, converted into a figure eight pattern, the motion, turning inward sliced the man's throat. She stepped back with her left foot, between her quarry's legs; the blade coming to rest on the quarry's throat. One small motion and he would be as dead as the fallen man. "So, we meet again at last," the man said. "Have you decided to take me up on our offer?"

Li Na looked fiercely into his eyes. There was no fear. Somehow, he knew that she would not kill him. At least not yet. While she peered at him, she suddenly realized he was not Asian, but English.

"You never introduced yourself," she replied.

"Excuse me. I am Aston Longfellow. I work for a corporation that does, well, different things. Do you mind, motioning to the sword?"

Li Na stepped back, lowering the short sword, kneeling

briefly to wipe the blood off on the dead man's clothes then, sheathing it and returning it beneath her long sleeve.

"Walk with me," Li Na said. "We will go eat something. There is a small restaurant on the next street."

Aston walked beside her, glancing at her when occasion allowed without bumping into other pedestrians. She was as beautiful as he had remembered. And the death of his man served as a reminder of her reputation. He had only found her through triad contacts before and it had been very difficult. He remembered that when he had approached her that he had been most unwelcome. Li Na had no time for uninvited guests and was very direct. They reached the small restaurant and were seated at a table away from the busy street. Li Na wasted no time getting down to business.

"I want to know how you found me last time?"

Aston did not know as much about her as he wanted to, only of her reputation and that she had been involved with Chinese intelligence with different groups. He knew better than to blow smoke so, he stuck with the direct approach realizing if he made a mistake, it might be his last.

"I found you through a triad contact," Aston replied. "Actually, I wasn't sure you were the person I was seeking because I had only a general description, nothing specific."

"You were not sure it was me then," Li Na said. "Why would you risk approaching someone you didn't know?"

"I was hired by an organization to find the best," Aston replied. "Your reputation precedes you. Did I make a mistake? Are you not the dark-haired assassin with the singing sword."

"I have heard that some call me that," she replied. "What kind of services does your organization require?"

"I am glad you are her," Aston said. "We or rather they, work with high profile clients. Their goal is both protection and sometimes kidnapping to effect it."

"Tell me about them," she demanded. "All that you can."

"I know very little in terms of intelligence," Aston said. "However, from what I know they are global and work with high-profile leaders both in governments and corporations. The have an extensive reach around the world, as well as resources to achieve their objectives."

"What are those objectives?"

"Truthfully, I don't know. I am only a go-between, a middleman to find people, technology, and other items of interest to them. They wanted me to find the best assassin I could, you. They told me specifically that an assassin who can get close enough to kill a high-profile target can also be very good at protecting them, no matter what it took."

"That makes sense," Li Na said. "How do they work?"

"Everything is kept on need to know, just like intelligence," Aston replied. "You, the agent, are assigned a client or target that they have already obtained the intelligence on. They detail what you are required to do with a time frame in which to do it. That is all I know. Payment is half up front and half upon completion."

"Who would I work with?" she asked.

Li Na watched him carefully each time he answered, her eyes slightly narrowed. She was staring at his pupils to determine if he was being truthful. His nervousness was apparent. Observing his mannerisms, eye contact, and the way he sat and tilted his head, she decided he was telling the truth. Still, she would be very cautious.

"From what I have been told, each agent is assigned one handler, perhaps two. That is all they would tell me."

"No doubt to prevent people from being able to sort out their organizational structure," she mused. "What is in it for you?"

"Money," Aston replied. "Simple. We agree on a price, and I find them what they want. Half up front and the rest on delivery."

"And if I agree, what then?"

"You set up a place to meet and someone will come to you.

Perhaps more than one. That is all I know. Once you meet, I obtain the rest of my payment, whether you are accepted by them or not."

"What do you mean accepted?"

"It is my understanding that they test the people they want to determine if they are suitable to work for the organization."

"Interesting. Tell me about the other items you procure for them?"

"I really should not."

"Then I will refuse."

"Very well. I will explain some, even though I have no clue about why they want such things. It's a wide range really. For example, I have gotten EKG units for them and other types of hospital equipment such as MRI machines and similar."

"Go on."

"I have also gotten them the most high-tech computers, metallic nanobots, various types of mother boards, large and small, pharmaceutical drugs and so forth."

"What kind of drugs?"

"Mostly sedatives, coma inducers, and that kind of thing. I don't know what they do with them and don't care. I have also purchased black-market arms, missile controllers, and all kinds of nefarious items used for anything from assassination to missile guidance systems. It is sometimes strange."

"In what way?"

"Well, I know that some of the drugs such as those used to induce comas and others are also used by intelligence organizations to control assets."

"How would you know that?"

"Because a friend does it for a European intelligence group and schooled me on the process. It's quite interesting."

"I have heard of these things done by the CIA, SVR, and other groups."

"It is a fact. How do you think they get a young man to shoot up a school full of kids or drive a car into a crowd or, take out a dozen people on a subway? It's not by accident. My friend told me that the assailants are assets waiting to be activated by their handler to push the political and ideological agenda of the agency or government they work for. I've heard the CIA and U.S. Government are particularly nefarious and experts at it, even the FBI."

"Yes. I am aware of what you say," Li Na said. "I have experience in the intelligence of such matters myself."

"What other services do you perform for this organization?"

"I just find whatever item they want and use whatever means are necessary to procure it. The last item had to do with biotechnology, some type of replication device. I suspect they do cloning, but it's only a guess."

"I should have asked you sooner," Li Na said. "Does this organization have a name?"

"They have only told me that it's an organization, no name."

"Now for the big question," Li Na said. "Suppose I accept, what happens next?"

"You will tell them where you want to meet them and when," Aston responded. "They will show up and you will have a conversation. Based on that, they will either hire you or you will never see them again."

"Will meeting them be dangerous?"

"Put it this way, I would trust a nose-horned viper more than I would trust them. Honestly, I have never been privy to the outcome of one of these meetings and I don't want to. Knowing would only be dangerous if you're not the one being interviewed. But then, I think if you are being interviewed it also would be dangerous. Watch your back with these people."

"Yes," Li Na said softly. "The first rule of assassination is to kill the assassin."

"Correct," Aston replied. "So, what will it be? Yes, or no?"

"I accept," Li Na replied.

"Good," Aston said, shoving a small business card across the table to her. "Call that number. Tell whoever answers you are the singing sword assassin. They will ask you when and where you want to meet and will require a 24-hour window."

"That's it?"

"Yes. But, like I said, watch your back. It was nice meeting you.

Good luck."

"Likewise," Li Na said, watching him make his way out of the restaurant.

While she watched, he pulled a cell phone from his jacket pocket.

"I have contacted the singing sword assassin. She will be calling."

"Thank you," a sexy voice replied. "Expect half payment tomorrow.

The conversation had been quite revealing. From what Colin and Henry had discussed about their hunches, she felt certain this was the same organization that held Jackson. Now, the question was why did they want an assassin when they had him and where should she meet them? Li Na would give it some thought. After a few minutes, she asked the hostess how to get to the delivery area and she slipped unnoticed out the back. It would be particularly important from now on to be extremely watchful. There was a good chance that Aston had been followed. And whoever might follow him would not be interested in him after a meeting. Li Na walked through several back streets to emerge onto a more frequented sidewalk, blending in with other pedestrians. She knew how to work a crowd and how to detect a tail. It wasn't long before she saw them. A man and woman, pretending to be lovers that shadowed her while she walked. Li Na had prepared for just such a scenario. They would be trying to follow her home and only her and Jackson knew where that was. These two would not find it just as others had not.

HENRY had been tracking traffic, energy use, and communications from every source he could find where the helicopters had landed that had taken Jackson. He was able to find a satellite that had passed over the area at the same time, it was American for which he could not gain the access code. He made a call to Colin.

"An American satellite passed over the area where the helicopters landed. I am certain they have a feed that shows where Jackson was taken. Can you get it?"

"I think so. You remember your counterpart in DARPA? He is a good friend of Jackson as well. Stay on the line, I'll make contact."

There was silence for about a minute then, a ringing phone.

"Mitch Daniels, how can I help you."

"Mitch, this is Colin Archer with MI6. Are you aware of what happened with Jackson?"

"They told me he was killed in the line of duty. That is all I know."

"I have Henry Payne on with me. Are you on a secure line?"

"No one is listening."

"Do you have a secure system that only you have access to?" Henry asked.

"Yes," Mitch replied. "Where do you need the IP sent?"

"Text it to +44748898517," Henry replied. "Great, I have it. Stand by."

About two minutes later, Mitch had the video feed.

"What am I looking at?" he asked.

"That is the missile strike Jackson was supposed to have been killed in. The CIA only used their feed for confirmation."

"Who are the men in the white suits from the helicopters?"

"We believe they are a clandestine organization we know nothing about," Colin replied. "We need to keep this between ourselves until we know more."

"They picked up a body and put it on a stretcher," Mitch whispered, looking around the room to make sure no one heard him. "Is that Jackson?"

"Yes," Henry said. "It has been confirmed. Notice the helicopters head back to Zatoka about sixty miles north-northeast. We lost our feed in that location."

"We have a satellite overflight of it," Mitch said. "It is highly classified. What are you looking for?"

"I have monitored traffic, energy use, and communications in the entire area. I think I have the location narrowed about twenty miles east of Zatoka in what looks like an abandoned industrial plant."

"But you don't want to chase ghosts," Mitch replied. "You want me to look for vehicles from where the helicopters landed?"

"Yes," Henry said. "The coordinates are 46°03'27" North; 30°24'44" East."

"Give me a moment."

Henry and Colin could hear the clacking of a keyboard while Mitch downloaded the visual from the satellite recordings.

"Okay. I'm in. I have the helicopters landing. The stretcher and several men jumped into a van. The other men got into two other vans. They are headed north intersecting P70. This may take a while."

"We have time," Colin said. "We will wait."

A few minutes later the vans changed direction.

"They are on E87 headed east," Mitch said.

About twenty minutes later they pulled off E87 heading south.

"Alright," Mitch whispered. "Looks like they are heading south to Kulevcha. They turned onto Vul Pryvokzal'na. They are turning down some side streets, seem to be in a hurry now. Picking up T1643. They stopped. It looks like an old industrial section, but there are some newer buildings toward town. The coordinates are 46°01'34" North; 29°54'38" East. You were correct Henry, it's about twenty-three miles from the landing zone. I see them taking the stretcher into the largest building."

"Excellent," Colin said. "At least we narrowed it down. For now, let's keep this to ourselves."

"You want to tell me what is going on?" Mitch asked.

Colin and Henry related all that had happened so far. It seemed a bit farfetched, but the fact that they had picked up Jackson and taken him to this location likely meant that he was alive. After all, a corpse didn't seem like it would be of much value to anyone.

"I believe what you say is true," Mitch said, when they had finished. "What can I do to help you?"

"Do you know how to disable a chip that can control a person?" Henry asked.

"I have some thoughts on it," Mitch said. "My former boss who was here for forty-five years anticipated just such a scenario. Let me check the research notes he left and see what I can come up with."

"Great," Henry said.

"It is likely we will need to go up the chain on this," Colin said. "We all need to be prepared for that."

"I understand," Mitch said. "But let's do our homework first. I would still like to stay on payroll."

They all laughed.

CHAPTER 4

SWORDSMANSHIP would be all that was needed to deal with the two-member team following her. Li Na had enough of their prying eyes. She cursed herself for not bringing her suppressed pistol. But she felt certain that she could handle them without it. Having lived in Hong Kong for years, she was more familiar than most with the backstreets and areas where there was privacy from prying eyes of which there were far too many. A misty rain had begun creating small puddles in the street; lights reflecting from them created a soft glare; it was just enough to make the night seem darker. The team was getting too close for comfort and pedestrian traffic was thinning quickly. No longer able to blend with others, Li Na crossed a small park to an alley beyond, hugging the shadows of the buildings. Dressed in dark clothing, she blended with her surroundings, standing next to a large drainpipe descending the brick wall. The man held his pistol in his right hand when he passed. With one swift movement, Li Na used an outward slice to his neck. The woman approached her quickly and Li Na was able to knock the pistol from her hand. She tried to sever the wrist, but the woman was too quick, only the pistol dropped to the concrete. Li Na heard the draw of the sword when it left its scabbard. Darkness was now the enemy rather than the friend. She placed herself so she could see the shadow of her opponent contrasted against the end of the alley. Circling each other, Li Na stabbed toward her assailant's center of mass, moving the sword slightly outward as the woman jumped back. Too late, the tip of Li Na's Wakizashi cut into the left bicep. Her opponent winched in pain while she circled left, slicing at Li Na's neck. Stepping forward, Li Na grabbed the left arm below the cut, which was bleeding heavily; she thrust her right hand out, the blade so sharp it almost severed the neck of the woman when it passed. Li Na's opponent fell, blood spurting from her with each heartbeat. The woman was dead before she hit the ground. It was unfortunate because Li Na had wanted to question her.

Li Na might have felt bad, but in the streets, there was no room for mercy. It was kill or be killed. Looking carefully around, she wiped her sword clean on the clothes of the fallen. Then, she searched each of them, found their wallets, picked up their guns and hurried quietly away in the falling rain, enveloped by the darkness. It was a long way to her apartment and despite the cover of night and falling rain, Li Na knew she could afford no mistakes so, she crisscrossed the streets and back avenues more than necessary to reach home. The last few blocks, she backtracked several times to make certain she was not followed. At one point, she stopped beneath the canopy of a tree and waited for thirty minutes. The rain had driven everyone inside. Most apartments and stores were darkened. It took another forty minutes to reach home, all the while continuing to stop, watch, and backtrack.

The door to their apartment was inset into a brick wall next to an old furniture making shop. The owner never came out during the day until he went home and there were no windows. Because of what had happened, she stood silently in the alcove, out of the rain, waiting and watching for a half hour. Finally, she unlocked the door and closed and locked it behind her. Feeling cold, she made a cup of tea, laying her collection from the two assailants on the table next to the kitchen. Sipping her tea, she looked over the items and decided she would take a shower first.

Li Na let her hair fall to her waist when she stepped into the shower, the warmth of the water cascading gently over her lithe, strong body. At this moment she thought about how beautiful she was. It was never something she really thought about. Her thoughts typically dwelled on strategy and the next danger around the corner. She put some body wash on a luffa sponge and meticulously rubbed her skin, feeling it rejuvenate; the sponge cleansing every pore. She lathered her hair and carefully rinsed it, dragging her hands from the scalp to the frayed ends to wring the excess water out. Stepping out of the shower, she grabbed a towel and dried herself then, slipped into a bath robe. Her thoughts drifted to Jackson. How she missed him. They had grown very close and despite their occupations, she was hoping he would pop the big question someday although a piece of paper would not define their love. It was a certainty he would; it was how he was raised. The question would never come if she could not find him. Walking back to the kitchen table, she began going through the small purse and wallet she had taken from her attackers.

There wasn't any identification on the man. His wallet was empty. The woman's ID was an expired drivers license with an English name. Since she had been Asian, it didn't seem to fit. The guns were both well used, which meant that likely, these two were a hit team. Li Na let out a sigh, stepping back to think. Suddenly, she noticed a white sliver in the man's wallet, the edge of a business card, which she carefully removed. Examining it, there was no information, only a phone number. The card seemed familiar then, remembering the one Aston had given her, she grabbed her own purse, pulling it out. Li Na laid both cards side by side on the table. They were exactly alike, the color and typeface. The only dissimilarity was that the phone number on each was different. She found it interesting and surmised that these two assassins worked for the organization that apparently wanted her.

"Why would they be following me if that were the case," she thought. "Was it a test or were they hoping, like many others, to find where she and Jackson lived? It was probably the latter. Making another cup of tea, she sat back in a chair, looking toward the table but not seeing it. Whoever this organization was, they were very clandestine. Working inward toward the leaders would be like peeling back a large onion. There would be many layers for protection. Unless they got lucky, it would be almost impossible to identify them. "It was simple," she thought. "They needed more horsepower." There was only one thing to be done, call Henry and Colin, as well as Mitch. They needed a conference call. The time to choose a path was now. It was late for her, 12:25 am so, it would be 5:25 pm in London and 12:25 pm in DC. They would all be up.

Taking her sat phone, she called Colin then, merged Henry and Mitch.

"Talk to me," Colin said.

"Do you remember the gentleman I told you about who approached me?"

"Yes, I do."

"I talked with him this evening," she said. "Afterward, I was followed and attacked by two assassins. Look at the pictures I just sent to all of you. The card on the left is the one Aston Longfellow gave me, at least that is who he said he was. The card on the right is one I took from the male assassin."

"We will check into them from both ends," Mitch said. "Right, Henry?"

"Yes, we will share our information," Henry said. "Need I ask what happened to the assassins?"

"I am still here," Li Na replied softly, while she explained what happened.

"Right," Henry whispered hoarsely.

"Gentleman, I think we need more people on this," Li Na said. "This organization, whoever they are, will be more than we can handle alone."

"You are correct," Mitch said. "I can get the NSA involved in tracking the numbers and things, but it would be better to go through channels. After all, being a loose cannon isn't exactly a good step to advance one's career in intelligence."

"Well said," Colin replied. "We have the satellite feeds, phone numbers, Jackson's pickup, and a few other things. I think we have enough to move to upper channels. What do you guys think?"

"I agree," Henry said. "We know that the missiles were launched to destroy a nuke. Neither the Russians nor Americans would want that to come out. The fact that we know that, and that Jackson's body was removed from the site, which they don't know, should be adequate to begin communications."

"I agree," Mitch joined in. "Why don't we put all our information together and send it up proper channels, stating that we wanted to make sure before we sent it up. The bosses will understand."

"I have a question," Colin said. "Li Na, do you know any of the top officials in Washington?"

"Yes, I have met the President and Vice President, the CIA director, and the Secretary of Energy. They got Jackson and I initially involved in this mess."

"Do you have their numbers?" Mitch asked.

"Yes, both the president and the CIA director," she replied.

"Good, call the director and explain what we are doing and who is involved," Mitch said. "Colin, Henry and I will go through proper channels. I think it wise that this doesn't broadside them."

"I understand," Li Na said, hanging up the phone.

She began to think about all that had happened and planned in her mind how she would approach the director. If this organization had as much capability as they imagined. They would be in a race against the clock. But what race, what were they planning? Whatever it was, for them to remove Jackson from the island meant that it was very important and that he was alive.

Phillip Ross was sitting as his desk thinking about the ugly havoc this new, secret organization could wreak upon the world.

"You have a phone call sir," his secretary said.

"Who?"

"She says her name is Li Na."

Phil's heart sank; he realized how much pain she must be in.

"Put her through and hold all calls until I'm done."

"Yes sir."

"Li Na, how are you?"

"I am doing well. Are you alone?"

"Yes," Phil replied, a feeling of apprehension falling over him. "What do you need?"

"I need you to listen carefully to what I am about to tell you," She began. "Do you remember our conversation about Jackson?"

"Certainly," Phil replied. "I'm so sorry."

"There is no time for that. He is alive and we are tracking him, at least trying to."

Li Na explained all that had happened, who was involved and what they were doing. While Phil listened, he realized this small group of agents had cracked a much bigger nut.

"Hold on a minute please," Phil said. "I'll get right back to you. "Maggie, get me Mitch Daniels at DARPA on the phone immediately. Put him through to both of us when you reach him."

"Yes sir," Maggie said.

"Continue," Phil told Li Na.

She had just finished the details when Maggie joined Mitch on the call.

"How can I help you, Director?" Mitch asked.

"I have Li Na on the phone with us. She has been explaining all the details about your small group working together. I need to know right now, have you put the information through channels?"

"No sir," Mitch said. "The packet will not be ready for another half hour or so."

"Very well. Do not go through normal channels. Bring it directly to me. I will tell your boss we are working on some technical issues related to Jackson's death. That's all anyone needs to know. You will not speak of this to anyone else that is not in your group that Li Na has divulged do me. Do you understand?"

"Yes sir, clearly."

"Li Na said you are working with Henry and Colin in MI6. Anyone else.

"No sir."

"Good, I'll call Sheena. She will keep this from normal channels there," Phil said. "How long will it take you to get here with all the feeds and other intelligence?"

"About an hour sir."

"Make it forty minutes," Phil demanded. "Li Na, I want to thank you for the information. Why don't you get some rest, and I will call you once I have everything. I need to take this directly to the President. You have managed to discover something we have been questioning. You'll be on the phone with some high-level leaders."

"I understand. I will rest now."

Phil began making calls and set up a meeting in the Oval with President Armstrong and Vice President Reisner. He would also help speed things up and merge in the British Prime Minister and MI6. Things were moving quickly. While contemplating the potential problem, Mitch walked in.

"Come with me," Phil said.

"Where are we going?"

"To the Oval! I'll fill you in on the way. I want your opinion. I suspect this is bigger than we imagine."

"That's why we brought it to your attention sir," Mitch said. "I have an uneasy feeling about these people or this organization."

"Join the club," Phil said. "There are powerful people involved and you're going to brief them. So, crank up your laptop and make sure you're ready."

JUST like Phil getting involved in the U.S., the information in London had gone directly to the Foreign Secretary and almost immediately to the Prime Minister. The intelligence revelation had shocked them to the core. The potential repercussions were unnerving in the least. They had sent for Henry and Colin to join them, as well as the head of MI6. They realized the small amount of information they had been privy to so far was the tip of an iceberg. In the conference room was Prime Minister Geoff Wilson, Foreign Secretary Jack Burton, and head of MI6, Sheena Harris. The technician had come in and set up feeds from both the White House and Kremlin. The group wondered what the Russian involvement was.

In the Oval was President Armstrong, Vice President Reisner, Director Ross, Mitch, and Admiral James West. Li Na stood by on phone. The Russian feed had President Sokolav and Andros Gusev, head of SVR. The screens came to life when each feed was fed in from the various heads of state.

"Gentlemen and Ladies," President Armstrong said. "All of you have the latest documentation that we have on a sinister group whom we have not yet been able to identify. You also have the satellite feeds. President Sokolav and I have agreed to show you this feed to put things into perspective. Please watch it."

The feed was the missile strike from the SSN Montana. It showed the missile launch and approach, as well as the impact.

"This missile strike was a joint operation between us and the Russians. A rogue general had gotten his hands on an ICBM that was being retired along with the launch codes. The target was Washington DC. We could not afford that to happen. I'm certain that you understand the politics involved. What we were not aware of is that an organization has arisen that can potentially take over world governments. It has come to our attention that the group MI6 destroyed last year worked for them. For whatever reason, they were exposed by this primary organization, at least intelligence seems to confirm that."

A hush fell over the conference room in Britain. They knew full well how difficult it had been to get rid of the organization, now they were being told there was another who controlled them.

"Diabolical," Burton whispered.

"What I would like to do now is for this small group to present the intelligence they have gathered so far. After that, we will discuss potential solutions. I will let Mitch begin here and Colin, Henry, and Li Na will join with their comments."

Mitch began by showing a shorter clip of the missile attack, followed by the helicopters landing and taking Jackson's body then, their flight to Zatoka and on to the industrial area.

"How do we know that is your agent's body that was retrieved?" Sheena asked.

"We were very close," Li Na broke in. "I would recognize him anywhere. Both Colin and Mitch will concur."

Sheena understood clearly that the two were lovers. It was

sufficient for her to know that they were not being pulled into something without vetted intelligence.

"Henry," Mitch said. "I think that you should tell them what you have uncovered on your end."

"I concur," Henry said. "We have two phone numbers for the organization. They appear to link to the same location. They were tracked to an abandoned factory in Budapest. We have been monitoring them but not with personnel. We need your approval for that."

"You have it directly," Jack Burton said. "Carry on."

"In addition to that, we have located where they took Jackson, which will also require agents on the ground. Further, Li Na was approached to work for them as an assassin. She has agreed but has not yet contacted them."

"From what we can tell," Colin joined in. "This group is highly sophisticated and likely has as great a capacity for intelligence gathering as MI6 or the CIA, which is most concerning."

"May I say something?" Andros cut in.

"Certainly," President Armstrong replied.

"We have talked about this with President Armstrong, President Sokolav, and Director Ross. We were not able to confirm what our suspicions were. This new intelligence helps. We have a grave concern in that we believe this group can clone both government and corporate leaders. Certainly, a group who controls the most resources and finances, as well as militaries will be very difficult to deal with."

"No one could have that kind of technological knowledge," Prime Minister Wilson said. "Could they?"

"Unfortunately, they can," Henry responded. "It's simple really. All intelligence agencies have worked on mind control for decades. With the advent of chips to join with drugs. I'm afraid is it not only possible but highly probable."

"I agree," Mitch chimed in. "My previous boss worked up a scenario to remove the ability of a chip to control an individual several decades ago."

"Ladies and gentlemen," Andros said. "President Sokolav and I concur with your technical experts. We have taken the precaution of not letting our leaders out of sight of their security, not even in the bathroom and have restricted public appearances except those we can strictly control. Also, our security has reverted to only those personnel we have known for at least twelve years."

"That seems drastic," Burton said.

"I don't think so," Sheena replied. "It is something all of us should do immediately. They took Jackson; that means they have a purpose for him. My guess is extraction of those they want to control since he is superb at that type of operation."

"You bring up a good point," Andros said.

"I agree," President Armstrong replied. "President Sokolav, you have been quiet. What are your thoughts."

"I keep thinking Mr. President. What all of you speculate is likely true. The question is, what kind of solution can we put in place to make certain we are not compromised? Also, we need to put ourselves in this organization's shoes."

"How so?" Prime Minister Wilson asked.

"If you were them, which world leaders would be most valuable to you?"

"That is an excellent point," Phil said. "Perhaps our agencies should draft a potential list, in order of importance."

"The question is where do we start the list?" Secretary Burton asked.

"May I say something?" Admiral West asked.

"Certainly," President Armstrong replied. "Everyone needs to speak up. The situation is too critical not to."

"All of you are old enough to be aware of global history for the last couple of decades," Admiral West said. "It is my opinion we should look at countries with strong militaries, as some have suggested, but more importantly, we should look at countries with great resources, especially in terms of water, food, energy, and precious metals."

"You mean like Afghanistan?" Andros asked.

"Precisely. We need not kid ourselves. Russia went in then, we went in with a coalition and now, the Chinese are going in. If we come clean with ourselves, we know all have gone in for the great mineral wealth the country holds. The problem was, there was no water to extract it. If the Chinese try to use the water from the head of the Indus, they are likely to end up in a serious war, perhaps nuclear with Pakistan and India."

"That is true," President Sokolav said. "But I do not think Afghanistan would be of interest to this group."

"I agree," Admiral West said. "The countries they would probably be most interested in are those with immediate wealth and or control abilities. Those with a capacity to control other nations and with the wealth or military apparatus to do so."

The group sat pensively for a few minutes, having private conversations among themselves.

"I believe the Admiral is correct," Prime Minister Wilson said, breaking the silence. Speaking with Sheena, a couple of the wealthiest countries to add to the list could be both Russia and Botswana. As you know Aikhal is in Sakha, Republic of Russia and is the world's biggest diamond mine. With various deposits, it includes the Jubilee Pipe, Aikhal Pipe, Komsomolskaya Pips, and Zaria pipe with and estimated 175 million carats. I think President Sokolav can be in danger."

"Also, don't forget Botswana," Phil joined it. "The open pit Jwaneng diamond mine near Gaborone is estimated to have about 165 Mct. and considered to be the world's richest diamond mine by value."

"I see where you are going," President Armstrong said. "I believe Admiral West is on point. I'm sure with such talented minds, we can come up with a list quickly. Phil, would you and Sheena and Andros cooperate to develop the list? While you are doing that, let's come up with a way to ensure the safety of us and the leaders of the countries on the list."

"Agreed," President Sokolav said.

"Mitch and Henry, you're the tech experts," President Armstrong said. "And part of the team that got us here. Any thoughts?"

"We have been talking Mr. President," Henry said. "One of the resources that we need to add to the list is high tech components and knowledge on how to use them?"

"Great idea," Sheena said. "We'll get on it but will need both of you to help us with that."

"I believe this is a great start," President Sokolav said. "I agree with President Armstrong. All of you work on that and we will concentrate on our security."

"Excellent point," Vice President Reisner chimed. "I suggest, with President Armstrong's concurrence that we adjourn and work on this for thirty-six hours then, meet again."

"Let's make it twenty-four hours," Prime Minister Wilson said. "Is that acceptable?"

The groups all nodded, the monitors going blank.

"We are up a proverbial creek, aren't we gentlemen?" the President asked.

"Not necessarily sir," Phil replied. "Henry and Mitch have a handle on Jackson's location. If we can track him then, perhaps we can circumvent what he will do for the organization."

"Yes," Vice President Reisner said. "With the combined resources of our countries, we can cut their capabilities."

"True," Phil said. "But I believe we should approach it another way."

"What are you proposing?" President Armstrong asked.

"Well, what the VP said is correct. But why don't we track Jackson and begin tracking the links then, crush the entire organization?"

"A sting operation?" the VP asked.

"In a manner of speaking," Phil replied. "After all, if we only track Jackson to the first target, it will not put us in a position to take this group down."

"You're the spymaster," President Armstrong said. "I like your thinking. Run this by the other two groups and determine the assets you need. If nothing else, this should prove very interesting."

JACKSON felt fully healed, even his broken leg didn't bother him anymore; it had fully recovered. After rescuing Antonio from the warehouse, he was in a good mood and out for a morning jog. It felt like he had been here for years and was comfortable with the people; they seemed to be his best friends. Because of the chip, he was completely unaware of his past. Jackson heard footsteps approaching from behind. He smiled at the man whom he considered to be his best friend.

"You are getting much faster my friend," Illiac said, jogging up beside him.

"Thank you," Jackson replied. "My leg healed. I still don't remember what happened."

"It was fate of the trade," Illiac said. "A grenade landed near you, and you took a bullet to the leg at the same time."

"Well, thanks for hauling me out."

"You would do the same for me. Antonio told me to tell you we are getting ready for a mission."

"What's up?"

"I don't know the details yet, but we are going after a figure who controls gold mines," Illiac replied. "I'll know more soon."

"Do I need to do anything to help you?" Jackson asked.

"Not yet, my friend. Just keep improving your fitness, you have the needed skills for whatever comes our way."

"I think I'm about one hundred percent," Jackson replied.

"I think so too," Illiac replied. "At least cardiovascular wise. I think you should hit the rappelling wall and some climbing ropes, so your forearms and shoulders are up to snuff."

"You think we will be climbing?"

"You know Antonio. Never underestimate the assignments. He seemed to hint that we may need to use ropes. I assume, perhaps wrongly, that means we may be scaling a wall or cliff. But who knows my friend? I must go; see you later."

Jackson watched Illiac take the road to the left leading to a large Quonset hut. He had never been in it before and had the distinct impression he was not wanted there. He wondered why but shook off the feeling and headed toward the ropes course. It was not his favorite training. Reaching the rappelling wall, he went up and down several times. It had always been easy for him. Having built up a sweat and warmed his upper body, he tackled his least favorite exercise, the rope climb, trying to remember where he had learned the technique but could not. All he remembered was the eight warm-up exercises that would help him from pulling a muscle. Jackson began with the assisted rope climb by stretching his legs out until they touched the corner of the log wall at the ground. His upper back was a few inches above the ground, his entire body in a straight line. His right arm grabbed the rope, his left at a ninety-degree angle. He began to climb the rope until almost vertical then, lowered his body back toward the ground. After doing six of them he stood erect and grabbed the rope like before and performed six pullups on the hanging rope. Next, he did hanging leg extensions, grabbing the rope and pulling himself up, bringing his knees to his chest and extending his legs until they were straight then, brought his knees back to his chest and lowered them for six complete repetitions.

He became irritated because he didn't like warmups. His irritation grew because he could not remember where he learned rope climbing. For his fourth exercise, he pulled up on the rope and did six straight legged raises then, moved onto rope hanging where he pulled himself up on the rope like the rope pullup and slowly lower his body, ten seconds for the first two reps, twenty for the second two and thirty seconds for the last two reps.

The next exercise was similar, rope eccentric lowering in which he did a pullup on the rope and slowly lowered to an extended arm position with both arms. Six reps and on to the rope plank walk. Jackson didn't know why, but inherently knew this was his least favorite warmup. He grabbed the rope while standing and lowered himself to a forty-five-degree angle while walking down the rope then, walked back up. He could feel a slight twinge of pain in his left shoulder. Rubbing it, he realized it was a shrapnel wound that had healed on the surface from his last mission but was still healing beneath the skin. Shaking it off, he performed the last warm-up. Grabbing the rope, with one hand, he lowered himself to a forty-five-degree position and performed six, one-arm pullups with each arm. He was really sweating but felt good. Looking up, thirty feet to the top was a long way. He began his first ascent.

Antonio and Doctor Bramahh were watching him through a hidden camera high in the trees behind him.

"He looks very fit to me," Antonio said.

"Yes," Bramahh replied. "We will keep watching him. So far, his memory block seems to be holding well."

"What happens if his memory comes back?" Antonio asked.

"From what you have told me about him, we will both be dead, or he will."

"Let's hope it holds then," Antonio grinned. "He is all I have heard and more."

"I agree," Bramahh said. "Were he not so fit, we may not have been able to do anything but clone him. Look, he has climbed the rope seven times. He is like a machine."

"Yes," Antonio replied, watching in wonder. "It is like he has a knack for everything he does."

"Especially killing, neh?" Bramahh responded. "He is a true assassin, justifying that those he kills are an enemy to the people."

"They are," Antonio murmured. "Either their people or ours. He is the piece of the puzzle we have sought that will allow us to get the control we seek."

"How so?" Bramahh asked.

"He has never failed a mission," Antonio responded firmly. " If you keep that memory block intact, he will not fail us."

"It will not be difficult," Bramahh said. "We can monitor his vitals through the chip 24/7. If it looks like the block is wearing thin, I have implanted another small container that will allow us to inject additional medication. He won't even know."

"Good," Antonio said. "Do not fail me."

"I will do my job," Bramahh said. "You just need to keep a close eye on him in the field."

"Illiac will."

MITCH and Henry had been watching the facility where Jackson had been moved to. From what they assumed was a small medical facility, he had been transported near the eastern border of the Ukraine to a heavily wooded area. While being unable to watch him 24/7, they were able to monitor him each day to some extent. It appeared the new facility was a training encampment.

"What do you think?" Henry asked.

"From the way Jackson behaves on camera, I believe he is under some kind of control."

"I concur. It is as though the people he interacts with are best friends."

"Is there a chemical that can do that?" Mitch asked.

"Several," Mitch replied. "If you combine those chemicals with current chip technology and biohacking, you can do an awful lot. We have come far since the early experimentation by the Russians and CIA."

"I don't think there is anything we can do other than keep monitoring him," Mitch said.

"'That and try to tap into their communications," Henry replied. "If we can intercept a phone call or two, we may be able to determine a better strategy."

"Let's keep at it," Mitch replied.

COLIN Archer was able to obtain information on the phone numbers. All had been rerouted from a small building in Berne to a location in Jamaica. One of their agents had performed surveillance on the building, a small warehouse and boat repair shop adjoining some boat docks adjacent to Kingston Harbor. The agent had sent photos of persons going in and out of the shop. Most were local fishermen who were having their boats repaired. There were at least three that promised more intelligence. One of them was the person Li Na had described Aston Longfellow. Looking up his history, he had no run ins with the law and was listed as the concierge officer of his own company. Simply put, he found things for people and seemed to be legitimate, at least in his periodic reports. Colin guessed that finding an assassin was not mentioned in them. He was sly, finding legitimate items for a wide variety of clients, all of whom were reported and verified. Of course, the shady ones like this organization would not be. Either way, his directions were not over the phone, but appeared to be from this shop. Considering that, then others who worked for them clandestinely would likely also be getting their orders here. It made logical sense. Assuming no one knew about them, which would be their premise, no enforcement or intelligence group would think of looking here. The field information would help them identify more members of the organization. Colin felt sure they were on the right track.

THE Oval was busier than normal. The President didn't want to move to the Situation room. There were only a handful of people involved and he wanted to keep things low key and off the radar of congressional snoops. Everyone was present. The monitors changed from black to reveal the Russian and British teams. They somehow appeared more upbeat than before and in better spirits, despite the gravity of the situation.

"Good day everyone," President Armstrong said. "President Sokolav, Prime Minister Wilson, and I have been talking about the security issues involved with this situation. Before we discuss that, we would like each of you to report on what you have found so far."

"I think it may be best is we begin with the tech group," VP Reisner said. "Henry and Mitch."

"Thank you, sir," Henry responded. "I've updated Prime Minister Wilson and the Foreign Secretary. You should have received my report. I will go over the gist of it. As you know, we followed Jackson and found out where their initial treatment or medical facility was located. You were made aware of that during our last meeting. Since that time, they have moved him to a training compound, at least that is what it looks like. It is on the western border of the Ukraine. We have been monitoring it closely and have been able to observe Jackson's interactions with others. They appear to be old acquaintances."

"I know Jackson," Phil said. "I have worked closely with him. He has none of those as his friends."

"We believe that sir," Mitch interrupted. "What Henry and I have assessed is that he is being controlled or manipulated. Not by threat of harm to anyone he knows, but through a computer chip."

"How is that possible?" VP Reisner asked.

"We have progressed much since the initial Russian and CIA forays into psychological control in its early days sir," Henry said. "My discussions with Mitch have led us to the same point. His predecessor envisioned just such an occurrence. Further, this organization has touched on something both our countries have been working on. We know we should not share such information, but given the critical nature, we believe there is a need for all to know. I am sure the Russians also have been making inroads into this field."

"You are correct," President Armstrong said. "Let's put our cards on the table. Otherwise, this endeavor is for naught."

"Mitch," Henry said. "I give you the floor."

"Thank you, Henry," Mitch replied. "We know that the technology is there to control a person with a chip. Henry told you that both our countries have been working on it."

"We have also," Andros said. "Just to be clear. Go on please."

"What if I told you that we can not only control the subject by changing genetic sequencing using computer generated signals, but that we can also do a onetime change using CRISPR Therapeutics, as well as change all biometrics, including fingerprints?"

"What is CRISPR?" President Sokolav asked.

"I will try to keep this simple," Mitch replied.

"Please do," President Armstrong interjected.

"It is a genetic engineering technique within the field of molecular biology through which genomes of living organisms can be modified. It is based on the bacterial CRISPR-Cas9 antiviral defense system. It works by delivering the Cas0 nuclease and complexing it with synthetic gRNA, the common term is guide RNA. This is done by cutting the cell's genome at a desired location, which allows existing genes to be removed or to add new ones *in vivo*."

"Are you telling us you can completely modify a person?" Prime Minister Wilson asked.

"Not only modify, but make them appear like someone else too," Mitch responded, everyone was shaking their heads in disbelief. "Let me continue. The technique is very significant in biotechnology and medicine. It allows the editing of gnomes in vivo with high precision. Not only that, but it is also relatively cheap and easy to do."

"What can it be used for?" Foreign Secretary Jack Burton asked.

"All kinds of things really," Henry said. "Items such as agricultural products, new medicines, all kinds of genetically modified organisms, as well as controlling pathogens and pests of various kinds."

"Does that mean you could develop a vaccine or germ warfare pathogen to control mass numbers of people?" President Armstrong asked.

"Theoretically," Mitch responded, but that requires much research and billions of dollars. Henry and I believe that although it is theoretically possible, no one has succeeded at that yet."

"This is most unnerving," VP Reisner said. "People directly around us could be influenced to kidnap or kill us."

"We concur," Henry replied. There is much that can be done. However, we do not believe this organization has that capability yet, but they may be the first to procure it."

"What I hear you saying is that this organization currently is using only chip control, but not alteration techniques as you just described?" President Sokolav asked.

"Correct," Mitch said.

"Thank you, gentlemen," President Armstrong said. "Because of this, I think our current security strategy will work. Now, the VP, CIA director and I have come up with a strategy that may help find and at least greatly reduce the capabilities of this organization.

"How so?" President Sokolav asked.

"A sting," Phil responded. "We need to follow Jackson and his group but take no action to stop them?"

"We have already found their headquarters location," Colin interrupted. "It is likely not their primary headquarters, but where their management and others come to get instructions."

"Yes," Phil said. "I saw that in your report. Kudos to you. That is a great step forward."

"You want to cast a net and capture or kill most of them," Andros said. "A good plan. What do you need from us?

"We need enough of all our countries best field agents," Phil said. "I have talked it over with the president. It is critical we work together on this. Mitch, Henry, and Andros have established a crises center that will fuse all our groups so that we can act as one."

"Where is it?" Andros asked.

"It is on the farm," Phil said.

"You refer to the Camp Peary Naval Reservation, AFETA, near Williamsburg," Andros said.

"Yes," Phil replied. "A crises suite is being set up there now and will be complete by the time your personnel arrive on site. Mitch and Henry will give you the details of the necessary skill sets."

"How many personnel will you need from us?" Prime Minister Wilson asked.

"We need six highly qualified personnel from each of your countries and a manager for the six," Phil responded.

"We have sent the details," Henry said.

"Good," Phil said. "We need you to select your personnel and send their pictures and identification directly to AFETA. We need them there within the next twenty-four hours. I will clear it. Once they arrive, they will be taken directly to the crisis suite."

"I have the list of requirements," Andros stated flatly. "The requested personnel will be airborne within three hours. You will see that our flight is cleared, correct?"

"Yes," President Armstrong replied. "It will be cleared through the necessary airspace and for immediate landing once it arrives."

"Thank you," Andros replied.

"We will follow the Russian example," Prime Minister Wilson responded. "Expect our personnel there within the same timeframe."

"Perfect," President Armstrong said. "It is my hope that we can continue to have great relations once this is over. I believe it is going to be a necessity."

"Why do you say that?" President Sokolav asked.

"If you look at global history, it shows that when one such organization arises, good or bad, at least two others will emerge."

"Then we had better learn well," President Sokolav replied with a smile."

MEETING in a restaurant always had its quirks. The upside was that it was generally public with enough customers so that the intent to do harm by those you met was curbed. One of the downsides was that there were places to hide within and without so that an assailant could come at you from any direction or easily put a bullet in your head. Li Na had set this meeting place because she knew it intimately, within and without. She also had placed several of her own men in the restaurant and two outside in the cover of adjoining high-rise buildings so that they had a good view while watching through the scopes of their sniper rifles. They had arrived under cover of darkness at 4:00 am. So far, nothing had been suspicious.

She entered the Chinese restaurant, acknowledging the hostess who seated her at her normal table. Li Na was wearing an elegant Hanfu skirt dress that had a pale peach top and light pastel green skirt. It looked like it was one piece because it was tied with a white sash around the waist. The sleeves were long and flowing and very loose down to the wrist, partially hiding her hands. The skirt was pleated and reached the floor. Her jet-black hair fell behind her back with two small braids beaded in front; stick pins that were barely visible held her hair in one long flowing cascade.

When she sat down the patrons in the restaurant gasped at her beauty. She glanced back; they withered under her gaze, going back about their business. Despite that, it was difficult for them to stop glancing at her stunning presence. Looking around, she counted ten patrons. She knew the entire staff who were going about their work. It was late afternoon and the patrons slowly left until only four remained. A couple and two men. She sensed immediate danger from them because they were the only ones who had not looked at her when she walked to her table. She didn't need a menu but took it anyway so she could examine them while she pretended to look it over. They were swarthy and their business attire did not suit them; they also seemed uncomfortable in it. Her eyes went to the left side of the menu to observe the couple. She noticed they did not seem to match. They neither seemed to be together or separate and appeared nervous. The hair on the back of her neck began to tingle. The waitress took her order. Placing her hands in her lap, she smiled at one of the staff and slowly moved the Wakizashi into position within her sleeve. A man walked in with a cane but didn't appear to be using it. He was dressed in a navy blue, wool blazer with gold and black buttons, and khaki pleated trousers that hugged his lithe frame, and an obviously expensive watch. Li Na identified it as a Rolex. His hair was black, as was his mustache with just enough gray to give him the appearance of maturity without too much age. He had a refined look and began walking directly toward her, his eyes piercing. Immediately, she instinctively knew he was the one she was supposed to meet.

"Permit me to introduce myself senorita. I am Antonio Raven. May I sit down?"

She nodded, carefully watching his movements. The cane was a sword cane. "Was it for protection or fighting?" she asked herself. His eyes were those of a predator, sharp, staring, and unblinking; blue, almost beyond blue.

"I am glad you accepted the meeting," Antonio said.

"What do you want of me?" Li Na asked.

"You killed our team," Antonio said. "They were one of our best."

"They were following me," Li Na replied, cautiously looking about, her head motionless. "I cannot allow anyone to know where I live. You must understand."

"Perfectly," Antonio replied, snapping his fingers.

Li Na's blade just missed his throat when he pushed himself backward. The couple and the two men were immediately on their feet, rushing her, swords drawn. Antonio stepped back against the wall. The couple reached her first, both holding their swords in the high-ready position. Li Na lifted her skirt with one motion. It fanned in front of the two, covering her movements. By the time they could see her, she had side stepped and in one motion stabbed the woman in the throat, the sword piercing through into the mans' neck. They fell spurting blood, to the floor. The two men began to circle her. Once again, she fanned her skirt, at the same time, she stepped by the man in front of her, using a technique from the legendary swordsman Miyamoto Mushashi. Stepping through with her right leg, holding the sword tucked against her elbow and at a ninety-degree angle, bracing it with her left hand on the hilt, the blade cut deeply into the man's right side. It was too late, she had walked past the effectiveness of the blade, which had lost its momentum and lethality; he fell to the floor, guts pushing out of the long, deep wound.

Without hesitation, she pivoted left, bringing the sword up to block the downward slice of the other man. Both hands on the handle, her left foot leading. She stepped slightly left; the blade slid off her, just nicking her sword hand then, with a quick snap of the wrist, moved her blade quickly forward, cutting the man's throat to the neck bones. She didn't turn to look instead, she did a front crossover leap, and her sword tip was at the base of Antonio's neck who had not moved from his original position. He let his sword cane fall to the floor, hoping she would stop her attack since he was now unarmed. Suddenly the door burst open. Four of Antonio's men began to rush in. Before they could clear the doorway, they fell dead from sniper fire. Four shots within 1.5 seconds.

It was like Li Na could see out of her right eye while she kept the left trained on Antonio.

"You are much more efficient than we have been told," Antonio said, lowering his hands.

The sword slowly pulled away. Her piercing eyes motioning to Antonio to sit back down. He picked up the chair and sat down, leaving his sword cane where it had fell. The restaurant staff were not surprised; they quickly cleaned up the mess.

"Why did you do that?" Li Na asked, her eyes glaring.

"Allow me," Antonio said, taking a handkerchief and wiping the few drops of blood from her hand. I had to test you. We can only hire the best. I gambled and played with fire."

"Playing with fire can get you badly burned," Li Na replied coldly.

"True," Antonio said. "But it was worthwhile to watch the show. You are like the emerald, green and black spotted frog in Peru, very beautiful yet very deadly. I was happy to see you at work."

"I was going to kill you," Li Na whispered through tight lips, her anger apparent.

"You would, but I was unarmed," Antonio said. "Assassins of your caliber do not kill the unarmed. May I have one of my men come in?"

"Unarmed," Li Na said, nodding to one of the staff.

The staff member walked to the door and waved, signaling the snipers not to fire. A short stocky man entered carrying an aluminum brief case that he sat down next to Li Na then, turned and left.

"You may open it," Antonio said. "It is your fee, which I am doubling because of your expertise. You will get the other half after the second mission of our man."

Li Na opened the case. Inside was $1 million US. There was a total of one hundred bound bundles, $10,000 each. She waved the owner over and gave him ten bundles then, motioned him away. He took the case and went into the back room where he and one of his staff passed a security wand over the case and cash to make sure there were no electronic tracking devices and then, carefully went through each bundle three times to ensure there were no embedded tracking devices. After doing so, they carefully put the money into a RFID signal blocking bag and placed it into another briefcase, which he took back to Li Na, placing it beside her and bowing.

"You do not trust me?" Antonio said, smiling. "That is wise. You were looking for an electronic bug, yes?"

"Exactly," Li Na said. "And in case you're wondering, this money will never go to my home. What is it you wish of me?"

"I do not want you to kill anyone," Antonio said. "I want you to protect one of our men. He is very important to us. I cannot let him be harmed unless it is from me."

Antonio passed a small photo across the table.

"I believe you have met before," he said.

"Yes, I helped him on an assignment once," she replied, hiding her happiness at the photo. "As I recall he was very good. I did not know he was still working."

"Yes, for us," Antonio said.

"Who is us?" Li Na asked.

"It is not important," Antonio replied. "I think he may be more than a colleague, yes?"

She knew he was digging for answers. He was troubled that he could not read her reaction. A typical Chinese woman he thought while he watched her.

"I wanted it to be," she replied carefully. "But he had love in his heart for another. Such is life."

The answer satisfied Antonio. He was unable to detect any attachment. She had only glanced at the photo and pushed it back to him. Had she kept it or run her fingers over it, he would have been certain something was between the two. It pleased him because he thought it best that they were not involved.

"Watch the morning puzzle of the Hong Kong Post," Antonio said. "When I need you, there will be a message reading – Pices, it was nice meeting you, please call."

"I do not have your number," she said.

"It is the one on the card," he replied. "Someone is always there to answer. When you call say you are Black Widow. You will then be given instructions. Adios senorita."

Li Na watched him exit the restaurant. Her men would tail him to discover any information they could, but she was certain little would be forthcoming. So, Jackson was indeed alive and active. Her heart beating faster, she stirred within, a smile spreading upon her face. She would see her love again, but would he recognize her. There were now too many unknowns. She picked up the case and walked outside, giving it to one of her men. It would be split into various amounts; some would go to her men; the rest would end up in a private account far from Hong Kong. So, even if the organization were smart enough to implant a tracker that was not detectable, it would never trace back to her home.

Antonio's vehicle turned left and right through the streets on its way to a helicopter pad near the harbor. He sat deep in thought looking at the photo of Li Na that had been taken when she entered the restaurant. His assumption that she would not kill him had been correct; he smiled. He was beginning to read people very well, even assassins. Still, it troubled him that he had been unable to read Li Na. She had glanced at the picture and passed it back in a manner that showed there was little interest there. His intelligence had said that Jackson and she were intimate. Maybe it was only during the one mission they had served on. She had confirmed that, and it would make sense because such a woman would probably not be able to have a long-term commitment to anyone. He had surmised that she was as ruthless and cunning as she was beautiful. She had dispatched his men like they were toys and they had been his best. He could not help thinking what she would be like in bed, a real panther probably. It was difficult to keep his mind off her. He resolved that he might need to do something about that. Perhaps he would have the good doctor prepare a chip for her. He pulled out the handkerchief, staring at the blood drops it had soaked up

CHAPTER 5

FORTUITOUSLY, the personnel from Russia and Britain arrived at the same time in two small vans each. They had been picked up at Andrews Air Base as soon as their transport planes arrived. Reaching Interstate 64, the vehicles headed south and exited at the junction of Highway 143, They were admitted through the security gate at the Camp Peary visitor center without a vehicle inspection because of Phil who was there to wave them through and make sure there were no glitches. An unmarked sedan led the vehicles northeast on a paved road that seemed to be about as inconspicuous as possible. Phil had jumped in his car and was following. The road abruptly turned north and about a half mile in they passed a large meadow on the right. There were so many trees it was difficult to see much, although both groups were straining to see what they could of the famous 'Farm.' About eight-tenths of a mile from the gate, the road had a wide bend turning back to the northeast. A moment later they saw Magruder Church off to the right across a narrow stretch that opened into a larger meadow with buildings scattered here and there. A few seconds later one of the Russians pointed.

"Look to the left," he said. "It looks like a gun range."

Both groups stared in the direction and could barely make out through the trees what appeared to be combined pistol and rifle ranges.

"I make the first range about fifty yards and the second about one hundred yards," a teammate said.

"Ummmm," the first grunted.

Directly after the range, the road swept back to the right and briefly they were at a Y-intersection. The lead car had stopped and made sure all four vans were close, then turned left, the vans following closely behind. About a mile later, they came to a cluster of about a dozen buildings with green tops and turned right, following the sedan ahead of them to the left and then right again until it pulled into a small parking lot in the northeast corner of what they felt was a compound. Phil pulled up right behind them. Mitch and Henry had already arrived and were waiting.

The groups stepped from the vans and were immediately assaulted by the smell of the salt marsh from Bigler Millpond a short distance to the southeast and the York River.

"It is great to have everyone here. For those of you who do not know me, I am Phillip Ross, Director CIA. I know that you have been told how critical this operation is. I want to ensure you it is vital to all our countries. Unfortunately, we do not know how long this operation will last so we need to make the best of it. About a thousand yards that way, pointing, a house has been arranged for each group. I'm not sure that you will be using them much, but we hope to make your stay as comfortable as possible. Due to the secure nature of this area, you will need to always be escorted when outside the building. I hope you understand. It is not an attempt to demean, but we have critical assets here that must remain secret. Let's introduce ourselves please. Who is leader of the British team?"

"I am sir. My name is Beatrix Adams. I am an expert in

satellite tracking, communications, photometry and intelligence collection and analysis via HUMINT, ELINT, and MASINT. This is my team, Blake, Edith, Sabrina, Felix, Jasper, and Trevor. They have the qualifications you requested."

"Excellent," Phil replied. "And the Russian Team?"

"It is a pleasure to meet you. I am Leonid Sobol and am expert in technological and bio tracking, satellite imagery, communication intercept and phone tracking, and sound interception. These are my team members Anton, Roman, Pavel, Vitaliy, Tatyana, and Elena. As Ms. Adams said, my team also has the skill sets you requested. Additionally, they all speak English okay."

"That is great," Phil replied. "It will make it easier to communicate. These two fellows, pointing, are Mitch Daniels from DARPA and Henry Payne from MI6. They are our tech gurus and will be helping you set up. You will be feeding them the information. Follow them to the inside of that building to the crisis suite. Food and beverages will be constantly supplied. If you have a request for specific types of food, the staff will comply as much as they can. For now, there is coffee, and a buffet with beef stroganoff, pizza, donuts, and cheeseburgers in plentiful supply."

"Follow us please," Mitch said.

The group entered the building and turned left down a wide corridor, passing rooms with large glass windows. There would be no privacy here. Everything was a critical operation with no room for error or chit chat with a friend on a cell phone. They came to a set of lockers with a couple of dozen small doors and locks.

"Please put your valuables, particularly your cell phones in one of the small lockers and take the key," Mitch said. "If you need to make a call later, you must go outside. No phones are allowed beyond this point.

Everyone took turns around the lockers doing as instructed. They were not unaccustomed to such policies, but it hammered home the importance of the mission. When they had finished, they walked through a locked security door with biometric identification of both hands, and facial and eye recognition. The guard stood aside to let them pass, scrutinizing everyone. He made them feel uneasy.

They passed large plate glass windows that spanned from about waist high to a twenty-foot ceiling. Behind it was a small room like an amphitheater found in most college settings; the door was at the bottom. When they entered, there was a huge monitor that covered the entire left wall and ten rows of seats that stretched to the top of the room. It appeared that the room could seat about sixty people. On the left and right sides were monitors and computer stations, about a dozen on each wall. Beyond the top row of seats was a walkway with tables set up with coffee and food. In the middle of the seats was a main walkway with several square pedestals for power blocks for hooking up computers and other communications equipment. The groups were staring in amazement at the set up. It was not new to them, but this room was exceedingly efficient. Phil had followed along and was watching. The looks on their faces pleased him. They would succeed or they would fail.

"Alright," Mitch said. "Henry and I will be taking up these stations in the middle walkway and will be putting your intelligence on the main screen."

"We want the Russian team on the right and the British team on the left," Henry said. "Our team will be taking up the inside seats along the middle isle. If you will notice, there is a white phone in the middle of each of the banks of computers. That is for you to communicate with your groups back home. Have them feed your intelligence directly to your IP addresses, which are listed on the bank of monitors at each station. You will note there are eight monitors at each station. Each is for incoming feeds for the intelligence type. It is listed at the bottom of every monitor."

"What types are we talking about?" Leonid asked.

"A good point," Mitch replied. "You are familiar with most of them that include Open-Source Intelligence or OSINT, Measurement and Signature or MASINT, Signals or SIGINT, Imagery or IMINT, Geospatial or GEOINT, Human or HUMINT. We have added one more called Linguistics Intelligence or LGINT."

"I have not heard of that one," Beatrix replied.

"We needed to do something with languages," Mitch replied. "It is fine if you have the ability of a personal translator within a group, like we have now. But when we monitor a language that we do not have an interpreter for and we need an immediate translation, we have gone to LGINT."

"You mean it is an algorithm to translate languages?" Leonid asked.

"More than that," Henry replied. "LGINT is run by a small supercomputer onsite that can place nuances, culture, etc. within the translation with a 99.5% accuracy. Samantha as we call it, utilizes one hundred sets of algorithms that are coupled together using neural network analysis and other advanced modeling techniques."

"LGINT is on the seventh monitor at each station," Mitch said. "If you hear a language that you do not understand, feed it into that monitor for immediate translation. Now, select your stations and we will go through some trial-and-error situations so that you can adapt on the go."

The teams took their places. Once settled in, they looked toward Mitch and Henry for directions.

"Okay," Mitch said. "I want the team leaders toward the middle of the computer banks and out onto the floor between the seats. This will allow your team to hear you and allow us to hear each manager. Please switch on the power to each of your stations."

Overhead lights were dimmed slightly while the banks of monitors flashed to life, adding additional light to the room.

The large monitor at the bottom turned gray and then, displayed all monitors in small arrays visible from anywhere in the room.

"You will notice your bank of computers are displayed on the large screen," Henry said. "Russian team, your banks, starting from left to right are on the left side of the screen, vertically aligned. British team, yours are on the right. Notice each bank of your monitors is assigned a color code, which you can see surrounding them in a square on the screen. That color is also listed on the bank. Please find your color so that you can constantly monitor it."

"What are we supposed to do with our intelligence?" Beatrix asked.

"Once you receive it, use your mouse to click the screen icon on the monitor," Mitch said. "When you click the icon, the data will be sent to the large screen from your bank of computers. Note that each of your monitors appears on the screen."

"What is the eighth monitor for?" Leonid asked.

"That is for live feed information," When you get something from one of your assets or agents, post it and it will appear on the room screen as well. Please do not use asset or agent name, only the information."

"Our team will take all your information and, doing a rapid analysis and then, post that analysis in the center, vertical row for all to see. If you see something that does not look correct, we will discuss and adjust."

"Also, if you have an idea or suggestion, feed it to us so we can change things in real time. Now, familiarize yourself with the equipment."

Both teams began posting intelligence from each of their banks, one monitor at a time. They watched the large screen change each time they posted an item. After about an hour they seemed very comfortable with the system.

"Leonid and Beatrix," Mitch said. "Do you think your team

has a good handle on things?"

Both team leaders nodded affirmatively.

"Very well," Mitch said. "Henry is going to begin feeding you information in all intelligence areas from different places around the world. Try to keep up with the changing feeds and post new information immediately upon arrival. If you have any questions, flag the information and send it to Jonathan here. Use code 11115. He will look at it and post it on the large screen within your array."

"Is everyone ready?" Henry asked. "By the way, the first run of information is to track a fictitious agent X. The first team to list final location gets the first break."

Henry began feeding the live information that was coming in from all over the world. Facial recognition hits and other information were being fed to the teams. The monitors began to change frequently while they tracked the fictitious agent using the seven forms of intelligence that appeared on the monitors.

"I have him," a Russian team member said. "He is in Madrid."

"No," replied a British team member, he is in Bogota."

"Keep going," Henry shouted. "Make sure of your information analysis before you jump to conclusions."

The teams kept feeding the information when it came in, analyzing it before posting on the big screen. Pictures from traffic cams, bank ATM's, security cameras, and cell phones were incoming at a rapid pace. The supercomputer Samantha whirred in a hidden room, analyzing and back checking the data, using interpolation and actual footage as the analysis was fed back to each team, including language nuances. Explosions, gun battles, assassinations, and economic activity were fed into the test to push each team hard and fast. At first, they were bogged down, but quickly got the hang of the system in real time and began laughing and chatting to each other, deducting what was happening before posting their intelligence.

"We have it," Leonid said.

"Agent X is in Santo Domingo," Leonid and Beatrix said in unison.

"Excellent," Mitch replied. "You have both earned a break. There will be two more tests. Each will increase in the amount of data, including frequency and intensity. Hopefully, we will then begin with our actual target or targets."

The teams took a break using the restroom, drinking coffee and taking advantage of the food, mixing within groups, laughing and chatting.

"They appear to be working well together," Mitch said.

"Yes," Henry replied. "I'm sure they were all read the riot act by their superiors before they arrived. Still, it is very nice to see them cooperating so well."

"They know as we do that without their cooperation, we will fail," Mitch said. "And we all want to go back to home and our families."

"In that we have commonality," Henry mused.

ILLIAC exited the main building on the compound and began jogging down a trail that led to the pistol range. He found Jackson shooting rapid fire at five-inch circles on a silhouette. Antonio was talking to him through an earpiece.

"What is he doing?" Antonio asked. "I do not understand this drill."

"It is the six-second drill," Illiac said. "He taught it to me the other day. It's quite fascinating."

"What is the purpose?"

"It is a magazine change drill for combat conditions," Illiac replied. "You select two magazines and put two rounds in each. Then, you insert one magazine into the pistol and chamber a round. Once you fire that round, you have six second to fire the next round, change magazines and fire the last two rounds."

"You are telling me it is a magazine change exercise," Antonio said. "But his pistol holds 15 rounds per magazine. I do not see the point."

"Yes, you are correct," Illiac replied. "But in combat, you often need to change magazines. This drill makes sure you can do it efficiently under pressure."

"Oh, I understand," Antonio said. "How is he doing?"

"I count about five seconds, which is very good."

"But of course, that is why we selected him. Prep him for the assignment. We need to get moving."

"Yes sir."

Illiac approached Jackson from the side to let him know he was there.

"How are you friend?" Illiac asked.

"Just tuning up," Jackson replied. "Any news?"

"Yes. We are going to collect a cash cow who will be great for our finances."

"I assume you mean person and not a real cow," Jackson said with a laugh.

"Yes. A real person who owns a very large mine in a very remote area. We have discovered that he will be on site a few days from now."

"I'm guessing he is well guarded," Jackson queried.

"Very well," Illiac replied. "We will need to quietly separate him from the herd. It is time to prep."

"About time," Jackson said. "This is a nice camp and all but lacks the excitement of the field."

"Don't worry my friend. You are about to get plenty of that."

Jackson put his pistol and ammunition in his range bag and the two walked back to the main building for a briefing.

"When are we going to leave?" Jackson asked.

"Directly after the briefing I've been told," Illiac replied. "It promises to be an interesting mission. Hurry, they are waiting for us."

The two men walked into the briefing room in the main

building. Their team of six more men were already present, along with the briefer, a formal NATO colonel. No one knew his name, only that he was called Six. He was a total bastard and a stickler for time and organization. It was probably why he was selected for the position he held, that of overall intelligence collection and analysis.

"I am glad you two could join us," Six said sarcastically. "Please let us know if you would like us to order you coffee and donuts."

The team laughed, but the point was taken.

"Now that we are all present, I will begin. Your target is this man, Luca Atkinson, head of Bergas Mines in West Papua, located in Mimika Regency. You will be a long way from home on this one. My intelligence sources say he will be visiting the mine in the next ten days. We will narrow the date. Two of you will shadow him to the location, the rest of you will already be waiting."

"This is a very isolated location, isn't it?" Illiac asked.

"Yes," Six said. "It has some of the roughest terrain in the world. The main team will be landing at Tabubil airport. It is remote to say the least. And, it is in Papua New Guinea, just across what some refer to as the border with West Papua."

"Is there a difference between them?" Jackson asked.

"It is mostly historical," Six replied. "For decades, West Papua was colonized by the Dutch as part of the Dutch East Indies. Of course, we know that now as present-day Indonesia. What became Papua New Guinea was originally colonized by Germany, followed by Britain and finally Australia. West Papua was listed as part of Indonesia in 1963 when the Dutch returned it. Later, Australia granted independence to Papua New Guinea and West Papua has been seeking separation. Because Papua is almost ten times larger in population, that is not likely. You're landing in Tabubil because it will bring less attention."

"I've been there once," Illiac said. "Roads are scarce."

"That is why you will be transported by helicopter to the target area. An out of the way hotel has been arranged for you in Timika, some twenty odd miles from the mine," Six said. "You will need to be as covert as possible. Even one person can stand out in the town. A group your size will start gossip."

"What is your plan?" Jackson asked. "Are you suggesting we take him at the mine?"

"No, that would be almost impossible," Six replied. "He will be staying at a hotel in Timika. You will also, but far from his. I do not have his hotel layout yet, but soon. You should also know that he will likely have a security contingent of at least a dozen personnel."

"We are not worried about that so much," Illiac said. "You said that we would draw attention as a group, how do you propose we maneuver?"

"One team member will check in the evening before," Six said. "The rest of you will arrive during the night. Most prying eyes will be asleep. During the day, you will need to work individually or in pairs. Be sporadic and make sure you don't group together anywhere until you are ready to take the target down. Spread out and do your surveillance. If you can do it at night, so much the better. We have paid the hotel manager and a couple of staff to keep their mouths shut, but you know how it is."

"Yeah," Jackson murmured. "They tell one person and everyone in Timika will know."

"The good thing is that they do not know how many of you there will be. That will help us."

"Will we have any backup?" Illiac asked.

"None," Six said. "The helicopter that will pick you up will have air to surface missiles if he needs to use them but on extraction only. He also has machine guns that are pilot controlled, which also, will only be used if needed upon extraction."

"Isn't there some other location we could get him?" Jackson asked. "This is one of the remotest areas on earth. With the number of security personnel he has, this is going to be a tough job."

"I realize that," Six replied. "But everywhere else he goes he has over twice the guards and travels in armored vehicles. There would be no way to take one of those out without risk of killing him or getting all of you killed. We need him alive because he controls vast funds that will be put at our disposal."

"We will accomplish the mission," Illiac said then, whispering to Jackson, "They're throwing us into a meat grinder. This guy must be more important to them than they let on."

Jackson nodded; the briefing continued. Suddenly, he had a sharp pain in his ear and put his finger on it.

"You okay my friend," Illiac asked.

"Yeah, just a jaw cramp," Jackson said.

He didn't want to tell Illiac that he had sharp pains a couple of times per day. He had a dream the previous night and saw a beautiful dark-haired woman who smiled at him. Her face was obscured but the smile melted him inside. He could not get her out of his mind, reviewing the dream over and over. Jackson heard Illiac asking a question.

"Is that a wise move?" Illiac asked.

"We are a clandestine organization," Six said. "Our ace pilot will land you in Tabubil and extract you. He will remain on the ground there until the mission is over."

"But the runway there will not accommodate the Gulfstream 650ER," Illiac said, loudly. "It needs around six thousand feet or more of runway."

"Actually, it only needs 3,200 feet of actual landing distance," Six said. "The rest of the six thousand is for clearway and stopway. We do not need those here. Takeoff distance should also be sufficient, correct?"

"Let me get fast Freddie on the phone," Illiac said.

"Why do they call him that?" Jackson asked.

"When he takes off, he revs the engines while standing on the breaks until the aircraft almost noses into the dirt. Then, he releases the brakes, and it is like catapulting off a carrier," Illiac said. "Yes, Freddie. We have a discussion about runway length and proper aircraft. The runway is 4,200 feet total. We are thinking of using the Gulfstream 650ER for it. Can that be done."

"No," Freddie replied. "Absolutely not. It would need 6,000 feet. How many in your group?"

"Eight," Illiac said.

"The best plane to use for that runway is our Cessna Citation Sovereign," Freddie said. "Where are we headed?"

"Tabubil, Papua," Illiac said.

"That will take two refuels and about sixteen hours of flight time on top of them."

"Thank you for the information, Freddie," Six said. "Prep the aircraft and we will be in touch soon."

"Yes sir."

"I appreciate your correcting me," Six replied. "As you know, the weight capacity of the Sovereign is less than the Gulfstream so, pack light. Now that we are on the same page with transportation, let's go over the aerial maps of the airport in Tabubil, Timika, and the hotels. The targets hotel is here, in the middle of town. Note the sparser vegetation and relative openness compared to the edge of town. There are still places to hide so, plan strategically. Your hotel is to the south just over a mile away on the east side of the Ajkwa River. The vegetation and undergrowth there is very thick, allowing good cover day or night. Also, I have arranged for three small vehicles. Using all of them at random should keep you from being suspects to the target's security detail."

"Obviously it will need to be a night operation," Illiac said. "Did we get the new thermal optics?"

"Yes," Six said. "You can begin training with them tonight. Time is short so you need to be ready at a moment's notice. As soon as I know the targets itinerary, you will deploy."

The group continued to review aerial photos and layouts of where the target would be, as well as potential entry and exit routes to and from the target location. The general plan was to abduct the target, extract to a remote field near their hotel via helicopter, back to Tabubil and return to base with the hostage. It seemed simple enough, but given the distance, security, terrain, and no backup, Jackson realized the mission could turn sideways in a heartbeat.

BOTH British and Russian teams had learned quickly and were able to rapidly go through live scenarios from the intelligence that Henry fed them. The targets that were being tracked and their final destinations were rapidly located by both teams – almost at the same time. Mitch and Henry knew they were ready. Potentially, the lives of millions could be at stake. However, with little information about the adversary, they knew it would be a tough assignment.

"Everyone," Mitch said. "Could I have your attention. You have performed admirably. Why don't you take a break; go back to your quarters and freshen up. Security will escort you. We will be discussing issues with the director and begin feeding in all the information we have so far on the real targets. It will take us a couple of hours to set up. The targets are eight hours ahead of us so report back here at 2200 hours."

The teams left the room, escorted to their quarters. They were beaming with smiles and enjoying the work. They felt some sadness that they could not always be allies, but for this moment, they were one team with one goal, apprehend the target then, deal with them as needed. The teams wondered where this would lead.

FLYING through several countries always made for a long trip. Li Na had begun at Hong Kong International Airport. It had been built on reclaimed land on the island of Chek Lap Kok. Formerly it had been called Kai Tak International Airport. From there she had a layover in Taipei at Taoyuan International where she managed to keep busy developing her strategy for a few hours then, it was on to JFK, spending almost ten hours in a luxury lounge before her final leg into Ian Fleming International Airport in Jamaica. The airport was not as high traffic as the two other major airports in Jamaica and was on the other side of the island from her destination. It had of course been named after author Ian Fleming who most famously wrote the James Bond novels and is a household name in the Caribbean where many of the Bond movies had been filmed. In 2011, the airport had undergone renovations and was now stylish, though its small size made it seem a bit off the beaten path and rural, which it was.

Li Na had chosen the airport because it would allow her to notice potential tails. Phil had offered to let her use a CIA jet, but she had declined. She knew these people were suspicious and good at intelligence. Had she used a CIA jet, it wouldn't take long for the clandestine group to realize she was a contractor for the CIA. Instead, she would keep them guessing. By using common airlines, it would keep them off balance and believing that she was indeed just an assassin who traveled like everyone else. She would thus be able to maintain her cover.

While at the airport, she collected her baggage and waited for a while moving from one location to another every ten minutes. Certain that she was not being tailed, after an hour, she made her way to the rental car agency and was on her way. Being on the opposite side of the island from her destination some sixty miles away, she took Highway 2000 taking her time to Kingston. The road was quite curvy and mountainous. About a third of the way to Kingston, she pulled into the Unity Valley Rest Stop to stretch her legs. It was a nice place to just stop and breathe, buy a sandwich and cup of coffee and relax. There were only a few vendors. After getting her sandwich and coffee she found a table and sat down. It was typical of the area, concrete and tile with three small, matching benches around it. The sky was a deep blue filled with cumulous clouds seeming to drift aimlessly and that appeared much whiter than in other locations she had visited, even Miami. Looking around, there were few people. After a half hour, she finished her sandwich and coffee and took a short stroll around the shops. She wasn't looking at them so much as her surroundings and the highway. Stepping back into the shade of a shop, she carefully looked back in the direction she had come. There were no parked cars or people. She was confident that she was not being followed.

Li Na began the final leg to her destination. Having chosen the Jasmine Inn from almost two dozen others, she checked in, took a shower and slept until 2200. She slipped into black jeans and a black knit blouse. The desk clerk nodded to her when she walked out the door. Climbing into her car, she made her way down Arthur Wint Drive heading west then, south where she picked up Camp Road West onto Caledonia Avenue and then, south on Slipe Road that changed to Orange Street. She turned west onto North Street a few blocks later. Two blocks down, she pulled into the parking lot of Kingston Public Hospital. There were few cars; Li Na parked midway into the lot. Turning her lights off, she exited the car and stood by it for several minutes inspecting her surroundings and watching for signs of trouble. She was just under a mile from her objective, where she would be meeting someone to go over her mission to protect Jackson. She picked up Slipe Pen Road at the corner of the lot and headed south to the harbor. Not wanting to stay on a straight path, when the street changed to Princess Street, she crossed to Matthews Lane on the west, traveled it a few blocks then, back to Princess Street for a few blocks and then, east to Luke Lane. She randomly went from one path to the other until she reached the harbor. Li Na meandered her way to the Ocean Boulevard Hotel. It wasn't long before she figured out why the group had chosen their location. It was only a mile and a half across Kingston Harbor from Norman Manley International Airport. With a good spotting scope, a surveillance team could easily read the tail numbers of any commercial jet. They would be able to immediately determine when a potential client or target arrived. Their strategy became apparent. A tail would follow their target to the destination airport, get the departing flights and track them virtually through various flight tracking apps in real time. Once the flight arrived with the target onboard, another tail would pick them up at their destination. While she stood in the parking lot of the hotel, the breeze off the harbor cooled her face. A chill suddenly came across her when realizing how effective this organization was. She must be very cautious.

Li Na walked quickly west along the harbor, her objective about six hundred yards distant. Not far down her path, there was a police station off to her right where Ocean Boulevard turned north. Meandering between buildings and other docks, she finally reached her planned surveillance point. Her binoculars were ten-power with thermal capabilities. At a mere three hundred yards, she could watch the rectangular building easily. The main entrance was on the harbor side, a small doorway on either end. She was certain both of those would be closed, locked from the inside. On the backside were separated bays for pulling boats in for repair. There was a chain link fence around them; several boats were visible. A lone security guard stood outside the front office door, the glow of his cigarette clearly visible. Switching to thermal, she detected another guard at the far corner of the building. After fifteen minutes, she was certain they were the only two. They were dressed in light colored trousers and loose button-up shirts; they looked more like tourists than guards. They would blend in well during the day. She made a note to herself. Watching closely while they slowly walked around the shop to inspect for intruders or signs of danger. Li Na could see bulges beneath their shirts when they walked beneath lamps at the front and ends of the building. There was likely nothing of real value inside. Phil had passed along information received from Colin that the location was a real boat repair shop, but also where orders were issued for the organization and where those that carried them out, came. About 1:00 am, she slowly headed back to her car, making mental notes of access points and retreat paths in case something went wrong and she had to flee from the meeting.

She climbed out of bed, took another shower and went downstairs. There was a small café about a block away, so she walked over and took a seat, ordering a traditional Bammy breakfast that was comprised of time-honored Jamaican cassava flatbread soaked in coconut milk and fried. Originating from the Arawaks', the island's original inhabitants, it was topped with shrimp and escoveitch fish, the latter being a sauteed sauce made of carrots, onion, peppers, and pimento seeds soaked in a mild vinegar. Along with her coffee and small glass of mango juice, she was quite content. Her phone dinged; it was a message from Colin:

Make sure you do not wear a listening device.

She replied with a thumbs up emoji and deleted the message.

It was then that she noticed the man, leaning against the end post of a bus stop that had a fast-food advertisement on top. Wearing jeans and an olive-green tee-shirt, he looked out of place. His attempts at pretending to read the magazine in his hands were poor at best. Sitting at the back of the café she could clearly see his eyes darting her way, the whites of his eyes in stark comparison to his dark skin. He wasn't a pro, just a tail. They had found her. She was sure they had expected her to arrive at Manley. The fact they hadn't seen her tail number meant they had no one at JFK to follow her. Perhaps they were not too worried since she had already been paid or, they may have thought she would be meeting someone before she met with them and wanted to know who. She surmised the latter while she quickly paid her bill and exited the café, getting into her car. Making a U-turn in the street, she saw the tail speaking on his cell phone as she disappeared from site. It didn't matter.

Li Na arrived at the boat repair shop and parked in the lot adjacent to Port Royal Street then, walked around to the front. A small boat dock led about fifty yards into the harbor. On the right was a chain link fence and gate with a security guard who stopped her.

"Who are you?" he asked

"I am Black Widow," she responded

The guards' eyes widened. Already, stories of her exploits had spread among the men. They were all eager to see what she looked like. He could barely contain his excitement while admiring her beauty. Her piercing gaze stopped his reveling.

"Come with me please," he managed to blurt out, constantly turning back to look at her over his shoulder.

The two reached the first bay door and he pointed, motioning her to a table about midway to the back of the building.

"The man with the hat will speak with you," he said.

While she walked toward the table, the guard returned to his post. The man at the table heard her clearly when she approached. Not turning to look at her, he spoke.

"Ah, the famed Black Widow at last. Please sit across from me. I am Conrad."

Doing as he commanded, she was able to finally see his face. He was relatively handsome. Dressed in Bermuda shorts and a tee-shirt, his straw hat covered four long scars protruding from under his scalp diagonally across his left cheek down to his chin. She could tell they were old. Combined with his gray eyes, the scars made him look both formidable and fierce.

"Don't worry about them," Conrad said. "I got in a fight with a wounded lion on safari in Africa. I thought he was dead but well, things happen."

"I was told to meet someone here," Li Na said, looking him directly in the eyes.

Most men would have wilted at her gaze, but Conrad didn't even blink.

"It is best to be wary of this man," Li Na thought.

"That someone is me," Conrad replied, sliding a manila-colored envelope across the table to her. "You have already been told the assignment. Your tickets and destination are inside the envelope. Destroy the contents when you have read them. Do not fail."

"You could have given this to me over a secure phone line," Li Na said, rising and walking around the table. "I came all this way to spend five minutes with you; it seems a waste."

"The meeting was for me so that I could assess you," Conrad replied. "I see that Antonio has judged well. I approve. That is all."

"You know, I could just skip out," Li Na said with a small smile, walking toward the door. "I already have the money."

"Black Widow."

She turned to face Conrad who also had turned in his chair to confront her.

"If you default, I will come after you and kill you. That is one of my primary duties for the organization."

"Don't worry," Li Na replied. "I was testing you. The job will get done."

"Finally," she thought, "A worthy adversary."

She was smiling when she exited the building, Conrad staring after her. Despite his better judgement, he liked her and had every confidence she would get the job done. After all, she was a professional and needed to uphold her reputation.

Colin Archer was part of the surveillance team watching the shop. He had seen Li Na enter and leave the building. He knew she would have the assignment and time was beginning to press them. She had sent a message earlier for a meeting. A half hour later, he pulled into the east end of the parking lot of the National Housing Trust, adjacent to Emancipation Park and wound his way around a couple of small buildings into the park. Li Na was waiting for him beneath a row of large trees. Both looking furtively about, making sure they had not been followed. Li Na sat on the grass, the contents of the envelope emptied out.

"I assume you received your assignment," Colin said softly walking up and taking a position beside her.

"Yes," she said. "I already had the basic assignment, now I have the location. There is not much here, a plane ticket to Tabubil and a couple of days later, from Tabubil to Hong Kong."

"Nothing else?" Colin asked.

"Just this note and another picture," she replied.

Protect Jackson at all costs. He will meet with the man in the photograph who will have his own security. You may need to kill several to fulfill your agreement.

"Do you recognize him?" she asked.

"He looks familiar," Colin said. "I seem to remember we collected information on him last year but found nothing unusual. Wait! Tabubil airport is in Papua New Guinea. One of the largest gold mines in the world is there. He is the CEO of Bergas Mines."

Colin arranged the tickets, note and picture and snapped a few photos with his smartphone. He immediately uploaded them to MI6 in London. Within minutes they would be sent to the intelligence teams in the crisis suite on the Farm.

"Keep me posted on your progress," Colin said, getting up. "We will feed intelligence to you when we can. Be discreet."

She watched him walk away and couldn't help noticing how professional and observant he was. He took a different path back to his car. Looking around, she put the photos and tickets back into the envelope and placed it in her purse. Certain that no one was present, she stood and took a different path back to her car. Having already checked out of her hotel, she turned left and right in a diamond pattern then, a snake to make sure she wasn't followed while she drove to Norman Manley International Airport where her flight would board in two hours. Sometimes being a clandestine agent was too tedious she thought to herself.

THE British and Russian teams had been practicing with more live scenarios when the information from Colin was forwarded from MI6 Headquarters in London.

"Listen up teams," Mitch shouted. "We have your first assignment. Airplane tickets to Tabubil in Papua New Guinea and a photo of this man, CEO of Bergas Mines. Find out everything you can about the location and Luca Atkinson. Feed it to the large screen when you get it."

"Also, feed your analysis as well," Henry replied. "Quickly, the clock is ticking."

The information began coming across the screen. Both British and Russian teams had become very efficient. Tapping into their intelligence sources, the wealth of information was nothing short of amazing. Phil had headed back to Langley and returned just when the information began flowing in. He began to realize what the organization was after. Within twenty minutes, the bulk of the actionable intelligence was on the screen. It turned out that intelligence agencies from all three countries had been watching the CEO and Bergas mining operations in attempts to determine if the company or CEO were hoarding gold from the world supply. There were suspicions, but no proof.

"Alright," Phil said. Leonid and Beatrix, what is your team's analysis of the information so far?"

"Leonid and I have discussed that," Beatrix replied. "If this organization is as complex as you have indicated and has the resources we suspect, this could be a move to garner cash."

"Explain," Phil said.

"The Bergas mine is the largest gold and copper mine in the world," Leonid replied. "Our country has suspected them for years of hoarding gold. Their CEO is a key player. We think they are making a move to kidnap the CEO and thereby control the mine."

"Interesting," Phil murmured. "Okay, start looking for connections to others and places. Let's ferret this out."

"Perhaps we should get Sheena on the line," Henry said. "I'll ring her in."

"Sheena," Henry here. "We have a question."

"What do you need?" Sheena asked.

"We would like to know if you have any information on Luca Atkinson of Bergas mines."

"We investigated him last year," Sheena said. "What's your intelligence telling you?"

"We think that the organization is making a move on Bergas for gold," Phil joined in. "If you wanted a cash cow, it would make since."

"That's very interesting," Sheena replied. "The numbers you gave us were also tracked to communications in Gaborone, Botswana."

"Is there anything of importance there?" Phil asked.

"The second largest diamond mine, Genji, is there," Mitch

said. "It is said to have reserves of over 160 million carats."

"Good God!" Phil exclaimed. "Even at wholesale prices that's well over $2 billion. Are you thinking what I'm thinking?"

"If you wanted to rule everything you need money, lots of it," Sheena said. "How would you get it?"

"Go after the richest and most consumed precious metals and gems, as well as energy?" Phil said.

"We need to be looking for connections among these with those phone numbers," Henry said. "Gold, diamonds and oil, right?"

"Yes," Sheena replied. "I'll get back to you."

"Teams," Mitch called out. "Begin looking for connections with your current intelligence to connections with gold, diamonds, and oil."

The teams nodded and began connecting intelligence in those areas with what they already had. They knew it wouldn't be enough, but with more information, the more accurate picture they could paint.

"You know there is an old saying," Henry said. "The person who controls the debt controls all."

"We need to change that," Phil replied. "The person or group that commands those who control the debt rules all."

"It would certainly be a giant step forward in ushering in the new world order," Henry observed aloud.

The comment was sobering. If the organization they were hunting could accomplish what they thought they were working on, it would change global reality. A dictator was one thing, a ruling entity with zero empathy was quite another.

THE plane made a bumpy landing at Tabubil airport. When Li Na looked out the window, she thought she had landed in hell. The runway was a mixture of gravel and dirt that seemed to disappear into the hills at the southeast end. The plane taxied off into a square inset about a hundred yards square in each direction and nosed to the right. There was only one other plane and it looked like it had been there for a few days. The rains had washed its tire tracks away. Her instructions told her to proceed to the terminal building. It was not far ahead of her. She only had the name of the pilot, Emil. The building had a forest green metal roof and light green concrete side. Walking in there wasn't much to the place.

"Small wonder," she thought while she looked for a place to sit down. She had no sooner grabbed a chair against the wall than a man with blonde hair and green eyes approached. He was slim, perhaps five feet seven inches. He stuck out his hand.

"I am Emil," he said. "I am also called fast Freddie or simply Freddie. You are the Black Widow."

"Yes," Li Na replied. "I was told to meet you here."

"Come this way please," Emil said. "We need to get going before the afternoon thunderstorms roll in."

They walked back down the same path she had come. Not noticing it before, a helicopter sat in the corner of the inset where her plane had pulled in. It was two-toned, forest green on top and dark gray on the bottom from the cockpit glass down. It blended into the surroundings as if it were part of them. Emil opened the door and threw her bag behind the co-pilot seat into the main cabin.

"It's an older AW139," Emil said. "It will transport fifteen men; not much to look at, but it gets the job done. The crew you'll be helping to protect will arrive tomorrow. I am instructed not to tell them about you. This is your hotel room key. I'll drop you off close as I can."

"How far is it?" Li Na asked.

"About 300 miles," Emil said. "We'll be there in less than two hours. This is the hotel where the target will be staying. Your hotel is only one block away. The team will be south of there."

Emil had handed her a folder with a layout of hers and the target hotels. They were airborne and heading west in a couple of minutes. While they flew, she began to develop her protective strategy. The number of potential security guards had been listed, as well as the number of rooms the party would occupy. Occasionally, she looked up from her study of the layout at the landscape below. It was green and very mountainous. She guessed the mountains average about 8,000 feet in elevation; they ran east to west off to the north. It appeared that it was jungle and one giant flood plain, much like the Amazon River Basin. There were large and small rivers running from the mountains to the Arafura Sea to the south. She kept studying the terrain while looking back and forth at the hotel schematics.

"We are now flying over Lorentz National Park," Emil said. "We will be there in about thirty minutes."

"What's our altitude?" Li Na asked.

"About 4,000 feet," Emil said. "Why?"

"Could you take us down to about 3,200 feet and fly one pass north to south and one east to west over the hotel area?"

"Sure," Emil replied. "Do you want me to slow down on pass by?"

"Yes," Li Na said. "I want to get a good aerial view and make some notes. I'm guessing I'm not getting a signal down there."

"No, you won't," Emil said, smiling. "There are a few spots with Wi-Fi, but even those connections are spotty. Besides, you don't want to go into any of them or you'll draw attention. Outsiders here tend to be followed."

"I understand," she said.

It was not long before they were making their pass in each direction. Li Na noted there was a church about eighty yards from the third-floor balcony and a small café directly in front of the church. The church had a bell tower. From there she could cover the insertion and extraction. From the layout, it looked like the balcony joined a major suite. She was certain that suite would be occupied by the target. Around the hotel was a steel fence. It looked low enough to hop over, but she would need to check it out. Parking was inside it, typical for the area due to crime. Her take-down sniper rifle would be more than sufficient for the task.

"I've seen enough," Li Na said.

"Roger," Emil replied. "I'll go to the airport and fuel up. Once darkness falls, I'll let you off in the small field near your hotel. You can walk from there. You will need to do a rope descent. You think you can handle that?"

"No problem," she replied.

They made it back to the airport and Emil refueled the helicopter. While they waited, Li Na kept going over her strategy to surveil the area more closely on foot during the early evening hours. The sun dipped low in the horizon behind dark gray clouds, punctuated by frequent lightning and rain. It was an eerie sight. Nightfall was advancing quickly but there was still the ability to see about fifty yards when Li Na descended from the helicopter to the ground thirty feet below. Waving to Emil, she walked hurriedly to a small grove of trees that hid her from view. For fifteen minutes, she watched and waited. An infrequent rain had begun to fall. A few blocks away she could hear a dog barking otherwise, the streets were deserted and low lit, a lamp here and there at the corner of intersecting streets.

She was about four blocks from her hotel on Pongtiku. Li Na thought it was ironic that it was named after Pong Tiku, a Torajan Leader and guerrilla fighter operating in southern Sulawesi who was shot dead in 1907. She made a note to avoid ending up the same way during her trip, a smile creasing her lips.

"Damn that Emil," she thought. "She hoped he could fly better than he could give directions."

His block consisted of multiple blocks between. Looking at

her watch, it was 7:00 pm when she arrived at the hotel. She traveled light with only moderate sized backpack and simple clothes. The desk clerk stared at her when she entered. She could tell that guests were not as frequent as at most hotels. But he was the only one present, which would help her while she covertly executed her mission. He spoke only broken English, a cigarette hanging out of the corner of his mouth, the ashes falling onto his black tee shirt covering an overly large belly. He was clean but smelled like the cigarette he was smoking. He slid a key to her room across the counter and pointed to the door making a locking motion with his hand. "Close 9:00 pm," he said. "Key work if late."

Li Na understood and headed to her room, which was down a narrow hallway on the first floor. She retrieved her 9mm and suppressor from the pack and then, placed it into a dark corner of the small closet. She washed her face and put on a dark green raincoat, just in case and a Fedora hat to keep the rain off her face. It was 7:10 pm, plenty of time to check things out. When she exited the door, the clerk was no longer behind the counter so he wouldn't know when she had left. Walking down the street, she made her way west just over a block and then, turned south about a hundred feet and west again to JI Budi Utomo. The targets hotel was just over a block to her right on the west side of the road. She had studied as much as she could, especially the streets and area around the target's hotel. She was surprised that JI was short for Jalan, meaning street and that Budi Utomo was Dutch meaning Prime Philosophy. It was not surprising it was Dutch since Boedi Oetomo was the first native political society in the Dutch East Indies, whom many considered the group responsible for the Indonesian National Awakening.

The street was a primary artery cutting through Timika, north to south. Li Na was relieved to find out she had dressed appropriately according to her research. Those she passed were friendly and wore the same kind of clothes, mostly dark and hard to see in the dim light along the street. She was on the opposite side of the street of the targets hotel and passing by the Jangkar; she decided to have a bite to eat. Requesting to be seated near the door on the south side, she had a clear view of the hotel less than two hundred feet away. The restaurant was very clean with dark wood table and chairs and white tile floor. Sitting against the wall, she sipped a cup of tea and began making mental notes. The waitress brought her food, which was simple, a flattened brown rice mound topped with two fried eggs, a couple of pieces of fried chicken, and a mound of green beans and local greens topped with what looked like cashew nuts. She was famished but ate casually not to draw attention to herself while she kept gazing back and forth to the hotel. She was interested in foot traffic going in and out. Now that she could see the fence it was easily low enough to hop, made of steel and painted black. She suspected it was to keep someone from stealing a car from the lot rather than for hotel security.

While she sat, four motorcycles passed by, the noise from their exhausts deafening. Many of the patrons waved after them, the riders waving back. Still hungry, she ordered a bowl of soup filled with vegetables and fish.

After about an hour, Li Na casually walked across the street and into the lobby of the target's hotel. A woman behind the counter asked if she could help her. The woman's English was poor, speaking Tok Pisin, a Creole language that evolved from English. However, she spoke well enough for the two to understand each other. Li Na explained that she wanted to wait for a friend who was supposed to check in and would it be okay if she sat for a little while. The woman smiled and pointed to the lobby area. It was quite nice with tables and chairs near glass windows facing the street. Well lit, she picked a corner table so she could get a better idea of the layout comparing it to the diagram she had. The stairs were much wider than those in most countries; she estimated them to be five feet, making it easy to run quickly up or down. About ten minutes later the clerk at the desk disappeared into a side room and Li Na made her exit.

The next location to recon was the church just behind Jangkar. Looking at its height and angle, she decided it would be unsuitable. She slowly strolled along the street back toward the hotel on the opposite side. It was then that she noticed a three-story building, concrete with a salmon-colored façade, just like the restaurant; it seemed to be a popular color. Continuing down the block, she compared the front of the building to the balcony on the third floor of the hotel. It was slightly kitty corner to it. The shot would be about thirty to fifty yards. A cake walk for her take-down sniper rifle. Li Na walked around the back and down a small side alley. There were stairs on the back that seemed to go all the way to the roof. Looking around, she slowly and cautiously walked up. Her running shoes were quiet; the metal stairs didn't make a sound. Here and there she could see through windows. Families were eating or watching television. On the top floor, the stairs ended in a platform about twelve feet from the top of the building. She would need a grappling hook to get to the top. Having anticipated it, she cautiously made it back to her hotel, just before the clerk locked the front door. The rain began to fall in torrents causing the streets to empty for the night.

THE British and Russian teams were up to their ears in intelligence. Wading through the breadcrumb trail of phone calls, HUMINT, and SIGINT and being reminded of the old saying in the intelligence field. "All intelligence is information, but not all information is intelligence." Beatrix and Leonid were comparing notes and approached Phil, Mitch and Henry.

"We think we have something," Beatrix said. "The phone number called people in these areas,"

The map was on the screen.

"As you suspected, the areas in yellow are near the Bergas mine and the CEO's headquarters; gold and copper kings."

"We see a similar pattern for the areas in blue," Leonid said

"What is in those areas?" Phil asked.

"The larger blue area is the location of the Romoshakin Oil Fields," Leonid replied. "The smaller area is the Tanfe Company offices, owner of the fields."

"It looks like we have gold, copper, diamonds and oil," Henry said.

"That's a potent mix if you're looking for cash cows to fund your organization," Mitch said. "All of them are the largest enterprises in those areas of industry."

"Leonid," Phil said. "Those blue areas are Russian, correct?"

"Absolutely," Leonid replied.

"Get on the horn to Andros," Phil said. "I'll contact the President and VP. We need to get them talking again. Let's fill them in on what we have found so far. Mitch, work with MI6 and the SVR, let's get surveillance teams to those areas as quickly as we can. We may be too late."

"I have a question," Henry said. "Why would they want Jackson on the mission in Papua rather than the other two locations?"

"Hmmmm," Phil mused. "It could be a scheduling issue or perhaps a level of difficulty? I'm not sure."

"May I?" Leonid asked.

"Go ahead," Phil said.

"The two areas our teams brought to your attention and the companies, would be easier to deal with," Leonid said. "From previous operations, I would say that the Papua location, combined with terrain and remoteness is a much more difficult location to achieve mission success. For that you would need the best you have. That is my operative opinion."

"Thank you," Phil said. "It certainly makes since. Okay, let's contact our people and get them moving on this. Also, retrace your steps and sift through the intelligence again. We don't want to make assumptions. Go only where it points."

President Armstrong and the VP were in the Oval when the call was patched through.

"Mr. President," Phillip Armstrong on the line sir. "He says it is urgent."

"Put him through and hold other calls," the President said. "Phil, how are things?"

"I have news to report to you and the VP sir," Phil said. "The chase is becoming muddied but taking shape. We're going to need more assets and may need your authorization."

"What's up?" VP Reisner asked.

"You already know about the gold mines in Papua sir. Our intelligence from the combined British and Russian teams appears to have uncovered a deeper plot. The same in a way, but two new targets. These include the Genji diamond mine in Botswana and the Romoshakin oil fields in Russia. We believe this organization is going after the CEOs of those groups as well."

"Before you mentioned it may be a cash flow drive for funding the organization further," Bill said. "Do you still agree with that assessment?"

"Yes, I do. If they can achieve their goal with all three, they can control a significant portion of world resources and commodities flow. It would be easy to blackmail various countries and corporations to get them to comply with whatever demands they may have."

"I'm not sure if they will have demands," Vice President Reisner said. "If they are going after these entities for their cash and can control them as you say, they would not need to make demands. They could simply change pricing or policies for crude oil and the other precious metals and gems and set the price globally. We would either need to pay or suffer any consequences."

"Correct sir," Phil replied. "What worries me is energy. If

they control this CEO, which we know they can, either by chip or outright cloning they would be able to control the price of crude and thus, the transportation of global goods."

"Yes, but wouldn't that only mean an increase in petroleum prices for them?" Bill asked.

"In a direct way sir," Phil replied. "But what if they guaranteed not to raise oil prices in return for a percentage of product sold in all areas? They could make it voluntary. It would simply become the cost of doing business without it being thought of as extortion."

"That's scary," the VP said. "Would there be a way around it?"

"I'm not sure sir," Phil replied. "I will keep working it on the intelligence side. I will let you know if we need more resources. I would suggest talking with the presidents of Botswana and Russia."

"Yes," President Armstrong said. "We don't need any surprises popping up. Keep us informed Phil."

"Yes sir."

CHAPTER 6

ILLIAC, Jackson, and their team landed in Tabubil. They walked directly from the plane to the helicopter. It had been almost twenty-four hours since Emil had flown Li Na to Timika. He did not understand why he could not mention her to the team, but orders were orders, and he didn't want to be found face up in a ditch somewhere. Very few of the men knew Antonio, but to know him well was to hate him because he was pure evil. He cared for nothing but money and the control and power it brought him. Emil had often thought of working for another company or even having his own helicopter business but knew that such a venture would be short lived and he as well.

The blades were already turning when the crew jumped aboard. Illiac gave a thumbs up and shut the door. Emil returned it and they were on the way. Despite being almost three hundred miles, the trip seemed short. No one talked; they all seemed preoccupied with their own thoughts. Like Li Na, the crew all had moderate sized backpacks with their gear and guns. When Emil landed, the team split into two-man pairs and took different directions to the hotel. They had adjusted their comm links on the helicopter and were able to stay in contact while they neared their rendezvous. Already dark, Jackson lagged while Illiac posed as a Russian tourist to register for the room. He got two adjoining rooms, requesting the first floor.

Illiac and the clerk were patient with each other's broken English, smiling about being able to basically communicate. "You have rooms 115 and 117 for you and party sir," the clerk said. "Down that hallway near end on right."

"Thank you," Illiac said.

When Illiac approached the room, he noticed there was an exit door in case of fire. It had no alarm so, he found a golf-ball sized rock outside and jammed it into the door frame. The door was open but not visibly so, especially in the darkness. He directed his men through the comm and opened the room door. The rooms each had two beds and a small table with two chairs. He quickly dragged the table and chairs from room 115 into room 117 so they could lay out their maps and plan strategy. The team began filtering in through the exit door one group at a time. Jackson was the first to join him.

"No place like home," Jackson said jokingly.

"Yeah, not a pleasure palace, but it will work," Illiac joked back. "By the way, how are your headaches?"

"They come and go," Jackson replied. "I haven't had one for a few days. I notice that they seem to happen most when I'm in a brightly lit area."

"That's good to know," Illiac responded. "This mission will be in the dark so, not much chance of one happening."

Illiac had been asked to keep an eye on Jackson and report his behavior and mood swings. Doctor Bramahh said that within a few more days, if Jackson didn't have any more headache episodes, the chip would have taken full control. It looked like that was going to be the case. Illiac was glad. He liked Jackson but knew if things were not successful it would be his job to terminate him. The last member of the team arrived.

Jackson was looking at Illiac and then switched his attention to the team. A few days earlier, he had noticed Illiac watching him intently. Something was odd about it. He was especially watchful when Jackson had a headache. Jackson was unable to shake the feeling that something was wrong. But what? He did not tell Illiac about his recurring dream of a dark-haired woman with a blade that seemed to follow him wherever he went. Still though, he could not see her face and wondered if the dream was recurring due to his stress levels, the fact that he liked dark haired women and his subconscious was suggesting it, or if the dreams were happening because the woman was someone he knew. He was in a daze, staring out the window when Illiac called his name.

"Isn't that right, Jackson?" Illiac asked.

"Sorry," Jackson replied. "Guess I was daydreaming. What is right?"

"That we would approach via the back entrance and go up the stairs to the target's suite."

"Yes," Jackson replied, his mind back to the business at hand. "This is the suite. We will approach from the back and up the stairs to the suite. We will leave two men on the back entrance, two at the bottom of the stairs and one at the top. Then, the remaining three will enter the suite, capture the target and exit the same way. We need to stay on comms and have the chopper pick us up in this small field. So, once we have the target, we exit south to the first street, west to the end and southwest to the next street then directly to the pickup point. It's just under five hundred yards. How far away is the helicopter?"

"About three miles," Illiac said. "Five minutes max for flight time."

"Alright," Jackson said. "Illiac calls the chopper when we get into position at the back and the pilot can warmup the bird. Once we exit the back door with the target, Illiac will call the chopper and we should be able to reach the pickup point at the same time and be gone before there is a response from the local police."

"Don't you think that's cutting it close?" Illiac asked.

"Normally," Jackson said. "But this is flat terrain, the men are in good shape, and we have a light load. We dope the target up and carry him on a stretcher, switching bearers every sixty seconds. We should be able to run half speed relatively easy."

"Okay," Illiac said. "You heard the man. Eat your Wheaties as the Americans say."

Everyone laughed.

"Let 's go by the numbers," Illiac said. "Count off, one to eight, twice."

The men did as they were commanded, each remembering their number.

"Now, one and two, you have the back entrance; three and four you have the bottom of the stairs. Five, you have the top of the stairs. Six through eight, we have the suite. It will be fast and furious. Make sure you don't shoot the target. Now, keep going over your assignments and prep your weapons and gear. We execute at 2300. Get some shut eye. It may be a long night."

L I Na had slept most of the day then, returned to Jangkar for a late lunch. She sat for over an hour sipping tea, watching traffic pass when she noticed a convoy of four vehicles stop in front of the target's hotel. She recognized Luca Atkinson at once. His blond hair and pale skin in stark contrast to those around him. She knew he had served as a mercenary in Africa for a few years and that he had friends in high political office in several countries, including Papua. He briefly glanced her direction as he looked around. Then, his security detail surrounded him while they walked to the front desk, disappearing from her watchful eye. His reservations made beforehand; the clerk passed his assistant key cards to the suite. They were upstairs in the suite within a couple of minutes. The day was breezy, one of those days where a person wanted to be outside and not cooped up. Her watchful eye caught movement on the balcony the instant the door opened. Luca took a seat in a wicker chair, turning it so he could watch the building across the street and the skyline. He pulled out a cigar and lit it, blowing smoke rings into the air; three security men stood at the corners of the balcony, so they didn't disturb his view. A few minutes later, a hotel employee brought some brandy and glasses, beer, and a large bowl of mixed fruit, placing it on the table next to him. The security detail each took a bottle of beer and returned to their original positions, taking a sip now and then and setting the bottle on the polished marble squared floor at their feet. She could tell by their mannerisms that they were experienced. Likely they had been fellow mercenaries with Luca in Africa.

Realizing she would not be privy to when Jackson's team would strike, Li Na decided to be in place on the roof top by 8:00 pm. She sat a while longer, watching down the street toward the building her sniper hide would be on. There wasn't much activity. If it rained tonight, the streets would be empty. She made it back to her hotel and locking the door, Li Na began checking her rifle. It was a 5.56 NATO with a sixteen-inch barrel that unscrewed at the end of the chamber. With an adjustable stock and 3.6 – 18 power scope with a 44 mm objective. She locked the bolt back on the rifle several times then, screwed on the barrel with its attached large, knurled nut that fixed it to the receiver. She put on a blindfold and assembled and disassembled the rifle five times, also putting in a magazine. Satisfied that she was prepared she separated the rifle into barrel, receiver and stock with scope, and suppressor.

There was so much confusion about suppressors and firepower she thought. Jackson had taught her the finer points so that she was proficient at longer ranges with a rifle.

He had told her to forget the subsonic ammunition and opt for a longer suppressor since subsonic ammunition typically would not recycle a semi-automatic weapon. So, she had a custom suppressor made for her rifle that would cycle the bolt every time it fired. She remembered Jackson's teachings like it was yesterday. At sea level, the speed of sound is 1,127 feet per second. When a moving projectile such as a bullet breaks that sound threshold, there is an audible shock wave that is like the crack of a whip. However, most of the sound is not from breaking the sound barrier but from the expanding gasses that rapidly escape the muzzle and it is that sound or bang that usually reveals the shooters position and that causes hearing damage. Thus, it is not the downrange crack that subsonic ammunition eliminates and does reduce muzzle noise somewhat, but a good suppressor that is key.

Li Na had opted for 55 grain bullets with a velocity of 3,130 fps. Her suppressor would reduce the bang at the muzzle and in a city situation, the sound heard would be the echo from the building she was shooting into. There was only seventy-five yards to target; instead of the typical one-hundred yard zero, Li Na had zeroed her rifle at fifty yards. Being less than one hundred feet above sea level, the round would strike one-half inch low and less than one inch at one hundred yards. She placed the rifle in her backpack and picked up her grappling hook, tying a thirty-foot cord with knots every two feet. She wrapped the hooks with a pillowcase to deaden the sound when she threw it onto the roof then, put the backpack on and picked up her hiking stick. Taking one last look around she exited and made her way to the main street. She walked about a block down skirting around the buildings through narrow alleys until she came to the building she had reconned. The rain clouds had moved in again, accompanied by thunder and lightning. It was perfect weather for a covert mission.

Being early, she knew there would be more activity in the

building, so she crept very slowly up the stairs, looking into every window. Twice she had to step back down a stair or two when she saw a person's face looking out at the lightning, the rain now falling in torrents. Reaching the last step, she pulled the grappling hook from her pack and threw it the twelve feet to the roof above. It made a dull thud when it landed. She heard the slide of a window and backed against the wall looking in the direction the sound had come, her heart pounding like a locomotive. Smoke exited the window in a large plume from a cigarette. It quickly closed when the rain began blowing at a steep angle through the open space. Li Na pulled on the rope; the hook had caught on a four-inch pipe, and she quickly climbed up using her upper body strength and feet on the knots to propel herself. Within thirty seconds she was on the roof and squatted, remaining motionless, her heart beating quickly from the quick ascent.

After a few minutes, she edged forward. Near the other side, facing the targets hotel, was a large swamp cooler the size of a commercial air conditioning unit. Standing next to it and looking at the hotel with her small monocular, she knew this was the best location. It afforded a good view of the target and would reduce the sound of the rifle when the bullets exited the suppressor at over 3,000 fps. The sound of a passing car drifted up from the street below. Taking advantage of a break in the rain, she quickly leaned her hiking stick against the unit and assembled her take-down rifle. It took less than a minute then, she laid a blanket atop the unit, placing her rifle on it. Crawling up, she covered herself and the rifle with an oversized poncho. At least she and her weapon would be mostly dry. Occasionally a patron entered the hotel. Enabling the FLIR on her scope she saw three men in the shadows, obviously a part of Luca's security detail. Li Na settled in for what could be a long wait. She knew when the team came, it would be fast and furious. Her thoughts drifted to the bliss Jackson and her experienced in

Miami. She was looking forward to experiencing it again.

JACKSON and the team had moved in pairs for what seemed like an eternity, meeting near the back of the target's hotel. The rain and lightning had kept almost everyone off the street. Timika was like a ghost town. They were certain that no one had seen them moving furtively about to get into position for the extraction. They waited until precisely 2300. Illiac entered to speak with the clerk, knocking her out and dragging her into the office near the front desk, locking her inside. The team took their respective positions. Rain soaked, four of them ran up the stairs on the balls of their feet, making almost no sound from their mid-height, flexible SEAL outsoles. The fifth man took the top of the stairs and the remaining three team members paused to barely crack the exit door to the stairwell and peer down the corridor to the target's suite.

Illiac pointed to his eyes with both fingers then, held up three. He described their position and pointed to each of them which guard they were assigned. Ready with their suppressed pistols, they flung through the door, Illiac standing and the other two kneeling. Three quick, silent headshots and the guards collapsed at once. The three quickly strode to the suite door, stopping and listening. Those inside had not heard the sounds from the hallway. They knew there were at least nine guards inside perhaps more. Picking up a key card from one of the dead guards, Illiac waved it across the lock, which turned from red to green. Immediately the three entered like a SWAT team, Illiac fanned left, and Jackson and his colleague fanned right. One of the guards saw the door opening and shot at them. The sound from the unsuppressed pistol was deafening. Two guards on the street ran to the front doors of the hotel. They had been posted outside as a perimeter security team to ensure Luca's protection from just such an attempt.

Li Na, watching from her hide, saw the door burst open and heard the gun shot. It seemed extra loud in the stillness of the night. Immediately windows began to light in nearby buildings from the sound. She shot each of the guards running to the door in the brain stem. They collapsed into lifeless heaps. Two guards who had been standing on the covered balcony were leveling their pistols at the assailants within. She took quick body shots wounding them. Falling to their knees they managed to get a couple of quick shots off, killing Jackson's teammate. Li Na shot both in the head and then another guard standing just inside the glass windows that had disintegrated from stray shots from within. Luca pulled a pistol and was swinging it toward Jackson; Li Na caught the motion and shot him in the right shoulder. She could not wait any longer. She took down her rifle put it and her supplies in the pack and got off the roof, leaving her grappling hook behind. Running like there was no tomorrow, she hoped that she was right about their exit strategy. Gun shots were still blasting out when she ran across the street into the darkness. Running a four-hundred-meter sprint, she was at the small grove of trees fifty-five seconds later, near where she thought the chopper would land. From her backpack she pulled a six-inch barrel, suppressed .22 pistol that had several special rounds reduced to a .17 caliber. They were tracker rounds that would send out a signal to Mitch and Henry, but only when they pinged the tiny transmitter inside the small pellet.

Jackson and Illiac moved quickly to restrain Luca, writhing in pain from the gun shot. Illiac pulled out a syringe containing 161 mg of propofol and 25 mg of meperidine. Within a few seconds Luca quit squirming and was out by the time one of the men had brought a folding EVAC stretcher. Luca was strapped to it and the three men exited the suite, leaving a fallen comrade behind then, moved down the stairs.

"That couldn't have been all of his security detail," Illiac said. "Keep your eyes open."

At the precise moment they reached the bottom of the stairs, two gunmen came through the front door of the hotel, all of them shooting. The team dispatched them before they could gain more than a few steps. The gun fire was waking up more and more people and some had made it to the street, peering into the hotel lobby. The team ran through the back door and shot two more guards. Both men they had left to guard the entrance were dead.

Emil was on the way with the chopper and had enough altitude to see the running gun battle.

"Illiac," he said. "There are at least four men on your tail, about a hundred yards back. I'll buzz them once to see if I can delay them then, will be waiting for you."

"Roger," Illiac said. "Hustle men, we are out of time."

Li Na heard the gun shots from the approaching team. They were just passing when the helicopter streaked toward the guards following behind and shooting at them. The machine guns on the helicopter opened fire, downing two of the guards.

"Perfect," she thought. "The helicopter will drown out the sound."

She saw them out of the corner of her eye and braced the pistol against the tree she stood behind. They were breathing hard. Not more than twenty feet away, she squeezed off three quick shots, two into Luca's shoulder, getting both into the wound area.

"What luck," she thought. "They won't notice them embedded in the wound and will suture it up without thought."

The third shot went into Jacksons right calf. Several bullets had hit nearby so hopefully he wouldn't notice it and just bandage it up.

"Damn!" Jackson exclaimed. "We underestimated them."

"Don't worry my friend," Illiac said. "We'll be gone before they can get any closer."

Emil, as promised, was waiting in the chopper, blades churning. They were in and had lifted off before the remaining guards could close the last fifty yards. To throw them off, the team headed north for fifteen minutes, the sound of the whirring blades dying completely. Then, Emil headed west back to Tabubil where the team's plane was already waiting.

Li Na watched them go. She had done what she was ordered by both parties.

"Goodbye my love," She whispered. "We will be together again soon."

"She was more efficient than we anticipated," Conrad said, stepping out of the shadows at the rear of the building, watching the helicopter disappear into the night.

"How so?" Antonio asked.

"She killed at least four or five guards from the rooftop across the street then, sprinted almost a quarter mile to cover the teams retreat."

"Did they see her?"

"No sir," Conrad replied. "She did what was required. I need to say that this time you outdid yourself. Her skills are unmatched."

"Very good," Antonio said. "So, you think we can use her again?"

"Yes sir," Conrad responded. "She did exactly what she was ordered to do."

"Excellent. Get back as soon as you can."

It was past midnight when Li Na sat down and pulled her satphone from her pack. Looking back toward the target hotel she could see the police lights reflecting against the buildings amid the light rain. Strangely, she felt at peace knowing that they would be able to determine the location where the organization was hiding their captives. She wondered allowed how many they already had and who they were.

"I put two trackers into Luca and one into Jackson," she said. "Five minutes ago."

"Standby," Mitch replied. "We have them. Phil says to be ready to deploy again immediately. You're booked on a charter flight at 0700 out of Mozes Kilangin International Airport."

"I'll be there."

Li Na took the back streets, moving cautiously. It didn't appear anyone was up yet, but caution was always a necessity in clandestine operations. It was also likely the police would be looking for anyone they found at such early morning hours and would question them on sight. The episode during the night was probably not a common one. The airport was over three miles away. Like still hunting for game, she traveled a mile about every two hours. She had predetermined a location to catch a taxi for the last mile. Right on time, she was dropped off at the VIP terminal. Its maroon walls and orange and black support columns were a welcome view. Once inside, she checked in and got her ticket then, went searching for a cup of coffee.

The team had made it back to Tabubil and boarded their private plane, the same one they had arrived in. Within ten minutes, they were airborne.

"Where are we going?" Jackson asked.

"A different training and medical camp," Illiac said, a sour look on his face.

"I have never lost that many men on a mission," Jackson said. "I feel like an amateur."

"Why do you think you were along?" Illiac smiled. "Antonio knew this would be the toughest of the three missions and

FOR PRESIDENT AND COUNTRY

you got the call. Were it not for you, we would all be dead."

"Thank you," Jackson replied. "But I don't deserve the credit."

"Yes, you do," Illiac said. "Thanks for my life."

"Thank you for mine," Jackson said. "If you hadn't shot Luca, I'd be a dead man."

Illiac looked at him trying to recall the mayhem in the suite. Did he shoot Luca? He didn't remember, but he or his dead comrade must have.

"Don't mention it my friend," Illiac said. "There will be more missions soon, hopefully not in such a hell hole."

Jackson didn't care where they were going. He was glad the mission had been accomplished. It would be difficult to get three men up to speed quickly unless Illiac had someone in mind. He leaned back in his seat and the dream began again. He had it constantly, almost daily. The woman was sitting on a boat, gliding across the choppy waves. It was a speed boat, off the coast of some major city maybe, he couldn't tell. She was leaning back, looking forward, her gaze cast across the ocean toward the sun set. She was wearing a colorful pale green and white sheer robe over her swimsuit. The sheerness of it unable to cover her lithe, athletic frame. Her jet-black hair blowing away from her while the boat sped across the waves. Her skin pale and smooth, and her face like a China doll, she exuded great confidence and grace. Jackson saw a smile begin to form on her face when she started to turn toward him.

Turbulence brought him quickly to the present.

"Are you okay my friend?" Illiac asked. "You looked so peaceful in your sleep."

"Yes," Jackson replied. "Yes, I'm okay. I was just getting to sleep. Damn turbulence."

"Dreaming again?" Illiac asked.

"No, just dead asleep," Jackson replied. He knew better than to say anything to Illiac. The nagging about things being out of place had grown stronger. Naturally, he had withdrawn into his security shell and began keeping things to himself. "I haven't had a dream for some time now. Besides, I do not put much stock in dreams. No one can interpret them anyway."

"Yes," Illiac said. "I once dreamed I was making love to four women in a Volkswagen Beetle. What do you think of that dream?"

"I'm no psychologist," Jackson said laughing. "But I'd say you were in dire need of sex."

The team got a big laugh out of the remark. It broke the tension that had been pent up and they began talking about the mission and the target. Jackson's comment had also thrown Illiac off his suspicious nature.

BEATRIX was the first to suggest the direction of the plane, Leonid quick on her heels. The two had been discussing potential options.

"Sir," Beatrix said. "Leonid and I have been discussing the intelligence we have so far. We believe they are not going back to the original training camp on the border of the Ukraine."

"We concur," Phil said. "Where to you think they are going?"

"They swapped to a longer-range plane in Kuala Lumpur, a Bombardier Global 7500."

"What's unique about that?" Phil asked.

"The plane is ultra-long-range sir," Beatrix said. "It can travel over 8,000 miles."

"It looks like they are going on a long flight," Mitch interjected. "Where, is the question?"

"It looks like the Caribbean," Leonid said.

"Why do you say that?" Phil asked.

"The new plane filed a flight plan to Mohammed V International Airport in Casablanca, over 7,000 miles from Kuala Lumpur."

"Sir, if I may," Beatrix stated. "Leonid and I discussed where they might go. From Casablanca, they have the range to go anywhere from the southern tip of Chile to Seattle. However, given what we know from their Jamaica operation, we believe it will land somewhere in the Caribbean. After all, none of our countries consider that a prime target area and satellite imagery is scant unless we re-task the satellites."

"What's your best guess?" Henry asked.

"Given customs, surveillance aspects, and tourism, we think it will land somewhere in the Lesser Antilles," Leonid replied. "Anywhere from Saint Kitts and Antigua in the north to Trinidad and Tobago in the south."

"What about Cuba?" Phil asked.

"That is a possibility," Beatrix said. "However, it's a nightmare for quick flights in and out if you're in a hurry. Besides, you don't go anywhere in Cuba without the government spying on you."

"We believe it will be a popular tourist destination," Leonid said. "Some place easy to mix with the crowd and remain unobserved but also be able to operate covertly. Given the heavy vegetation on all these islands, it will be easy for them to hide from the general populace."

"I concur with their assessment sir," Henry said. "It is logical and makes perfect sense."

"How long before we know the flight plan from Morocco?" Phil asked.

"In about three hours sir," Beatrix replied.

"Ok, pull up a map of the Caribbean," Phil said. "Let's try to narrow it down."

"We have a pool if you want to get in on it," Beatrix said. "$10."

"You're on," Phil said. "What are my choices?"

"Martinique, Barbados, and Saint Lucia sir," Beatrix said, smiling.

"Which one did you choose Leonid?" Phil asked.

"St. Lucia," Leonid said. "Hewanorra International Airport is at the southern end of the island and there are lots of places to hide. My wife and I spent a vacation there once learning how to make chocolate. The beaches and towns are widely dispersed and very private in most places."

"You sold me," Phil said. "I'll go with St. Lucia also."

The two teams continued linking intelligence sources together to get a leap on their targets and the organization that so far, was nameless. One of the Russian team members yelled out "It is St. Lucia commander."

Phil and Leonid smiled at each other. The hunt would be on quickly. The other teams in the field were also reporting activity with the oil and diamond CEOs. There would be no rest in the crisis suite for some time. The teams buckled in for the long hall.

A CIA team had gotten a visual on Malcolm Okeke, CEO of Genji Diamond Mines, at Sir Seretse Khama International Airport about five miles north of Gaborone.

A tail inside the terminal followed the CEO when he exited the airport. Two CIA agents in a rented sedan outside the terminal recognized the CEO standing in the passenger pickup area.

"He's out," Agent 1 said. "Getting into a black luxury van. He's all yours."

"We have them in visual sir," the agent said. "You just want us to follow them?"

"That is correct Agent 2," Mitch replied. "We need to find out where they are going to take Okeke once they grab him. We suspect back to the airport to a private jet. Have your men do a full recon so that you are ready."

"Okay sir, we will surveil as you request," Agent 2 replied.

They followed Okeke from the airport passing Airport Junction Shopping Centre on their left just before picking up A1 heading south. About five miles later the agents continued to follow about a half mile back when the van turned east onto A10. Agent 2 was watching the van through binoculars. The further they traveled from the city, the sparser the traffic. It was midday and quite warm. He picked up a map and began looking at the distance and route, knowing that by the time they reached Jwaneng that it would be close to dark.

"In about 45 minutes they'll reach the junction of A2," Agent 2 said. "Hang back a little more. After all, we know where they are headed."

"Will do," Agent 3 said. "You know, this soil reminds me of the red clay of the Southern Piedmont in the U.S. Lots of clay and likely iron. A bitch to grow anything on."

"Maybe that's why we don't see any fat people."

The two laughed relieving the tension.

They kept an eye on the van ahead while they passed Gabane and about thirty minutes later, Thamaga. The area was surrounded by dry brush and washed-out rills where heavy rains had caused gullies of varying size. Once they passed Thamaga, the dryer brush gave way to green shrubs and taller, lush grasses. Acacia trees with their flat looking tops seemed to dwarf most of the shrubs, excepting the very large sycamore fig trees. Sparse green grasses along the highway in areas stood in stark contrast to the red soil. Nearing Mosopa, the landscape changed to small hills with large boulders and shortly back to the flat terrain more common to the area. Directly after swinging northwest on A2 the target vehicle stopped at a small roadside vendor who was selling bottled water, soft drinks and local fruits. The Agents didn't want to raise suspicion and pulled in a short distance behind them before getting out. They stretched some and walked around the car as if inspecting it. The security detail, four men, had surrounded Okeke while he bought a bottle of water and some mangos and papayas. He was quickly ushered back to the van that took off quickly. Agent 1 could see the passenger side security guard looking back at them in the outside mirror. He pretended not to notice while they walked to the vendor and bought a couple of bottles of water and several oranges. The security guard appeared satisfied and turned to face forward. Waiting a few minutes, the agents climbed into their sedan and sped after the van.

"Don't worry," Agent 2 said. "They will be climbing that rise in the distance. Their elevation is higher than ours so we will be able to maintain visual and close the distance."

"If you say so," Agent 3 replied, slowing down. "What I don't get, is why we aren't allowed to off this CEO?"

"I'm talking directly to Mitch who is with the director in a crisis suite on the Farm," Agent 2 said. "He said they are conducting a sting. I'm guessing wherever they are taking Okeke is when we will be able to do our thing?"

"Seems like they could just track his passport," Agent 3 said.

"This mystery organization has more brains than that," Agent 2 said. "They are going to nab the target tonight from what Mitch said. What we need to do is get close enough to do our job."

When they neared Jwaneng, the agents closed the distance. It was quickly apparent the target would check into a previously arranged hotel, but which one? There were only a few upscale hotels, so the agents cruised past the first one and got lucky. The targets van was in the parking lot in front of registration. Okeke and his security detail were already headed to their rooms. The Caster Inn was laid out well. From the registration desk, ornate concrete pathways led to multiple room small buildings with green roofs, red trimmed joists and red brick walls. It was a great setting with a friendly, professional staff. The two agents opened the trunk of their car and put on different shirts that were between subtle and wild, playing the part of tourists. Agent 3 walked into the registration area. There was no one at the desk so, he looked around. The name of the hotel was behind the registration desk on a greenish wall with a fax machine on the far right. A computer monitor and POS machine was to his left sitting on a dark, marble type countertop. The wood on the front of the desk, which stretched across the end of the room, appeared to be mahogany with the matching wooden diamond outlays across the front. Though the inn had a computer, they also kept a ledger of guests, which was laying right next to the monitor. Agent 3 was able to get a quick glance at it before the clerk rounded the corner.

"May I help you sir," the clerk asked.

"Yes," Agent 3 said. "Some friends arrived ahead of us, about six of them. We wanted to know if we could sit by your pool and have a few drinks before we met up?"

"Certainly sir," the Clerk replied. "Take the path around the end of the building. Sit at any of the tables in the northwest corner kitty corner from the large boulder waterfall on the opposite side of the pool. I'll have a waitress from the Nedali Restaurant and Bar sent right over to take your order."

"Thank you, sir," Agent 3 said, leaving a tip. "You've been most helpful."

"Sir," the Clerk asked. "Will you be staying for the night?"

"I'm not sure," Agent 3 said. "One of the men is our boss. He will let us know."

"Ah, yes," the Clerk said with a broad smile. "I know bosses."

Walking back to the car, the agent looked down the path at the end of the building. It was well lit and lined with palms on either side. Motioning to his colleague who brought baseball caps to wear, the two made their way as directed by the clerk. Sitting down, they had put their caps on and were sure that with those and the different colored shirts that Okeke's security men would not recognize them. They had no sooner sat down than a lovely waitress from the bar took their drink order. She had a very pleasant attitude and lovely smile.

"Were you able to get any information?" Agent 2 asked.

"They are in bungalow 13 and the one on either side," Agent 3 said. "Don't look too hard, but 13 is that one directly across from us, inset about ten feet back from those on either side. Let's keep our eyes on the three. My hunch is Okeke is in the middle one assuming they follow typical security protocols.

The sun hung low in the horizon, a beautiful orange red glow surrounding it, casting a golden light over the tops of the palms next to them and onto the opposite end of the pool. The water shooting out of the large boulder in a flowing spray formed a small rainbow. Agent 3 was wondering if it was a real boulder or made by some construction workers being some eight to ten feet high and about twenty feet wide. Motion behind and to the right of it caught his eye. Through the trees beyond the boulder, he caught a glimpse of Okeke and his security detail.

"You were right," he said. "There they are."

The two agents watched the group closely who were visible here and there on the pathway behind the trees. It was obvious they were headed for the restaurant.

"They may be in there for a while," Agent 2 said. "Keep an eye out, I'm going to check around the bungalows."

About fifteen minutes later he returned.

"The other team is here," Agent 2 said. "They are in the parking lot in two vans, feigning a breakdown."

"How do you know it's them?"

"Their clothes are all wrong," Agent 2 said, smiling. "Looks like they're going to an all-black ball. Two of them were walking around the area near the restaurant. They'll hit him later tonight."

"While you were away, I was looking at a map of the hotel the clerk gave me," Agent 3 said. "My hunch is they will take Okeke down this path to the west into the parking lot. We can position ourselves in two different locations behind these trees and we should be able to fulfill our mission."

"Hmmmm," Agent 2 murmured, looking at the map. "I like it."

The sound of voices on the other side of the pool made

drew their attention. It was Okeke and his men, they had decided to eat outside. Being across the pool, the two agents knew they were too far away for the men to recognize them. In the spur of the moment, the waitress returned, and they ordered another round of drinks and Seswaa, which is regarded as a national dish of Botswana, consisting of a variety of meats including beef, chicken, goat, or lamb. Agent 2 had eaten it before and loved it. The dish was cooked slowly over a few hours until it was completely tender and soft. He knew that being a restaurant and being a very popular dish in the area, that the chef would have begun preparing it about midday, before the restaurant opened. The fatty meat would be boiled with onion and pepper in a traditional three-legged cast iron pot. They ordered it as a sandwich. Agent 2's mouth was watering just thinking about it. By the time the waitress had brought their food, darkness had fallen. The group across from them were having a great time laughing and talking.

It was about 10:00 pm when the two agents positioned themselves behind the shrubs that masked the bungalows from the pool area. With small openings here and there, they picked two spots that would give them the opportunity to accomplish their task. Using the same type of six-inch barrel .22 with a suppressor and subsonic rounds Li Na had used, they readied themselves. About an hour later, six black clad operatives approached the three bungalows Okeke had reserved, two of the men to each. The outer bungalow doors were breached quickly, and the suppressed sound of 9mm pistols were barely audible, followed by thuds of bodies hitting the floor. Clearing each bungalow, the four operatives joined the other two just outside Okeke's door and burst through. It was then that the agents heard the familiar chopping sound as the blades of a helicopter sliced the night air. In less than thirty seconds the operatives were dragging Okeke's limp body from the bungalow and down the path toward the parking lot. The exact route the agents had determined. When the operatives passed, both agents were able to fire several tracking rounds striking Okeke in the right arm and leg and lower torso. Agent 2 grinned, "Mission accomplished he thought." The sounds of the helicopter drowned out the muffled shots.

The two agents moved toward each other and out onto the walkway. Standing in the edge of the shrubs, away from the light cast by the lamps along it, they were able to see Okeke loaded into the helicopter; it was quickly airborne and heading toward Gaborone. The operatives leapt into their vehicles and within seconds were out of sight.

"They are headed your way," Agent 2 said, speaking into his cell phone. "Tracking devices operative."

PRESIDENT Sokolov walked into his office, Andros closing the door behind him.

"How much do we know?" President Sokolov asked.

"Leonid said they had some good leads and that the organization just nabbed Okeke," Andros replied.

"It seems that President Armstrong and the CIA Director were correct," Sokolav said. "Any news on where they may be operating from?"

"Phillip Ross said it looks like they are taking the hostages to St. Lucia. Leonid confirmed that. In fact, it was he and his team that deduced the location."

"You have an incoming sir," his secretary said through the speaker. "It is President Armstrong."

"Put him through," Sokolav replied. "President Armstrong, how are you? I have Andros here with me."

"I am well and hope that you both are also," President Armstrong said. "I'm sure that Andros has filled you in with the details to date. I wanted to let you know what we had so far. Okeke has just been taken. He was tracked to the Seretse Khama International Airport in Gaborone. From there, field officers tracked him to a private jet. Phil said it is bound for St. Lucia."

"Does the jet have the range for that?" Andros asked.

"Yes," President Armstrong replied. "It's only about 6,400 miles I'm told."

"So maybe about twelve hours flight time?" President Sokolav queried.

"Good estimate President Sokolav," VP Reisner said. "We approximated the same. Also, we have field officers being dispatched to St. Lucia now. We have not narrowed the exact location but hope to soon."

"What can we do to help?" President Sokolav asked.

"Can you spare any SVR agents from Nicaragua or any area nearby?" President Armstrong asked.

Andros and President Sokolav looked at each other, wondering how they knew about their field operatives in the region, although they were not surprised.

"We have Sgt. Melor Dominik and his men in Managua," Andros said.

"Oh yes, the men from the Snake Island assault," Reisner said. "That's less than 2,000 miles away. How soon can you have them in St. Lucia?"

"They were about to return home," Andros said. "They can be in St. Lucia in four hours."

"Good," President Armstrong said. "Let's have them coordinate with the crisis suite and our agents on the ground. I'll have someone meet them at the airport."

"Very well," President Sokolav said. "I need not remind everyone that we must tread lightly here."

"Good point," President Armstrong said. "We must respect the sovereignty of St. Lucia; at the same time, we need to be very covert."

"Agreed," President Sokolav replied. "We should come up with a cover story just in case."

FEDOR Semenov, CEO of Tanfe Company, in charge of the Romoshakin oil fields near Tyumen Oblast, sat down in the back of his large SUV. He could tell winter was not far away, a chill already in the air. He was so engrossed in the well production data he held in his hand that he didn't look up when he sat down. The man next to his driver in the front seat and the man next to him went unnoticed.

"To the office Alek."

"Yes sir."

"You may want to put your papers down," the operative said, a pistol leveled at Fedor.

"Who the hell are you?" Fedor asked, his voice quivering.

"That is unimportant. Do you wish to live?"

"Yes."

"Then, do as we say, and you will," the operative replied. "Otherwise, you will die."

"Alek, the Plekhanovo Airport," the operative said. "Obey the speed limits."

The Romoshakin oil fields were in Western Siberia surrounded by hemiboreal forests of broadleaf and coniferous trees. The density of the trees made for limited visibility. The airport was only ninety miles away, but the twisting, unkept roads made for slow going. It would be a three-hour trip. Fedor didn't understand what was happening. In a country like Russia, nabbing rich oil executives usually didn't end well for the kidnappers. Like the Special Operations Police in Turkey, the Russian Federal Police Service didn't care about collateral damage. These men were taking a huge risk. Fedor felt a sharp twitch of pain in his neck. He looked at the operative who was holding a syringe and was just forming the words he wanted to say when he fell against the door, out cold.

"That will keep him out of our hair until we reach the airport."

"Do we stop them sir?" the SVR agent spoke into his phone.
"No. Our orders are to keep them under surveillance only. They are cleared already for takeoff. Did you place the tracker in his suit?"
"Yes sir."
"Very well. Tell me when you reach the airport."

The sedan reached the airport, pulling off Tkad road and circling back to the northeast, parking in a small lot where a van awaited them to escort them to the plane. The operative jabbed the driver with another needle; he passed out at once. Fedor was coming around when the two agents helped him ionto the waiting van, which made its way around the tarmac to a row of planes two-hundred yards northwest of the runway. Driving down the row, the van stopped and pulled around the side of a twin engine King Air 350ER that had almost a 3,000-mile range. Within minutes, the plane was airborne, on its way to a small field in Belarus where they would refuel and make it safely to Morocco, switch planes and then, fly to the Caribbean.

The SVR agent called in. "They are on the plane sir. It just became airborne."
"Good," the commander replied. "Find the driver and question him. Report back with any information. I'll pass the information up the chain."

MITCH met Li Na at the airport. Waiting in the main terminal area, she wasn't hard to spot. Like most men, when he noticed Li Na, his eyes became riveted on her. She noticed him immediately and walked right to him.
"The wild shirt, sunglasses and Fedora are not a clever disguise," she said, smiling.
"Hey, I'm a tourist," Mitch replied with a laugh. "What did you expect? This way please."

The two were met at passenger pickup by Mitch's driver in an ordinary gray sedan. Li Na threw her bag into the trunk and the trio were off.

"Where are we headed?" Li Na asked.

"We will pass through Soufriere," Mitch said. "It's only about twenty miles, but the road is along the coast and winding so it will take us an hour to get there. Once we do, we will head toward a resort on the beach below Jade Mountain."

"You have a room for us?" Li Na asked.

"Yes," Mitch replied, unable to keep his eyes off her. "We're posing as a married couple on vacation, but we won't be staying in the room. As soon as it gets dark, we will head around Grand Caille Point and to 'The Keyhole", a spot in the small cliffs behind a hotel that juts out into Soufriere Bay and begins the horseshoe that forms it. By the way, this is Frank, he will be meeting us there."

"Please to meet you Frank," Li Na said, smiling.

"Likewise," Frank replied.

"His team of four will rappel down the cliff face and climb aboard our small raft. It's not fast, but it's quiet."

"Where are we going?" Li Na asked.

"It's a surprise and very closely guarded secret," Mitch said.

About forty-five minutes later they passed through Soufriere. Li Na was surprised at the lack of amenities and shops she thought she would see.

"It's bleaker looking than I anticipated," Li Na said.

"No everyone flourishes from the tourist trade," Mitch said. "It is a continual progress. Things are much better now than a decade ago. Jobs are scarce still, but more are opening. It is one of the reasons we chose this location. Still, it is advisable to pay attention to details."

She understood him. They would stand out if they ventured into town. Nothing would happen to them, but many eyes would be watching, perhaps more curious than anything else. But gossip was gossip and when there wasn't much to do it was the main topic on many islands in the Caribbean. The resort was not far from Soufriere; Li Na guessed about three miles or a bit more. They checked in and were led to a small bungalow down near the beach. One of the few that was air conditioned. The room was more lavish than Li Na had expected. If it were not for the current situation, she could picture spending a week with Jackson, lounging on the beach and having fun. The room was immaculate with a red tile floor, balcony with a hammock and flowers, wooden shutters, and an awesome bed with colorful spreads and pillows and mosquito netting tied to the corners that could be closed at night.

Like most tourists, they put their bags in the room, changed into swimwear and headed the short distance to the beach where they were greeted in a friendly manner and directed to one of the many palm-thatched Tiki huts with two reclining lounge chairs having nice cushions for relaxing. Between them was a small wooden table attached to the supporting center post. They each took a chair and laid back, looking at the ocean. Scarcely having sat down, a waiter in a white shirt and matching short pants took their order for drinks. Li Na had noticed on the walk down from registration to the bungalow, the Pitons off to her left. They rose like great monuments from the ocean. The one further south called Gros Piton and the smaller one, closer to Soufriere, Petite Piton. Once the waiter had brought their drinks, making sure no one was within distance to hear them, they struck up their conversation again.

"See the rental building off to our left?" Mitch asked. "That small, rubberized boat is what we will take about midnight to meet with Frank and his team."

"Where are we going?" Li Na asked.

"We will round Grand Caille Point there and turn back left following the shoreline to the Keyhole, pick up the team and travel about three miles across Soufriere Bay into Pitons Bay toward Gros Piton. There, you and I will drop overboard while the men remain on the boat, putting several ashore to guard us against potential adversaries. I don't think there will be any, but we must take precautions. You will speak to no one about this ever, except Jackson, if we can get him back."

"How are we going to do that?" Li Na asked.

"How good are you with your sword?" Mitch responded. "By that, I mean how deep, or shallow can you cut."

"My instructor taught us how to cut as shallow as a piece of paper or deep as the bone and beyond."

"Excellent," Mitch said. "Our former boss knew that something like this would happen. You will need to cut about one-quarter inch below the skin while another operative helps you with the body. I'll explain more about that later."

"What is the intent of my cut?"

"Deep enough so that it severs the signal connection," Mitch said. "At the same time, we must short circuit the chip. I've been studying all the theory behind such mechanisms and feel certain I know what type they are using. So, it will all depend on your skills."

Li Na stared into the distance. The sun was sinking lower in the western sky. Looking to her left, the point jutted southward into the Caribbean, its lush green foliage in stark contrast to the blue green water that shimmered in the afternoon sun. There were few people out due to the balmy heat, which she rather enjoyed. Li Na wondered how they would be able to carry out the mission because they had to find Jackson first. She was frustrated by the circumstances. The organization had not called her so, she determined they had no need for her services since she had fulfilled the contract. She had put her cell in a Faraday bag that would prevent signal tracking and prevent spying on her. She had done so as soon as she had shot the men from the roof top in Timika. She knew that having her number, the organization would keep tabs on her. Or maybe they were not interested.

Her men at the restaurant confirmed the remaining amount of payment had been delivered.

"How do we find Jackson?" Li Na asked.

"We already have," Mitch said, looking into her eyes. "Don't get excited, but their plane is on the way. We have trackers on two of their targets. Our problem is that we do not know where they will be going. Intelligence suggests an area near us but you can see it is quite rugged. I will take you to our laboratory tonight and that is where we must get Jackson to go, one way or the other."

"Will he remember me?" Li Na asked.

"I don't think so," Mitch said. "They probably have a chemical memory block in place. However, once I do my thing, his original memories should come back almost instantly."

"Good," Li Na said. "The suspense is killing me."

Mitch could tell that the female assassin had feelings for Jackson like most other women would have for their men. The difference was that he was the only one she had ever loved. Mitch could appreciate that. He realized that Li Na could not only be very unpredictable, but ruthless, letting nothing stand in her way to be reunited with the best spy ever. His men would need to keep a close eye on her lest she kill every one of the organization's men. That would blow her cover and their only chance of finding out more about this powerful covert group. Mitch decided it was time to make the call.

"Falcon 1, Osprey," Mitch said. "We are in place. Do we have coverage?"

"Osprey," the voice replied. "Overlapping coverage in place. Proceed with mission."

"Roger," Mitch replied. "We are in luck lady assassin. Live feeds will be available from both drones and satellite."

"Why do you think the organization has a base near here?" Li Na asked.

"It is remote and not remarkably important from a global security perspective," Mitch replied. "Also, one of our more obscure field operatives has noticed a helicopter coming and going. It appears then, disappears for several hours or more and reappears."

"That would suggest going into a narrow canyon or deep forest, landing and coming back out," Li Na replied.

"You are a quick study," Mitch said, realizing she was very sharp.

"I wasn't head of my old Chinese intelligence group for nothing," Li Na replied, a sly look and smirk on her face.

"Look at this aerial map," Mitch said. "If you were them, where would you likely be?"

Li Na studied the map for a few moments, sipping her drink while enjoying the breeze. She studied the map for about twenty minutes.

"How certain are you that their base is nearby?"

"Ninety percent."

"I have flown helicopters before and been on many missions using them for stealth," she said. "The problem is that when you climb in altitude, the sound carries a great distance. Look at this area, Mahaut Bay."

"I see it," Mitch said. "What of it?"

"I'm guessing your field man sees or hears the helicopter near dawn or dusk."

"How do you know that?"

"Look at the east end of the watershed here. It climbs from sea level to around 1,400 feet. Then, look at these two small canyons south of it. If a helicopter flew up either one, they would be relatively quiet and by going in early or late, they would avoid hikers that may see them from this hiking trail."

"But they could go beyond that point," Mitch replied.

"True, but if they do, they will be above the road at a higher elevation. That would mean more people would be likely to see them. Besides, the seaside of this rugged terrain would be ideal for concealment."

Mitch began looking at the map more closely including areas further out. Li Na was correct, flying up either of the two canyons early or late meant the only likely visual would be from a lone hiker; a tourist who probably would not think twice about seeing a helicopter figuring it was on a tour of the island. The organization had been very strategic placing an operation here. He continued to look north and east. The more he looked, the more convinced he became that Li Na was right. Further north and west were more populated. Further east meant longer flight times and more likelihood of being discovered. From the coast to the west side of the area was just over two miles. A quick in and out. He picked up his phone.

"Frank," Mitch said. "Send one of your extra men to the cutoff going west to Mahaut. Yes, it's about a half mile north of the Morne Tabac Rain Forest Trail. Then, tell him to perch along the road to Mahaut about one-half to one mile from the west face of the large ridges in the Belvedere area. There are two canyons coming in from the coast. Watch for a helicopter coming up either of those toward the west face of that large ridge."

"Done," Frank replied. "We still on for 2300?"

"Yes, see you then."

JACKSON'S plane landed at Hewanorra International Airport and taxied to the flight support area northeast of the terminal where they deboarded and carried Luca Atkinson to the waiting helicopter on the edge of the tarmac. Illiac, Jackson, and two other men got aboard, and they were off to the facility. He was tending to Luca, deep in thought. Jackson was curious about where they were going. He knew that Illiac was being cautious and seemed somewhat suspicious of him. The question was why?

"He's not in the best of shape," Jackson said, turning to Illiac.

"Lost quite a bit of blood, but he will live."

"That's all we need," Illiac said. "Our job is to deliver him alive. The doctors at the facility will take care of him."

"How long will it take us to get there?" Jackson asked.

"About twenty minutes, maybe a little longer," Illiac replied. "Why? Do you have plans?"

The comment was almost cold, like Jackson had suddenly become the enemy. He looked out the window briefly to throw Illiac off while he determined the best answer he could give to what now seemed more and more like a predicament. His covert senses were tingling. Something was wrong. Until he figured out what, he would be friendly but guarded in his responses in such a way Illiac would not suspect anything.

"No, just curious. You know me."

"All too well," Illiac thought.

It was only a few minutes later that the helicopter turned and headed away from the coast in almost complete darkness. Jackson saw a large opening appear in the side of a hill directly in front of them when the helicopter slowed. A very tall chain link gate swung open on either side; the helicopter flew between them. Inside was a huge cavern so low lit that the pilot needed to use night vision goggles to maneuver. Several medical personnel were at the door before the chopper's landing skids touched down. They hurried Luca onto a gurney and rushed as fast as they could to a room with the familiar red medical cross by the door. Jackson pretended to stretch and watched the gates close. He could just make out the purple-colored flowers of the vines on the outside. They appeared to be liana de cuello, a woody vine whose flowers had a trumpet shape. Because of the opening and closing of the gates, they had to be artificial to keep from being rooted up or dying. The group had flown low in the canyon away from the coast and just above treetop level into the facility. There was no doubt it was well hidden. On the inside of the chain link was a black-out geotextile type material. The lights slowly grew brighter in intensity so the team could see well enough to look around. The cavern was enormous. On one end were two more Cobra gunships, fully armed. Jackson wondered how they had gotten them. The rest of the cavern was full of various kinds of equipment ranging from medical supplies to food stuffs, and more weapons. All along the inner wall were rooms that appeared to be used for offices, sleeping, and medical work. The top of the cavern was at least one-hundred feet above him. It was then that he noticed a small, blinking red light in a uniform array spaced about fifty feet apart. The cave was armed to self-destruct and destroy evidence and any opposing force trying to breach it. These people were very shrewd.

"I see you like my toys," Illiac said, grinning. "One can never be too cautious. You taught me that."

"That's right," Jackson replied. "We need to constantly be prepared for the unexpected."

"Follow me," Illiac said. "The boss wants to see us."

There was a small hallway in the middle of the cavern that led past the rooms intersecting another larger hallway running left to right then, continuing. The hallway ended at the beginning of another cavern. There was a blast door directly in the middle with observation rooms on either side. The windows were covered. Jackson assumed that the windows peered into the depths of the rest of the cavern he could not see.

"Take a seat in the far room," Illiac said, pointing. "I'll be back in a few moments."

Illiac walked away and disappeared through a locked doorway that he input a code for. Jackson walked to the room and took a seat. It had a small conference table with a half dozen chairs. In the middle was a basketful of fruit and drinks to the side. He grabbed a banana and wolfed it down. Then a soft drink to get his energy up. He ate a mango and a papaya while sipping another cola. When he first entered the room, he had noticed the camera that was very small and almost unnoticeable. He knew that for some reason this group was suspicious of him, maybe they were just paranoid of everyone.

"Tell me what you noticed in his habits," Doctor Bramahh said.

"He initially had some headaches and then some dreams," Illiac said.

"Those are both normal," Bramahh replied. "Did he say what the dreams were about?"

"Just that he was on a beach and saw some people in the distance swimming."

"That is very good," Bramahh said. "It appears that he has been totally converted."

"Are you going to zap him again with the medicine you implanted inside him?" Antonio asked.

"I don't think that is necessary," Bramahh replied. "The dreams are merely a representation of common circumstances. The headaches were a symptom of his brain adapting to the chip. I will keep monitoring the frequencies of the chip and if I deem it necessary, will introduce more of my serum into his blood stream."

"You're the doctor," Antonio said. Let's go talk to our boy. And Illiac, well done. I'm sorry about your men, but we all knew the risks. Atkinson will give us all we need. We will be in control of global finances once we spring the trap with him and the other two. That reminds me. They will be arriving in the next two days. The Russian part was giving us problems, but they have been resolved. Let's go see Jackson."

At the top of the adjoining ridge to the south, the field operative had been dozing from the heat and humidity when he suddenly heard the muffled sounds of the helicopter. It had no running lights and took him almost a full minute to find it in his binoculars. Once he did, he estimated its destination on the west slope of the larger ridge.

"What the hell," he thought. "There is nothing there. Wait, I see it. Pretty damn dim."

He continued to watch while the seemingly invisible gates opened and the helicopter landed inside, the gates closing quickly behind it. The agent could barely see the inside before the gates closed, enough to determine it was a large cavern of some sort.

Moving his binocular straight up to the silhouette of the large ridge, he calculated the location from the western edge; the third small peak over. Loading up his laptop, he was able to determine the exact coordinates.

"Sir," the Agent spoke into his phone. "You were correct. A helicopter flew into the ridge and disappeared. I was able to get a visual before and during landing. Sending you the coordinates now."

"Excellent," Frank replied. "I'll send someone to relieve you. You will remain hidden in the area until we get a team out there."

Antonio, Illiac and Doctor Bramahh walked into the room. Jackson was finishing off another cola and banana.

"Sorry," he said. "Just found that I was hungry. How are you Doc and Antonio?"

"We are fine," Antonio replied. "Illiac tells me that you were stellar in planning and executing the mission."

"Thank you," Jackson replied. "But I wouldn't be here if Illiac hadn't saved my ass."

Illiac still could not understand why Jackson thought he had done so, but if it made him trust him more, he would go along with it. Illiac thought that perhaps the chip had sent some mixed signals but decided not to bring it up to the doctor since Jackson and he were getting along so well.

"Regardless," Antonio said. "You both did a great job and deserve some R&R. Why don't you take tomorrow off and go to the beach, sightseeing or something? It will be good for you."

"I have other plans tomorrow if you know what I mean," Illiac said, grinning.

The men laughed knowing he would be with his girlfriend.

"Alright," Antonio said. "We will have Scott show Jackson around. He has some favorite haunts on the island and I'm sure you'll enjoy some of them. Once you return, I have something of importance to show you. For now, get some sleep. The Doc may want to give you a brief checkup. If so, he'll catch up with you shortly."

The two operatives walked away laughing and joking. When they had turned the corner, Antonio faced the doctor, his eyes narrowing."

"I need your honest assessment," Antonio said. "Can we count on Jackson moving forward?"

"Based on what Illiac told me, he has no symptoms out of the ordinary," Bramahh said. "Everything appears normal like I told you before. Let me give them both a checkup and I will decide. However, all the readings from the chip are within standard operating norms. You worry too much my friend."

"That's what I'm paid for," Antonio said. "If we fail, I won't be happy, and you know the consequences."

"All too well," Bramahh said, walking away and scratching his chin. "If I introduce more serum into his blood, it could make the headaches worse for Jackson. It could also trigger the return of dreams that would take him back to some of his former memories. I must tread carefully."

He decided to give Jackson a checkup. At least he would be able to tell Antonio he had done his best, but that may not be enough for him to retain his head on his body.

HENRY was in the crisis suite. It was time to do one ping on Luca's tracker. Once he did so, they would turn it off so that it would not register a measurable frequency.

"Send one signal," Phil said.

"Roger," Henry replied, working on his laptop. "Signal sent and ping back received. He is at the coordinates the field operative sent."

"Good," Phil replied. "We know where they are so, turn it off and let's get all the teams in place. Leonid, calling across the room. How far out is Melor's team?"

"They just landed sir,"

"Good, I'll have Frank meet them and get them near target.

One of the doctors at the cavern was removing bullets and their fragments from Luca's shoulder. An X-ray had pinpointed all of them and he deftly removed each fragment. Pulling out a couple that looked odd, like they were made of Teflon wrapped with a lead jacket at the tip. He wondered it they were some type of poison meant to kill Luca so if someone kidnapped him, no company secrets would be revealed. Working before as a researcher, he knew there was nothing that could dissolve Teflon. He had even tried Dioxygen Difluoride, the gas of Lucifer, as well as fluoroantimonic acid that had a pH of -25; nothing worked. So, he walked over to the fume hood where there was a beaker of nitric acid sitting atop a stir plate. He picked up a small pair of double action bone cutters and lowering the glass door on the fume hood, clipped off the end of the Teflon capsule and dropped both parts into the beaker, along with the other fragments he had removed. The sensitive electronic device inside the capsule rapidly dissolved, leaving no trace. Unknowingly, the doctor had destroyed any evidence of a tracker.

In another room, Bramahh was giving Jackson an exam. He placed EKG tabs onto the chest, arm, and back of the neck where the chip was located so he could easily access the reading. The machine was not an EKG machine but a similar modification to adjust the tiny electrodes attached to

Jackson's brainstem.

"Looks like you took a couple of fragments," Bramahh said. "I'll remove those for you."

"Oh, they're just scratches," Jackson said. "I took one out already. If there are more, I'll take them out too."

"I suppose you are pretty adept at removing fragments judging from all the scars on your legs and shoulders," Bramahh said. "Alright, looks like you're good to go. Send in Illiac on your way out."

"Roger."

"How are you Illiac?" Bramahh asked.

"I'm good Doc. How long will this take?"

"Do you feel okay?"

"Yes, fine."

"Then we are done but stay a few moments so that Jackson thinks you were examined too."

"I take it you hooked up the chip?"

"Yes. Everything appears normal. I think our patient is okay and believe that the chip is performing well. If not now, within a few days his memories will be permanently altered."

"Good," Illiac said. "I don't want to kill him. We have become friends."

"That shouldn't be necessary," Bramahh said. "Keep an eye on him just a little longer."

Bramahh knew that he had done his job to the best of his ability and would state so in his report which would go up the ladder quickly. He did not know for sure, but felt that Antonio, despite his audacity, was not the big boss. Despite not knowing the extent of the organization's leadership, it was his belief that Antonio was one of several leaders that answered to someone else. He was not about to snoop around to find out who that was. The last doctor had been thrown into a vat of acid. Word had it the leadership group had thrown in life preservers, laughing when the victim grabbed them while they dissolved in his hands, his blood curdling screams echoing off the walls. Bramahh shuddered to think about it.

IT was 11:00 pm when Mitch and Li Nah hopped into the motorized raft. There were several sets of SCUBA tanks, masks, and swim fins in the bow. Within a few minutes, they rounded Grand Caille Point and headed for the Keyhole where Frank and several members of his team met them. They rappelled to the waiting raft below then, headed toward Pitons Bay to coordinates two and one-half miles away, coordinates that only Mitch and two others were privy to. No one talked while the boat sped across the water, barely visible in the moonlight that reflected off the froth behind the raft and the larger waves around them. About ten minutes later they reached their destination, dropping Frank and one of the team off on the nearby shore. Then, Mitch steered the boat back onto the bay, dropping anchor one hundred yards from the shoreline. They could just make out Frank and the other team member.

"Suit up," Mitch said. "You two, keep a sharp eye out. You know what to do if we get an intruder."

The two put on their tanks and fins, followed by their masks. Falling backward into the water and diving toward the bottom. Mitch turned on his SCUBA flashlight, which lit up the water surrounding them. It was only when the brilliant colors displayed themselves that Li Na realized they were in a coral garden. The intensity of the vibrant colors was amazing, taking her breath away. There were reds, greens, purples, orange, pinks, yellows, and browns; everywhere she looked the colors were breath taking. It was so different than walking along the beach looking into the water. There were so many fish and coral species. Some she recognized, angelfish, sea bass, parrotfish, snapper, and many others. The coral was magnificent too – hidden cup, fire corals, stony corals, and more, as well as a wide variety of plants, lichens, and anemones.

Mitch stopped about forty feet below and moved some rocks out of the way. Li Na wondered what he was doing and then noticed he was uncovering a hidden circular door that the coral had attached itself to. Assured it was clear, he accessed a hidden panel and punched in a code; the door swung open to the side, and they swam in, Mitch closing the door behind them. There was a small tunnel that led in the direction toward shore then, cut back to the right. Li Na could see a red glow above them. They surfaced, emerging into a cavern that surrounded them on all sides. Moving over to the edge of the well-formed pool, Mitch took off his mask and fins, climbing out and giving Li Na a helping hand.

"We keep the lights red, so our night vision stays intact," Mitch said. "Welcome to my laboratory. It was my bosses before and now mine. When we need to do something that only a few people need to know about, we do it here."

"Is this where we can help Jackson?" Li Na asked.

"I hope so," Mitch replied. "It will depend on both skill and luck in several areas. As I said, my former boss anticipated what is happening now. Fortunately, we talked about it and what could be done."

"I gather it is difficult," Li Na responded.

"It is not difficult technically if you know what you're doing," Mitch said. "The difficulty is making the modification so that this organization doesn't know it's been done. Come, I'll show you."

The cavern was in three levels with walkways. Climbing the stairs to the third level, they could clearly see the pool below. From above it looked like a backyard water feature with the same type of edge a typical pool had. Beyond it was a large circular desk with several personnel manning computer monitors.

"What are they doing?" Li Na asked.

"They monitor all our intelligence data," Mitch replied. "They are looking at the latest updates from the crisis suite, as well as satellite feeds, motion detectors, and other security assets. If something happens, we will know immediately."

The two kept walking and entered a room with double, stainless steel doors that said 'authorized personnel only' below the viewport in each. Mitch swung them open to reveal several hospital beds and monitoring equipment. Li Na felt like she had walked into an emergency room.

"What is all this for?" she asked.

"We have every type of equipment needed for surgery on patients that have embedded chips, nanobots, and other advanced technology running through their veins. My predecessor drew a schematic of what control chips for a human could look like today. While we haven't seen Jackson's, I'm guessing it's close."

"What is the working premise?" Li Na asked.

"Basically, the chip will be about an inch square, give or take. To effect mind control it would have been programmed to block out previous memories and use a type of nanobot technology along with medication on occasion to inject into the bloodstream to help enhance the chip modification."

"From what I've seen Jackson is an active operative," she replied. "How would they be able to inject him with medication to ensure the memory block?"

"Easier than you think," Mitch replied. "All they would need to do is place a small reservoir in his body somewhere that would receive a signal from the chip, which would then inject a small amount, perhaps a microgram or more."

"But wouldn't the patient know the reservoir or cylinder was there?"

"Not at all. If I were to put it in, I would place it under the armpit much like a breast implant then, a pouch type reservoir could easily be inserted behind the pectoralis major where it joins the clavicular part of the pec muscle. The patient wouldn't have a clue it was there. Rather than rely on a signal, two small wires could be run under the skin to the chip."

"Where would the chip be located?" Li Na asked.

"The best place would be as close to the brain stem as possible. At least that is where I would put it. Now time for you to practice."

"Practice what?"

"We took the liberty of bringing several swords like yours, both katana's and Wakizashi's. Come."

Exiting the laboratory, the two walked to the far end of walkway and entered a room. Inside was a martial arts training room. The floor was covered with bright blue training mats with four 'rings' set in red and a three-foot square directly in the middle of the room. The walls were covered with every conceivable type of martial arts weapons. At the far end of the room were seven flesh-colored punching dummies with their faces toward the wall. Next to them was a rack of a dozen swords; six long and a matching number of short swords. Li Na gasped at the cleanliness of the room and the training apparatus all around the perimeter. The two walked to the punching dummies.

"We set these up for you to practice," Mitch said. "I'm not sure you need any but given the critical nature of the mission, every edge we can get counts. Look here; we have modified the back near the brainstem area to replicate the chip and its location, as well as probable depth."

Opening the back of one of the punching dummies, a small chip could be seen, along with four tiny wires attached to it; they were scarcely larger in diameter than a thick hair.

"What do you want me to do?" Li Na asked.

"I want you to slice through the epidermal layer and sever these wires leaving no more than a one or one- and one-half inch incision. Can you do that?"

"Yes."

"Good. Start practicing and I'll return shortly. There is some high-density foam over there if you want to practice on that first."

Li Na watched him until he had closed the door then, turned back to the punching dummies. She decided to place some of the foam on the back of the neck of each one. On a table against the wall, she found some or the practice chips and inserted them halfway into the foam which she attached to the neck with electrical tape at the top and bottom. From the sword stand she took a katana and Wakizashi and compared the two to the job that needed to be done. Just what she thought; she settled on the short sword. They were eerily uncanny, like her own and she wondered how Mitch had managed to duplicate them so closely.

Standing behind the dummy she placed the sword inside her left belt and put her left thumb on the Tsuba, pushing the sword from the Saya about one-half inch to unlock the blade. Most people never guessed that a Samurai sword is worn with the blade up to prevent dulling and for ease of draw for the varying cuts a short or long sword could perform. When she drew the sword, she twisted the Saya (scabbard) outward about 35 to 40° allowing the Kissaki or tip to clear it. The draw was silent when it left the Saya, the sign of an expert draw, and the swing so quick the blade sang while it sliced the air. Mitch has quietly slipped back through the door and stood watching while Li Na cut several of the high-density foam targets, inspecting each before practicing another cut. He did not realize that Li Na had felt him enter.

"What do you think?" Li Na asked, startling him.

"I'm not a master swordsman, but looks like you're hitting your mark well," he said.

"The sound of a singing sword could be the last sound you ever hear if you're the target. I believe the task is very doable."

"I heard the sound when the blade cut the air," Mitch said.

"Could you explain more to me about swords and how they

work? I've always been curious."

She looked at him for a moment to determine if he were earnest or not.

"I will explain it like my instructor did for us," Li Na said. "The sound or sounds a sword makes reveal whether it will or will not cut through a target. The key goal of what I do is achieving the proper edge line or hasuji as the Japanese call it. If done properly, the sword's edge should be the same angle as the cutting path. If it tilts one way or other while the sword is swung, the cut likely will not make it through the target. That's important if you're trying to sever a head. The sound will tell you if you did it correctly or not, the sword wind or tachikaze in Japanese. Done correctly the tachikaze will sound like a sharp whistling; if wrong, the sound will be a flat whoosh or no sound at all. Ideally, the tachikaze should be heard from the beginning of the swing to the cut. That is when the power is needed to initiate the cut."

"Why do you get different sounds?" Mitch asked.

"My instructor was a Japanese aeronautical engineer," Li Na said. "In a sword, like an airplane wing, the blade generates a thickness noise and a loading noise. When air is pushed out of the way by the thickness of the spine of the blade, that is the noise that occurs when the blade pushes the air and then, the air reoccupies the same space once the blade passes through it. The faster the blade moves the louder the thickness sound. Loading noise is generated when the blade acts directly on the surrounding air. It generates forces that cause the air to literally speed up, change direction, or slow down. The noise generated from unsteady loading is the dominant source of the sound from a blade moving at relatively low speeds."

"That's seems very technical as a requirement for learning the sword," Mitch grinned.

"You must know every part of it," Li Na replied. "It is an art and a science, not a Hollywood movie. When hasuji is good, the sound is an Aeolian tone, names after Aeolus, the Greek ruler of the winds. Think of air passing a cylinder; vortexes of air are shed from top and bottom in an alternating sequence at a regular frequency. This is known as a von Karman vortex street. When a blade cuts the air, you hear a tone, like that of wind passing electrical transmission lines; the tone is due to the unsteady loading noise, which is very uniform or regular, but only at a few specific frequencies. And, because the back part of a katana or Wakizashi is not tapered, the sound is a similar vortex street to a cylinder. If the sound is bad, the flow over the blade is separating in a chaotic fashion, which means it has a larger region of turbulent flow. Of course, turbulent flow is randomized, which generates the whooshing sound. Therefore, the thickness of the blade and its geometry, especially of the edge are key to generating tachikaze when swung. If the blade has a groove along the back edge, what is called a bo-hi, the sound generated is louder than swords without it, but because of this it can be difficult to know if your hasuji is proper."

"Sounds like an awful lot of information to determine if a cut is a good one or not," Mitch said, grinning.

"The knowledge is a component part," Li Na replied. "Hearing the right sound means I can forget that opponent because he is dead before he hits the ground."

"So, with multiple opponents, it is crucial?" Mitch asked.

"Exactly."

"How do you feel about the proper technique so far?" Mitch asked.

"Let's see."

Li Na went to the furthermost punching dummy on the right and took off the high-density foam collars she had put on each. Then, standing about five feet behind the dummy, drew her sword and re-sheathed it; stepping left, she repeated the action on three dummies. Ten seconds later she had finished. The two looked carefully at each of the chips and wire leads. They had been severed perfectly without touching the chip.

"Outstanding," Mitch said, looking at her in admiration.

He knew if they could get to Jackson, somehow that he could make him whole again.

CHAPTER 7

F RANK met Melor at the airport. With their combined teams, they had sixteen well-trained operatives. Their plane of course was private; Frank had two vans nearby. Loading their gear into them they headed toward the rendezvous with the rest of Franks men.

"Good to meet you Melor," Frank said, climbing in. "I'll explain things on the way."

"Nice to meet you as well," Melor replied.

"We are about twenty miles from target," Frank said, showing Melor the map. "I will drop you off here then, I need to come back. Your team will work with the three operatives on site, and they will bring you up to speed."

"The only information I have is that there is a cavern or cave where this group is located," Melor replied. "Do you have more information?"

"Not yet," Frank said. "The location has a camouflaged gate of some sort that they open and close. It blends in so well during the day it is virtually impossible to determine the outline. At night there are red lights to maintain night vision when the gates open, but even they are difficult to see if you're not looking right at them."

"Any idea about how large the cavern is?" Melor asked.

"It appears to be quite large," Frank replied. "From what our field operatives relayed, it is about four hundred feet long minimally and at least two hundred to three hundred feet deep."

"Much larger than I expected," Melor said.

"Us to," Frank replied. "Both Phillip Ross head of CIA and Andros believe this is their main operational base. By the time we get there, my full team will be on site. It will be up to you to recon the entire area and determine a way in without being seen."

"That is a asking a lot," Melor said, smiling.

"I know," Frank replied. "We have surprise on our side so far. However, I suspect there are motion detectors, booby traps, and other potential hazards awaiting you."

"That's what we are trained for," Melor replied.

"To assist you, I have two technicians coming out that should be able to find motion sensors or anything else with a signal."

"That will help," Melor said. "It looks like it will be a night maneuver."

"Correct," Frank said. "Find what you can during the day and plot your route so you can find it. As you know, it gets mighty dark in the jungle at night."

"Right."

Illiac had taken Jackson out the back side of the facility. He was on his way to see his girlfriend. It was obvious he was in a hurry and did not want to be a babysitter to Jackson. Just outside the door, hidden in the undergrowth, was a slim man smoking a cigarette.

"Ah Scott," Illiac said. "This is Jackson. Antonio wants you to show him around some of the island today. Show him a good time. He needs to relax. I'll see you later."

"Pleased to meet you," Scott said, holding out his hand.

Jackson shook his hand while looking into his hazel brown

eyes. He saw no fear in them, only professionalism. Scott's eyes looked like those of a tiger.

"What's first on our agenda?" Jackson asked.

"Would you like a woman?"

"No," Jackson replied. "Some other time perhaps."

"I had to ask," Scott said humorously. "Don't want Illiac or Antonio breathing down my back because I didn't. Well then, how about I show you around parts of the island. Do you like sea food?"

"Yes," Jackson replied. "I love it."

"Good, after a tour of some of the scenery, I'll take you to a great restaurant at a hotel that serves the best I've found. It overlooks the bay. There are some good walking trails below that we can check out too."

"Lead the way," Jackson said. "Where are we going?"

"First, we will head to Cape Moule à Chique," Scott replied. "It is on the southern tip of the island. The views are spectacular. When I want to relax, it's a nice place to go."

In minutes the two were headed toward Vieux Fort on the south end of St. Lucia.

"Frank," the agent said. "Just picked up Jackson in a car headed south; him and a driver."

"Roger," Frank said. "Mitch, we spotted Jackson, heading south from the facility area."

"Good," Mitch replied. "Activate Jackson's tracker, he shouted across the cavern to the personnel at the monitors. "Give me minute by minute updates."

"Will we be able to follow him now?" Li Na asked.

"Yes," Mitch replied. "We could have tracked him inside the facility but did not want to risk discovery of the tracking device. Since he is outside, they won't be able to detect it and we can follow him everywhere he goes."

"What do I need to do?" she asked.

"Be ready at a moments notice. We will only get one chance."

Li Na understood all too well and readied herself for what she needed to do. She yearned for Jackson to be by her side but could not let on how she felt, even around these professional colleagues. She returned to the martial arts training room and performed one more cut to the back of the punching dummies, checking her work. Satisfied, she donned a cover-up dress with brilliant embroidery and breezy ladder trim. The dress had an empire waistline with open ladder trim on a bodice front and lantern ¾-sleeves. Lined with linen, it felt comfortable and was easy to pull over her head with a V-split round neckline. It had a classic Caribbean pattern with red flowers to match the embroidery and light blue petals with green stems. The pattern was elegant and blended well with tourists. In the dark, it looked like shadows of the night. Li Na would blend in perfectly in a subtle way and not be overly gaudy. The hemline was about five inches above her knees. She grabbed her fashionable dark gray leather backpack and attached her sword to it in its bag. She looked like she was going or coming from the beach. Decked with sunglasses and hat, she looked quite the opposite of the deadly assassin she was.

Mitch entered the training area and secretly gasped at her beauty. Jackson was a lucky man he thought.

"Time to get going," Mitch said. "I have a man waiting on the raft to take you ashore where you'll meet Tim, and two more of our agents. We will send you the tracking information."

"Do you have a waterproof bag?" she asked.

"Yes, waiting at the pool with your SCUBA tanks."

They made their way back to the pool and Li Na took off the dress to reveal a plain, two-piece, royal blue bikini beneath. The men and women performing their tasks couldn't help looking at her. The looks were not lustful but in admiration. Placing her sword, pack, dress and sandals in the waterproof bag, she slipped on the single tank and fins and slid into the pool. Taking a light from Mitch, she sank below the surface and emerged from the door surrounded by the coral garden. She looked carefully around like she had been instructed. Seeing no one, she swam in the lower areas and out from the shore. Now that it was daylight, she was overwhelmed at the beauty of the coral and sea floor. Finally making her way to the surface, helping hands quickly pulled her aboard the raft and they were off to nearby Sugar Beach Resort, just over a half mile distant.

She jumped off the raft with her bag and quickly walked through the huts and lounge chairs, grabbing a quick shower along the way, drying herself while she walked. The Bayside restaurant was to her left across a pool, not Olympic size, but considerably large. She always wondered why someone would put in a pool right next to miles of endless beach and swimming. The beauty and peace of the sea and landscape surrounding her made her think about Jackson. This was such a beautiful resort that she wished the two of them could come back to once this mess was over.

About two hundred feet later, she turned left, winding around back to the right past the Rainforest Spa and out to a small, unmarked parking lot where the three agents waited. She made her way back to the trunk, which was ajar; taking the items out of her bag, she slipped on a dry bra and thong then, the dress. The driver could see just enough through the opening where the trunk joined the body of the car. He got his eyes full of her alabaster skin and pert firm breasts; a tiny glimpse before she pulled the dress over her head. She opened her leather bag and checked her suppressed 9mm and two spare magazines, making sure she had one round in the pipe, or chamber as the uninitiated called it. Satisfied, she opened the front passenger side door and climbed in.

"I'm Li Na," she said, shaking all their hands.

Fresh in from Botswana, the agents had been well briefed on her exploits and were thankful her sword was in its bag.

"Any updates?" she asked.

"You can follow him on this," Tim said. "The red arrow. By the way, this is John and Ken."

The two men nodded.

"You'll notice he is on the southern tip of the island."

"That's not far from here," she replied. "Can we approach closely?"

"Not close enough without binoculars," Tim replied. "I have been ordered to not get too close until we can come up with a strategy to nab him."

"I agree," Li Na replied. "He is too skilled to be taken easily so, it must be plausible. Are we the only group?"

"I have three more men we can call in quickly," Tim said. "They'll be tailing us a little way back."

"Why are you all dressed so shoddily," she asked.

"The island is poor in many areas," Tim said. "We need to blend in. Not too poor or too rich. Too poor looking and you cannot get into any of the restaurants or hotels; too rich and you'll be a target of criminals, just like in Chicago or New York."

"Makes sense," Li Na murmured.

The group made their way to the southern tip of the island, past the airport, about halfway between it and Moule à Chique where they turned to the right and parked near the Chique Retreat. With their binoculars, they could clearly see Jackson and Scott who appeared to be exploring the light house and airport radar and antenna arrays then, disappeared.

"What do you make of that," Li Na asked. "They're beyond our view."

"From what Mitch and Frank told us," Tim replied. "They just came off a mission so I'm guessing they're sightseeing, trying to relax."

"This is a great place to do it," Ken said. "Look at that view, you can see everything from here. It's spectacular."

"I don't disagree with you," John replied. "Makes me feel like we're not on a mission."

"But we are," Tim replied sternly. "Don't lose focus and don't forget who we're up against."

Li Na could tell the team had great respect for Jackson and his prowess in tight, dangerous spots.

"How well do you know Jackson?" she asked.

"We have all served on various missions with him," Tim said. "Like most others, he's pulled out butts out of a sling more often than we care to admit. If it were not for him, you'd have three other agents with you right now. What about you, how did you meet?"

"I first met him on the Big Cypress, Seminole Indian Reservation in Florida," she replied. "Initially, I was the adversary, in a good way. I ended up helping him rescue a business partners daughter and then went on another mission against the Chinese. Both ending in success. Like you, I have come to admire his skills."

Tim knew the relationship between the two was more than admiration, but it was never discussed among the men. The agents could sense that she was as cunning as she was beautiful, as calm as she was deadly. Looking at her, she seemed concentrated totally on Jackson. Her face was calm, only a slight wrinkle of the brow. She was planning already. Tim knew no matter what happened she would not fail the team or her man.

SCOTT and Jackson were admiring the view from the top of Moule à Chique. They had parked the car and walked up the steep concrete path next to the old light house on their right. Jackson was enamored with the architecture of the building, which seemed well kept compared to the rusting lighthouse beyond. Right next to the lighthouse on the concrete path was a chain link fence surrounding a military olive-green communication module with a radar mast on top. He supposed it had something to do with the airport radar system. Jackson particularly admired the black stone walls with white mortar between the bricks and a white trimmed fascia, the corners of the building painted aqua blue. The view was spectacular. It was a photographer's paradise. A clear day and light breeze allowed views for miles. The airport was as clearly seen as if it were right next to them, despite its distance of just under two miles. He had clear views of Maria Major Island a short distance to the east, along with Anse Des Sables and Sandy beaches. To the west were St. Lucia Marine terminals and a cruise ship at dock. Further west were Noir Bay and Laborie. The darker blue of the deep sea, blending into a light aqua green as it neared shore was like those in splendid landscape photographs and paintings that while magnificent, never really captured the vivid colors of nature as witnessed by the naked eye. He inhaled the fresh air like it was the first time he had ever breathed it. It made him feel alive and worry free. Then, the nagging feeling came back. It was always something he could not put his finger on but deep down, he knew something was wrong. Despite his friendship with Illiac, it was a subject he dared not discuss until he could put his finger on it and so, kept the nagging feeling bottled up.

Finished admiring the view, he caught Scott on his cell phone. Immediately, the operative in him wondered what was up.

"Good news," Scott said. "How would you like to do a pick-up game of soccer or run at a nice stadium?"

"Either or both would be great," Jackson replied.

"Great. I have a friend at the Soufriere Mini Stadium that can let us in, and we can have fun for the afternoon then, take a swim and eat dinner."

"Sounds great, but I'm starving now," Jackson said. "Can we stop someplace and get a quick bite?"

"No problem," Scott said. "I'm starving too. I know this great joint that sells finger foods over on Clarke Street near

Independence Square."

Scott called ahead and ordered take out French fries, breaded shrimp, and a small salad. Only a short drive away, Scott ran in to pick up the food and was back in an instant. The smell from the white Styrofoam containers wafted up to their nostrils and made their mouths water. Parking the car next to the park, they walked through the wrought iron gates, down a red brick, herringbone path leading toward the monument in the center, which looked surprisingly like a smaller version of the Washington Monument. They were about to set on one of the benches along the path closer to the water feature but instead, opted to sit in the shade at the top steps of a pavilion to their immediate left.

Sitting, they wolfed down the food and drinks. To their immediate right, directly across the Clarke Street was St. Paul's Church, its red trimmed windows set against a white wall with a white cross on top, somehow matched the design of the park and stood like a sentinel overlooking the front gates.

"This is not as pretty as Moule à Chique, but it is relaxing," Jackson said. "What time is the pick-up game?"

"In about thirty minutes," Scott replied. "We better hurry."

Tim and the team had parked kitty corner down the street across from Martin Luther King Street where they could monitor the target. They had even followed their lead in getting lunch from the same location, casually eating while Li Na used her binoculars to keep a close eye on Jackson and his companion.

"They're finished with their food and moving," Li Na said. "Walking to their car. Don't get too close."

"This ain't my first radio sister," Tim said, grinning.

They tailed about a half mile behind the target, watching it turn left on St. Judes Highway. After about six miles they reached the area near Laborie Beach and were still headed up the coast road toward the direction of Soufriere. There were enough cars on the road for them to blend into the traffic and maintain a leisurely pace. Because the tracker was working, they fell further behind not wanting to be spotted.

"Do you think they are headed back to the facility?" Li Na asked. "That will be a big problem for us."

"I don't think so," Tim replied. "What do you think Ken?"

"I was wondering the same thing, but isn't it too early in the day?"

"Let's put ourselves in their shoes," John interrupted. "If we had just come off a mission and were relaxing, what is the one thing we would really enjoy doing?"

"Have a beer and dinner," Tim replied. "An interesting thought."

"I agree," Li Na said. "Maybe they are headed to a beach and then dinner? It would fit John's hypothesis."

"Well, let's not speculate too much," Tim said. "I'll just follow them and see where they go."

The four rode in silence, watching the tracker on the small laptop.

"John, get out your map of Soufriere," Tim said. "Looks like they angled up to the north and slightly west. What's there?"

"It looks like they stopped at the Soufriere Mini Stadium," John said. "That's a match to the streets and location of the tracker. Guessing, I'd say they're going to play soccer."

"That sounds like something Jackson would do," Li Na said, a smirk on her face. She knew him too well. He would be excited to burn some energy.

"We better not use the same route," Tim said. "Give me an alternate way to get a visual."

"The road turns into Church Street," Ken said, following the map with his finger. "Once we are in town, take the second street left, it's Sir Arther Lewis Street. Okay, good so far. Now, one block down, take a right on Cemetery Street. That's good. The fourth street down is Palmiste Road, turn right."

"Where will that take us?" Tim asked.

"It bends right and the first street on the right is adjacent to the stadium," John said. "There is an inn just before on the right. We should be able to park near there, maybe in the inn's lot."

"There's also a copper factory across the street on the northwest corner of the field," Ken said. "Can't be more than about fifty yards from the track."

The group made a quick pass by the factory and came back a few minutes later, parking near the inn in the corner of the Shoppers Choice strip mall. Tim and Li Na walked the short distance to the copper factory. Making sure no one was around, they quickly hopped the fence and squeezed between two of the buildings on the east end of the factory where they had a clear view of the field. Beyond it, the tops of houses blended into the far part of Soufriere Bay, the Pitons jutting skyward into an azure sky. In a few moments, John and Ken joined them. Li Na had brought her pack and pulled out a monocular. She could see Jackson clearly; a tear almost escaped but she kept her composure.

"I see a group approaching from the other end of the field," John said. "I think it's a pick-up game."

"Hmmmm," Tim mused.

Jackson and Scott were standing in the middle of the field when the group walked up with smiles on their faces looking forward to a friendly game.

"I see two of you," the Leader said. "We only need one more man. You can change up if you want."

"No need," Jackson said. "Scott, you play, they're your friends. I'm going to run sprints."

"Are you sure?" Scott asked.

"Certain," Jackson responded. "I never was the best skilled at soccer anyway."

"Okay," Scott replied.

The group chose their team and began playing while Jackson walked to the west end of the field and checked out the track. It was 400m; a MONDO, one of the best made. Surveying it, Jackson paced off a few distances. He took off his pants to reveal a bathing suit beneath, hoping to go for a swim later. He began performing split squats and walking lunges, stretching his legs and warming up with short jogs, faster and faster while he readied for the exercise. He determined he would do eight 40s, 60s, and 80s. The pickup game was underway by the time he had warmed up and started his first 40m sprint.

"What's he doing?" Tim asked.

"He's doing a routine his friend Lunadi taught him," Li Na said. A 20x40x20 or jog-sprint-jog with a 15-second rest between."

"You mean he jogs the first distance then sprints?" Tim asked

"Yes," Li Na replied. "A great fat burning and conditioning exercise. He will continue without a break, except a small rest interval between and will finish in about forty minutes."

The four continued to carefully watch. While Tim and Li Na watched Jackson and the game, Ken and John checked out the surrounding area looking for spotters from the organization just in case; there were none. It was likely they felt secure and secretive on the island and that no intruders could have tracked them.

Nearly an hour later, Jackson began drinking from a large water bottle he had brought with him while sitting on the grass watching the game. Scott and a couple of his friends approached, the first forty-five-minute half ending in their friendly match.

"Do you want to play?" Scott asked.

"Not now," Jackson said. "I'm burned out from the sprints. Are you done with the first half?"

"Yes," Scott said. "Another half to go. The restaurant I was going to take you to is over on Hummingbird Beach about a half-mile from here. Maybe you could wait there and swim?"

"That's sounds great," Jackson smiled. "I could use a good swim to cool off."

"See that strip mall down there," Scott said, pointing. "Walk down the street to it and then left on Palmiste Road. Keep going, you'll come to Cemetery Road, there's a fire station on the left corner so you can't miss it. Cross the street and walk down to the beach then right along the shore. About three hundred yards up you'll be on Hummingbird beach. Ask a local if you get lost."

"Are there any landmarks?"

"Yeah, there's a group of buildings with red roofs and the one past those is the restaurant with a green roof. You can't miss it; the beach ends just past them."

"I'll see you there."

Picking up his pants and water bottle, Jackson began walking. The streets were not like back home with sidewalks, so he followed locals along the road, mimicking their movements when cars passed.

"John and Ken," Tim spoke into his comm. "Follow him, keep a long distance. Do not make him suspicious."

Jackson walked, enjoying the crowded neighborhoods and the salt air. Although humid, it was pleasant and had a sweet smell from so many natural flowers. He reached the fire station and had to wait a few minutes because of heavy traffic then, like the locals, dodged quickly across the street and walked until the road ended. There was a cemetery to his right. Continuing, he passed a fisherman's gas station and a group of buildings that looked like boat repair shops. He walked onto a small dock; looking to his right, he saw the red roofed buildings Scott had mentioned. Across the bay on mirror smooth water rode a five-masted schooner. At least he thought that was what it was called. It's blue and white paint made it look like it was made for the bay in which it sat. Backtracking on the dock a few yards, he jumped down onto the beach, which seemed rockier than he expected and wound his way around the end of the boat repair buildings.

There was a long grove of trees to his right through which he could see the cemetery, the graves seemed very old; he reminded himself to check up on their history. Past the trees, the beach quickly opened, and he could see the beach end about two hundred yards distant. Not wanting to wait, he jogged forward. Jackson knew he was in the right place when he saw a sign for Hummingbird Beach Resort when he passed their grass thatched Tiki huts and lounge chairs. Just past them he dropped his pants and shirt and ran into the warm waters of the bay. Backstroking from shore the water felt soothing after the intense sprints. He was barely able to reach the bottom with his feet, his toes digging into the sand and pebbles. Treading water, he slowly turned, taking in his surroundings. The Pitons were magnificent, rising to touch the sky. He seldom saw nature in such splendor, and it relaxed him. He swam for a little while and then, exhausted and relaxed, made it back to shore and lay on the sand, falling asleep.

John and Ken had made it to the end of the dock, sitting on its edge, pretending to look into the water. They watched Jackson discreetly until he lay down.

"He was swimming and now laying on the beach," John spoke into his comm. "I think he is asleep."

"What's near him?" Tim asked.

"He's in front of a resort, not sure which one," John replied. "There's a restaurant with a large veranda covering a seating area just beyond."

"They may eat in one of those locations," Tim said. "Maintain surveillance."

"The game is ending," Li Na said. "We better get to our car."

"Roger."

The two had no sooner reached their car than they noticed Scott speed by. Hurriedly, the two followed a discreet distance. Watching their target pull into the parking lot of the resort, they went up a little way, made a U-turn and found a place to park then, walked to the dock and met up with Ken and John. On the way, Tim called for the rest of his team.

"What do you think?" Tim asked.

"Our guess is they will eat here later," Ken replied. "They'll likely head back to the facility after that. This will be our only chance to get him."

"I agree," John said. "We may need to take out his companion."

"You know him better than the rest of us," Tim said. "Any ideas?"

"I'm not sure he will act the same," Li Na said. "If he does, they will eat early and then, enjoy the scenery until dark before they head back. Didn't you say that Mitch implied he may have recurring dreams?"

"Yes," Tim said.

"I think I have an idea," Li Na told them. "What is around the restaurant, the one with the large, covered dining area?"

"Only the Hummingbird Resort," Ken said. "There is a road that goes past it leading to what locals call the Keyhole on the northwest side of Rachette Point; that point there, beyond the beach."

They stared as a group, each trying to come up with a strategy. The silence became intolerable.

"I think my idea will work," Li Na said. "We will need a boat near the point and the rest of your men up top."

She explained her strategy in detail, the men nodding in approval with smiles on their faces. They thought it just might work. Regardless, it would be their only chance. The group watched while the two targets swam until late afternoon. Resting in the sun then, swimming, back and forth until they had their fill. Tim and his men had anticipated where they would go and had guessed correctly.

Already sitting under the veranda of the restaurant, the team was seated at various tables when the two targets walked up the beach-side stairs and were seated by a waiter wearing a light pink shirt and dark jeans. He took a drink order and reappeared a few moments later with a tray of fruity alcoholic beverages and began serving several tables. There were about twenty patrons spread throughout the dining area. Tim marveled at the view of the Petite Piton to the south. The targets were setting just to the right of it and wouldn't consider him a threat looking past them at the sharp volcanic mound.

The mix of people was perfect for surveillance. He just hoped Li Na's strategy worked. His men were all in place and it would soon be go time. The table and chairs were a mix of polished wood and wicker and wood. The red squares of the Terracotta tile floor softened the rays of the sun, scattering them around the tables, where the sun's rays reflected off the tops of the tables and glasses while shadows began to lengthen. It was a beautiful setting, with palms and banana plants adjacent to the dining area and the lap of the waves hitting the beach barely audible over the clank of glasses and soft conversations. Tim had spoken to a waiter earlier to reserve a specific table and gave him a generous tip to sit an Asian woman who would be coming in.

Li Na watched the dining room from the hostess area. She spotted Tim and the rest of her crew. Then, she saw Jackson with his colleague. Her heart and body yearned for him. She let her hair down and shook it out, so it was soft and flexible, running her fingers through it. Tim had instructed her where to sit based on target position. The angle at which she sat to the targets would make it impossible for them to see her face. It was obvious to the other patrons that she wasn't the typical dowdy tourist. Li Na walked slowly to the table, mincing a little, slightly and provocatively swaying her hips. The entire group of patrons, men and women, almost in one unit, paused when she stood by the table to be seated, gasping at her elegant beauty. Jackson, noticing everyone looking the same direction, glanced up. His heart stopped. Li Na shook her head so that her hair fell across her left cheek. The sun's rays having softened, reflected like gold off her jet-black hair. Jackson could not keep his eyes off her. He stared at her at every opportunity. Scott could see he was distracted.

"Caution friend," Scott smiled. "A woman has always been the downfall of an agent."

"True, but this is a special woman," Jackson replied. "It doesn't take a rocket scientist to see that."

"Still," Scott said. "Focus on the food first, women later."

The two men laughed softly though Scott's words didn't keep Jackson from becoming lost in thought. His dreams came back to him, everyone of them in clear focus. While he stared at Li Na, the images were a match. He kept hoping she would turn his way so he could finally see her face. The hair and skin and the outline of her face were a perfect match to his dreams. He slowly ate the seafood linguini he had ordered that promised a mix simmered in a dreamy herb and cream sauce tossed with hot pasta, mozzarella and parmesan cheese. It was delicious. Having ordered coconut cake, he savored it with a cup of coffee, all the while taking every opportunity to watch this beautiful woman. She was the woman he had seen in his dreams, of that he was sure, and he determined that no matter what, he would meet her face to face. She ate only a small salad with a glass of water. He was suddenly alert when he overheard her ask the waiter a question.

"Sir," Li Na said. "I have heard about the Keyhole on Rachette Point. Where is that?"

"It is just over there ma'am," the waiter said, pointing. "You can walk up the road; it's about a ten-minute walk. The walking trails are easy to see. There's just enough time to watch a magnificent sunset."

"Thank you, I'm going right now," Li Na said, standing and leaving cash and a generous tip, bringing a beaming smile to the waiter's face. She deliberately turned the opposite way from Jackson while slinging her hair to the right side of her face, the sun's rays again bouncing through and off it with a golden sheen. Being a sexy woman, she exuded it deliberately while walking toward the exit. And again, the patrons gawked at her, like they couldn't help it, her own colleagues among them.

"Damn," Ken said. "That is one sexy woman."

"Don't forget who she belongs to," John retorted, a broad smile on his face.

Tim was right behind her, out the door in a non-obvious manner.

"I'm going to meet this woman," Jackson said. "You can come or not but let me talk to her privately."

"Okay," Scott replied, paying the bill. "But don't say I didn't warn you."

The two followed Li Na out of the restaurant, Ken and John not far behind. Other patrons and locals were also walking to and from the point. The steady number made for discreet and easy surveillance. Jackson was walking faster and passed Tim on his way to Li Na. He slowly gained on her and finally caught up at the top of the point in a small pull off, the trail just behind.

"Excuse me Miss," Jackson said, Li Na turning to face him. He froze in his tracks. He knew her, but how?

"Yes," she said. "Can I help you."

"You seem so familiar to me," he said. "Have we met?"

"I don't think so," she said. "I am Li Na and you."

"Jackson, Jackson Black."

"I think I would remember if we had met," Li Na said. "I'm going to watch the sunset. You seem nice enough. Would you care to join me?"

"I would love to," Jackson responded.

They walked down a trail and sat on a large rock, facing west, watching the sun sink toward the sea. Li Na, excited, engaged him in conversation and they began telling each other how they had grown up.

"Would you like to go for a swim?" Li Na asked.

"But you don't have a suit," Jackson said.

"Yes, I do," she replied. Lifting her dress and revealing the suit beneath. "See. What are you waiting for?"

Jackson quickly took off his pants and shirt revealing only a pair of shorts.

"Oh my," Li Na whispered. "Aren't we in shape."

It was not quite dark when Scott approached, the setting sun momentarily blinding him from a clear view of Li Na and Jackson. Tim and his men walked up behind him, pistols in hand.

"Don't move," Ken said. "Give us your money, watch, and wallet."

Scott stared at them. He had no weapon and realized he would not be able to take them on.

"I don't have much," he said. "You can have it all."

Hearing the voices, Jackson turned, confronting the men behind him. He and Li Na had been standing below the top of the Keyhole, about twenty feet above the high-tide level.

"You there," John said sternly. "Give us your money or we'll throw you in. We want the woman too."

Jackson stepped forward, throwing his wallet toward them.

"You get the woman over my dead body," he said.

"If that's how you want it," Tim replied.

The small group walked closer to him, pushing Scott ahead. Time seemed to stand still in anticipation. Jackson heard the sing of the blade and the sting as it sliced open the back of his neck. He began turning his head to look over his shoulder, a surprised look on his face. He had barely turned when the hilt struck the side of his temple. Stunned, he stumbled and fell twenty feet into the bay below, the salt water rushing into the incision Li Na's sword had made. Scott, taking the opportunity, made a run for it. The agents fired three shots, making sure they came close, but didn't hit him. Below, Tim's other agents pulled Jackson's body from the water. One of the agents immediately pulled out a syringe and stabbed Jackon in the neck, injecting him with 30 mg of esketamine.

"You sure that's not too much," an agent asked.

"A little more than normal, but he's very fit."

Tim, Li Na, and the others had dove into the water and climbed aboard. The boat headed to the laboratory as fast as it could. Jackson's vitals were good despite the ventilated foil covering they had slipped over his head to prevent signal tracking in case the sword had missed its target. Two- and one-half miles later they anchored directly above the coral garden then, put Jackson's unconscious body into a waterproof life pod with ballast control and ushered him to the lab. Surfacing inside, technicians quickly removed his limp body and rushed Jackson to the medical room, prepping him for the work Mitch and his team would execute to alter the damage of the chip.

MELOR'S SVR team arrived on site to join with Frank's CIA team. This wasn't the first time that American's and Russian's had worked together. The CIA agents had kept the area under surveillance for the past twenty-four hours. During that time, they had taken magnified satellite photos and flew a small drone overhead to get a better look at areas that might provide a way into the facility.

"Susan, this is Melor," Frank called out when the group got out of the vehicles.

"Pleased to meet you," Susan said, shaking Melor's hand and nodding to his team members. "These are the rest of my team, I'll let you introduce yourselves.

The group chatted among themselves, getting to know each other a little while Susan continued to observe the opening of the facility. It was so well camouflaged that it was difficult to determine the entry despite knowing where it was. Looking directly at it, she could only make out a couple of details on the gates.

"What do you have so far?" Frank asked.

"Well sir," Susan began. "We know where the opening is, but it is difficult to determine the boundary of the gates. Melor, take this other pair of binoculars and I'll try to dial you in. Counting from the north, go to the fourth peak to the south."

"I have it," Melor said.

"Good. About fifty yards more south there is a crevice that appears to be quite deep, the one in dark shadows."

"I have it," Melor replied. "It looks like it may have been an old waterfall."

"Yes, that is it," Susan said. "The entrance is midway between the fourth peak and that crevice. It is difficult to see."

"I see a row of orange flowers almost vertical, but not quite," he said.

"That's it," Susan said. "The flowers mark the right edge of the gate as near as we can tell. It has only opened one time, at night."

"Is there a path to it?" Frank asked.

"Not that we have found," Susan said. "My men did find a few booby traps and marked them. I didn't want to go further until we had the full team and the tech people to scan for electronic devices."

"What's the slope?" Melor asked.

"If you look from that point directly across from us, the elevation changes from about 800 feet to 1,150 feet, perhaps a bit more."

"That's almost twenty percent," Melor said. "Fairly steep but

239

we can handle it."

"Our maps and photos are there on the trunk of the sedan," Susan said. "We can potentially plot a line of attack from them."

"Let's have a look," Melor said. "May I?"

"Certainly," Frank said.

"Both teams, gather around. We need to come up with a strategy and timeline. Susan."

"Right," she replied. "This is what we have so far."

She began to explain the area, allowing the SVR team to familiarize themselves with the terrain and geography. While she was explaining it, two technicians arrived with sweepers and other devices to scan for any gadgets that gave out a frequency and to help detect other booby traps. The discussion continued for over an hour. Finally, with input from the men, Susan and Melor chose a potential route for reconnaissance.

"This looks like our best shot to the gate," Melor said.

"I agree," Susan replied. "Mark it on the topographic map and let's send up a squad of four with the two techs."

"Good idea," Melor said. "Can we scout it with your drone first?"

"I don't see why not," Susan said. "Tom, come over here."

"How can I help you?"

"We need the drone to get a close-up video and photos of this route. Can you plug in the GPS coordinates?"

"Certainly, give me a minute."

"Oh, and make sure the drone is high enough, so it won't be heard or seen," Melor added.

"Roger that."

In no time, Tom has set the mission route and the drone was airborne, relaying video footage to the controller. Susan and Melor watched, directing Tom when to take a close-up photo of specific points.

"Now, back up to a forty-five degree and zoom in as close as you can where the gate area is," Susan said.

When the drone was finished, both teams went over the video footage and pictures several times. Pinpointing kill zones and finalizing the route for a better recon of the area around the gate and what looked like two entrances into the facility. Once they were satisfied, Susan chose two of her men and Melor two of his, along with the technology experts. The six men began a full recon of the path. A matter of waiting, most of the men tried to relax in the shade while the sun climbed the sky, increasing the effects of humidity. Sweat was dripping from every pore; the lack of a breeze served only to enhance the effect. It was like being in a greenhouse on a hot day with all the vents closed and fans off. They waited for what seemed hours for the recon team to bring back their final report.

The facility was quiet. Antonio was trying to determine what to make of Scott's story.

"Explain it to me one more time," Antonio said. "I want to make sure I have it correct."

"We were sitting in the restaurant," Scott said. "Jackson kept staring at this beautiful woman. He couldn't see her face but was determined to talk to her even though I cautioned against it. So, when she left, we followed; he finally caught her at the top of Rachette point and was talking with her when three men walked came up behind me pointing pistols and took my wallet. They looked and dressed like locals, two black and one white."

"Where was Jackson?" Antonio asked.

"Talking to the woman. When he heard the commotion, he turned toward me. The men said they wanted his money and the woman. He said something like over my dead body. The woman then hit him over the head with something, I couldn't see what it was because the sun was in my eyes. He fell over the edge into the water. I heard his body splash when he hit."

"Are you sure it didn't hit the rocks?"

"No, it was water. Besides it was high tide. Anyway, while their attention was diverted, I got the hell out of there. I figured I couldn't help Jackson. They fired several rounds that almost hit me."

"Do you think Jackson is alive?"

"I don't know," Scott replied. "He was unconscious, and it was a long way down. I'm guessing he didn't make it."

"What about the woman?" Antonio asked.

"She appeared to be part of the gang. I think the way she sat in the restaurant was to get our attention and lure us to that spot. It was isolated and we were outnumbered. They were armed and we were not."

"Would you recognize her if you saw her again?" Antonio asked.

"I doubt it," Scott replied. "I was not able to see her face, even when she turned. It was too bright behind her for an identification. Besides, long dark hair grows on trees all over the world."

"Very well," Antonio said. "You may go. I might have more questions later. Send in Doctor Bramahh.

"What do you think?" Antonio asked when Bramahh sat down.

"Everything matches with what Scott told you," Bramahh said. "The time the tracker in the chip went dead coincides with the time frame he gave you."

"Do you think Jackson survived the fall?" Antonio asked

"Probably," Bramahh replied. "It's not the fall that concerns me. If he didn't wake up when he hit the water, he will have drowned. A search so far of the local hospitals doesn't show anyone matching his description having checked in."

"Damn," Antonio said. "I was counting on his skill set to take us to the end."

"You should start looking for a replacement."

"Is there a chance he made it somehow?" Antonio asked.

"There is always a chance," Bramahh replied. "The tracker could be damaged, or he could be wedged in a crevasse or have some type of other interference. I'll keep monitoring the frequency and let you know if we receive the signal again."

"Do that. And Doc, make sure you have another chip ready just in case. I'm thinking of a replacement."

"I have quite a few if you require us to use them."

THE orange and silver life pod surfaced in the pool within the confines of the laboratory, divers surrounding it while pushing it to the edge. Four medical technicians pulled the pod out of the water onto the floor. In less than a minute they had Jackson's body strapped to a gurney and dashing to the medical room where all the needed equipment had been prepped. Li Na got out of the pool quickly and caught up with Mitch, already in the room. The medical team rolled Jackson face down onto a surgical table, so they had ready access to the chip near the top of his spinal cord. Mitch had recruited a retired CIA surgeon for the task, James McElroy.

"I thought you may want to see this," James called out. "Whoever made this cut did it with surgical precision."

"Let me see," Mitch said. "It is exactly what we needed. Thank you, Li Na, well done."

"How did she do it so well?" James asked.

"With a Wakizashi, an eighteen-inch blade," she said softly.

"Is she the one called the black widow?" James whispered into Mitch's ear.

"The same."

"She is certainly deserving of her reputation," James whispered. "I couldn't have done better with my scalpel."

"Can you explain what you're going to do?" Li Na asked.

"We will do several things," James said. "First, we will carefully remove the chip. Mitch's team already has the schematic and details. The replica will be exact so, we will be able to counter any commands the organization may give him if we need to. They have a serum of various medications in a small tube under his armpit; I will empty that and fill it with an adrenaline-based derivative. We will know what dose they are injecting once we analyze the chip. Then, a pause, perhaps you should tell her Mitch."

"Then what?" she asked.

"To pull off the rest of this mission, we are going to do something that no one else has ever done," Mitch said. "We are going to insert a different chip, covered in TEFLON that will allow him to change his appearance at random by changing genetic sequencing with computer generated signals that only he can access using this specially modified Rolex Deepsea. It has the inside thickness we needed for the technology we packed in and is a duplicate of the watch he always wears."

"I asked him why he wears that particular watch," Li Na said. "We were getting shot at and I never got an answer."

"He's Jackson," Mitch said. "His watch needs to be as tough as he is. The Rolex Deepsea fits the bill. If any watch can take a licking and keep on ticking, it's that one. That reminds me, team, yelling, make sure the new watch has the same wear points and scratches as the one he's wearing now. Anyway, as I was saying, this sort of thing has been done on a one-time change using CRISPR therapeutics. I have refined the process using research notes from my predecessor. Not only that, but Jackson will also be able to change all his biometrics and fingerprints on demand."

"That is scary," Li Na said. "I'm not sure I like it."

"I have tested it over a hundred times," Mitch said. "It works like I designed it. If you're worried about the technology getting into the hands of someone else. Don't worry, I have very specific safeguards. Only Jackson and I will be able to use it, which requires four factor authentication."

"That's a relief," Li Na replied. "But still scary if I understand you correctly."

"I see where you're going," Mitch said. "You're on the right track. He will be able to change his fingerprints, eye color, and other biometrics at will. The other part of the technology will allow him to change his appearance to look like one of any three individuals he chooses. I could add more, but in this case, less is more."

"We're ready," A tech called out. "Come see."

The three gathered around the technician while he explained everything.

"This is the chip he had implanted. This is our chip. They are identical. Even the original maker wouldn't be able to tell them apart. We have the same signal circuitry, as well as the doping reservoir. It's already been changed to an adrenaline base like you instructed Doctor McElroy. The neat thing is that anytime they send a signal, it will get relayed to us first and we can counteract, modify, or mirror it so that it looks like the signal was received and will perform as intended."

"Excellent," Mitch said. "Doc, time to do your thing."

"Let's get this inserted," James said while he and the tech gathered around the surgical table."

"How are you going to make it so that they don't know you tampered with the chip?" Li Na asked. "If I were them the first thing I would look for is a fresh incision."

"Not to worry," Mitch smiled. "We have it covered."

About an hour later the new chip had been inserted and James called them over to look.

"How did you make the incision look old?" Li Na asked.

"Elementary," James said. "Nanobots did the job. Even the surgeon who operated on him before won't be able to tell. See, lifting the hair. There are no fresh wounds of any kind, but we've added some to his legs, arms and a few on his face to make his fall seem real. We will roll him into the recovery room and you two can watch him until he wakes up."

"How long will that take," Li Na asked.

"Ordinarily, several hours," James replied, smiling, picking up a small syringe, tapping the side of it then slightly depressing the plunger until a couple of drops oozed out. He jabbed it into Jackson's upper deltoid. "Give him about twenty minutes."

Mitch and Li Na were sitting in chairs on either side of Jackson when, about thirty minutes later, his eyelids began to flutter, and he slowly opened them. At first his vision was blurred and then cleared while he looked left and right.

"What are you two doing here?" he asked. "Where the hell am I?"

"So, you recognize us?" Mitch asked, smiling.

"Of course, you are Mitch, and she is Li Na, my best friend."

Li Na quivered with excitement inside, her eyes wide and bright in the surety that her lover was hers again. She had been holding his right hand and gave it a firm squeeze when he answered.

"It's a long story," Mitch said. "But here goes."

Both related all that had happened to him since the missiles exploded and almost killed him. He told them all that he remembered including the inside of the facility where the organization was on St. Lucia. The men, Antonio, CLUB DREAD and everything else, including his recurring dream about seeing Li Na but not her face. The discussion continued for several hours. James and another medical technician interrupted a couple of times to make sure that Jackson's vital signs were normal and that everything was functioning properly. When they finished, Mitch and Li Na briefed him on what was going on.

"I feel like crap," Jackson said.

"You've been through a lot," Mitch replied, pulling the Rolex Deepsea from his pocket and rotating the bezel clockwise one click.

Suddenly, Jackson perked up; it was like he had never been through his ordeal.

"I feel great," Jackson said. "What did you do?"

"Oh, just turned the wheel one click and let it stay for five seconds," Mitch said, smiling. "You have a small tube in you that was implanted, which we replaced with an adrenaline-based medication."

The operations of the watch and what it could do were explained to Jackson, who compared the two watches side by side. Unlike a normal Deepsea, this one was specially modified so the bezel could also turn right. Every scratch and nick were identical. The duplication was nothing short of perfect.

"I see that look," Mitch said. "You know that T-Group would never let you down."

"That's one thing I have never worried about," Jackson said, getting out of the bed. But I do have a question. How come I remember everything now, even all the people from CLUB DREAD?"

"They blocked your memory," Mitch replied. "We removed the block, and you now remember everything."

"How do you feel?" Li Na asked.

"I feel refreshed, like a new man," Jackson replied. "Except for the scratches all over my body, I would never have believed what happened to me like you described it."

"Sorry," Mitch said. "We need to keep up appearances. What's your gut feeling about this Antonio fellow?"

"He is ruthless as they come," Jackson said. "But also charming, shrewd, and strategic. Illiac told me there is a group of those in charge of CLUB DREAD. Something has kept bugging me though."

"What's that?" Mitch asked.

"I think he is the head honcho. Don't ask me how or why, it's just a gut feeling I have, and it keeps gnawing at me. He is not easily fooled either. What are your plans for getting me back into their good graces?"

"Thanks to Li Na, the link was severed completely," Mitch said. "If I were in their position, I would believe it was either damaged sufficiently to cease operating or that you had landed in a place where the signal couldn't escape. You know, the way a cell signal drops."

"There is a small crevasse just below the water line at high tide," Li Na said. "We will place you there and wait for someone to come get you?"

"What if they do not?"

"Let us worry about that," Mitch replied. "I'll leave you two alone for a bit. You have one hour."

Mitch was smiling and humming when he walked out the door, closing it gently behind him. Li Na quickly walked over and locked it. Turning, she rushed into Jacksons arms, hugging him firmly, tears streaming down her cheeks while she looked into his eyes. He gently wiped them away and kissed her long and hard, their tongues exploring each other.

"I thought I had lost you my love," Li Na whispered. "When I saw the video of the missile strike, I broke down inside."

"I'm lucky to be alive," Jackson said. "This organization saved my life. Sometimes I think I owe them."

"You must remember they only saved it to use you in their attempt for global domination," she retorted. "But enough of them for now."

The two spent the next hour getting reacquainted and exploring each other's bodies. They were laying on the small bed together when he slipped his manhood into her heavenly chamber, and they made passionate love. He could not get enough of her sweet smell, cupping her breasts in his large hands and licking her nipples; she likewise explored his chest with her tongue. Time was up; they got out of bed and put their clothes on. Li Na had scarcely finished, when someone knocked.

"It's okay," Jackson said, opening the door. "We were just catching up."

"I'm sure," Mitch smiled. "It's time."

"How are we going to keep the signal from reaching them

before I'm in the crevasse?" Jackson asked.

"We made a modified diving helmet," Mitch replied. "It's very light. It will block the signal until it's removed."

MELOR and his team, along with the American team were busy assessing the latest intel from the techs and their four-man team. The path they had chosen turned out to be the only path up the mountain side.

"Our assault will not be easy," a tech said. "There are motion detectors and anti-personnel mines located at each of the red dots."

"There are also natural booby traps marked by the orange dots," the other tech said. "The problem is that despite our great care and the skill of your operatives, we cannot guarantee that we found all of the devices."

"I had not anticipated this," Melor said. "What do you think Susan?"

"It's a real fluster cluck," she replied. "It rules out a night assault. We will need to ascend during daylight and wait."

"Agreed," Melor replied. "If we leave in the next hour, we can make it to the gates or thereabouts by nightfall."

"Yes," Frank said. "I'll tell them. Melor and Susan, great news; Jackson is back. He will be our inside man. At least we hope so. T-Group has fixed him up and everything looks good."

"I knew that bastard was too tough to die," Melor said, smiling. "It will be nice to work with him again."

Both teams saddled up with their gear and slowly, patiently, started down the trail. They were able to communicate with each other through their comms; Frank had told them that Jackson would be able to transmit to them as well. He would use the code words 'we in di lime tonight' at first contact. The team asked what it meant, and Frank had explained, it's a Caribbean saying meaning 'we're going to the party tonight.' Everyone laughed and joked about it, even humming the words. The techs kept rotating drones overhead to avoid potential dangers. The teams moved like they were still hunting, pausing every two or three steps to recon the area directly around them. Twice they found anti-personnel mines and marked them with bright green, fluorescent flagging tape. The point man was rounding a bend in the trail when his hand moved a branch triggering a booby trap, dropping a four-foot-long Fer-de-lance with a string attached to its tail. The snake bit him on the right forearm. He yelled in pain, the other team members quickly gathering around, killing the snake in the process. Susan administered anti-venom at once and put a tourniquet above the bite about four inches. Calling for two support personnel from the base camp, they waited until they arrived with a stretcher and more antivenom, taking the wounded operative away.

"Let that be a lesson to all of you," Susan said. "Don't lean on a tree or touch anything you have not carefully inspected. We are now down a man when we cannot afford to be. Move out."

The teams continued moving, sweating from every pore, it dripped down their faces and stung their eyes, while mosquitos attacked from every angle.

"Complain about the desert and its heat all you want," an operative said. "I'll take it anytime over this crap."

Operatives always understood the danger of a mission, accepted it; it was the only way to succeed. The distance to the gates seemed further away somehow. Though not more than a half mile, the steep terrain and constant stress and strain from looking for potential danger took its toll. About halfway up, they took a much-needed break, kneeling in place. The normal banter that would sometimes accompany a mission was absent; all eyes continually pivoting from tree line to forest floor and into the deep shadows cast by the undergrowth among and beneath the trees. The smell of the dampness and from rotting vegetation hung heavily in the air. The odor, different from that found in the desert or typical conifer forest was pungent, not sweet, despite the many natural flowers that surrounded them. Like being on a battlefield, they struggled every step, constantly alert for the enemy who for now, was the reptiles and mosquitos of the forest rather than mines and men. After a fifteen-minute break, the teams resumed their movement.

CHAPTER 8

WITHIN the facility, one of the technicians heard a soft beeping sound. Turning to look at his computer monitor, he noticed it was a signal from Jackson's chip.

"Doctor Bramahh," the tech said. "The tracker is working again."

"Where is it coming from?"

"Looks like this area sir," the tech said, pointing to a map.

Bramahh ran to Antonios office, out of breath by the time he got there.

"Good news," Bramahh said. "The tracker is on again."

"Where?"

"Rachette Point."

"That's where Scott said they were attacked. Find Illiac, get him there now. Tell him to take a couple of men with him."

Less than thirty-minutes later, a helicopter hovered above the end of Rachette Point. Illiac was peering below, hanging out the door.

"The locator is right below us," the pilot said.

"I don't see anything," Illiac replied. "Take us out about fifty yards so I can see the cliff face better.

The pilot turned the chopper to the right and flew about fifty yards away over the water. Illiac motioned with his hand to stop and began scanning with binoculars. Remembering what Scott had told him, he noticed a crevasse full of trees from the top that ran down to the bottom, stopping just below the high tide mark. Looking closely, he saw Jackson's arm and hand protruding from the shadows. Illiac assumed that Jackson had probably hit the water at high tide and been washed into the trees and settled with the water as the tide subsided. No wonder they had not received a signal. He directed the pilot to the proper spot and swung the cargo hook out. Attaching himself to the cable, he lowered himself to Jackson. The rotor wash blew the trees and shrubs in the crevasse back and forth, allowing Illiac to judge the situation. Seeing no real danger, he lowered himself the rest of the way and put a harness around Jackson, who struggled to sit up and seemingly alert. Hooking Jackson's harness to the end of the cable, the men in the chopper reeled them in. Jackson plopped like a dead fish onto the floor of the chopper.

"I thought you were a goner," Illiac said, laughing. "That'll teach you to stay away from strange women."

The other men and pilot burst out laughing. Seeing that Jackson was okay, he was passed a bottle of water and the bird headed back to the facility. Mitch had purposely not fed him or given him water so that he would appear in the proper condition. One of the men passed him a chocolate bar. Thanking him, Jackson wolfed it down like he hadn't eaten for a week.

"I thought we had lost you," Antonio said. "Tell me what happened.

Jackson reiterated everything, following the woman, getting robbed and then the pickup. Antonio listened carefully comparing what was said to the report Scott had given him. Always paranoid, he seemed satisfied and turned his attention to other details.

"I want you to go with Scott and get something to eat. Also, Doctor Bramahh will want to check you out. Send Illiac in please."

Illiac smiled at Jackson when they passed. He was glad to have him back. Watching him, he felt relieved somehow.

"What do you think?" Antonio asked.

"Aside from some scrapes and bruises, he seems fine?"

"That's not what I meant. Do you think he is on the level with us?"

"Yes," Illiac said. "He is in the shape I thought he might be, cold, wet, tired, dirty, and hungry. The location where I found him coincides with what I thought may have happened and with Scott's story. Do you suspect something?"

"I don't know," Antonio replied. "Go eat with him and see if you notice anything different. He won't lie with Scott there. We'll know more once the doctor examines him and the chip.

An hour later Doctor Bramahh examined Jackson, along with a tech expert. He lifted Jackson's hair so he could see where the chip had been inserted. The incision was the same as he remembered. Satisfied, he had the tech run diagnostics on the chip. Everything the tech did was monitored by Mitch's team.

"How does it look?" Bramahh asked.

"Everything is working 100%," the tech replied. "The GPS tracking is on, and the rest of the chips functions are well within design parameters."

"Good," Bramahh said. "Complete your diagnostics and let me know if you find anything out of the ordinary. I need to report."

"Roger that."

"Give me an update," Antonio said.

"I just checked him," Bramahh said. "The chip has not been tampered with and appears to be working as designed. The tech is running more diagnostics. The only thing I noticed is scrapes and bruises all over him, on his legs, arms, back, and face. They are consistent with a fall. He does have some hair clipped smooth right around the scrape on the back of his neck. I'm sure it was from the rock that caused it."

"You're certain no one tampered with the chip?" Antonio asked.

"Absolutely," Bramahh said. "Had they done so, there would be a new wound around it. The incision is aged, not new. Why are you so paranoid?"

"It keeps me alive," Antonio said, narrowing his eyes. "Is he fit enough to do what I need?"

"Without a doubt," Bramahh said. "He was somewhat dehydrated and famished, but he's recovered completely. I had him on an IV drip so no worries about his ability to perform. He's totally ready."

"Good," Antonio said. "I need him to begin moving clones of the leaders."

Antonio began walking to the breakroom where he found Scott, Illiac, and Jackson eating, drinking and joking. Jackson acted like nothing was wrong. He was one of the men, that was all he need portray.

"Boss," Jackson said with a grin. "Any work for us?"

"Yes, there is always work to do," Antonio replied. "I need the three of you to come with me."

The three men immediately stood and followed. Jackson had always wanted to know what was behind the huge blast doors. They were even larger than those at Cheyenne Mountain. When they reached the door, Antonio nodded, and a technician opened the door just enough to admit them. It was immediately closed. The three men stood in awe. Neither had ever had access to this part of the facility. They were above and looking down on rows of plexiglass pods reinforced with titanium columns on the outside of each. There were four rows on either side of the catwalk they walked down. The pods were lit from within; a low lumen, blue-green light that emitted an eerie glow. Atop the pods were lit consoles containing a small monitor that controlled the temperature and life functions within, presumably via electrical cables hooked to a master computer somewhere within the large room. There were at least one hundred of the pods perhaps more. Within the pods were clones at varying stages of a lifecycle. Jackson immediately recognized clones of the U.S., British, and Russian presidents in the front row. They looked identical to the real person.

"This is my masterpiece," Antonio said. "Why try to control the outcome of war when you can control the person in charge of the war machine?"

"I do not understand," Scott said.

"My dear employee," Antonio said, turning. "This chamber took over ten years to build. There on the first row are clones of the most powerful rulers on earth. They have been programmed with every memory, news articles, personal relations, and any other piece of intelligence we could garner. When put into operation, they won't even know they are not themselves. And it will be me who controls them. I will not only control the nations and their debt, but I will control the rulers of every major army, communist or free makes no difference. The decisions they make will come from me."

"You will be master over all boss," Illiac said.

"More than that," Antonio replied. "CLUB DREAD will rule the world; it will be our new world order. Anyone who does not cooperate will be punished."

Jackson watched Antonio intently. He was like a proud parent and madman all at the same time. Nothing good would come from the power this man would potentially wield if he were able to activate the clones. Jackson pressed a small button in his right pocket on the bottom of a mint container. He was hoping that the signal and voice would make it out of the chamber to Mitch's team. Live or die, this place needed to be destroyed. The faster, the better.

"The three of you will take the three new hostages and the clones of President Armstrong, President Sokolav, and Prime Minister Wilson to our other location. You will not know where it is until you reach it. Go down the stairs and work with my team. They will help you get to Soufriere and then to the airport. You should reach your destination in just over three hours once you depart. I will meet you there."

Jackson and the other two were looking all around. Finally, Jackson looked at the ceiling. It was domed and perfectly smooth. He realized it was manmade and not the natural rock that the walls had been hewn out of.

"Ah," Antonio said. "You see my masterpiece. It was designed from research and deployment of the American's bunker buster bombs. By understanding exactly how they work, their technology can and will be defeated. They may eventually find this chamber, but they will be unable to penetrate it. Go now."

The three men descended the metal stairs to the floor below where workers were already moving the pods to a four wheeled trailer. Instructed on what to do, the three assisted in hoisting the pods with an electric winch and lowering them into recesses inset into the trailer floor. Several other men had brought the three hostages they had taken from Papua, Africa, and Russia. They were blindfolded and placed into a seat in in front of the pods. It didn't take long to remove the clones and assemble everything.

"We in di lime tonight," Jackson said.

"It's a party alright," Scott replied."

The entire team got into a four-man electric towing tug, like those used at airports. It was then that Jackson noticed another set of large blast doors that opened outward onto a combination monorail, car track. The doors were so huge it took about ten minutes to open and close them. The tunnel was well lit with a steep descent. Within a few minutes, they had exited into a large warehouse, the entrance closing behind them, leaving no trace of the tunnel. Waiting for them were a box truck and two vans. The prisoners were loaded into a van with a couple of men, and it took off. The pods had wheels on them so that when the winch lifted them out of the trailer and lowered them to the floor, they were easily rolled onto the lift gate of the box truck and moved inside. The entire process worked smoothly and efficiently. Jackson discreetly pressed the button on the bottom of his mint container.

"Have you ever seen such a thing?" Illiac asked.

"Never," Jackson replied. "How about you Scott?"

"I'm still trying to wrap my head around what we're doing." The three laughed.

"Mount up," the head tech said. "We're off to the airport."

When they exited the building, Jackson and Illiac were surprised. It was the copper factory across from the stadium.

"Hell, we could have walked up to the facility from here," Scott said.

"Yeah, but we'd never get through those doors," Jackson said. "Neither a nuke nor bunker buster would do us much good."

"Got that right," Illiac said. "I gather this has been planned for a very long time. You don't build a facility like that overnight."

The three rode in silence to the airport.

"We're getting a signal from Jackson," a tech called out. "He's on the move. He gave the code words."

Mitch listened to the conversation while they watched the GPS tracker on the monitor.

"Get a team over to the copper factory," Mitch said. "I'm guessing it is deserted. Tell them to be discreet and see if they can find the tunnel that was mentioned. I'll contact DC and let them know what is going on."

PHIL drove from the crisis suite and was in session with the President and VP. Everything had been moving so fast it was difficult to keep track of it all.

"What do we have?" President Armstrong asked.

"It's not good sir," Phil replied. "Jackson is back with us now and transporting some clones to an as yet undisclosed location."

"Do we know who the clones are?" VP Reisner asked.

"They are Presidents Armstrong and Sokolav and the British Prime Minister. There are others including you sir, but those have not been moved yet."

"Damn!" Bill exclaimed. "Can we destroy the facility and other clones?"

"Uncertain sir," Phil replied. "We know where it is but not the design. I recommend sending in the two teams."

"Martha, get me President Sokolav. Tell him it's urgent."

"Yes sir."

About a minute later, Sokolav appeared on the monitor, along with Andros.

"What have you found out?" Sokolav asked.

"They have clones of you, me, and the British Prime Minister," President Armstrong said. "They are moving them. We do not know where yet. They also have many others of world and corporate leaders. What we discussed before with you and Andros needs to be put in motion now. We cannot afford for this organization to replace us."

"What is our best course of action?" President Sokolav asked.

"We have discussed it with Phil, and we believe the teams need to go in now."

"I agree," Andros said. "What of the facility?"

"There is a problem with it," President Armstrong replied. "It appears the facility has a huge back chamber where the clones are kept behind a blast door."

"Then we must take it out," President Sokolav said. "What are our options?"

"We are looking at bunker buster bombs," VP Reisner said.

"The 30,000 pound, GBU-57 is too large," Andros interrupted. "We cannot shake the entire island. Which one are you thinking about? The new 5,000-pound bomb?"

"Yes, the GBU-72B," VP Reisner said. "It should penetrate up to one hundred feet. We use two of them dropped from F-15E Strike Eagles; they have a ferrying range of 3,500 miles and can accomplish a midair refuel."

"I agree with your assessment Vice President," Andros said. "The Presidents will need to clear it with the Prime Minister of St. Lucia."

"I have been talking to him," President Armstrong said. "He wants concessions from both of us."

"What concessions?" President Sokolav asked.

"So far, building his coast guard with a dozen new boats and some money," President Armstrong said.

"How much?" Sokolav asked.

"One hundred million," President Armstrong replied.

"Okay, what if we give him the boats and you pay him the money?" President Sokolav said. "After all, it's a small price to save the world, neh?"

"Done," President Armstrong said. "The Strike Eagles are already on standby at Eglin. They will be launched to coincide with a 2:00 am strike. At most a few of the residents will see part of a fireball."

"Very well," President Sokolav replied. "Keep us posted."

The monitor went blank. The President, Phil, and the VP sat in silence for a moment, looking back and forth at each other.

"This can turn into a very sticky mess," Reisner said.

"Yes, but that is why we have Phil," Bill replied, smiling.

"I will make sure it goes according to plan," Phil said. "The problem is, where is this other location and who controls it? Until we know the answer to that, launching another operation will need to wait. This Antonio Raven told Jackson that they would reach the new destination within three hours. The plane initially headed east. Intelligence being put together in the crisis suite is predicting anywhere from Panama to Mexico. The location will narrow with time."

"Stay on it," President Armstrong said. "The VP and I will hold down the fort here."

THE two teams steadily worked their way through the thick undergrowth up the would-be trail. Two more men had been sent back to the base camp, victims of punji stakes and a tree whip, reducing the number to thirteen. The tree whip was fastened out of a flexible tree limb consisting of sharpened wooden spikes tied to the end of the limb that was pulled back in an arc using a catch attached to a trip wire. When tripped, the catch disengaged and sent the foot-long sharpened sticks toward the victim at a hundred miles per hour. Fortunately, the victim was hit in the shoulder rather than the chest and survived.

After what seemed like hours of sweat and toil, the teams were mere yards from the gate; they saw five sentries on duty, all armed with AK-47s.

"What do you think?" Susan asked, holding up her fist for everyone to stop.

"We need to take them all out at one time," Melor whispered.

"We can use knives or suppressed M-4's," Susan said. "With all the undergrowth, the rifles may not work as well."

"Yes, I have read about how they worked in Vietnam," Melor said. "Some things never change. Let's take out the end sentries by hand and the middle three with the rifles; they are the more exposed."

"Good plan," Susan replied, circling her hand and pointing down.

The team members gathered around her and Melor while they explained the strategy. Two men were assigned to each of the sentries to ensure total success. It took almost an hour to get into position due to the steep slope. Finally, their men were in place. Susan's men had the outside sentry's and Melor's had the middle three. They waited patiently while the sentry's moved about; finally, they all stopped moving at the same time.

"Now," Melor spoke into the comms.

The three middle sentries were each taken out by suppressed rifle fire, falling with thuds to the ground. Susan's men had crept behind the other two. One of her men grabbed each of the enemy in a choke hold while another stabbed them beneath the rib cage into the heart. Quietly and quickly the sentries were replaced by their own men. Moving the rest of the team forward, they began searching for an entrance into the cavern. The last light of day had disappeared when the team found a small opening in the vines that led inside. Melor and Susan eased through the opening to observe the cavern. It was much larger than they anticipated, with multiple floors and at least thirty armed personnel and another dozen or more support personnel. Susan quickly shot video with her smart phone then, the two returned to their team. It was pitch black. The team gathered around to watch the video. They were outnumbered by at least two to one.

"We cannot move until Franks clears us to go," Susan said. "Any ideas?"

"We could creep inside and use grenades to reduce enemy strength," a team member said.

"That could work," Melor replied.

"I do have these," Susan said, opening her bag and pulling out an autonomous killer drone. "Each one has a three-gram shaped charge in its frame. The only problem is that I only have twelve of them."

"How do they work?" Melor asked, surprise on his face.

"They need to either be thrown or dropped from a height to initiate movement," Susan said. "I suggest throwing them given our situation."

"Do they kill indiscriminately?" another team member asked.

"They can, but I will program them to kill only those with weapons. It only takes a few minutes."

"What then?" Melor asked.

"One of us sneaks in without a weapon and throws each drone as hard as he can then, retreats."

"What about using two team members?" Melor asked.

"That will work too, but remember no weapon, not even a knife."

While Susan programmed the drones, Melor and the team discussed who had the strongest throwing arms. One of his men and one of Susan's had played baseball at a near professional level. They were selected for the task.

"Yes sir, I understand," Susan spoke into her phone. "Jackson sent the code words; Melor, we are a go."

The two men took the drones and snuck inside the cavern. There was minimal light against the wall, so they inched their way to the right and each laid six of the drones in front of him on the floor then, stared at each other.

"Let's strike them out," the CIA operative said with a smile.

"With pleasure," Melor's man said. "Throw them as fast and hard as we can."

They each grabbed a drone and threw it toward the third level directly across from them. The first drone was followed by the rest in quick succession. Within ten seconds they had tossed the drones and five seconds later were outside the cavern.

"Count the sounds," Susan said. "They will sound like faint gunfire then, move in."

No sooner had she spoken than they heard the first faint sounding shot. While they counted, they could hear panic and chaos inside the cavern, the personnel running in an attempt to escape the killer drones. Twenty seconds later, they moved quickly through the door and began engaging the remaining enemy. One of the pilots made a dash for the helicopter and was gunned down. Three men came running at them firing fully automatic. But it was too late, the team's bullets ripped through them like punching paper on the range, knocking them off their feet while their eyes faded with their last breath. Another group of the enemy were behind a metal barricade raining hell on them with a .30 caliber machine gun; it was quickly taken out with a grenade, gun and body parts flying. The teams moved from the ground floor to the next two levels. Civilian prisoners were brought down and sat near the helicopter. Five minutes later the last shots were fired just outside the large blast doors to the clone chamber.

"We have the facility secure sir," Susan said.

"Good job Susan," Frank replied. "Give my thanks to Melor and his team as well. Mitch and I, along with a few of his technicians will be there shortly via helicopter. Open the gates when you hear it."

"Understood," she said. "Melor, Frank wants to pass on his thanks to your team. They will be here soon to determine what we need to do next."

"Good," Melor said. "I'll contact my people and let them know what is going on."

The familiar sound of a helicopter was not long in coming. Red lighting inside the cavern made it easy for the pilot, using his night vision, to land. Frank and Mitch hopped off before the helicopter set down.

"Show us the blast doors," Frank said. "Hurry."

The group ran up the steps to the third level and back toward the middle going deeper into the cavern.

"Have your men examine it," Frank said. "We need to know if we can get in."

Mitches team spent about an hour using drills, ground penetrating radar, thermal scopes and other equipment to get an idea of what was behind the blast doors and wall.

"You're not going to like what we found," Mitch said.

"Tell me anyway," Frank replied.

"The outer wall appears to be fifteen feet of reinforced concrete followed by six, four-foot layers of steel with concrete between those. Behind that appears to be another fifteen-foot layer of reinforced concrete and another fifty feet of natural rock. It all correlates with the inset distance to the blast doors."

"Remember what we discussed. Can we do it?"

"There is no way to get a bunker buster bomb from the front of the cavern to this point. Even if we did, it wouldn't penetrate. I doubt the 30,000-pound bomb would be sufficient either."

"Okay tech man," Frank replied. "What is our best option?"

"We determine the exact coordinates and hit it with two GBU-72B's. Given what Jackson could relay. I believe the chamber beyond is almost the size of this cavern. Anything inside should be destroyed."

"And if not?" Frank asked.

"Then, we have a serious global problem."

"Phil. Frank here. I'm sending you coordinates for the GBU's. Execute when ready. We'll be gone."

"What's going on?" Susan asked.

"We need to leave at once," Frank said. "Our men have brought a couple of box trucks and the base camp vehicles. Get all your men aboard and get the hell out of here."

"You're going to bomb it?" Melor asked.

"Yes, bunker busters," Frank said. "Move out now."

Two F-15E Strike Eagles, each with a single GBU-72B had left Eglin over two hours before. Once the coordinates were received, they were programmed into the targeting computer of each jet. The teams moved franticly to clear the area and were several miles away when they stopped. Frank stepped out of the lead vehicle.

"Lance 1, Lance 2, Spearhead" Frank spoke into his sat phone. "We're all clear. Start the symphony."

"Concerto 5000s on the way Spearhead," Lance 1 spoke. "Have a splendid day."

The F-15s turned northeast and headed home, the targeting computer guiding the bombs to detonation. Forty-three seconds later, they struck the area above the chamber at a speed of 1,389 ft/s. The kinetic energy alone was staggering when the two 5,000-pound bunker buster bombs struck the ground. The bombs were fitted with a delayed fuse connected to a small antenna in the point that retained the signal while the oscillator-amplifier detector sensed what was happening during penetration so the bombs would not detonate on impact, but only when they had entered a chamber below ground. Such fuses are known as a hard target smart fuse (HTSF).

All the team members had stepped outside the vehicles, looking back toward the facility. There was a bright orange flash and a sound like loud thunder when the bombs hit. The ground shook momentarily from the concussion then, the sky went dark again. Satisfied, the group loaded up and headed back to base where they would be immediately deployed again as backup to Jackson. What the teams didn't know was that when the bunker buster bombs exploded, seismic detectors that Illiac had wired to his explosives, initiated a chain reaction inside the outer chamber and the tunnel, collapsing both. It made it appear the bunker busters had done their work and would seal the inner chamber so no one could ever get to it.

In Moscow and Washington DC, both presidents watched the bombs strike; the monitor went blank. They felt relief that at least one major problem had been resolved.

"Where is your man now?" President Sokolav asked.

"The plane headed west," President Armstrong said.

"Unless it changes course radically, the British and Russian teams in the crisis suite have the destination narrowed to somewhere in southern Mexico, south to El Salvador," Phil interjected.

"We will keep you informed President Sokolav," President Armstrong said. Both our teams are on standby in St. Lucia; they are ready to move when we know where the plane is going."

"Very well," President Sokolav said. "Andros will follow up with Phillip from this end."

The crisis suite buzzed with activity. Henry was clearing information and posting relevant intelligence on the large screen while the teams kept searching for possible landing strips for the plane Jackson was on. Henry hesitated to ping the tracker for fear it would give him away and the mission would fail.

Leonid and Beatrix called out almost in unison, "the plane disappeared."

"What do you mean it disappeared?" Henry asked.

"One minute it was there, now it isn't," Leonid called out from across the room.

"Where is the last known location?" Henry asked.

"Over the Corn Islands east of Nicaragua," Beatrix yelled over the din of activity.

"Try to relocate it," Henry said, picking up a phone. "Mitch, we have a serious problem. The plane disappeared off our radar near the Corn Islands."

"Damn!" Mitch exclaimed. "Another area we do not have major assets. We do have one option, an MQ-9 Reaper on standby in Guatemala City. It sounds like they are using an old smugglers trick from the drug war flying into Florida."

"What's that?" Henry asked. "Cartel pilots would fly at normal altitude and about one hundred fifty miles from the coast would drop down to around five hundred feet for the remainder of the trip. When we began using AWACS, it solved the problem. Let me get back to you."

The small, private hangar on the edge of GUA airport had a great view of the four volcanoes Agua, Fuego, Pacaya, and Acatenango. Manny, Chief of Guatemala Station, was daydreaming, watching the cloud cover hanging over Agua when the phone began ringing.

"Manny."

"This is Mitch. How long would it take you to get the Reaper airborne?"

"We just completed maintenance on it," Manny said. "Maybe ten minutes. What's up?"

"We are in desperate need to track a plane. It disappeared over the Corn Islands. I think it's using the old smugglers trick. Get it airborne now."

"You want us to head it toward the islands?" Manny asked.

"No, I think they are headed into Nicaragua proper. Take a south-southeast heading at 50,000 feet and look for anything suspicious. You know the drill. Maybe we will get lucky."

While Mitch described the plane Jackson was on, Manny waved his hand to a colleague standing next to the Reaper near the middle of hangar then, pointed up. The 950-shaft-horsepower turboprop engine roared to life. The remote pilot sat in a thirty-foot trailer at the back of the hangar in front of the pilot operator console. She fired up the UAVs satellite link to the on-board avionics for navigation, instrumentation, and communications with local and enroute air traffic control. Two synthetic aperture radar workstations together with satellite and line-of-sight ground data terminals were already at work controlling the Reaper while it rolled down the taxiway with expedited takeoff clearance on Runway 01. Heading into the wind at 18.6° North, the Reaper was airborne 2,000 feet later, turning easterly toward the coast directly after liftoff. The remote pilot quickly ascended to 50,000 feet. Every plane that appeared on its radar was checked and analyzed in the crisis suite. Looking for a needle in a haystack was never easy.

"Falcon 1 airborne," Manny spoke into the satellite phone. "Data is being sent directly to the crisis suite for analysis."

"Is it armed?" Mitch asked.

"It has four Hellfire missiles. Will we need them?"

"Not yet, I hope. Thanks Manny."

EVERYONE aboard noticed the change in course and the steep descent. The pilot said nothing, flying as instructed. He knew that the air density would rapidly increase and fuel use with it, when he descended. By the time they reached their destination, the plane would be on fumes. It would take all his skill to land the large plane on a 4,920-foot runway without running off the end. Coming in from the east the pilot circled into the landing pattern. The airport wasn't much more than a two-lane highway, with a red and white checkered control tower and a small beige terminal with a matching red roof. It was visual landing. The aircraft continued west and made a slow banking turn, lining up to the runway, which started almost at the edge of Lake Nicaragua. From his pilot seat, it looked like the lake was greater in elevation than the runway. He gritted his teeth; lowering the landing gear, he descended not more than ten feet above the water, skidding down on the apron right at the beginning of the asphalt. As soon as the wheels touched down the pilot adjusted the propellers to produce rearward thrust while he stomped the brakes, rapidly slowing the aircraft. There were about fifty yards to spare by the time the plane came to a stop and turned to taxi toward the terminal where two trucks that looked like throwbacks from the 1950s, their beds covered with a green canvas, awaited them.

"Where the hell are we?" Illiac asked.

"Welcome to OMT," the pilot said, the plane stopping on the tarmac not far from the trucks.

"What the hell is OMT," Jackson queried.

"La Paloma Ometepe Airport," the pilot yelled over the

sound of the engines. "Welcome to Ometepe in the middle of Lake Nicaragua."

Jackson and Illiac were staring toward the looming volcano about three miles east of the runway. It seemed to leap toward the sky, covered in a blanket of white clouds that cloaked the top almost to ground level in the appearance of an upside down 'V.'

"You think we're headed there?" Jackson asked.

"I believe we are," Illiac smiled. "Looks much like the last place but more barren."

The group quickly disembarked, taking the three hostages while the clones, the containers covered for concealment, were hurriedly loaded onto the second truck. Motors revving, the two trucks gunned it and were off. Within a couple of minutes after leaving the airport, they were bouncing down a narrow rocky road bounded by banana trees. Although the forest was more open than on St. Lucia, it still afforded plenty of cover for anyone or any group to conceal themselves. The road was far from smooth, winding around to the southeast and joining NIC-64 just west of San José del Sur, it began to slowly bend to the left past Urbaite. Making a quick turn left and then back right, about two miles past the small town, they crossed an old lava field. Directly after, the trucks turned into the undergrowth between the lava flow and some farm fields adjoining it to the north. Two guards dressed in camouflage stopped them, checking the trucks; it was the first of three checkpoints. The drivers quietly talked to them in Spanish; the trucks were admitted through a swinging gate with razor wire on top that had been overgrown by vines.

The road was again rocky, more so than before. Jackson noted it was almost invisible due to the vines and trees overhanging it on one side and bananas and papayas bordering it on the other. The rocks were not black, but a dark brown that blended with the grass and bordering plants. The road was so curvy it was unlikely it would show up on satellite. He knew it was time. He could not risk waiting for Mitch. Everyone was looking out the back watching a small SUV following them for security reasons. He unsnapped his leather protective watch cover and turned the bezel on his Rolex Deepsea one click to the left. He found the cover was particularly protective given the harsh environments he always found himself in. This one was also lined with a RFID blocker that would prevent signals in or out when closed. The tracking device embedded inside the watch began broadcasting a signal. Five minutes later, the trucks stopped; Jackson turned the bezel back to the 12 o'clock position. Being specially redesigned, it was the only watch of its kind that allowed turning the bezel right, as well as left. He re-snapped the protective cover. Illiac hearing the snap, turned.

"Are you getting itchy about the time my friend?"

"No, just curious because my stomach tells me it's time to eat," Jackson said with a grin.

"I couldn't agree more," Illiac said.

The security guards walked to the back of each truck and lowered the gates so everyone could get out. The clone pods were placed on hand towed lifts in front of the trucks. The three operatives looked around. The road had ended and there appeared no place to go.

"Open," a guard said.

Not more than twenty feet in front of them, the hillside began to raise, revealing large hydraulic columns that supported an iron base with earth, rocks and vegetation planted on top of it. It was so well made and camouflaged that neither of the three operatives saw it. Cunning indeed. The area beneath the opening was smooth, with a small rail car that the clones were loaded onto. The guards took the three hostage CEO's to a room at the far end of the cavern, which was almost identical to the last one, but at least twice as large. Scott, Illiac, and Jackson surveyed the new facility, which contained considerably more men and supplies than the last one. Then,

Jackson saw them, a set of huge blast doors almost two hundred feet away inset into an oval shaped hallway that was more than one hundred feet long.

"You'd think he was expecting World War III," Scott mused.

"You think there are more clones behind those doors?

"I'm guessing so," Illiac replied. "This facility looks just like the last one, but even more reinforced."

"Come forward gentlemen," a voice called over the intercom, the red door on the third level at the end. Hurry please."

While they walked to the end of the giant cavern, Jackson was able to get a good look at the layout, number of men, almost all armed, and the armaments. Unlike the last facility, there were three machine gun nests on each side on each of the three levels. The guns were trained on all those below. "It would take an army to drive these men out of here," Jackson thought, interrupted by Illiac.

"I wonder what he has planned for us now. I have a bad feeling about this."

"Me too," Scott said. "I get the feeling we're suddenly expendable. Why?"

"Not to worry my friends," Jackson said, attempting light banter. "As long as Antonio has a use for us, he will keep us around."

B EATRIX and Leonid had just put their information up on the large screen in the crisis suite. There were good visuals from original satellite images.

"Is there any clue where they are?" Henry asked.

"They disappeared near this point," Leonid said. "It is the same coordinates that Mitch sent to us from Jackson."

"There has to be a hidden entrance," Beatrix said. "Otherwise, we would have picked up some shape or at least something."

"Grid it out and go over every inch with a magnifying glass," Henry said. "Also, have your teams work on communications and see what they can dig up. By the way, did your teams look at the feeds prior to Jackson landing? I would like to know how this Antonio fellow got there so quickly."

"We'll get on it right away sir," Beatrix replied.

About an hour later, the team had come up with an array of photos and maps they had been scanning.

"Look at this," Leonid said. "This plane was caught in aerial imagery when it took off from St. Lucia, a couple of times in midflight, and upon landing at Ometepe. The inflight software also follows the same track."

"Antonio landed on Ometepe quite some time before the others," Beatrix said.

"The question is, can we track him to this new facility?" Henry asked.

"We were able to track him through Urbaite," Leonid replied. "We lost coverage after that."

"Show me where Jackson's signal disappeared," Henry said.

"Here," Beatrix said, pointing. "Just beyond this curve and west of the highway."

"That was also Antonio's last track," Leonid said. "We therefore assume they went to the same location."

"The question is, where is that location?" Henry asked, picking up his phone. "Manny, Henry here. Do you still have the Reaper up that Mitch requested?"

"Yes," Manny replied. "We've have about 24 hours left on its run. What's up?"

"I'm sending you coordinates," Henry said. "Jackson's signal disappeared there. We need a sweep of that area. Pipe back the video to us. How soon can you do it?"

"The Reaper is about twenty minutes away," Manny replied. "It's an odd, shaped area so, we'll do a polygon search pattern with sixty percent overlap and bring down the bird to three thousand feet."

"Can your crew also analyze the video?" Henry asked.

"Certainly. They are experts. I'll pipe it to both locations."

"That'll work," Henry said. "We have an ops team arriving soon. They can target anything that looks suspicious with their small drone. Thanks, I owe you one."

"No worries."

THE plane bumped onto the tarmac, wheels screeching, at OMT in strong winds. Three vans awaited Melor and Frank's teams. The flight wasn't overly long, but the ops teams were accustomed to long hours with little sleep. By the time they arrived, three hours hard sleep had helped refresh them for the next part of their mission. Mitch arrived just before them and already had a good idea of the area where the facility might be located. The Reaper had not finished its search yet but would soon. By the time the teams arrived at the potential location, they would all be up to speed.

"Welcome," Mitch called out. "Everyone needs to climb into the vans. I'm glad you didn't wear ops black, or we'd stick out like a sore thumb."

"Where are we headed?" Li Na asked.

"I'll show you on a map once we load up," Mitch replied. "Frank, it's good to see you."

"Likewise."

It took only a few minutes to retrieve their gear from the plane and load it onto the vans. Before long they had reached El Quino along Highway 64 and passed it to take a break near Sarren. Pulling off the road behind some trees, they noticed a farmer skinning a pig, scrapping the hair off the carcass to reveal white skin beneath. He barely glanced at them; his goal was simple survival. The undergrowth and forest grew thicker after Urbaite, lending itself to covert movement. The teams crowded around Mitch and Frank in the last van, where Mitch was able to display the feed from the Reaper overhead, of the area to the west.

"Okay men, and women," Mitch said. "We have a Reaper overhead on a search pattern of this area. It is where we believe Jackson entered the new facility, and his signal was lost."

"Any idea where it is?" Melor asked.

"Only this general area," Mitch responded. "We have a British and Russian team going over the same video feeds we have here, as well as a CIA team in Guatemala City. The goal is to identify the entrance."

"Are there any roads toward that direction leading off the highway?" Li Na asked.

"Only three that we have found; all appear intermittent," Mitch replied. "Why?"

"The last mission Jackson and I were on had the same type of scenario." Li Na said. "The roads were so obscured that visuals from airborne drones nor satellites could find them."

"If we can see those three roads, even intermittently, it would help," Melor said. "Perhaps we should have the drones concentrate on where they end. If the facility is as well-hidden as you suspect, the end of the road would be a logical entry point."

"You may have something there," Mitch said. "Falcon 1, Osprey. Can you send us videos and pictures of where those three roads end that you see?"

"Osprey, Falcon 1. We will conduct a tight grid search of each area. Standby for visuals."

About ten minutes later, visuals of the first roads end displayed on the monitor. The entire team looked at it closely. There was nothing out of the ordinary. The only recognizable sign of human trace was a small beat down area where vehicles had probably parked and a small trail leading to the farm fields directly north. Visuals of the second road showed the same. The team was running out of options. Finally, the end of the third road was displayed on the monitor. Just to the east were a couple of guards by a gate.

"That looks like mercenaries," Melor said, pointing.

"I agree," Mitch replied. "Falcon 1, Osprey. Can you make a

small grid search of the area surrounding end of road three and try to trace that road back to the highway."

"Roger. Conducting new search."

The team again watched the live feed. The teams at the crisis suite, as well as Guatemala Station were also glued to the visuals. Once the sweep had been made, the team slowed down the recorded video and compared parts to still images along the roadway and at its end.

"Osprey, Falcon 1. My team said to concentrate on the end of the road. There appears to be inconsistencies with the flora there. Also, the trace shows three gates, all guarded, back to the main highway. The other roads don't have anything like that. I would say you have found your area. We will continue to monitor."

"Thank you," Mitch said. "Alright team. Let's relocate temporarily so that we can launch our own drone and concentrate on that area."

The teams climbed back into the vans and backtracked about a half mile. Finding the third road, they began looking for a location in the undergrowth where they could pull off the road. They finally found a good spot that led to a small clearing surrounded by Paradise and Laurel trees and here and there, small Kapok trees with spikes large enough to impale a person. Several of Melor's team walked back and brushed up the grass so that a passerby would not be able to recognize that vehicles had pulled off the road. No sooner had the vans halted than the two techs with them, launched a 6K camera drone sending it up to eight hundred feet where it would not be seen or heard. Using FLIR, they were able to pinpoint each of the gates and guards. Frank's team marked the locations. Then, the techs traced the road from the highway to the end. At the end of the road, they hovered the drone, taking wide angle photos of the area, then a video, gradually increasing magnification to full. Using overlapping shots, they recorded a collage of pictures for the team to analyze before retrieving the drone.

After over an hour of searching, the team was unable to identify an entrance of any kind into the facility, if indeed they were in the right location.

"It has to be there," Li Na said. "The farmers aren't using those men to guard their crops of papayas and bananas."

"Exactly," Melor said. "We just need to spend more time to find it?"

"We will need to wait until dark," Mitch said.

"Why?" Frank asked.

"If there is a facility there, perhaps our thermal imaging will be able to see at night what we cannot during the day."

"But if that is the case, why don't we use that technology now?" Melor asked.

"The temperature is too high during the day," a tech said. "At night, the temperature of the facility will be higher than the lava rocks, which will allow us to identify it."

"Hmmmm," Melor said, shaking his head.

"On the bright side, we can use the road as an avenue of approach," Li Na said. "It won't be difficult to remove the sentries."

"Agreed," Melor replied. "Once we find an entrance."

JACKSON also had misgivings about Antonio and his plans. For such a ruthless man, their lives meant nothing, only a means to an end. But Jackson knew he was indispensable if his secret was kept from Antonio otherwise, the man would have never spent so much time trying to capture the world's leading spy. The end game of the organization seemed clear, to replace leaders and control those countries. However, Jackson felt there was something more. Something that he couldn't quite put his fingers on. It kept nagging at him, despite constantly pushing it to the back of his mind. Jackson also knew that by now, there was a team of operatives somewhere outside. Getting in was another problem. They would need his help and to give it to them, he would need to transform; he hoped that Mitches technology worked. And if he wanted to find out what the end game was, he would need to play along with Antonio and his crew until he found out and discovered a way to stop them. CLUB DREAD was no joke. They had embedded agents everywhere. It was going to become a long-term mission to ferret them out. Somehow, he knew that they had agents in each government close to the leaders of America, Russia, and Britain. How to identify them would depend on whether Jackson succeeded. As much as he hated it, the only way to discover the end game was to go deeper into the rabbit hole that the organization controlled. That also meant that he would be able to rely only on himself, outnumbered with no backup in a perpetually hopeless situation. He was not looking forward to it.

The three men had reached Antonio who stood near the blast doors, constructed exactly the same as the previous ones. They were already open.

"Ah," Antonio said. "You finally made it. Come, I have something to show you."

The four walked into the large chamber, which had several hundred clones that appeared ready to implement. Technicians were attending to each clone tube, uploading programs via the control panel on the outside of each tube.

"What are they doing?" Illiac asked.

"They are programming the clone with memories and orders," Antonio said. "We can override the system any time we need to, but the orders are those they will execute when needed. They will be autonomous to some extent."

"That's ingenious," Scott said. "They will obey at will and you will control them."

"They are not the only ones," Antonio said. "Follow me along the catwalk. Look down there."

The men focused on the left side of the walkway. Below them were other clone tubes, row after row. The first section was corporate leaders. They recognized each one; some of the richest and most influential men and women in the world.

"What do you need these leaders for if you already have control of the governments?" Jackson asked.

"A good question," Antonio replied. "Sometimes, one leader isn't enough. You need to persuade his or her followers. These leaders can control supply chains and commodities, shipping, trucking, and airlines. We can manipulate them, like lobbyists, to put pressure on those in league with the leader. A little coercion now and then works wonders. Because governments are seldom run by one person, persuasion is the key to cooperation."

"You mean blackmail," Jackson said.

"A nasty word, but yes," Anthony said. "We must have full cooperation to carry out our plan."

"What plan is that?" Scott asked.

"You need not concern yourself with that," Anthony said. "Look there."

Past the corporate leaders were at least fifty more tubes, all duplicates of several operatives. They were evenly divided between clones of Illiac, Scott, and a woman.

"Why that's me," Scott said. "Why do you need clones of me?"

"They will serve my purposes," Antonio said. "Your services are no longer required."

Without flinching, he drew a pistol and shot Scott in the forehead who fell without making a sound. Antonio motioned with his pistol and a half dozen guards came running down the walkway.

"You see, once I have a clone of a person, I no longer need them, especially when they put valuable assets at risk."

"I suppose you're going to shoot me too," Illiac said.

"No, my friend," Antonio said. "We have been through too much together. You will undergo the same treatment Jackson did. Take him to the doctors."

Jackson didn't know what to make of the situation. It appeared Antonio had gone quite mad. Antonio leveled the gun at him.

"What are you waiting for?" Jackson asked. "Pull the trigger."

"There is no need," Antonio replied, holstering his pistol beneath his sports jacket. "You have been monitored since you entered my service. I find your loyalty admirable. Not once have you flinched or failed to carry out your duty, despite the danger. You will control all of those below. They will be operational in three days, except the woman, she is in the beginning stages. We will send them after more targets that we need to control to accomplish our purposes."

"Why do you need so many to control the major countries and corporations?" Jackson asked.

"We are not after control," Antonio stated flatly. "We are after world domination and population control. Our new world order will be one of strict obedience or death. Like that of Fidel Castro but on steroids. You don't approve."

"It seems a bit drastic," Jackson said. "The rationale also is somewhat short sighted."

"Look at the earth," Antonio said. "The carrying capacity is nine billion, which we are approaching. Globally there are water, food, and energy shortages that grow worse daily due to incompetent management. California is perhaps the best example; with a Mediterranean climate they can only support about five to eight million people. But what have they done? They have grown to forty million. Half the water supply of the Los Angeles basin is almost gone due to deficit of Lake Mead and the Colorado River. The governance there hasn't even thought about solutions, just taxes and their greed for more money. The result is waves of homeless on the streets, car homeless, and rampant crime. No, my friend, it is time to stop the nonsense."

"By eliminating the population?" Jackson asked.

"There is no other way," Antonio said. "The moronic actions of those in control have chosen this path for us. Either we save what we can, or all will perish."

Jackson thought about what he said. It was true. Already around the world there were not only rolling energy blackouts, but also rolling water blackouts because many locations didn't have the energy to distribute water on a city-wide scale. Within another year or so the U.S. would experience national rolling energy blackouts just like California. There was no getting around it. But, despite all the faults of narcissistic congress critters and those in city and regional governments, acting like God to give and take life was inhuman.

"It must be done while time is on our side," Antonio said. "It is the only way."

"So, you will reduce the population to save the world."

"Yes. But we will have control of the world's wealth. People talk about monopolies all the time and how bad they are. The government broke up Ma Bell decades ago because they were a monopoly. Current monopolies are allowed to exist because they control congress with blackmail, extortion, and other means of control. We will eliminate all of that and, we will control the wealth. Think about it. For the first time, constitutions of countries will work like they were designed. They will work because we will control them, as well as the population. We will end starvation and diseases like cancer."

"Do you really believe the people will accept you?" Jackson asked.

"Certainly not," Antonio replied. "But they will not know of our existence. You are a specialist in hand-to-hand combat. Thus, you know that both Yin and Yang must exist and coexist. We will be both. Now, look below."

The two had been slowly walking along the catwalk. When Jackson looked where Antonio was pointing, he saw ten clone tubes with the same woman in each. He gasped; it was Li Na.

"Who is she?" Jackson asked, hiding his recognition.

"She is called the Black Widow," Antonio said. "She is the most exquisite death machine I have ever met. A master with a sword. You worked with her before, but we blocked that memory. You will work with her again. After we distribute the current clones, you will bring her to me."

"Why do you need her?" Jackson asked. "You already have her clones."

"Correct," Antonio responded. "I met her to give her the money to protect you. She was ever so slightly wounded, and I was able to collect a minute sample of her blood, but it was enough to develop what you see here. I do not need her; I want her. She will be programmed to become my mistress and mine alone. Such a beauty is too rare to let others possess."

It took all of Jackson's control not to break Antonio's neck and throw his lifeless body over the rail to the floor thirty feet below. In his mind he saw him striking him in the throat with a left-hand serpent's paw, followed by a right punch to the rib tips to take his breath away and then, striking the right side of his chin with a left-inverted palm heel twisting the neck while his right hand snaked behind the head to grab the chin with a left-hand checking brace. He heard the neck snap; Antionio fell lifeless to the floor.

"Get a grip on yourself," he thought. "I suppose if I had your resources, I would do the same," managing to choke back his hatred. "What do you need me to do?"

"Not her yet," Antonio said. "We are preparing the clones you brought. You and a teams you select will replace President Armstrong and President Sokolav, as well British Prime Minister Wilson, all within the same time frame. The Chinese President will come later. Those will give us the clout we need for success."

"When do I leave?"

"You will leave within three hours give or take. Trucks will arrive to take you to the airport. Our men are on the first floor, many of whom you have worked with. Choose from among them and ready yourselves. I will am heading to Washington DC within the hour. All our facilities are on communications lockdown until these three leaders are replaced. Do not fail me."

"Have I ever?" Jackson asked. "Besides, I don't want to end up like Scott."

"No," Antonio said, smiling while he watched the men below drag Scott's body out the door. "I just needed to reiterate it. I must go. Look around some more if you wish, the men will close the door when you leave."

Jackson watched Antonio walk down the long catwalk. Below, looking on either side, lay the fate of the world, a bad fate. These clones must all be destroyed. How could he pull it off? He sensed the presence of Li Na and the team she was with. Jackson began looking at his watch then, at the armed techs by the blast door. He knew that they would not know when Antonio had left, along with Doctor Bramahh. Jackson had been surprised to see the doctor, thinking he would have gotten taken out by the teams on St. Lucia. Knowing he would be closely watched, he devised a strategy to cripple the tubes below. He would deal with the President's clones later. Walking down the stairs, he looked closely at the tubes. There was a console on each that displayed the temperature, heart rate, brain activity, and other body functions. The light was green, meaning everything was normal. A light on a nearby tube turned red setting off a continuous, softly blaring alarm. Two technicians were at the tube within a few seconds.

"Damn," a tech said. "It's the voltage again. It's dropped too low. Turn up the knob to boost it while I go find the analyst."

"Tell him to hurry," the other tech said. "This is only a temporary fix."

"What happens if you cannot fix it?" Jackson asked.

"The clone will die within three minutes," the tech replied, watching the panel carefully.

"Is it a problem with the main electrical system?" Jackson asked.

"Yes. It has been giving us problems the past week. We recommended a backup generator on the floor, but Antonio and Doctor Bramahh said no."

The tech was busy attempting to adjust the voltage and keep it in nominal range. Jackson walked away, meandering around the tubes until he came to those with clones of Li Na. They looked exactly like her although they had not reached maturity; he found himself wishing she were in his arms. Slowly, he cleared his mind to focus on the task at hand. Electricity was the key. Shut it down and the clones would be dead. His plan began to develop.

CHAPTER 9

DARKNESS having fallen, the two techs launched the drone and sent it up to six hundred feet. The buzz of its rotor blades was barely audible, so they increased altitude another one hundred feet. No longer able to hear it, they slowly flew it toward where the team had narrowed the entrance of the facility to be. Hovering, the zoom camera was set to its lowest power while they slowly adjusted the yaw to the left then, ever so slowly back to the right. The thermal imaging camera picked up the bodies of the guards left on duty. Zooming in, they could watch them while they talked and smoked cigarettes. Adjusting back to about four power, they inched the drone forward examining the slope where it climbed toward the top of the volcano. One hundred yards upslope they spotted several heat plumes. Flying the drone closer, using ten power, the camera could clearly make out air vents.

"Do you have something?" Susan asked.

"We do," the tech said. "Air vents but they are too small for a person to enter."

"Keep looking," Melor said. "If there are air vents, there is an entrance."

"Should we take out the sentries?" Susan asked. "The sooner we do maybe the better."

"It's not my place to tell you your jobs," Li Na said. "I would wait until we find the entrance."

"Quite correct," Melor said. "We can leave no gap in time once the assault begins."

"All teams," Susan spoke into her comm. "Double check your gear. Be prepared to move in."

With darkness, mosquitos had arrived in abundance. The men were constantly slapping at them while they made certain their gear was ready to go, talking softly amongst themselves.

"Hey Grigori," Ivan said. "Haven't you oiled your pistol enough?"

"You can never have it too clean," Grigori replied. "It is my life."

The answer sobered both teams because they knew he was right. There was a flurry of activity while each checked the condition and cleanliness of their weapons. Waiting was always the hard part for black ops teams. Like a trained athlete waiting to go out on the field of play, they were accustomed to action and much preferred it rather than waiting for something to develop so that they could do their duty. Their gear was as ready as it would ever be. The teams looked toward Susan and Melor. Some of them admiring Li Na. Even in the dark, her beauty stood out.

"We have something," a tech said. "A vehicle just came out of the mountain. It is driving without lights on."

The teams heard the tires on the road, crushing small rocks during its approach to the dead end; it slowly drove past them. The techs yawed the drone to follow it with the camera, which displayed a visual on the monitor. When the vehicle reached the highway, it turned right and turned its lights on.

"Aren't you glad you didn't kill the sentries?" Li Na asked with a smile. "Since we have a point of reference for an entry, now may be the time."

"I agree," Susan said. "Let's send both teams up each side of the road and take the sentries out along the way. You two, find us that entrance."

"We are working on it," a tech replied. "Ah, there it is, now clearly visible. It was around the ridge line, which is why we missed it before. The road to it is so little used it didn't stand out either."

"Li Na," Susan said, "You, ..." Her voice trailing off.

Li Na was gone.

"Did you see where she went?" Susan asked.

"No," Melor replied. "Men, move out."

Both teams began moving up opposite sides of the road. Staying behind the undergrowth as much as they could, using their night vision goggles to find the sentries. Reaching the first gate, they found the sentries dead, laying on the ground, blood oozing from the necks where their heads had been, which lay beside them, eyes staring lifelessly into the dark. As much blood as the men had seen in operations, the sight sickened them.

"Li Na?" Susan asked.

"Yes," Melor replied. "And think, she doesn't even have night vision."

Susan shook her head in disbelief; the men opened the gate and moved forward. The next gate was about one hundred yards away, just around a sharp bend in the road. Reaching the bend, two men moved forward to kill the sentries. Stepping on a twig and snapping it in two, only a few feet from them, the sentries turned, one of them shooting a CIA team member in the shoulder. The wounded man fell while the other operative, shot the sentry in the chest twice with his suppressed pistol. Turning it on the other sentry, he realized he was too late, the sentry was leveling his AK-47 at his chest. He was just pulling the trigger when the sword penetrated his neck from left to right, severing his spinal column. He dropped in a heap to the ground.

"I thought I was a goner," the operative said. "Thanks."

Li Na was already gone. The rest of the team had caught up and were tending to the wounded man.

"How did they see you?" Susan asked.

"He stepped on a branch that snapped," the man said. "If it were not for the Black Widow, we'd both be dead."

"Where is she?" Melor asked.

"Hell if I know. She was gone before the sentry she killed hit the ground."

"Keep moving men," Susan spoke softly into the comm.

The men moved past the next gate; the sentries were already dead. One had his entire shoulder and arm cut off. The scene was ghastly.

"That woman is on a mission from hell," one of the men said. "I'm glad we're not her enemy."

Within a few minutes the teams had reached the end of the road. Li Na sat atop a large pile of volcanic rock, listening intently for any sounds that would lead her to those within. She detected nothing. It was deadly calm.

"Any signs of others?" Melor asked.

"No," Li Na replied. "That's what concerns me. If this place is so important, why aren't there more than those few sentries protecting it?"

"A good point," Susan replied. "Men, keep your eyes open. The entrance is about fifty yards away."

"I agree with Li Na," Melor said. "We need to be extra cautious. All teams, ten-meter spread, thirty-second intervals."

"That's a long distance in the dark," Susan said. "You sure we want to do that?"

"No," Melor replied. "But if they come at us, we won't all get wiped out. Is there any way to tell if they have hidden cameras?"

"No," Susan replied. "I asked the techs. They won't show up

on the thermal scans."

The teams began to move, Li Na taking up the rear. When they rounded a bend on the nearly invisible road, a small ridge had formed that ran from midway up the volcano and flattened out nearby. About fifty feet further was another. Looking left through their thermal vision, as directed by the techs who had a sky's eye view from above with the drone, the team was able to see the opening where the car had exited. They studied it for quite some time before deciding to move further forward to find a way in. Appearing from nowhere were about a dozen men just to the right of the entrance. Bullets rained down on the team while they dove for cover.

Having developed his strategy, Jackson needed to move quickly before anyone became suspicious. The hostages were ready to be moved again, along with the clone tubes of the three world leaders. He had at most twenty minutes while Illiac finished the loading. First, he went to the armory. Twisting the dial on his Deepsea to the right, a total transformation took place. He felt a little dizzy for a few seconds and had to lean against the wall. Looking in the glass pane of a door when he passed, he couldn't believe what he saw.

"Illiac, I thought you were gone," the armory guard said.

"I should have been but needed to pick up a couple of things."

"Okay, but hurry. Antonio told me to lock the armory a few minutes ago."

"Thanks. It will only take me a minute."

The armory was a duplicate of the one on St. Lucia so he where to go. At the end of the row of automatic weapons were a couple of chests. In them were grenades and C-4 explosives already affixed to timers. He grabbed several of each and placed them into his bag and set the timer of another for fifteen minutes, dropping it back into the chest and closing the top. He also picked up a 9mm pistol and suppressor and four loaded magazines. Quickly exiting, he nodded to the guard who closed and locked the door behind him. The inside of the cavern was massive with three levels, and he wasn't sure how to get to where he needed to be next. Standing in the shadow of a support column, he looked around carefully. Finally, he saw what he was looking for, conduits leading from each area. They converged at the far end of the cavern in a corner above a doorway marked maintenance. Staying in the shadows, he moved furtively, reaching the door and entering just when two guards passed.

"We thought you were gone," a maintenance man said. "What are you doing here?"

"Antonio sent me down to see if you needed anything on my way out."

"No. Everything is fixed. Two of the men are checking all the clone tubes. That'll take them about thirty minutes. I'll spare you the technical jargon, but we are normalizing the voltage regulators to prevent another surge."

The man turned, walking between the regulators to his colleague who was kneeling beside the last one. Jackson pulled his pistol from the small of his back and shot each man twice, center mass. Putting his pistol back, he dragged each to the darkest corner of the room. Having a basic knowledge of electricity, he planted two charges and set them for twelve minutes then, just before exiting, shot out the lights and closed and locked the door. Remaining in the shadows, he twisted the bezel on his watch and became himself.

"One more stop," he thought.

He felt slightly queasy and leaned against the wall for support while turning the bezel two notches right. Feeling a little dizzy again, he made his way to the blast doors. The two guards looked a little surprised when he approached.

"We thought you were gone Mr. Raven," one said.

"Before leaving I want you to look at the locking mechanism behind the door; make sure it is impregnable."

The two guards walked in front of their boss to the control mechanism on the left side behind the three-foot thick door. The control was lighted with a green light on a small mechanical panel with several cogged wheels. When the two men began inspecting it, the Mr. Raven imposter, having looked around to make sure no one was watching, shot each in the head. It was so dark behind the space between the door and wall that it was difficult for even him to see them. He placed the next charge, on a five-minute timer, behind the locking arm of the panel. The blast would render the locking mechanism inoperable, leaving the doors open. Readying himself, he leaned against the wall and turned the bezel counterclockwise; Jackson Black emerged from behind the blast door. Looking carefully around, he walked quickly to the stairs and down and out into the tunnel where Illiac had just finished loading the last clone tube.

"Where have you been my friend?"

"I had a stomachache, from too much food I guess," Jackson replied.

"Hope you're better now, we need to move," Illiac replied.

The clones had been loaded onto a small flat trailer that sat upon narrow rails leading into the tunnel in front of them. They jumped aboard the instant it began moving. It was like riding a train, the click, click of the rails speeding into the night. Jackson could not tell where they were, riding for several minutes before stopping. A wall directly in front of them slid to the left to reveal two box trucks, lights on, engines running. The men Jackson had selected were in the first truck. The hostages and clone tubes, along with Jackson and Illiac loaded onto the second. The truck headed away from the volcano to the north. About five minutes later they were on the highway headed west. Jackson turned the bezel on his watch to send a signal.

The explosive on the door lock detonated, the thickness of the door obscuring the sound. Near the entry, the guards had delivered a hail of bullets toward the team, killing several men. There was no way to flank them. Moving forward would put them in a funnel of death. Suddenly, several columns emerged from the ground, the top of each opening like a four-sided flower to reveal fifty caliber machine guns that locked onto thermal images and began firing. The entire team retreated behind the ridge for protection.

"Falcon 1, Osprey. Are you airborne?"

"Osprey, right above you. Looks like you're in a jam."

"That's an understatement. Help us out, will you?"

"Two conductors enough?"

"Roger, start the music."

"Target acquired, coming down."

"Everyone cover," Mitch yelled.

The two Hellfire II missiles delivered forty pounds of blast fragmentation and incendiary explosives on target. The sentries and guns were destroyed. A small hole had been created in the entry and the men poured through.

"You saved our ass Mitch," Susan said. "Thanks."

"You'd do the same for me."

There was no time to judge targets, all enemies were indiscriminately shot while the teams advanced through the cavern. Medical technicians poured out various doors in the rooms above to meet a hail of bullets. Bodies dropped left and right as the teams maneuvered to clear each room floor by floor. Just when they reached the upper floor, the armory and electrical bombs Jackson had set went off; the lights went out leaving everyone in total darkness. The team had begun putting on their thermal vision when the backup generator kicked in, turning on the emergency lighting, most of it red. Moving through the cavern, having cleared all outer areas, the team ran through the blast doors.

"The explosions couldn't have been an accident," Susan said.

"They were not," Li Na replied. "Jackson was the only one who would have set them."

"Guess the transference technology worked like we planned," Mitch said.

"What is all of this?" Melor asked.

"It's the clones Jackson told us about," Mitch replied. "We need to get rid of them. Falcon 1, Osprey. Remain aloft and track anything around the area that could have left the facility."

"Roger."

"It looks like the power outage will take care of them soon enough," Susan said.

"Let's make sure," Li Na replied.

The group walked down the stairs then, among the clone tubes. They were amazed at the number and who the clones were. When Li Na saw her own clones, she froze. They were an identical likeness. Only pure evil could come from such work. She grabbed an M-4 from the nearest team member and began firing. The liquid and bodies in the tubes crashed to the floor. Melor motioned and the rest of the men destroyed the remaining tubes.

"They won't be impersonating anyone," Melor said, laughing.

"What bothers me is the missing tubes," Mitch said. "They had to be someone important."

"Are you thinking what I am?" Susan asked.

"Yes, the Presidents and perhaps the British Prime Minister," Mitch said.

"Let's search the entire chamber and cavern again," Melor said. "We cannot let them get away."

Both teams began a thorough search of the chamber. There were dead and wounded laying on the floor. The wounded were too far gone, bleeding out.

"You need to come see this," a team member spoke into the

comm.

The entire team as a unit rushed to him. He stood by another set of blast doors to reveal a small set of tracks leading into a tunnel cut into the volcano. It was lit with red lights.

"You four men," Susan directed. "See where it leads, quickly."

"Osprey, Falcon 1. Looks like a couple of trucks just getting on the highway. Not sure if they came from your location."

"Follow them."

"Roger."

"Let's clean this place up," Frank said, breathing heavily from his jog through the facility. "I'll post some guards outside."

"What about the local police?" Mitch asked.

"It's so late I doubt they heard the missiles strike and the road to the facility is not visible," Frank replied. "I'll take care of it. Go do your thing and track down those tubes."

PRESIDENT Armstrong was on video feed with President Sokolav and Prime Minister Wilson. They were obviously irritated and tired.

"Melor relayed to us that several clones are missing," President Sokolav said.

"We have the same information," President Armstrong replied. "Our expert from T-Group believes the clones are duplicates of the three of us. I'm sorry, but we have no way to confirm that at present."

"What is your next step?" Prime Minister Wilson asked.

Phil was in the room and leaned over the Presidents shoulder, whispering in his ear.

"We may have good news," President Armstrong said. "The Director just told me that Jackson turned on his locator. Our best bet is to follow him to his destination. Meanwhile, we lost about half the teams on each side. We need reinforcements as soon as possible."

"Where do we send them?" Andros asked.

"Let us follow Jackson's signal and we will know shortly," Phil replied. "But we need to get ahead of this somehow. Let's put ourselves in their position. What would you do if you were attempting to replace three world leaders?"

"I would replace them at the same time," Prime Minister Wilson said. "Doing it one by one would greatly increase the risks."

"I agree," President Armstrong said. "We need to determine where they are going and if they are splitting up. T-Group informs us that the GPS tracker is continuous now. When they near their intended destination it will be deactivated again."

"Then it's settled," President Sokolav said. "We wait and be ready to move at a moment's notice."

Those in attendance nodded agreement; the monitor went blank.

"Phil," Bill said. "Stay on top of this with Mitch. What do you need from us?"

"Nothing at present," Phil said. "I just got word that three planes left OMT."

"That means they split into three teams," Vince said.

"Likely," Phil replied. "We need eyes on them at all times. So, I may need to re-task some satellites. With the issues in the South China Sea, North Korea, and Latin America it could become critical."

"Do what you need to do," Bill said. "Those issues will be rendered moot if CLUB DREAD succeeds."

"Yes sir," Phil replied, leaving the Oval.

"I don't like this at all," Bill said.

"Neither do I," Vince replied. "Waiting has never been our strength."

BEATRIX and Leonid were whipping their teams to a frenzy to keep up with the increasing intelligence threads coming in from multiple assets around the globe. The information relayed from Falcon 1 sent the teams scurrying to try to link all of it together. Separating information from intelligence was beginning to overcome Henry who kept changing intelligence posted on the big screen.

"Enough," Henry yelled across the room. "Let's take a deep breath and a short break. What do we know, just the basics, Beatrix?"

"We know that three planes have taken off from OMT and are headed in different directions."

"Leonid?"

"We also know the basics of their intent and thus, we should be able to initially guess what country the planes will head for."

"So, we look for leads, links, and intelligence for the U.S., Russia, and London," Henry said. "Concentrate your efforts on those points then, plug in additional intelligence received to either confirm or deny your hypothesis."

The two teams settled down and began tracking the planes that had left OMT. Several hours passed while they analyzed the planes routes matching them with incoming intelligence and potential paths mapped out by Samantha. The inflight software made it relatively simple. However, the flight plans didn't match the routes consistently.

"The second plane is headed toward Europe," Leonid said. "So is the third."

"What about the first plane?" Henry asked.

"Sir, it disappeared off radar about ten minutes ago?" Susan replied. "Near Ciudad Acuna. We thought it may be trying to avoid detection by flying beneath five hundred feet. It has not resurfaced."

"Is there an airport there?" Henry asked.

"A small one," Susan replied. "The pilot could land the plane if he has the guts to tackle the short runway."

"Damn!" Henry exclaimed. "That's near the border, isn't it?"

"Yes sir," Susan replied. "Do you think they're going to try to cross the border in a truck?"

"That would be risky," Leonid said. "The clone tubes cannot be easily hidden. Besides, they're likely more nefarious than that."

"I agree," Henry replied. "Are there any U.S. assets we can use nearby?"

"Laughlin Air Force Base is only twenty miles to the east," Susan said.

"We need help," Henry said, picking up the sat phone. "Mitch; we lost the first plane near Ciudad Acuna. It's about twenty miles west of Laughlin AFB. Can you get a bird up to help us find the targets? Roger that. We will stand by."

The short wait of twenty minutes seemed like an eternity when Henry received the call from Laughlin.

"This is Harpy 2. We are airborne and searching. Do you have the tail number?"

"Yes," Henry said, reading it. "We believe it landed at ACN."

"That is almost ten miles inside the Mexico border. We will send photos your way. Any other requests?"

"Harpy 2," Leonid said. "Patrol along the Rio Grande River from the box canyon bottleneck on the west end to U.S. Route 377 on the east end. Can you make several passes?"

"Harpy 2, standby."

The drone was cruising at 40,000 feet and relaying pictures and videos to the crisis suite. It had made three complete passes from east to west. The lake was busy with boats, which had become a constant problem for border patrol agents trying to do their job without harassing those on the water.

"Mission complete. Let us know if you need further assistance. Harpy 2 out."

The videos and photos taken by the drone were high resolution and very clear. The camera system and lenses on it were a closely guarded secret, but the results spoke for themselves.

"Alright everyone," Henry called out. "Look for anything that may indicate the target. Given the size of the clone tubes, you'll be looking for something larger than a basic motorboat."

It was a daunting task sorting through the array of videos, which the teams separated into shorter lengths so that they could analyze them as quickly as possible. Henry looked across the suite knowing the teams would do the best they could and that in the end, there would be some clue. If there was not, it was going to be a very long night. He picked up the phone to report to Sheena Harris, Director MI6.

JACKSON was surprised they had reached their destination so quickly. Looking out the window all he could tell was that the plane had landed at a small airport surrounded by an arid landscape.

"Off the plane quickly," Illiac said. "We have ten minutes to be out of here."

"I don't suppose you would care to fill me in about where we are headed," Jackson said.

"All in good time my friend," Illiac said, grinning. "Welcome to Acuna airport in Mexico. We are headed to Lake Amistad and from there eventually to Washington DC."

"Why all the covertness?" Jackson asked.

"You should know the boss by now," Illiac said. "He doesn't trust anyone. After what he did to Scott, I'm not sure we can trust him."

"What does your gut tell you?"

"That we cannot."

"I feel the same," Jackson said. "However, if I'm going to be responsible for replacing the president with the clone, it would be nice to have some background information for planning."

"We discuss it soon," Illiac said. "We need to make a couple of transfers with our vehicles first."

Their team was much smaller now since they only had one clone. The three hostages had been taken by the other two teams. The airplane taxied to the small terminal, parking on an apron about the size of a football field. Moving quickly, the team loaded into a waiting box truck as soon as the plane stopped. The control tower and airport personnel looked the other way when the truck pulled up, unloaded the passengers and took off past the end of the runway, dust boiling behind it toward the lake. Jackson noticed that the driver took a winding route, mostly on backroads and some with asphalt. Judging from the time and estimated speed of the truck, they had gone about twenty miles by the time they reached lake. The driver picked up a two-lane asphalt road with guardrails on either side. Jackson saw a sign reading Río Grande Presa La Amistad and about five miles further a sign reading Tlaloc Playa. He knew playa meant beach; he kept trying to place where he had seen the name Amistad before after Illiac mentioned it. Suddenly it dawned on him; he remembered it from a border patrol story on the news. Presa was the word for dam. Lake Amistad; they were near Del Rio, Texas.

"So," he thought. "They are going to attempt to smuggle us into the U.S. across the lake. Not a good idea considering how few roads there were in the area on the U.S. side and the fact that U.S. Customs and Border Patrol agents set up temporary roadblocks on a rolling basis. It was impossible to tell where one would be, especially along the two-lane highways. A poor idea indeed."

Illiac was watching him and began to smile broadly looking at the consternation on Jackson's face.

"You are worried my friend," he said. "If you are thinking we are going to take the boat across the lake and hit the highway, you are mistaken. We are here."

The truck had turned right, off the pavement into an area that jutted into the lake and that had quite a few short roads where people walked down to fish or launch a boat. About a mile in, there was a long cove that jutted toward them, the driver skirted the north edge and stopped a half mile down, next to the lakes edge. Two boats had pulled up to the shore. The first was a standard fifteen-foot motorboat, the second was a large, rubberized craft. The clone tube was immediately put into the rubber boat, along with its life support electrical box. Three of the men jumped aboard and covered the tube with a fishing net and green tarp. Jackson and Illiac, along with the remaining operatives hopped aboard the lead boat. The boats headed east along the lake, hugging the southern shore; they traveled about three miles before stopping. It was growing dark.

"I'm guessing we are at the border," Jackson said.

"Yes," Illiac replied. "See that bridge in front of us? Here, use my binoculars."

Jackson focused on the bridge. It was at least two miles away. "It looks like a railroad truss bridge and another bridge just past it for cars."

"You are sharp," Illiac replied. "The first bridge is Lake Amistad Bridge for the railroad, the second is Governors Landing Bridge. We must make the railroad bridge so we can wait beneath it until our transport arrives. When it is fully dark, we will cover our boats with these foil lined tarps to reduce our heat signature."

"Quite ingenious," Jackson thought. "These guys were shrewder than he imagined; he had underestimated them and wanted to kick himself. It was important that he try to get ahead of their strategy."

The skies had clouded over, blocking a quarter moon that shone through silvery occasionally against the blackness of the water. Jackson could barely make out the dam on the Mexico side of the border about a half mile to his right. The distance to the first land fall was about three-quarter mile. Adjusting the lined tarps and anchoring them onto the boats, as well as a framework that had been built around the outboard motors, they sped forward about ten miles per hour to cover the large space of open water. At the slow speed, the motors were hard to hear more than a hundred yards away. It was far from that of a Navy Seal operation, but effective none-the-less. The team closed the distance in under ten minutes then, pulled close to the shore and waited, motors idling. The short rocky cliffs rose about ten feet above them. A mile away to their right, the men could see the glow from the U.S. Customs and Border Protection check point. It made their hearts race while they moved along the shoreline, in and out of the small coves that would have been finger canyons on land. The tortuous path of the boats almost doubled the distance to their destination.

Hearing the throaty roar of a boat exiting the Southwinds Marina onto the lake, the boats stopped near the harbor mouth, cutting their motors. Even in the darkness, they were able to identify it, passing only yards in front of them. The insignia for U.S Customs and Border Protection, broad diagonal green stripe and large letters reading Border Patrol were clearly visible. Jackson guessed the boat at about seventeen feet. The throaty roar of the dual, 250 horsepower Mercury engines that propelled it echoed loudly across the water. Two agents sat beneath a flat-topped frame that housed the boats radar and communications equipment. Leaving the mouth of the small harbor, the patrol boat turned left, no doubt heading toward the invisible border in the lake that marked the Pecos River. Illiac carefully watched it through his binoculars. Scanning right, no other boats were visible in the harbor.

"Let's move," he said.

Gunning the motors, the two boats crossed the two-hundred-yard-wide mouth of the small harbor in a couple of minutes. Then, slowing down, skirting in and out of the small coves, reached the truss bridge. A small inlet, leading to the right and narrowing at the end two hundred yards away paralleled the railroad tracks about twenty feet above them up a steep embankment. They cut the motors and drifted to the very end then, jumped ashore. Illiac whistled. A replying whistle floated down from above. They heard footprints scuffling slowly toward them. Suddenly, they saw two men making hanging onto a knotted rope that had been knotted every two feet.

"Good to see you," Jose said. "We must hurry before the patrol boat passes by again. We will run a cable and winch down from the side-by-side for the tube."

"Will it hold it?" Illiac asked. "That vehicle is not very heavy."

"Yes, we anchored it with a cable and a steel shaft driven into the dirt. Hurry."

A cable was lowered alongside the knotted rope and anchored near the boats about five feet above ground. Another cable was thrown down. Jose and a couple of men strapped the clone tube to the first cable while the second cable was attached to the end; someone unseen from above, began winching the tube upward. Despite the short distance of 150 feet, the tube was awkward to negotiate and winch up the steep slope. It took almost an hour. Finally at the top, the team rested on the base of the ballast, the rocks that hold the ties or sleepers in place for the rails. Jose sent two men down to the boats who untied the cables, which were pulled up. A couple of minutes later, Jackson heard the boats heading east under the bridge.

"Thank you," Illiac said, shaking Jose's hand.

"No problem. We will leave you now."

Jose loaded his cables and gear into the back of the side-by-side and headed south along the track. The low sound of the engine disappearing into the night. It had become deathly quiet. No one spoke while they waited. A couple of hours later, it sounded like a truck was coming toward them but was the rumble of the train still five miles away.

"They must have paid an engineer to stop for them," Jackson thought. "It would be the only way arrange a pick up."

Moments later, the train passed, slowing to a crawl, not stopping. The entire team lifted the clone tube into an empty box car, keeping pace with the train. No sooner had the tube been loaded than the train began picking up speed; the men hurriedly scrambling aboard.

"We will be getting off soon men," Illiac shouted above the sound of the rails. "About an hour."

Warriors always hated the wait, but this time it would be short. Fifty miles down the rails, the train slowed, barely moving; the team jumped off, removing the tube while the train sped up again. The movement was so efficient that someone not standing next to it wouldn't notice the decreased speed. Waiting a few yards from the tracks was a flat bed truck. They loaded the tube onto the truck and sped toward Spofford, lights out.

"We need to get to the plane while the train is passing through town," Illiac said. "It will drown out the sound of takeoff."

The truck sped down Standard Lane that ran parallel to the tracks, until they reached South Avenue A and turned right. The locomotives pulling the train were a few hundred yards behind. Three blocks later, the truck turned left onto third street and pulled up in front of a Quonset hut. The field was small and unmanned. In front of the hut, lined up on the 4,000-foot runway was a twin engine cargo plane, cargo doors open; the men rushed the clone tube and gear aboard. Immediately the pilot cranked the motors, small clouds of smoke pouring from each while the propellers picked up speed. Idling for a moment, building oil pressure, the pilot stood on his breaks, pushing the engines to take off speed and almost nosing the plane into the runway before releasing them. It was Emil, fast Freddie. The plane shot down the runway and was airborne before the end, banking left and staying below radar, heading southeast toward Washington DC 1,500 miles away.

THE second team with the clone of President Sokolav, landed outside Orsha, Belarus on a dirt strip next to a deserted farm. Inside an old barn, a three-person medical team had set up a sterile room. Doctor Bramahh had shown them exactly what to do. The clone was brought to life and dressed like President Sokolav. The team programmed him with specific commands to order troops at checkpoints to make sure the team would make it to Moscow. Using three sedans, with the clone and three team members in the middle, they crossed into Russia at Krasninskiy Tamozhynnyy Customs Office. Using credentials that the organization had prepared, the team was ushered through without delay. The team followed the E30 route the rest of the way toward Moscow, two hundred miles away.

"Did you see who that was," a guard asked.

"Obviously," his supervisor replied.

"I wonder what he was doing so far from Moscow with such a small security detail?"

"Do you want to ask him?

"Certainly not."

The teams in the crisis suite had tracked them well, despite having flown under radar and eluding intelligence channels throughout their flight. The Russian team in the crisis suite contacted Andros who had already detailed an agent to the customs office check point. He was on scene a few minutes after the sedans crossed into Russia. Flashing his credentials, he approached the supervisor.

"Did you notice the President travel through here?" the agent asked.

"Yes sir," the supervisor replied. "They passed not more than ten minutes ago in three black sedans. Is there a problem?"

"No," the agent replied. "I am working on an extra layer of security for them. May I see your cameras please?"

"Certainly," the supervisor said, leading the way to the monitor bank.

"Thank you," the agent replied. "I require privacy."

The supervisor walked out the door leaving the agent alone.

"Sir," the agent said. "There are three sedans, black. The target is in the middle sedan with three other men. There are two men in the lead sedan and three more in the follow sedan."

"You are certain the middle car has the target?" Andros asked

"Yes sir, clearly visible on the monitor sir."

"Very well," Andros replied. "Sir, we cannot let them get to the city, there are too many potential evasion routes if they do."

"Did you put out the story of my visit to the Bolshoi Theatre to see Swan Lake?" President Sokolav asked.

"Yes sir," Andros replied.

"Do you think these men know that?"

"Without a doubt. It would be the best place to replace you. I fed the media the story you would be there to watch and to congratulate the dancers and the company and that you would be sitting in your usual box in the Belle-etage, the second level."

"We have a choice then," President Sokolav replied. "We can let the mice come to the cheese or, we can remove them from the maze beforehand. What do you recommend?"

"You know me sir," Andros said. "I believe in shooting first and asking questions later. There are two things to consider, the knowledge of the team with him and the clone's knowledge."

"I don't follow," Sokolav replied.

"Sir," Andros said. "From what the CIA and President Armstrong said, the clone has your basic knowledge and other programmed knowledge to efficiently carry out the organizations plan and your duties. He has only just been awakened so knows nothing of our intelligence yet."

"And the team?" Sokolav asked.

"They are expendable sir," Andros replied. "They likely know nothing of the organizations plans. Jackson Black filled us in as much as he could."

"Your assessment?"

"Don't give them the opportunity to succeed. Our team in the crisis suite can fill us in on any intelligence gaps we may have. These operatives are of no value to us."

"Is your team in place?" Sokolav asked.

"Yes sir," Andros said. "Already enroute to destination, eighty miles from Moscow on A100."

"Give them the green light."

The three sedans were under surveillance of a Thunder stealth combat drone that had picked them up minutes after contact from the SVR agent at the customs checkpoint. The drone was carrying four Kh-50 guided missiles and requested permission to fire on targets.

"Negative Goshawk," the voice replied. "Surveillance only. We need to keep this mission very covert."

The SVR team jumped from the helicopter before it hit the ground. Several police cars were already on scene. Within ten minutes, they had rolled a dump truck on its side with a controlled fire in the engine compartment. The helicopter then, took the SVR team to its next location. Meanwhile, the police officers had placed flares along the road before the accident to detour traffic from E30 to A100 to circumvent the scene. They initially let traffic through, past the rollover. About twenty minutes later, Goshawk contacted them.

"Target is ten minutes out."

"Roger," an agent said. "Any cars ahead of them?"

"Negative."

"Excellent," the agent said, dressed as a police officer. "Maintain surveillance until mission is complete."

"Roger."

"Men, target is approaching," the agent spoke into his comm. "Stay alert, it will take them about fifteen minutes to reach your location."

"What's that?"

"Looks like an accident sir," the driver said.

"Everyone be alert," the operative spoke into his comm.

The three sedans slowed and were stopped by the agent wearing the police uniform.

"What's going on?" the driver asked.

"A rollover," the agent replied. "You'll need to detour to A100. Take 46K there and go about three miles to pick up A100. It will be on your right."

"How long is the detour?" the driver asked. "We are rather in a hurry."

"The detour will only take you an extra ten minutes," the agent said. "I can't let you through yet. Not until the recovery vehicle arrives; no one is allowed to pass. That could take another hour. You're welcome to wait of course."

"We'll take the detour."

The driver turned onto 46K, and three miles later had to slow down, almost to a standstill to make the ninety degree right turn onto A100. The second sedan was making the turn directly behind them when the SVR team opened fire with their suppressed AK-105 carbines, a short-barreled version of the AK-47. The team had staggered standard military rounds with armor piercing rounds. Within ten seconds, all personnel in the vehicles were dead. Obeying an order given specifically by Andros, the lead operative walked up to the second vehicle and shot the clone in the head three times then, placed a black bag over it, tying it around the neck.

Several flatbed trucks were already on scene to pull the cars onto their beds. Fifteen minutes later, the cars were on the trucks, covered with tarps and headed toward Moscow. About three hundred yards down the road the team passed the Uspenskiy Monastery. A couple of the agents made the sign of the cross when they passed, feeling somehow that God would forgive them for what they had just done. But, after all, it was their duty to their country.

"Mission complete," the agent spoke into his comm.

"Roger," Andros said. "Report for debriefing. I will send a team to pick up the main target."

"Inform the Americans," President Sokolav said.

COLIN Archer, the best agent MI6 was focused on the satellite feed. The information on the tracking had come in late and the third team from the organization, with a clone of Prime Minister Wilson had eluded them. All they knew from Beatrix in the crisis suite was a lost signal off the coast to France near Nantes.

"How many airports are around that area?" Colin asked.

"At least twenty to the northwest," Beatrix replied. "There are too many planes for us to track. It looks like they dropped to sea level. Where they landed is anyone's guess."

"Damn it!" Colin exclaimed. "Chelsea, come here please."

"Yes sir. How can I help you?"

"You know the coast very well."

"Yes sir. I spent my whole life working with my father who is a marine biologist. What are you asking?"

"If you landed in France, how would you enter the UK and make your way to London?"

"Hmmmm. If I were these operatives, I would stay off the roads. They know our surveillance capabilities and that London is the most camera dense city on the planet. What do you know so far?"

"All we know is the plane they were flying disappeared from

radar somewhere around Nantes, France. Nothing else."

"They would not be able to land in the UK easily. If it were me, I would opt for a sea plane then, I could land at almost any location around our coasts."

"Is there a way to narrow the location?"

"Sure," Chelsea responded. "The intel says they have a clone tube and maybe other hostages. I assume it would be heavy so the location would need to be somewhere they can have easy access to land, less populated area, and a passable road."

"What about somewhere along Bristol Channel?" Colin asked.

"That could work," Chelsea replied. "Swansea would be ideal with less steep slopes but it's too risky due to population. The rest of the area has fifty-foot cliffs that would be almost impossible to negotiate unless the operatives are spiders."

"From all the places you visited with your father, where would you attempt entry?"

"The place I believe would fit the criteria is Tremadoc Bay. There are nice beaches there and, on the west shore from Pwllheli to Criccieth, the terrain is low lying with quite a few isolated spots. The closest areas to the nearest road are in each of the end locations."

"That means they would need to come through Birmingham to get to London," Colin said. "At least that narrows it down."

"Not necessarily sir," Chelsea replied. "If they are as sharp as we think and agent Black trained them, they will skirt Birmingham, to the south most likely, and enter London from directly west or southwest where we wouldn't be looking for them."

"Good point," Colin said. "Get all eyes and ears up and looking. Until this is over, no breaks."

"Yes sir."

Chelsea began calling every available agent, putting London and French Police on alert, and tracking every camera. The only face they knew was Prime Minister Wilson's, which she entered into the biometric and visual tracking system. It would be a long shot at best.

"Sir, everything is in place," Chelsea said. "Anything else?"

"Not now," Colin replied. "I'll be in the field if you need me. Call me or Sheena if you find anything."

Minutes later, Colin arrived at #10 Downing Street. Sheena was already with the Prime Minister.

"Any news?" Prime Minister Wilson asked.

"No sir," Colin said, sitting down. "We have put alerts up everywhere and are actively looking for the team. We have drones in the air and teams standing by to intercept if they pop up on radar."

"You're telling me that with all our technology we have nothing?" Prime Minister asked.

"Well sir," Colin said with a smile. "Like my former instructor used to tell me, computers are simply high-speed idiots; they are not infallible. We do have one lead sir. Chelsea and I think they will land by sea plane in Tremadoc Bay. It's about three hundred miles from where we lost contact and makes sense."

"But it could be anywhere else," Sheena said. "We cannot afford to guess."

"I agree," Colin responded. "But so far, that's the best scenario we have."

"If we cannot pick up the trail things will go sideways quickly," the Prime Minister said. "We can ill afford that. Also, President Sokolav called me," the Prime Minister said. "They stopped the clone about an hour outside Moscow."

"Killed?" Colin queried.

"Yes."

"Sir, we should follow their example," Sheena said. "As far as I'm concerned it's not really a person and better gone than escaped."

"I agree sir," Colin said.

"Let it be done," the Prime Minister said. "But first we need to find it."

One of the prime minister's staff walked over and handed a phone to Colin.

"A call for you sir," the staffer said.

"Colin here."

His eyes widened slightly while he looked at the other two.

"When?" Covering the mouthpiece. "Do you have a map of southern England? Spread it out on the desk please."

"We caught a break," Colin said. "One of our security cameras obtained a visual on the target just outside Gloucester headed toward Cheltenham."

"How did we get so lucky?" Sheena asked.

"A fisherman called local police in Tremadoc Bay, said he saw a sea plane land," Colin replied. "A few minutes later police questioned a driver who said that he saw two sedans, white and gray, racing at high speed past him."

"That doesn't make since," the Prime Minister said. "Why would police question a random driver?"

"The sedans sudden appearance made him crash," Colin said. "Sheena, get me Waddington field."

"Yes sir," Sheena said, dialing. "They are on hold sir."

"General Lockley," the Prime Minister. "I need you to get a Protector airborne immediately."

"Armed sir?" General Lockley asked.

"To the teeth," the Prime Minister said. "It specifically needs Hellfire missiles and whatever ordinance that will be high impact with lesser collateral damage. How long?"

"We have a Protector on standby sir," General Lockley responded. "It will be airborne in ten minutes sir."

"How long will it take to reach the Oxford area?" the Prime Minister asked.

"About forty minutes Minister."

"See to it immediately. MI6 will send intel when we receive it."

"Understood."

"Sheena, get all your people on this. Colin, we need to slow the target down somehow to give the Protector time to get overhead."

"Do you remember Operation Lorry sir?" Colin asked.

"You mean striking truckers who would block the highway for an indeterminable amount of time so we could carry out discreet operations with less chance of collateral damage."

"That's it sir. The target would not have made it to Oxford yet, they'd still be a half hour or so out. I can have it operational on incoming arteries A40, A41, M40, A34, and M4 in ten minutes sir. I just need to send out a code word."

"Do it," the Prime Minister said. "Whatever it takes. How are you following the cars now?"

"Helicopter sir," Colin said. "It will need to pull off due to low fuel before the replacement arrives."

"What about police on the ground?" the Prime Minister asked. "Can they keep an eye on them before the replacement arrives."

"Already on it sir," Colin replied. "They are to keep visual only and stay a half mile or more back."

"Good," the Prime Minister said. "Perhaps we will be as fortunate as our Russian friends."

"How did they take out the target?" Colin asked.

"A fake rollover accident," the Prime Minister said. "They detoured; an SVR team took them out at close range with automatic weapons. It was convenient. Remote, dark, and no witnesses."

"Fitting," Colin murmured.

"Keep me up to date," the Prime Minister said. And Colin, you know what to do with the clone."

"Yes sir."

BASED on information coming from the crisis suite, Li Na and the two teams were on their way to Andrews Air

Force Base. More team members would meet them to replace their fallen ones. They had been in the plane, A C-17 Globemaster for what seemed hours. The plane was so large it seemed like overkill but had been on stopover in St. Lucia ferrying supplies somewhere into South America. Li Na was obviously frustrated. The constant frown on her face kept the men away from her lest her sword decide to take another blood bath. Jackson's tracker was sending out a locator signal every ten minutes. Frank and Mitch were aboard, along with other members of T-Group to keep the signal as strong as possible. They knew that once the plane landed the signal would be turned off again. It was a safety precaution to keep the organization from finding it. Multiple law enforcement agencies had been brought in for surveillance. Because the CIA could not officially operate in the U.S., even though they did so constantly, the operation had fallen under the guise of the Department of Energy and a potential nuclear threat. That would keep local and federal law enforcement on their toes and off balance about the real reason for the surveillance. Later they would be told it was a drill to determine how well the agencies had worked together. Of course, they would slap each other on the back never suspecting they had cooperated in a live operation. So far, everything was working efficiently. The Russians had stopped their clone infiltrator, the British were tracking their clone and the Americans were doing the same. Still, too many things could go wrong and despite the intelligence network, the dirty business always fell to the agent in the field where often, there was no backup.

"Where do you think they will land?" Frank asked.

"I'm guessing a remote field outside DC," Mitch replied.

"That would make the most sense," Melor said. "They need privacy from prying eyes."

"Correct," Susan interjected. "The real problem is that when they land, the network of highways gives them a large number of routes to their destination."

"Hopefully Jackson can send a signal intermittently," Mitch said.

"What if he cannot?" Li Na asked.

"Once they reach the Whitehouse area, he has a communications device," Mitch replied. "We will be able to hear him, and have agreed on code words to help coordinate our movements. It's a bit risky, but the only way."

"Why weren't the rest of us informed about that?" Frank asked.

"We didn't know who we could trust," Mitch replied. "This organization has spies in many places. We needed to make certain."

"At least we know their final destination," Frank said. "Our men and others are waiting but we will keep them at a distance so that Jackson can do his job."

"It will not be easy to get the clone in to replace the president," Mitch said. "That will be difficult not to mention the detail of Secret Service they need to bypass."

"That's why they have Jackson," Li Na said. "He and the president are close friends."

"You don't suppose, no forget it," Melor said.

"What are you thinking?" Frank asked. "Speak up."

"I was just thinking aloud," Melor replied. "Remember the body we found in the facility? I believe his name was Scott from our information. It was our understanding he was a key operative in the field, yet he was shot in the head."

"I thought your men did that," Frank said, eyes widening.

"No, not us and not your men," Melor replied.

"Which means he was expendable," Mitch said.

"Exactly," Susan interrupted. "It also means that Jackson was chosen specifically for this mission from the beginning. It must, doesn't it?"

"Strategically, you are correct," Li Na said. "I have a feeling that Jackson is well aware of that fact."

"He better be," Frank said. "Else, we're looking at failure and big trouble. I don't want to plan the assassination of a fake president."

"Don't worry," Li Na said. "Jackson has never failed to accomplish a mission."

The others nodded agreement.

The plane touched down at Andrews on Runway 01 Right. The 9,000 plus foot runway was more than sufficient for the Globemaster. It didn't have far to taxi before it turned right at the end of the runway and circled back south on the tarmac in front of the two large military hangars adjacent to Patrick Avenue. The rear cargo doors opened, and the team walked down the ramp. The replacement members for each team and others awaited them. The waiting group looked very official; normal pleasantries were shoved aside while they got down to business.

CHAPTER 10

COLIN and his team had positioned themselves along the route they believed the target would travel and pulled off A40 at Church Road, waiting.

"Sparrow, Goshawk. Suspect vehicle getting off M40 and appears to be headed onto Denham Road. Standby."

"That's about five miles from here," Colin told the driver. "Punch it."

The van the MI6 team was traveling in entered the A40 freeway heading west at high speed.

"Sparrow, Goshawk. Suspect vehicles on Denham Road approaching roundabout, circling, going straight, taking A412. Hold on, tracking. They are slowing, taking a right turn onto Seven Hills Road. Are these guys secret agents or something?"

"Goshawk, Sparrow. In a way, why?"

"Sparrow, Goshawk. Because Seven Hills Road leads to Pinewood Studios where they make all those secret agent films. Maybe they'll make one about this mission."

"Goshawk, Sparrow. Gotta laugh at that one."

"Sparrow, Goshawk. Wait. Suspect vehicles turning right, the second right before M25. It appears to be a car body shop, very spread out. Sending you live view now."

"Goshawk, Sparrow. How long can you stay on station?"

"Sparrow, Goshawk. Another twelve hours."

"Understood Goshawk. Keep an eye on them and send us live feed."

Colin directed the van to pull into a commercial plant nursery southeast of the body shop. The team gathered around the back of the van, watching the monitor.

"I don't like this," Colin said. "Why would they pull into a dead-end street?"

"Look at the area," an agent said. "It's farm to the north, another industrial yard to the east, and between is dense forest."

"A good place to lay low," another agent replied. "Maybe they are going to switch vehicles."

"That is a good possibility," Colin said. "Despite the studios and other traffic, the location is out of the way and secluded. With cars frequently going in and out it would be easy for them to elude us."

"What do you want us to do?" an agent asked.

"We need to position the team along the road going in," Colin said. "Look for anything suspicious and if you think one of the targets is in a car, we will have the police stop and search it."

While the van dropped the team off and went back to the nursery entrance, Colin called Chelsea arranging for police backup. They were on scene a few minutes later.

"Officers this is a critical situation," Colin said. "It is a matter of national security. If my men tag a car, your job is to stop it and search it. Do not let it pass without my approval. We need a car on the other side of M25 and two more near the intersection of Seven Hills Road and Denham Road. That should confine them. Just in case, have backups near A40 and Denham and Bangors Roads junction."

The police dispersed to the locations and waited. It

wouldn't be long before dark, the friend of clandestine operatives and criminals, overtook them. Colin anticipated a potentially long wait, which he hated. He kept his eyes glued to the laptop screen and ears attuned to the comm.

"Sparrow, Goshawk. My radar is showing a slow-moving bogey coming from the east. Likely a helicopter. It's ten miles out at three hundred feet altitude."

"Goshawk, Sparrow. Do you have authorization to fire?"

"Sparrow, yes, if we can minimize collateral damage. Do you want me to shoot it down?"

"Goshawk, Sparrow. Not yet. Only if it appears the target is going to board it."

"Team, move toward body shop," Colin spoke into his comm.

The entire eight-member team slowly moved through the adjoining lorry and container yard and down the street toward the body shop at the rear. Looking at them, Colin was thankful for Operation Lorry; it had slowed the organizations operatives down just enough. The shop had closed moments before according to intelligence, and it appeared most of the workers had left. They covered the first hundred yards to the body shop, which occupied another length of one hundred yards before reaching the forest. Colin directed his driver to block the road about twenty yards in and ran to catch up with his team. He was on comm with his men and Goshawk, as well as the local police. The team split with four proceeding down the east side of the main building and the others on the west side. The windows were too high to get a visual on what may be happening inside.

"Sparrow, Goshawk. There is a small group, maybe a half-dozen men or more. My sensors picked them up when they emerged from the trees at the north end of the shop. They are entering into the edge of the farm field and appear to be waiting for the helicopter. It is a half mile out."

"Goshawk, Sparrow. How close can you zoom in on their faces?"

"Like they are standing right in front of me. Standby. Visual sent."

Colin looked at the image on his laptop and zoomed in. Although a bit hazy, there was no mistaking the clone of the Prime minister. While he was looking, the helicopter landed, and the men began running for it.

"Goshawk, Sparrow. That is the target. Do not let them board the helicopter."

"Understood."

The group of men were running full speed toward the helicopter, which disintegrated into a ball of flame still ten feet to touchdown. Three of the men were killed instantly from fragmentation, the others ran for the cover of forest. Colin motioned for his men to circle through the trees and hopefully surround the target. He ran as fast as he could to the dead bodies. Neither was the clone.

"Never a lucky break when you need one," he murmured.

His team checked in one by one. Occasionally, he could hear the thud of a bullet striking a tree and return fire from the targets team. A recent rain had made the earth soft and forgiving under the weight of foot. One of the operatives had barely reached the cover of a large beech when he heard a branch break nearby, under the darkness of the trees canopy. He could scarcely make out the figure in the growing darkness. Bracing his pistol, he fired two rounds, killing the man. Suddenly, automatic weapons fire began, the tree and area around him erupting in flying shards of wood and leaves. The rest of his team closed in and were returning fire. Seeing the primary target running, the agent gave chase, catching his foot on a log and falling flat on his face. By the time he had gotten up the target was gone.

"Sir," the agent said. "I think we got the other team members, but the primary got away."

"Good, keep a sharp eye out," Colin replied. "Maintain search."

Colin had quietly made his way to the industrial facility east of the body shop and was slowly maneuvering around old broken-down lorry's and Connex shipping containers, stopping to listen every few feet. The sound was soft at first but continuous; the panting of someone breathing hard from running hard. An inner voice told him to put his Walther PPK away, so he slipped it under his shirt. From the sound, which grew louder as it grew closer, he knew where the man would emerge and slowly made his way past a blue shipping container, which he pretended to be locking, muttering to himself.

The primary target emerged from the woods exactly where he thought he would; Colin stood up, facing the container at first then, slowly turned.

"Damn lock," he said aloud.

"You there, can you help me?" a voice asked.

The clone had a pistol in his hand, holding it casually.

"What do you need?" Colin asked.

"Do you work here?" the clone asked.

"Yes, I was just making sure the containers were locked," Colin replied.

"I need your keys and your vehicle," the clone said. "Quickly."

"It's right around the fence there," Colin said. "Keys are in the visor. Hey, aren't you the Prime Minister."

"Yes," the clone said, waving the pistol. "I need your help and will fill you in once we drive away."

Colin walked ahead of the target, feigning a limp in his right leg, letting the knee bend deeper every other step, wincing each time.

"Are you okay?" the clone asked.

"Just a soccer injury from the weekend," Colin replied.

When they rounded the fence, a car was right in front of them. Colin took a deep breath hoping it was unlocked. He began to pull on the handle of the driver side door, which opened smoothly; he breathed a short sigh of relief.

"You drive," the clone said, waving the gun above the roof of the car.

Colin had already pulled the door open and the instant he began to sit down, pulled his pistol. Bending down to enter the car, the clone's eyes widened; at once Colin put two bullets into his chest and two into the head, propelling the clone away from the car where it collapsed to the ground.

"Sheena," Colin. "Tell the Prime Minister, final part of Operation Lorry is complete. Target removed. A helicopter was shot down in a farm field near the shop. You'll need to spin a story to the media."

The media had already jumped on the story because frankly, there was no other interesting news. They were disappointed when the Civil Aviation Authority made a statement to the press that the accident had been caused by a rotor malfunction and the helicopter had crashed into an empty farm field, killing all on board. Any new findings would be released if any were uncovered.

JACKSON and his team landed. They were an hour from Washington DC and a date with destiny. When the cargo door opened, there was nothing but a long dirt strip in the middle of an open field surrounded by hardwoods. Anyone watching would have noticed the plane getting lower but would not be able to see it land. It was likely a common enough occurrence that no one would pay attention to it. Jackson turned off his tracker by rotating the bezel back to the 12 o'clock position just in time. Antonio was waiting nearby; one of his assistants began sweeping the plane and occupants for bugs.

"Is something wrong," Illiac asked.

"We have lost contact with the other teams," Antonio replied. "They have not responded to our messages."

"Why is that a concern?" Jackson asked. "You told all teams

not to make contact until the mission was complete. If you were not here to greet us, you would not know where in our mission we were."

"True," Antonio said. "But it pays to be paranoid."

"I did not expect to see you," Illiac said. "Do you need us to do something?"

"I wanted to go over the plans one last time," Antonio replied. "From the three clones, this one is the most important. Failure means a great delay, which the organization cannot afford."

"Very well," Illiac said. "The basics of the plan are to travel from here to Hagerstown Regional Airport, meet the next plane, our pilot takes control, get to altitude, and then use our specialized suits to reach target area, locate the target, eliminate and replace."

"You make it sound so simple," Antonio said, laughing. "You know the price if you fail. I have two men who are going to shut down the motion detectors. You must stay on your schedule to make this work."

"We won't fail you boss," Illiac said. "Load up men."

The trip to Hagerstown took about an hour and a half, picking up Highway 522 to I-66 and onto I-81. The plane was parked on a concrete apron close to the terminal, adjacent to the taxiway for Runway 9; 7,000 feet of asphalt. Illiac and Jackson walked into the terminal to find the pilot.

"Excuse me," Jackson said. "I need to use the restroom, be right back."

"Hurry," Illiac said, greeting the pilot.

In the bathroom, Jackson entered a stall and pulled his sock back and retrieved a small box, half the size of a typical matchbox. From within he grabbed the tiny earpiece and put it into his left ear. It was invisible unless the ear canal was closely inspected. Pressing the button, he began to whistle the chorus of the William Tell Overture then, said. "What a beautiful day."

Immediately, the signal was picked up at the crisis suite.

"Henry, we're live," Beatrix called out.

"About bloody time," Henry said. "Everyone up, track the signal. Where are they?"

"Hagerstown, HGR," Leonid said. "Satellite imagery coming up."

Illiac had come into the restroom after meeting the pilot and was surprised to hear Jackson whistling.

"You seem happy," Illiac said. "What's that tune, it sounds very familiar."

"I'm tired of being bored so thought I'd whistle some to buoy my spirits," Jackson replied. "The song is the William Tell Overture. You know, Hi Ho Silver Away."

"Ah yes," Illiac said. "The old western, Lone Ranger and Tanto. I used to watch the reruns with my parents. It brings back happy times."

"Yes, pretty good for its day," Jackson replied. "Law and order and all that stuff. Glenn Campbell played the song on his guitar. He was awesome."

"Well, we better Hi Ho Silver Away," Illiac replied, laughing. "Else we'll be joining Scott."

"Got you."

The remarks were sobering. It brought back the severity of the situation. While they walked to the plane, a veil of silence overcame them. Jackson was trying to think ahead. This would be no picnic. They could all end up dead or worse. He hoped his message had made it to the President. They had only once chance to thwart the replacement plan. Entering the plane, the men were ready. The pilot lay dead on the floor, already replaced by Emil, the organizations top and trusted pilot. His skinny frame and quick laugh made him easily likeable, a trait that most psychopaths shared.

"Alright men," Jackson began. "Let's go over the specifics once more. First, the problem with the flight path.

Washington DC has several layers of very strictly controlled airspace. We're going to cross into the 30-mile layer. As soon as we do, air traffic control will contact us to move out of it. The pilot will do his job and we will jump out at the prearranged coordinates, which will be on the perimeter of the SFRA, the Special Flight Rules Area that extends about fifteen nautical miles from Washington National Airport. There is no way to get closer without getting a military jet on our ass, which could potentially shoot us down. We won't get close to the other prohibited areas fly space that we discussed before; those are P56A, and B. So, it is important that when the jump light comes on you get out of the plane as fast as you can."

"This seems very risky," a team member said, yelling over the sound of the propellers."

"It is probably the riskiest thing you will ever do," Jackson replied. "It's live or die. Now, let's go over the wing suits one more time. You will recall from training these are electric powered. It is the only way to jump from 20,000 feet and get to our target location. I used one on a mission a while back. Its weakness was the distance. Your jet packs have expanded batteries to overcome that. The cloth webbing between the legs and underneath the armpits make them very light. The electric impellers are for extra thrust. In case of a malfunction or once you reach 12,000 feet, pull the quick-release harness. Do not be afraid, fear is the mind killer. Your packs are lightweight carbon fiber jetpacks with electric impellers and weigh about twenty-five pounds, including their 60-volt lithium battery. By the way it has a 15-kW output. To reach our target on a glide path of a 3:1 ratio of length to height, we will initiate thrust as soon as we exit the aircraft. When you reach 12,000 feet, jettison the pack and glide to target from there. We will get exactly six minutes of thrust from the packs, which will put us about four to five miles from target at hopefully, 12,000 feet."

While Jackson was talking, the men were doing the math in their head.

"We will reach speeds of up to 180 miles per hour," Jackson continued. If you get into trouble, jettison the pack, land, and get out."

"Evade capture at all costs," Illiac interjected.

"I will be first out," Jackson said. "Follow my lead and you'll be just fine. Look at your aerial photos again so you have a good feel for the geography of the area. You must not make a mistake about where you are."

The President received the coded message that Jackson had sent him. He was going over it in the Oval with the Vice President.

"What do you think?" Bill asked.

"It's a big risk sir," Vince replied. "Still, it is the only way to be sure."

"Do you think these men can actually pull this off, I mean make it to the target?" Bill asked

"You tell me," Vince replied. "I have only heard stories of his operative adventures. But from what I witnessed in the last operation, he saved the nations ass so, I'm guessing he can."

"Yes," Bill replied softly. "He is better than anyone suspects. Let's follow his instructions. Let's get to the situation room and brief the team."

The team stood at attention, like they were in the military when the President and Vice President walked into the room.

"Welcome everyone," President Armstrong said. "I was left a coded message from Jackson. We received it two hours ago. Who are the team leaders?"

"It is Susan and Melor," Phil said. "Also, we have Mitch and Frank working with them with communications and support."

"Very well," President Armstrong said. "You will be

replacing my normal Secret Service agents when I exit. They will have your backs. It is important that we capture or kill this clone."

"I prefer the latter," Phil quipped. "There must be no future risk."

Listening to him, the team clearly understood the repercussions and high risk of the situation.

"I second that," Vice President Reisner said.

A secret service agent poked his head into the door.

"Excuse me sir," the agent said. "The crisis suite said they are on the way."

"Thank you," President Armstrong said. "I'll make this quick. What the agent referred to is that Jackson and the organizations team is on the way. Let's go over the plan and Phil, make sure it's quiet. We don't want the media getting wind of this."

"Yes sir."

The teams were briefed by the President and Vice President and assumed their positions. The wait would not be long, but like a stakeout, minutes could drag like hours. Unlike other waits, this one promised to be exceeding suspenseful. The teams were stationed around the White House and grounds. Although they knew the basics of Jackson's plan, he had not relayed the specific target location. To fulfill the President's orders to keep things quiet, the teams and Secret Service suppressed all weapons and posted a small white, solid circle onto their front and back. Anything more might be too visible to the rapidly approaching intruders.

"Sir," the air traffic controller called out to his supervisor. "We have a plane entering restricted airspace between Dickerson and Leesburg."

"What's the problem?" the operations supervisor asked.

"The pilot says the plane's rudder is giving him problems.

The flight line has been erratic."

"What's his number?"

"NS336LX."

"NS336LX, air traffic control Washington National. You have entered restricted airspace. What is your situation?"

"Washington National, NS336LX," Emil said. "I have rudder control issues. I'm not sure what is wrong."

"NS336LX, you must attempt to land at the nearest field out of the SFRA. Those are Leesburg Executive or Front Royal-Warren. Can you make one of those?"

"Washington National, NS336LX. I am not sure. The rudder is forcing me left, I may hit the edge of the SFRA but will try to avoid it. Leesburg is too populated. I will attempt Front Royal-Warren. Please have emergency vehicles standing by."

"NS336LX, Washington National. We are handing you off to Front Royal-Warren.

The crisis suite patched the conversation through to the team and the White House.

"What do you make of that," Susan asked.

"Sounds like the plane is in trouble," Melor said.

"I believe it's a decoy," Li Na interrupted. "The plane is using the excuse of malfunction so the team on it can get close enough to make their target area, wherever that is."

"What do you mean?" Phil asked, breaking in.

"Remember the mission against the Chinese base?" Li Na asked.

"I remember," Phil replied. "He used a wing suit to get in."

"Yes," Li Na said. "I think he may be using the same again."

"Makes perfect sense," Phil replied. "All teams, look sharp."

The President and Vice President were listening as well.

"See Vince," Bill said. "Jackson at his finest."

"You know," Vince said. "I'd hate to be his enemy. Time to get you dressed sir."

Jackson's team jumped out of the aircraft right on cue. Emil flew toward Front Royal-Warren, gaining altitude to about 20,000 feet where he cut power and bailed out. Reaching a terminal velocity of about 100 miles per hour, the plane crashed into a farm field two minutes later. Air traffic control immediately dispatched emergency services to the area. The tensions of invading the NFZ relaxed, traffic patterns returning to normal.

Jackson gave the signal to turn on their jetpacks by rolling over twice. All team members engaged the impellers, and the team hurtled through the air at over 150 miles per hour. They had exited the plane over Poolesville. Jackson watched the town below them, his team in staggered formation behind. Next, they passed Dawsonville on their left then, Darnestown, over Travilah, Glen Echo, and Georgetown. Having already jettisoned their electric packs the team was on its final glide path with two miles remaining. The target was very small, but every team member had been able to land in areas half the size during training. It was a tribute to how good Jackson had been as an instructor. The Washington Monument was their anchor point, shining like a beacon in the night, clearly visible for most of the route.

Descending on the last leg of their path, each member put both hands behind his back causing a more rapid drop and then, pulled to release their pilot shoots, which pulled out the main ram-air chute. Dark in color, they were invisible against the night sky. The team was nearing the south lawn, east gate adjacent to W Executive Avenue NW. Pulling down on the toggles pulled the back edge of the entire parachute downward, slowing descent. Each of the team members softly touched down between the pool and the tennis court, surrounded by trees and darkness. The south side of the White House was well lit, including the south lawn fountain, everywhere else was obscured in shadows. Three of the men stood guard while the rest of the team took off their suits and rolled them up, stuffing them beneath shrubs along the fence. When all were ready, Jackson and Illiac briefed them one last time.

"The President always takes a walk around the oval path between the fountain and back of the Whitehouse," Jackson said. "He is very regimented. Assuming his schedule has not changed, we will have just enough time to get into position."

"What do we do if we see him?" a team member asked.

"Kill him on site," Illiac replied. "Our clone with Antonio is close by."

The teams at the crisis suite were receiving the discussion live and transferred it to Susan and Melor's teams so they could hear and adjust their strategy.

"I want two team members to stay here, beneath the trees in this small triangle north of the tennis court," Jackson continued. "The rest of you circle around by the fountain. Half of you position yourselves in the trees north and near the fountain, the other half in the trees and around the Secret Service vehicles in the northeast corner."

"Why there?" Illiac asked.

"Because I don't know which way he will turn when he exits," Jackson said. "Either way, each group has a backup. I will circle around between the pool and putting green near the front of that white supply truck you see there. That way, I can be behind them. Beware, he may or may not have Secret Service or the Vice President with him."

"Okay, I understand," Illiac said. "Once they pass either team, they'll be in a pincher movement."

"Exactly," Jackson said. "Take your positions."

Melor and Susan were in position on top of the central structure of the Whitehouse for better visibility. Susan also had three snipers atop the east side of the Eisenhower Executive Office Building.

"Everyone on their toes," Melor said. "Jackson will be moving alone past the pool. Snipers, ready yourselves. Don't fire unless you can get every person in the group. Snipers one, two and three you have the northeast area. Snipers four through six, you have the southeast area."

"I'll mirror the other side," Susan said. "Snipers on my team you have the southwest areas. Follow Melor's lead. Don't fire unless you can take out the entire group. Be careful not to shoot our man. He will be the only one approaching the northwest area. You heard what he said. Stay on your toes, acquire your targets right to left."

Jackson could hear the conversations in his earpiece while he crept between shrubs and shadows, slowly making his way toward the box truck, which looked more like a command vehicle the closer he got to it. Suddenly he stopped, dead still. He thought he heard a scuff, like someone had slipped on the path. After pausing a few minutes, his heart racing, he decided it was his ears playing tricks on him; slowly, he moved forward. The snipers on the roof of the Eisenhower building picked him up while he crept beneath the trees in the northwest corner of the south lawn. They carefully watched when he slowly moved forward to the right front of the command vehicle. Looking across the lawn, he could barely make out the figures of Illiac and his other team members.

"Sniper 3 on EB. Be aware our agent is standing near the front of the command vehicle."

"Roger," Susan said. "All snipers, eyes on targets."

The president and vice president walked out the back of the Rose Garden exit and along the sidewalk next to the roses, turning right at the end of the small grassy area that separated the roses on either side. Within a minute they were walking alongside the command vehicle. Jackson turned off the comm to his group.

"Gentlemen," Jackson whispered. "The raven flew into the darkness."

"Never to be seen again," President Armstrong replied.

The President and Vice President disappeared into the shadows in front of the truck.

"What is going on?" Vince asked.

"I need Bill to change clothes with me," Jackson said. "Hurry. Did you bring the vests?"

"Yes, there," the President pointed.

"Get them on, quickly. Mr. President, you stay here. Do not move until we give you the all clear. Where's your Secret Service?"

"At the end of the truck," Vince said, snapping his fingers.

Two secret service agents quickly crept forward standing behind the president.

"Agents. Don't take your eyes off the president and if anyone approaches you other than your fellow agents or me, shoot them."

The agents nodded affirmatively. Uncovering his Deepsea, he turned the dial to the right several clicks. Within seconds he looked like the president. The men gasped.

"How the hell did you do that?" President Armstrong asked.

"Long story sir," Jackson replied. "I'll tell you later."

Jackson, wearing the presidents coat and pants stepped out of the shadows along with the vice president.

"Vince," Jackson whispered. "I hate putting you in danger like this, but there is no other way. Stand behind me a little and to my left in case bullets start flying."

"I understand, let's go," Vince whispered hoarsely.

Jackson turned his comm on again. "President and Vice President heading south past pool nearing putting green."

"Snipers do not shoot the executives," Susan whispered. "Wait for the others to reveal themselves."

The two were nearing the first large tree on the right past the putting green when Illiac stepped out of the shadows raising his pistol and pointing it.

"Mr. President," he said. "It's a pleasure to meet you at last." He fired the first-round center mass, knocking the President off his feet then, approached for a second round to the head.

"It's better to go out honorably, no?"

There was a soft singing sound that cut the air.

"Good..."

Illiac's voice suddenly stopped the pistol dropping to the asphalt, a look of surprise on his face. Collapsing to his knee he looked behind him to see Li Na re-sheathing her sword.

"Black Widow, how?" he gasped.

Jackson stood, twisting the dial on his watch, returning to normal.

"Damn that hurt," he said, turning Illiac onto his back.

"You double crossed us," Illiac said. "I thought you were my friend."

"I am old friend, but President and country come first."

"At least I die a warrior," Illiac said, barely a whisper, the last breath of life passing his lips.

Jackson closed his eyes with his hands. "Goodbye old friend."

"That was close," Vince whispered. "Your reputation is well deserved."

"Don't thank me," Jackson said. "Thank Li Na. She has always had my back."

"Thank you young lady," Vince said. "It is a pleasure to see you again."

When Illiac fired the first round, every sniper, scope on target, squeezed their triggers. The entire team of CLUB DREAD was dead before Illiac hit the ground.

"All snipers stand down," Susan said. "Converge on south lawn."

The south lawn filled with Secret Service agents and the teams. The dead were already being lined up and covered, waiting for a truck to carry them away.

"You saved my life again," President Armstrong said, shaking Jackson's hand.

"We're not done yet," Jackson said. "Do any of the guards know about this?"

"No," President Armstrong replied. "Only Vince and my Secret Service on duty tonight. Why?"

"Because Antonio needs to replace you with the clone," Jackson replied. "That means he needs to bring the clone here."

"How will he do that?" Vince asked.

"He knows your security protocols," Jackson replied. "Mr. Vice President, call down to the northwest gate off Pennsylvania Avenue. Tell them the President snuck out again and you're expecting him back shortly."

"Okay," Vince replied, complying with the request. "Mr. President, I need to borrow your clothes for a little while longer and position the teams around the shrubs surrounding the north entrance. You must remain inside away from what will happen next."

"Quiet, Jackson said dialing. "Mission complete, president dead. Everything went without a hitch except that Illiac, and two others are severely wounded. Entrance is secure."

"We will be there in fifteen minutes," Antonio replied.

"We have fifteen minutes," Jackson said. "All team's outside north entrance. All Secret Service inside with the President."

Susan and Melor's teams moved into position, hiding themselves behind the shrubs and trees adjacent to the driveway in front of the north entrance. Others were hidden among the shrubs near the guard house on the east side of the entrance. They had been in position for only a few minutes when the guard at the gate admitted the clone and Antonio through. The black Suburban and duplicate of the 'beast' looked exactly like he would have expected. Seeing who he thought was the president, the guard motioned them through after checking the drivers' credentials.

The vehicles made their way up the drive to the north entrance stopping directly in front of the steps leading to the doors between the columns on the corner. Six men got out of the Suburban, the driver remained, opening the oversized sunroof from which appeared another man panning a minigun. The minigun, also known as the M134, a 7.62 mm, multi-barrel heavy machine gun was capable of firing 6,000 rounds per minute. It would tear the operatives to shreds with its bullets flying from the gatling-style rotating barrels.

"Heads up everyone," Susan said. "Snipers one, two, and three. At the first sign of trouble, take out that minigun."

Jackson wanted to take Antonio alive, but not the clone; that would be too risky. He had walked down the steps and approached the sedan. The minigun was trained on him, while he slowly opened the door.

"We're ready Antonio," Jackson said.

"Where's the rest of the team?" Antonio asked, suspicious.

"Inside guarding the Secret Service agents."

"What about Illiac?" Antonio asked.

"So sorry to tell you sir. He didn't make it."

"I wouldn't say that old friend," Illiac replied, getting out of the driver's side of the car."

"How, ..." Jackson's voice trailed off.

"He was a duplicate or, am I the duplicate?"

"This is getting confusing," Jackson said. "You'll tell me later I suppose."

"Yes, later," Antonio said. "Mr. President, step out please."

The clone stepped out of the car looking very presidential. Jackson examined him carefully. He quickly realized he would not be able to recognize the real president versus the clone if they were standing next to each other. With every step the clone took, the risk grew. Without warning, Jackson drew his pistol and put two rounds into the clone's head, killing him instantly. The minigun began to elevate slightly when three sniper rounds found their way into the gunner's chest and head. The entire team opened fire. Antonio's men were all dead in less than five seconds. Jackson had pulled Antonio to the asphalt to avoid the bullets that flew in every direction. Giving all clear, several Secret Service agents ran out the door and down the steps, securing Antonio with zip ties around his wrists behind his back.

Quickly running down the steps were Mitch and Phil who had searched the dead team on the south lawn and then, remained behind the scenes during the foray. Mitch used a handheld metal detector, scanning Antonio for weapons. Another colleague scanned him with a trace detector to determine if there were any explosives, nodding negatively.

Given an all clear, the President and Vice President were watching through the windows while the scene had unfolded before them. For the first time they saw Antonio Raven, both thinking it was great to finally capture him.

"He's clear," Mitch said.

"I didn't come to blow myself up," Antonio smiled. "You think you have won. What did I tell you the first day we met when you were waking from your operation? Our organization grows more powerful each day. The biohacking, cloning, and other technology we use is superior to even DARPA. Did you think you could just eliminate us?"

"The organization is large yes," Jackson said. "I agree, but now we have the mastermind."

"Do you?" Antonio asked, smiling broadly. "Or do you have something else. Events are coming your way that will be almost impossible to stop."

Antonio bit down hard, breaking the cyanide capsule in a false tooth. When the President and Vice President saw what happened they ran down the steps as fast as they could, secret service agents on their heels.

"Did he kill himself," President Armstrong asked.

"Yes," Mitch replied. "We checked him and the other man by the car, Illiac, both are clone's sir. By the way Jackson, the Illiac on the south lawn was not a clone. Sorry. There are likely more of them from what we discovered in St. Lucia and Nicaragua."

"That leaves us in the dark about this organization?" Vice President Reisner said. "Still, all considered, it ended well."

"Phil, you'll need to get on it right away," President Armstrong said. "However, our man Jackson needs a short break. I just spoke to Li Na. Thank you for saving us and the nation. We will call on you again, perhaps sooner than you want us to. Vince."

"These are for you," Vice President Reisner said. "Two tickets to where Li Na wishes to go, a two-week resort stay."

"I don't know what to say sirs," Jackson replied softly, Li Na now standing beside him."

"There is nothing to say," President Armstrong replied. "You timed everything just right; your strategy was perfect. I just got off the phone with President Sokolav and Prime Minister Wilson who wish to pass along their congratulations."

"I wouldn't have been able to pull it off without Mitch, Frank, Susan, and Melor sir."

"They will have their rewards too," Vice President Reisner said. "You need a break. Sam, take care of these two, will you?"

"Yes sir. Follow me please."

"Wait," Melor called out, walking over. "I am glad you are alive friend. I thought you were a goner when those missiles hit. Perhaps we shall work together again. I wish I had you in Directorate Z."

Jackson and Melor shook hands then, hugged each other. Combat had a way of making lifelong friends, even among enemies. They had shared something that many never would; they had looked death in the eye and remained alive.

Sam led the two away to a waiting car. Most of the bodies were already gone; all traces of bullets and blood were quickly being removed. The cover of darkness had hidden the potential danger and covert action from the media. Two hours later, the spy and Black Widow were airborne.

AZURE blue sky's always looked so peaceful, especially when they were filled with large cumulus clouds, bright white from the rays of the sun. Jackson and Li Na fell into the sheet the night before and made passionate love after arriving back on the island. They fell asleep, exhausted by the stress and anxiety of the mission. When morning came, a fresh basket of fruit and breakfast had been brought to their room, which they devoured like they had not eaten for days. Jackson began caressing Li Na's smooth skin, kissing her abdomen, the urge overpowering while falling into another hour of blissful physical intimacy, their bodies intertwining. About 10:00 am they finally got up, took a shower and walked down to the beach, laying on a couple of lounge chairs beneath the palm frond shade of a Tiki hut looking across Piton Bay.

"Did they ever find the team that had the three CEO's?" Li Na asked.

"Mitch said they lost them near the coast of Spain," Jackson said. "The third team headed to London dropped them off in Morocco. I suppose they are somewhere in Europe."

"Do you think CLUB DREAD will replace them with clones?"

"Yes. But it won't matter. When they resume their duties, they will be eliminated as a routine precaution. The major powers cannot afford to lose those industries to criminals."

"I understand," Li Na replied thoughtfully. "Do you think Mitch is over there in his lab?"

"He's probably back at DARPA examining the chips the two clones had in them, along with the clone of the president. He'll be happy doing that and will let us know if he finds anything of interest. We all know we have not heard the last from CLUB DREAD. But enough talk about work, let's enjoy this wonderful resort."

"I thought you'd like Sugar Beach," Li Na said smiling.

She grabbed his hand and held it tight, both sipping on rum punch enjoying the sun and the breeze from the bay. They were slowly lulled to sleep.

Behind the two, sitting in the outside area of the Bayside Restaurant, obscured by palms breaking the back of the beach, sat two agents, a couple. They were watching Li Na and Jackson intently.

"How are they doing?" Phil asked.

"Just relaxing sir," the female agent said.

"Good, stay out of site and keep an eye out for danger. Let them enjoy their well-deserved vacation. We have trouble brewing in China. Their break will be a short one."

END

ABOUT THE AUTHOR

James Tindall is the author of Jagged Grass, The Transparency, Indian Law, Sun God's Treasure, Alas Omega, and other books, including two best-in-field textbooks. He grew up on a Florida reservation wrestling alligators and training horses to earn money. He is a U.S. Army veteran who served in intelligence and is an expert in sharpshooting and hand-to-hand combat. He has five martial-arts black belts of advanced rank including a 9th degree in Kenpo, as well as four college degrees. As a federal scientist, he specialized in water, energy, and food security, engaging him in the areas of homeland and international security and counterterrorism. His assignments have taken him from Latin America to Brazil, Mexico to Alaska, Turkey to China, and many points between. When not writing, he consults and helps solve tactical and strategic problems for international governments and SOGs.

www.ingramcontent.com/pod-product-compliance
Lightning Source LLC
Chambersburg PA
CBHW070842260626
47170CB00007B/2473